Agaziga

(The Rising Crown)

D.L. Roley

DEDICATION

To my wife Jenny. Your continued support allows me to pursue this dream of mine.

Contents

Characters

- Vlad Yanov
- Frederick Garin
- Stefan Grigoriy
- Adam Piccoli
- Aslan Tekin

Hand of the Shadow

Darius Kabir

Cheung Po – The "Pirate King"

Jenna Allister

Rose Thatcher

Arnon Porter

Karl Olsen

William Bratt

Rhys Allister

The Barons

Bedria Kess – Baroness of Magora

Aisha Kess – Bedria's daughter

Kofi Kess – Bedria's son

Eshe Kess – Bedria's brother, Commander General of Magoran forces

Lord Misrak – Captain of the guard in Magora

Chan Haitao – Baron of Yapon

Elias Harmenos – Baron of Chugoku

Cordelia Kabir – Darius's mother

Cordelia's wards

- Kal Cherian
- Anna Cherian – Darius's fiancée
- Ander Stone
- Lianna

Cult of Kisha

Empress Ullani Hailu

Ahmed Hussain Khan Al-Saad – First Chancellor

Muhammad ibn Abdullah – Second Chancellor

Ava – Captain of the imperial guard

Fatemah – Member of the imperial guard

Randa – Imperial advisor

Ubad Faran – Imperial advisor

Ubad Cawlan – Imperial advisor

Ubad Dafo – Imperial advisor

PART I

Crushing weight,

feet pressing down.

Skin bursts, dark liquid flows,

sweet succulence overwhelmed by bitterness.

Resilient essence,

transformation begins.

Acceptance, integration, metamorphosis,

true nature emerging from the broken remnants.

Fermenting vestiges,

extraction through force,

refining, fusing, amrita assembled,

broken fragments left behind as new purity evolves.

Fragrant aroma,

decadent savor brings delight.

Fruit, chocolate, and tobacco on the tongue,

fine wine comes not from subtlety but from a laborious birth.

Summer – 35 A.E.

Chapter One

Kasha Marka

General Abdul Hamazi leaned back against the elaborately embroidered leather of his camp chair. His wife had given it to him as a present the last time he was home. *"A general deserves a comfortable place to rest while he is drinking his morning kaffe."* She had playfully slapped him on the backside and then dodged around the table when he tried to sweep her into an embrace. He chased her around the kitchen, laughing. She eventually let him catch her, then he pulled her into a deep embrace and a passionate kiss that ended with her resting her head on his chest while he held her tightly.

He smiled at the memory. *How long ago was that? Nine months? A year? Or more?* It must be more. It was spring then, just before the emperor had ordered them to assemble for the march south to invade Shalanum. Now, it was the following summer, and

Abdul had led the army to set up the siege on Kasha Marka while Commander General Sharav helped Emperor Lao negotiate the surrender of Shalanum's high ministers.

Abdul's attention was drawn back to the valley as the reward for his quiet rumination was rewarded. The shadowed mist that covered the basin around Kasha Marka suddenly came alive with streaks of gold when the sun broke free of the horizon. The blacks and grays of the hulking city turned purple as they reflected rising light. He sat and watched in awe, silently sipping from his clay mug until the spell of color ended and the sun bathed the valley in new light.

With a sigh, Abdul stood and folded up his chair. He carried it in one hand and his cup of kaffe in the other as he strode back to his tent. The aroma of bacon was already drifting through the gap in the tent flaps.

"General Hamazi, good morning!" Captain Tilgman, Abdul's aide-de-camp greeted him as he entered. "I've prepared bacon, beans, quail eggs, and fresh tomatoes for you this morning, sir."

"That sounds great, Porter," General Hamazi said as he unfolded his chair next to the table. It was okay to break decorum a little bit in private.

Porter poured Abdul a fresh cup of kaffe as he sat down and then hustled away to retrieve the steaming breakfast plate. "A few messages arrived for you while you were out, General."

Abdul stretched out one hand for the messages while he

scooped a spoonful of beans into his mouth with the other. He could tell by the feel of the paper that one was different from the others before he saw them. Four of the messages were just battle reports from the various generals in charge of the siege troops at different sections of Kasha Marka's six-league perimeter. One message was from Captain Kabir inside the city—he would read it next. But the final message was a thicker, folded paper and was closed tight with the emperor's wax seal.

General Hamazi tore open the seal and scanned the contents. "Interesting," he mumbled and then read through the letter a second time, more carefully.

"What is it?" Captain Tilgman asked. "Anything I can help with?"

Abdul suppressed a grin. This letter must have been driving Porter crazy all morning. It was rare to receive a sealed message directly from Emperor Lao. It would have been more traditional to receive orders from General Sharav. Abdul briefly considered teasing the young man but relented.

"Emperor Lao has appointed Commander General Sharav governor *pro tempore* over Shalanum Province. The emperor has ordered me to assume command of the expeditionary forces for the foreseeable future. My first order is to secure the city of Kasha Marka and the larger province of Magora." General Hamazi summarized the contents of the letter.

"That's amazing! Congratulations, General." Captain

Tilgman was visibly excited. The promotion for Hamazi meant an equally important promotion for him, though the captain didn't mention this.

"Thank you, Porter," Hamazi said with a smile. Captain Tilgman had served as his aide for many years, and the occasional use of his given name was warranted—only when they were alone, of course.

He opened the note from Captain Kabir. It was a simple message: "+2 grain burn. K.M. on ½ rat per Kess. Cows sick from psn. +2 target next week."

"That boy is amazing." Hamazi held out the note for his aide to read.

"Lieutenant Kabir has been a commendable leader for the Night Birds," Porter agreed. "I wasn't sure when Emperor Lao first appointed him, but I see now that it was an inspired choice. Emperor Lao truly does have an eye for talent."

"Especially when it comes to tactics," General Hamazi added. He returned to his breakfast and scanned through the other missives. There wasn't much of note in any of them. They were standard morning reports.

"General, if you are done with your breakfast, it is nearly time for this morning's council meeting. The other generals will be arriving soon at the command tent."

Abdul took another sip of his kaffe and then walked to his private section of the tent to don his uniform. Once he was dressed,

Captain Tilgman took a horsehair brush to the front and back of the uniform to remove any wrinkles. Tilgman made some final adjustments to the general's cuffs and collar before nodding his approval.

The tent was already full when General Hamazi arrived, and the other officers were crowded around a central table that showed a map of the surrounding area. Several large blocks were stacked in the center depicting the city of Kasha Marka. Gilded blocks depicted each of the city's four gates. Groups of wooden figurines were assembled outside each gate showing the position of Hamazi's army.

The smallest contingent—a single horse, soldier, and archer model—represented General Malik's forces north of the Crown's Gate. General Kandiba's group of three infantrymen, two bowmen, and two horses formed a semi-circle around the western gate, also called the Wadi Gate after the dried riverbed that passed nearby. An identical group represented General Volkov's forces outside the Spice Gate to the south and General Soliman's men at the Merchant's Gate on the eastern side of the city. Half of Volkov's figurines faced the city, and the other half faced south toward a caravan of blue painted figures that Volkov had just added to the map. The new troops showed two cavalry, four infantrymen, and two archery units marching north from Kantibar.

General Hamazi waited for General Volkov to finish adjusting the figures before catching his eye with the unspoken question.

"Scouts have reported that Eshe Kess, general of the Magoran army, has marshaled their forces and is moving north," General Volkov addressed the assembly. "He leads a sizable force. They are no match for our army as a whole, but spread out as we are, they could create a significant disruption to the siege. We have no more than a week to prepare for their arrival."

General Hamazi considered the new information. "General Kandiba, I want you and General Soliman to each send an infantry division south to reinforce General Volkov's lines. I also want you to each reposition one of your cavalry divisions at an oblique and be prepared to harass General Kess's flanks when I give the order. We must prevent them from joining forces with his sister on the field as well and stop them from crushing General Volkov's men against the walls."

The other officers nodded their understanding.

A sudden commotion of muted voices outside the tent broke Hamazi's concentration. The apologetic face of one of the guards poked through the tent flaps. "Apologies, generals, there is an urgent message from the front."

General Hamazi waved his hand, and a panting messenger was allowed to pass.

"Doves, General." The messenger bent over, slightly resting his hands on his knees while he breathed hard. "Hundreds of them."

Hamazi gave the man a moment to recover before saying, "Please explain, son."

The messenger took a deep breath and tried again. "We was watching the woods to the south when, all of a sudden, hundreds of doves and pigeons start flying out of the forest toward the city. We took shots at a few, just for fun, and maybe to add a bit of meat to the gruel. But then someone noticed that they had little messages tied to their legs. They was all carrying the little notes. We started shooting at them for real, and we must have shot two hundred of 'em, but there were so many—a bunch of them made it past the walls."

General Hamazi resisted the urge to roll his eyes at what was surely an exaggeration and addressed the messenger in an even tone. "You mentioned notes. Did you bring any with you?"

"Yeah, they was all the same. But I brought one for you to see." The messenger held out a crumpled piece of paper.

General Hamazi took the note and then dismissed the messenger. "Thank you, Corporal. You can return to your post."

The runner bowed briefly and then exited the tent.

General Hamazi smoothed the paper and then read the haiku printed on it out loud. "River's memories. Crimson sky, two gibbous moons. Fly free, little dove." He raised his eyes to see the equally baffled stares of his subordinates.

"Well, it's obviously a code of some kind," General Kandiba offered.

"Great observation, Titus," General Volkov muttered under his breath.

Hamazi gave his second-in-command a warning glance before turning to a flustered Kandiba. "Agreed," he said, trying to set the junior general at ease. "The line 'Fly free, little dove' seems to indicate an escape plan. Any other thoughts?"

Hamazi listened while the others added to the speculation. If it was an escape plan, then General Kess would need to communicate a location and time. Crimson sky could indicate sunset, but they couldn't reach agreement on the rest.

"Assign a few officers from the signal corps to puzzle it out," General Hamazi commanded. "The ones that show a knack for code-breaking. What else do we need to consider?" He turned his attention back to the map.

Understanding that the discussion about the haiku was over, the other officers studied the defensive positions and offered additional suggestions to prepare for General Kess's arrival.

Chapter Two

Cheung Po

Darius opened his eyes slowly. His head ached and the light filtering through the handsewn curtains felt like nails being driven into his skull. He felt a combination of pain and relief in his legs and back, fully straightened for the first time in more than two months. He lay in a bed that felt like a cloud. The downy softness felt familiar somehow.

He fluttered his eyelids, trying to blink away the fire. Little by little, the room came into focus. The room was familiar, and Darius remembered the many trips that he and Arthengal had taken to visit the Cherians on their farm during his youth. He had slept many a night in this very bed.

His fingers danced over the patchwork quilt that Elsie Cherian had made. His neck protested as he turned his head to see the handcrafted dresser that Hanish Cherian constructed for his father decades before. His eyes drifted across the hand-hooked rug where he'd played games with Kal, Nasha, and Anna. He turned his head the other way, looking for the rocking chair that Arthengal helped Hanish build.

A figure sat in the chair. Darius's brain took a moment to reconcile the shape. It wasn't Arthengal, as he'd half expected. This man was smaller, and though his darkened skin reminded Darius a little of Arthengal, his leathery visage had been burned by years on the open sea rather than natural pigmentation. His hawkish features and straight dark hair were much different than Arthengal's rounder face and long wavy hair.

The man rocked in the chair reading a book on his lap. Darius didn't know the man well but had met him often enough to recognize his face. He was married to Gabriella Portor, the owner of Sew Elegant, Darius's favorite clothing store in Eridu.

"Arnon?" Darius's voice croaked.

The old sailor looked up from the book.

"Ah, he's awake," Arnon said. "How do you feel?"

Darius touched his throat. "Thirsty."

"Of course, of course." Arnon stood from the rocking chair and crossed the room. He poured water from a porcelain pitcher on the dresser into a tin mug. He held it to Darius's lips while he sipped. Arnon pulled the cup back as Darius broke into a fit of coughing. Once the spasms settled, he helped him drink some more.

"Better?" the older man asked.

Darius nodded.

He tried to speak again, but his throat was raw, and he only managed to get out a few words. "Why am I here?" His eyes signaled around the room.

"You mean at the Cherian place?" Arnon asked.

Darius nodded.

"That's a long story, but suffice it to say, we're looking after Hanish's place while he and his family are away," Arnon answered. "We rescued you from that prison wagon the imperials had you in the night before last. You've been pretty much sleeping ever since." Then, he changed the subject. "You hungry?"

Darius's stomach growled at the mere mention of food.

Arnon laughed. "I'll take that as a yes. You rest…I'll get you something to eat."

The man exited the room and Darius struggled to sit up. His muscles screamed with every motion. After a labored battle, he was finally able to leverage his body into a half-sitting position with pillows propped against the dark cherry headboard.

Arnon returned with a tray and a steaming bowl of porridge. "Elsie would have fits over how we're abusing her poor kitchen, but ain't none of us here that can cook like her." He laughed.

Darius took a bite. It was bland but he could swallow it easily, and his stomach didn't mind the lack of flavor. He had grown accustomed to a lack of seasoning during his two months in captivity. The imperials mostly fed him hardtack and water and the occasional mutton stew.

"Go easy to start," Arnon cautioned. "I don't know what they've been feeding you, but it doesn't look to have been much, and

Elsie would kill us if you threw up all over her nice quilt."

Darius nodded and took small bites. He was surprised that he was only able to eat half the bowl before his stomach felt full. He pushed the tray away and relaxed into the pillows.

"That's enough for right now," Arnon said. "You want to tell me how you ended up in that cage?"

"I was captured when we tried to rescue Anna outside of Kasha Marka," Darius said. "I think they were bringing me down here to show off their prize to Emperor Lao."

Arnon nodded. "Sounds about right. How did Anna end up in their hands?"

"Micah had her," Darius growled at the memory. "Brought her with him when the imperial army set up their siege around Kasha Marka." The memories flooded back, and his head began to throb.

"Micah, your brother?" Arnon asked, surprised. He knew the name, but Darius had always implied that Micah was killed when the imperials raided his town and captured their mother.

"It's a long story," Darius said. He rubbed his eyes. "Do you mind if we get into it later?"

"Of course," Arnon said. "You rest some more. I'll be here if you need anything."

Darius nodded, closed his eyes, and drifted back to sleep.

"You look better today," Arnon announced as he entered the room.

"You're getting some of your color back."

It had been three days since Darius awakened to find himself convalescing in the Cherian family farmhouse. After two months of being locked in a cage too small to stand up in, he didn't feel like he was looking better. His entire body was sore, and his muscles didn't feel like they worked right. He had tried to get out of bed a couple of days before to go outside and relieve himself, but his legs collapsed underneath him as soon as his feet hit the floor.

Arnon had helped him back into bed, and then, to Darius's embarrassment, had to help him piss into a bucket. The next day was worse, and Darius felt mortified when Arnon was forced to clean Darius's backside once the prior day's porridge had worked its way through.

"You fancy a walk around the room?" Arnon asked.

Darius cringed. He didn't want a repeat of his prior attempt.

"Come on," Arnon urged. "You've got to start using your legs again. I'll help you." He came to the edge of the bed and held out his arms.

Reluctantly, Darius reached out. Arnon draped one of his arms over his shoulder and then wrapped his own arm around Darius's waist. With a grunt from both of them, Arnon dragged Darius out of bed to stand on wobbly legs.

"Good, good," Arnon said. "Now, let's try a step."

With Arnon's help, Darius was able to lift his foot enough to shuffle it forward half a span. They repeated the process with the second leg. After ten short steps, they turned around and made their way back to the bed. Darius collapsed, surprised at how exhausted he felt. Arnon helped him swing his legs up onto the mattress.

"Here, let's see if we can get your legs to move while lying on the bed." Arnon lifted one of Darius's legs. "Pull it toward your chest like you're stepping up onto the back of a wagon."

Darius tried but failed. His legs ached, and when he willed them to move, they flopped uselessly from one side to the other. After a moment, Arnon made him try again, except, this time, he pushed on Darius's foot, forcing the knee to bend.

"Aaaaah!" Darius cried out in pain. Fiery spikes radiated through his lower back, hip, and knee.

"Okay, now straighten it out. Try to push against my hand."

He tried, but Arnon ended up pulling the leg straight more than Darius pushed it. They tried several more times before Arnon switched to the other leg. By the end, the motion caused dull aches rather than shooting pain, but Arnon was doing most of the work.

"Okay, I think you earned some mutton stew. What do you think?"

Darius laughed half-heartedly and gave an exhausted nod.

The mutton had been overemphasized, and the term "stew" was a stretch for the contents of the bowl that Arnon brought. It was mostly a cloudy broth with a few small chunks of carrot and potato and two thumb-sized chunks of meat.

Little by little, over the next few days, Darius's strength

returned—with the help of Arnon's ministrations. By the end of a week, Darius could walk around the room, holding on to Arnon's shoulder, and by the end of the second week, he could shuffle down the hallway unaided.

"How's our boy?" a gruff voice sounded from the door of the bedroom.

Darius had been practicing sitting in a chair and standing, holding onto Arnon's arm for support. The sound startled him, his hands slipped from Arnon's wrist, and he sat down hard, nearly toppling from the chair. He'd heard voices of other men outside in the farmyard, so he knew that he and Arnon weren't alone on the Cherian farm, but he hadn't actually met any of the other men. The deep timbre of the voice sounded like gravel scraping along the bottom of a boat. The man that belonged to the voice was a heavily muscled man with a graying beard and long mustache. His eyes were narrow and he had a thick head of salt-and-pepper hair tied into a loose braid. His face was thicker than Arnon's, but he had the same look of a lifelong sailor.

"Uh, hello. Who are you?" Darius didn't mean for his voice to squeak, but it did just the same, making him sound intimidated by the hulking figure. He cleared his throat and tried again with more confidence. "I'm Darius. And you are?"

"Did Arthengal ever tell you the story of Nasu Rabi and the Pirate King?" Arnon asked.

"Of course, many times," Darius answered. "It was one of his favorites."

"Darius Kabir, may I introduce you to Cheung Po, also known as *the Pirate King*."

Now Darius was intimidated, more by the legend than the man. His eyes widened and he took the old sailor in with new comprehension. "I don't understand," he said simply.

Cheung Po laughed. A deep hearty laugh. "A bit out of place and time, yeah? Like a villain stepping out of a fairy tale?"

"Something like that," Darius said.

"Well, let's start with the fact that I'm neither a pirate nor a king," Cheung Po explained.

"I think the imperial captains that you faced over the years would disagree," Arnon interjected.

"Okay, maybe a bit of a pirate," Cheung Po relented. "But only insomuch as it was necessary to protect the people from the cruelty of the Tyrant King."

Darius's thoughts were a jumble. His eyes darted between the two men.

Cheng Po saw the expression and laughed again. "Don't worry, we'll get into all of that later. For now, suffice it to say that Arnon and I have been friends for a very long time, and I helped him rescue you from the imperials. We'll work out the finer details of who was a villain and who was a hero another time." He chuckled again and then turned to leave the room.

Arnon turned a sympathetic eye to Darius. "It will all make sense soon enough. Fancy a try at the stairs?"

Chapter Three

The Wadi Gate

General Hamazi watched the field with satisfaction from his position on a tall hillock west of the city. The sun was creeping over the horizon in the east. He could just make out the shadowed outlines of General Volkov's defensive barricades in the south. The early morning mist obscured battalions of General Kandiba's horsemen spread out across the plains, east of Hamazi's position.

The rest of Kandiba's forces stretched more than a league, the length of the western wall, with the bulk centered near the Wadi Gate. He could still see the last remnants of the enemy's campfires, which had dotted the southern tree line like starlight only a few hours before.

Eshe Kess had arrived more quickly than anticipated, but the imperial defenses were strong. In Hamazi's opinion, General Kess would have very little chance of breaking the siege. He seemed determined to try, though, however fruitless it might be.

The Magoran forces launched their first assault as the sun rose above the distant desert hills. Rather than attacking the heavily entrenched forces near the Merchant's Gate, horsemen rode across the open plain to strike at the western edge of Kandiba's forces. The angle of attack gave them the advantage of having the sun at their backs, and General Kandiba's right flank paid heavily. He quickly adjusted, however, and drove the Magoran horsemen back to the edge of the forest with a well-delivered counter-offensive.

The clash of arms rang out sporadically across the valley as, over the course of the day, General Kess continued to test the imperial defenses. First, he tried to outflank General Kandiba on the west, but the terrain was not ideal for a cavalry assault. Next, he tried to bring his forces close to the wall of Kasha Marka in order to use the archers on the wall as cover. But this took him too close to General Volkov's forces in the south, and between Volkov and Kandiba, they were able to squeeze Kess's lines and force him to retreat or risk being cut off from the bulk of his army.

Meanwhile, archers from the city walls attacked in support of each of General Eshe's assaults. General Hamazi's army easily defended, locking shields to block the majority of the arrows that flew from Kasha Marka. It was an ineffectual distraction at best.

The dance continued throughout the day. As Hamazi watched the battle play out, he began to suspect that General Kess was toying with the imperial army. This theory was reinforced by the fact that reports of casualties on either side were minimal. Hamazi surmised that Kess was trying to get him and his generals to overcommit in their response. General Volkov was smart. He saw that he had the advantage, and there was no benefit to pressing the attack. He took advantage of opportunities to deal damage to the Magoran forces but didn't overcommit.

General Kandiba, on the other hand, seemed to be getting frustrated with the constant harassment. Kess had outmatched him during several confrontations, and now his responses were emotionally charged.

Hamazi looked at the sun. Within the hour, it would settle behind the mountains in the west. The moon was rising in opposition to the sun, moving counterclockwise across the sky. The sun was still too bright and Hamazi could only make out a faint outline parallel to the ground.

Hamazi signaled to one of his runners. He hadn't needed to give his generals much instruction throughout the day, but he was concerned that Kandiba may do something rash as dusk approached. Even as he thought this, he noticed some of Kandiba's forces being redeployed from near the Wadi Gate to offer additional resistance against Kess's next charge.

He's planning a large counterassault before nightfall to try to break Kess's forces. This is what Kess has been waiting for.

The messenger arrived.

Hamazi scrawled a quick note on a messenger's scroll: "Hold the line. Do not go on the offensive."

He handed the note to the runner. "Deliver this to General Kandiba immediately."

The soldier gave a quick bow and then began sprinting in the direction of General Kandiba's standard.

The sky darkened from pale blue to vermillion as if the sun was painting the horizon with a final burst of color before bidding the world goodnight. The words from General Kess's haiku message to his sister played back in his mind:

"River's memories.
Crimson sky, two gibbous moons.
Fly free, little dove."

Hamazi glanced at the moon. It hung, a pale reflection in the sky, midway from the horizon to its apex. If the sky was a sundial, the moon would be resting near two o'clock. A million thoughts came together at once in Hamazi's head. His eyes flitted to the battlefield, then back to the sky, then to Kandiba's forces slowly shifting position.

River's memories, river's memories, he thought. He was still missing something. The memory of a river…a dry riverbed? *Wadi!* Realization exploded in his mind like a fire burst.

"The Wadi Gate!" he shouted out loud with a mixture of pride at solving the puzzle and fear that it was too late.

His aides looked at him in confusion.

Just then, their attention was drawn back to the battle as a war cry started low along the southern line of trees. Infantry poured from the forest, and the low rumble became a roar that echoed through the heights as thousands of men turned the distant plain black. Hamazi saw General Kandiba's troops immediately assemble along the wall in preparation for the inevitable archery barrage, but it never came.

Instead, the sky to the west turned dark with arrows that fell like rain on Kandiba's flank. Cries of alarm echoed from the valley floor. General Hamazi realized that the constant aggression from the city walls had not been designed to damage his troops but rather keep the shield walls engaged as General Eshe's archers took the heights behind them. The imperial forces were not expecting the sudden, vicious attack from the rear. Hamazi watched as dozens of his men were cut down by the black shafts as they scrambled to adjust their defenses.

It must have taken them all day to get archers into position to attack that flank without being detected.

The Magoran infantry moved toward the weakened flank, and Kandiba's forces began to move to bolster their defenses. The imperial troops, who had been slowly marching from the Wadi Gate toward Kandiba's defensive positions to help with the counterassault, quickened their pace and moved double time to try to intercept.

As the last of the infantry cleared the tree line, the raucousness of the war cry was drowned out by the thunder of hooves. All of Kess's cavalry seemed to emerge at once. They were attacking in force, intending to break Kandiba's western line.

"Where do they plan to go?" Hamazi heard one of his aides ask.

Another shrugged. "Even if they make it to the city, they'll be trapped inside like the others."

Hamazi groaned. They had not yet connected the attack to General Kess's pledge to rescue his sister.

"Issue orders," he shouted. "Reinforce the Wadi Gate. Don't let the Magorans—" he cut off, saw the towering panels of wood and iron begin to move, and realized it was too late.

The city gate opened slowly. Hamazi was sure that men were turning furiously on the cranks inside the walls, but a thing as massive as the gate did not start moving quickly. As soon as the gap was wide enough, horses charged through. What started as a trickle turned into a deluge and the imperial lines closest to the city wall were quickly overrun.

The baroness's banner appeared in the center of the charging forces. Men on foot followed the horse charge across the field. However, rather than engaging, they merely followed the cavalry through the hole it had created. The imperial forces, expecting an aerial assault, were unprepared for this type of massive ground attack.

For the first time, the scene below them devolved from the boring game of cat and mouse that had played out all day into a truly brutal battle. Baroness Kess's forces clashed with the assembled infantry with the sudden fierceness of a late summer storm. Thunder of hooves, clouds of dust, and sparks of iron striking iron that lit the gloomy landscape. The narrow strip of grassland soon became slick with blood, but the city forces didn't slow. Kandiba's lines shattered at the focal point of the attack, and Baroness Kess turned her long column southwest.

Eshe Kess's charge struck with a similar ferocity. The war cry that had signaled the onset continued and grew louder. The constant noise made it impossible for General Kandiba's shouted orders or trumpet calls to be heard and he had to switch to flag signals to rally his men. In the confusion, it did not take long for General Kess's forces in the southwest to meet his sister's forces as they fled the city. As soon as the two groups met, the Magoran forces turned south. They hit Kandiba's western flank again, in force. Faced with a second brutal assault, many of Kandiba's men turned and fled toward more secure defenses.

Kess didn't pursue, however—he just widened the gap and allowed the massive army to escape into trees to the south. The initial assault took thirty minutes at most, and within another thirty, the field was clear of Magoran forces. A bewildered Kandiba could be seen riding from one commander to the next trying to organize a counter. Then he stopped (Hamazi's runner must have finally arrived) and began reorganizing his defenses.

General Hamazi glanced around at his own command staff.

They seemed as dumbstruck as Kandiba. The gates to the city remained open and unmanned. General Hamazi realized too that the ever-present archers no longer manned the walls. The Kess's had just executed a full military evacuation, leaving the city open for the imperial forces to take over. It was obvious that they depended on Emperor Lao's goodwill to protect the welfare of its citizens even though they remained at war.

Hamazi nodded to himself in appreciation of the maneuver. It was a safe bet. Emperor Lao had not molested the citizenry following similar victories in Shalanum. Emperor Lao had no desire to punish or alienate the people of the empire for the sins of their leaders. Emperor Lao saw the campaign as liberating the citizens rather than dominating them.

"Send in troops to secure the city," Hamazi ordered. "Make sure none of the citizenry are harmed. Organize a pursuit force to harass the Magorans as they flee south. I doubt they will try to reorganize and attack but make sure they don't. Keep them moving south until they reach Basara."

"What just happened?" a baffled Captain Tilgman asked.

"Eshe Kess just rescued his sister and surrendered Kasha Marka to the empire," Hamazi answered simply and turned his horse back toward his command tent to await reports.

Chapter Four

Reunited

Darius unsheathed the borrowed sword and set the scabbard down in the dusty courtyard. He let his hand mold around the leather wrappings on the hilt and flexed his wrist, adjusting to the unfamiliar weight. The weapon was slightly unbalanced, but nothing he couldn't adjust to. The blade was broader than usual, which created an almost imperceptible drag as he swung the sword back and forth through the air.

His eyes drifted around the familiar square. The Cherians' house, behind him, where he had spent many a night surrounded by comfort and laughter. The barn and stock yard to his right where he had learned how to milk cows under Elsie Cherian's watchful eye. The orchards and fields to his left and all around the surrounding property where he and Arthengal had helped Hanish, Kal, and Nash harvest their crops. The stone well in the center of the courtyard and the road beyond, which led south to Eridu and north to the mountain home he had shared with Arthengal near the abandoned city of Anbar Ur.

He started to move, slowly. He pushed past the screams of his aching muscles and forced a slow but precise version of Lazy Viper. It was the first sword form Arthengal ever taught him and the one his muscles remembered most easily.

There were so many memories in this place, now made unfamiliar by the absence of those he had made them with. Arthengal was dead, killed by the new emperor. Anna Cherian, his betrothed, was in Kasha Marka, safe under the protection of Baroness Magora—at least he hoped that was the case. He had been captured before he could confirm that her rescue was successful.

Kal Cherian was with Darius's mother, most likely on a boat bound for Ito. Hanish, Elsie, and Nash were living on a cattle ranch with Elsie's brother hundreds of leagues to the east. In their place, unfamiliar men moved around the property, tended the crops, drew water from the well, and slept in the house.

Movement through the sword form stretched his muscles. They resisted at first, but soon settled into the comfortable motion and were even soothed by it. Darius fought the urge to pick up speed, knowing that what his body needed now was long, exact movements to build back his strength and flexibility.

"You do that very well," a now familiar voice called from the steps of the house.

"Thank you," Darius responded to Cheung Po's compliment without interrupting the form.

"I wonder, though, if you have been taught to depend on the

wrong tool." Cheung Po's voice had a tone of genuineness.

"What do you mean?" Darius asked. He was only nineteen, but he'd been praised by many as the most naturally gifted swordsman since his mentor, Arthengal.

"Do you understand that the sword is a tool and is not the weapon?"

Darius couldn't hold back a laugh. "I've found the sword to be a pretty effective weapon."

"No," Cheung Po said simply. "You have been deceived."

"How so?"

"The weapon is not the sword; it is but a device, an extension of the weapon, if you will. The true weapon is you, Darius."

Darius laughed again.

"I promise you that you can be just as dangerous without the piece of metal as you are with it, but you have been trained to use it as a crutch."

Darius finished the sword form and turned to face the other man. Cheung Po was tall, his skin bronzed from a lifetime on the open sea. His thick arms, exposed by the short sleeves of his loose cotton shirt, were etched with scars and painted with tattoos. Cheung Po's black hair was straight, short at the front to keep it out of his dark, penetrating eyes, and tied into a long braid at the back. Calloused hands pointed at the sword.

"It is like a rope or block and tackle. Both make it easier for me to load cargo onto my ship. I recognize their value, but I do not depend on them. If the ropes break or the block and tackle jams, I can still load my ship."

Darius shook his head, not understanding the analogy.

"Let me ask you this," Cheung Po continued. "If I were to take the sword away and replace it with a stick, could you still defend yourself?"

"I suppose," Darius said. "It would be like a practice sword."

"And if I take the stick away and replace it with a shield?"

"Yes," Darius nodded. "Many of the forms work with a shield as well. I could defend myself."

"And if I replaced the shield with a length of rope?"

Darius sniggered at the thought.

"You think I jest? Allow me to demonstrate."

Cheung Po crossed the yard and retrieved one of the thick lead ropes for the horses that was hanging over the fence to the stockyard. He stretched his arms out to full width, jerking on the rope to test its strength. A little bit of extra rope dangled from each of his outstretched hands.

He held the cable more loosely as he approached Darius.

"Attack me," Cheung Po ordered.

"What?"

"Go on, attack me. I assure you, I'll be fine."

Darius moved forward suddenly with Wild Horse Leaps. He watched as Cheung Po's feet responded with Rose at Sunset—a natural defense to the attack. It was the man's hands that caught

Darius by surprise. They moved in short, quick circles, causing the rope to form a succession of loops that wound around Darius's weapon hand. Cheung Po gave an abrupt jerk. There was a stab of pain in Darius's wrist. His hand went numb and the sword fell from his grasp. It clattered to the ground at his feet, stirring up clouds of dust.

"Again." Cheung Po pointed with his chin to the weapon.

Darius rubbed his wrist and then retrieved the blade. He assaulted the man with Striking Adder. Cheung Po moved incredibly quickly for a man of his age and rolled under the thrusting blade before popping up in a standing position behind Darius. He gave a jerk on the rope again, and Darius felt his legs get yanked out from beneath him.

"Again." Cheung Po let the longer end of the rope dangle from his hand.

Darius stood and brushed himself off. He charged using Dancing Mongoose, bouncing quickly from one foot to the other, keeping both his hands and his feet free to avoid the previous counterattacks. The rope suddenly thrust forward, striking like a living snake. The nob at the end of the rope struck Darius between the eyes, making his head jerk back involuntarily. Before he could recover, the other end crashed down like a whip on his right shoulder. The impact almost made him drop his sword again. He transitioned to Dragon Whips his Tail, attacking the rope now rather than the man, and then it was over. Cheung Po's foot thrust out, striking Darius's extended knee—a hand like iron struck his right arm just below the wrist, making his hand go numb again. The sword was easily knocked away with another counterstrike, and then a palm to the chest sent the unbalanced Darius sprawling to the ground.

"You turned your focus to the tool and ignored the weapon." Cheung Po extended a hand to help Darius up. "You see…the tools are useful, but the weapon is here." He clutched Darius's shoulders. "And here." Cheung Po touched a finger to Darius's forehead. "And here." Finally, he placed a hand over Darius's heart.

Darius was dumbfounded. He had never encountered an opponent who could so easily disarm him—repeatedly. He had studied with Arthengal for years, and trained on dual sword forms with the Magoran Lord Misrak during his months in Kasha Marka. Both men were sword masters, but Cheung Po made short work of the skills they had taught him.

"Do you understand?" Cheung Po asked as if not sure how to read Darius's expression.

Darius considered the words. "Teach me."

Cheung Po cocked his head, studying the boy. "You have a lot to unlearn."

"Teach me," Darius repeated.

Cheung Po nodded. "Very well…under one condition."

"Name it."

"You must not touch a sword again until I say you can."

Darius ran his fingers through his long blond hair, brushing it back over his ears. He felt a surge of panic at the thought of being defenseless this close to an imperial stronghold. He took a deep breath and let it out slowly before nodding. "Agreed."

The exchange was interrupted by a clamor near the gate. Cheung Po's men were shouting and rushing to arm themselves. At first, Darius thought it must be an imperial scouting party attacking the farm, but as his eyes lifted above the gate to the field beyond, he saw a solitary shape moving toward the farm. It was brown and nearly the size of a horse and moved in an unconcerned manner toward the farmhouse.

"Antu!" Darius shouted. He ran across the yard and through the gate.

The bear stopped and sniffed the air at the second shout.

Darius rushed across the field and leaped at the bear, enfolding the massive neck in an embrace.

The beast grunted but otherwise didn't move. When Darius released the embrace and stepped back, Antu raised his muzzle to sniff Darius's wounded eye, then extended a long pink and black tongue to lick the side of his face, leaving a trail of saliva from his chin to his hairline.

Darius laughed. "I missed you too."

The bear grunted and continued walking toward the farm.

Darius turned to join him and was confronted by a dozen shocked faces scattered across the courtyard in various stages of armament. Cheung Po, however, showed no reaction other than the faint trace of a smile that drifted across his lips for an instant and then was gone.

Chapter Five

Divine Light

The desert sun had baked the clay soil into a patchwork of misshapen bricks separated by a spiderweb of cracks that stretched into the infinite distance in front of Ullani. Her throat was parched and her horse had been reduced to slow, plodding steps. When she first agreed to transport the reliquary to Kasha Haaki, she had not anticipated such a difficult journey. Initially, Baroness Kess arranged for her to travel with Prince El' Nasir and his retinue, but she had been forced to separate from them when imperial troops tracked down the caravan.

Shapes began to form out of the heat waves to the south. Striated red hills towered above the shimmering veil in sharp contrast to the broken brown gray below. Ullani's eyes had a difficult time focusing. The hills first seemed close, magnified in her vision, and then they were suddenly far away. The shimmer that separated the shattered landscape and the towering hills began to form colors of its own. Shades of green and blue emerged from the blinding white. She tried to urge her horse forward at a faster pace, but the horse had no more will left than Ullani did. Instead, the steady, muted *clop, clop* of horseshoes against clay drummed in her ears.

Something unfamiliar tickled her nose. The scent was heavy and wet but also sweet. It was like smelling a bouquet of flowers through a burlap sack soaked with water. It took her a while to realize that she was smelling the plant life that had sprung to life along the banks of the river. She could literally smell the humid air as water evaporated from the river mixed with the aroma of decaying leaves, stunted conifers, and sage.

Her horse stopped at the edge of the waterway, its front hooves submerged in the flowing water, and its back hooves on the rocky shore. The mare lowered her muzzle to the water, letting it just dance across her skin before finally drinking. Ullani dismounted and dropped to her knees in the water next to the horse. She scooped the water in her hands, raising it to her mouth, and took a long, satisfying drink. Her belly started to recoil after a few gulps, so she paused to splash water on her face and arms.

Ullani pulled her horse's nose away from the water to prevent the mare from drinking herself sick. She guided the animal across the waist-deep river to the flattened shore on the other side. A road of sorts had been cleared through the underbrush on this side of the river, and she knew from the maps that she'd been provided that there was a walled waypoint no more than a league or so downriver from this crossing. She was afraid that if she remounted the horse, it would just return to the water, so she continued to walk, leading the animal.

The air beside the river, while humid, was cooler than the surrounding desert. Ullani found her energy returning the further downstream they traveled. After an hour, she could see the open archways of the wall that surrounded a man-made pool and several small adobe structures. Taller trees grew around the small lake, offering more shade to travelers.

There were other visitors to the waypoint either traveling downstream to the Ziindi Bay where they could secure ferry passage to Kasha Haaki or traveling upstream to trade with the nomadic tribes of the Ziyandi Desert. Ullani picked her way past other groups until she found a somewhat isolated spot on the southern side of the lake to set up camp.

The mostly male travelers gave her quizzical—and sometimes hostile—looks. The idea of a woman traveling alone was foreign to most of them. She wondered if she would have any trouble tonight. She loosened the knives in the sheaths hidden beneath the folds of her clothing along her forearms and at the base of her neck so she could easily extract them if she needed to defend herself.

Once she was settled and a simple meal of rice and beans was simmering over a campfire, she surveyed the scene on the opposite side of the small lake. The adobe buildings seemed to be permanent trade establishments where people could restock supplies. She was running low on a few things and would have to visit the traders before she continued her journey downstream. The rest of the journey should be easier now that she was out of the alkaline flats and could follow the river.

The night was quiet with the exception of the occasional screech of a nighthawk and the hooting of owls. Ullani slept lightly and was pleasantly surprised when her rest went uninterrupted. Maybe there was a code among the desert traders or maybe the oasis was just busy enough to secure her safety. Whichever the case, she was grateful for a good night's sleep.

She awoke early just as the sun was starting to peek over the eastern horizon. Light reflected off the buckles of the saddlebag that had served as her pillow. Ullani reached for the bag and then pulled back her hand. She reached again and tentatively loosened the straps that secured the flap. Sifting through her spare clothes, she unwrapped the dark box and set it on the ground in front of her. Her fingers stroked the pair of keys underneath her tunic as she stared at the box.

Every morning since she separated from the caravan, she had repeated this ritual. Part of her wanted to remain loyal to Saria and the baroness and deliver the box, unmolested, to Kasha Haaki and then on to Kasha Nisir. Also, inside her was an insatiable curiosity to know what was in the box. She pulled the chain from under her shirt and looked at the keys.

"Maybe just a quick look," she said to herself. "There's no

harm in that, right?"

She removed the keys from the chain and inserted them into the matching locks. Her breathing began to quicken. She turned the keys as one. The sound of the twin clicks sent a shiver of excitement down her spine. Reaching forward gingerly, she lifted the lid.

In the shadows of the trees, the bejeweled objects in the box looked dull. There were two objects inside. The first was a golden diadem adorned with a variety of beautifully cut gems and crystals. In the center of the crown was an ovular jade carving of a dragon circling back on itself. The second object was a crystal about the size of her fist. She could only describe the shape as a pyramidic teardrop. There were four semi-flat sides, but overall, it was rounded. There were many facets cut into its surface.

Ullani lifted the bejeweled circlet out of the box and placed it on her head. It fit perfectly, resting atop her tight curls. She looked at her reflection in the pool. Twin sapphires dangled on pendants next to each of her ears. The crown was spectacular and seemed to magnify her beauty. She stood and looked at the pyramid, examining its chiseled edges. It looked like it was intended to be mounted atop a scepter or something similar. She held it aloft, trying to catch the reflection of the sun to make a rainbow with the prism.

Ullani was standing on the edge of the small lake, holding the prismatic orb at arm's length when she caught the perfect beam of light. The light shone through the prism and settled on the gems of the diadem. The crown seemed to grow warm, and she felt like she was being bathed in light. It was an almost holy experience.

A gasp echoed across the water. Ullani turned to see more than a dozen faces staring at her in wonder. She lowered her arm and the bathing light receded. She quickly returned the items to the box and hurried to pack her belongings. She needed to put some distance between her and these people before anyone got the idea to steal these treasures from her.

She had just finished securing the saddle and bags to her mount when she heard a branch snap behind her. She spun in a flash, a throwing dagger appearing in each of her hands. A crowd of men were emerging from the trees at the edge of her camp. She saw that many of them were armed, but none had their weapons drawn.

"Back off," she warned loudly. She held her knives ready to attack. "Just let me be on my way and nobody needs to get hurt."

"Empress," the closest man spoke. "Please allow us to serve you." With that, all of the men sank to their knees and lowered their heads in deference.

Ullani took a step back in surprise. She didn't lower the knives immediately. *Serve me? What in the blazes are they talking about?* She let the tips of the knives drop, studying the assemblage. *It could be useful to have an escort to Kasha Haaki. There's no harm in a little deception. Right?*

She tucked the blades back into their hiding places. What was she supposed to say? "Rise." Her voice was louder than intended. She was nervous, and it almost sounded like a shout.

The men scrambled to their feet but still refused to look her in the eyes.

She cleared her throat and spoke in what she hoped was a casual tone, "I will allow you to accompany me on my voyage to Kasha Haaki."

Chapter Six

Fallen Jewel

The crowd gathered around the *La Dame d'Miracles* fountain was growing restless. Micah and his men did their best to maintain order while they waited for General Hamazi to address the crowd.

The murmur in the crowd increased as Micah saw a wave of movement to the east. The throng parted briefly to make way for the general and his honor guard and then immediately closed behind him once he had passed.

General Hamazi arrived at the fountain and mounted a small platform that had been hastily erected. He stood, silently surveying the crowd and waiting for the chatter to die down.

"Good people of Kasha Marka," Hamazi spoke. His voice, born from years of addressing large groups of soldiers, carried over the crowd. "Emperor Lao Jun Qiu is most happy to have liberated you from the dominance of the illegal rule of *Baroness* Kess."

A ripple of uncomfortable laughter rippled through the crowd, then was quickly silenced.

"Our Holy Emperor wants you to know that he had nothing

but love and sympathy for the good people of Chungoku and its provinces," Hamazi continued. "We will remain to ensure a peaceful transition of power and to ensure that the emperor's people have what they need to return to a happy, prosperous life of freedom out of the clutches of tyranny."

This time, the tone of the murmurs was one of confusion and uncertainty.

"I will personally oversee the installation of a regional governor who takes his responsibility to the emperor and the empire's people seriously and is not devoted to the greed of his own selfish desires. We will ensure that free trade is restored to the province of Shalanum. Once we have liberated the port cities of Kantibar and Basara, we will also restore free trade throughout the imperial kingdom. Our goal is to aid in the prosperity of the empire and its people."

The mumblings sounded more excited with this wave.

"We understand that Baroness Kess destroyed many of the city's reserve provisions prior to fleeing with her brother to the south. No doubt to stir up resistance against the rightful emperor and his followers. I assure you that we have wagonloads of meat and grain on the way from the Taspin Plains as we seek to restore this city's supplies to provide respite for the good people of Magora while its own farmers and ranchers work to restore their livelihoods. Furthermore, I understand that the normal planting and harvest season was disrupted by our arrival and the baroness's resistance. I have been authorized to dispatch soldiers to help you plow and plant and harvest through the summer to get you back on track and independent."

This time, there were actual cheers in the crowd.

"Finally, in order to promote the full restoration of commercial interests in the good city of Kasha Marka, the emperor has authorized the distribution of a gold mark to every loyal citizen and his family. We will set up registration points throughout the city. You only need to record your name in the rolls, sign a pledge of loyalty, and the mark will be yours. His Holy Emperor has also authorized the issuance of a silver drach to all widows and orphans under the same conditions if they don't have the patronage of a loyal citizen."

"Long live Emperor Lao!" a man shouted from the crowd. Micah scanned the crowd, looking for the speaker. Another man shouted from nearby. Micah was sure that he recognized the man as one of Hamazi's field commanders. A third man shouted and then a fourth. Micah recognized Captain Zima in plain clothes. After a few more plants echoed the cheer, the actual citizenry tentatively picked up the chant until, slowly but surely, more than half the crowd was chanting, and "Long live Emperor Lao!" echoed across the marketplace.

General Hamazi let the chant continue for several minutes before raising his hands in the air to signal for silence. "Thank you, good people of Kasha Marka. Emperor Lao will be humbled by your passionate tribute. Now, please return to your homes and celebrate with your families. You are finally liberated! You live once again as free people of the empire! We will begin distribution of provisions and registration for the stimulus gifts in the morning."

Micah arrived outside the offices that General Hamazi had taken over in the palace. He had not been waiting long when one of the general's aides escorted him into the office.

"Ah, Lieutenant Kabir," the general said with a smile. "Thank you for coming."

The general stood behind a large oak desk. Several reports were spread out across its surface. Micah had only met the general on a couple of occasions, but he always exhibited the epitome of order and discipline. The disarray on the desk caught Micah by surprise and spoke volumes of the stress the general must be under while organizing the occupation of Kasha Marka.

"Of course, sir." Micah stood at attention.

"Lieutenant, you and your men did an excellent job during the siege. Your efforts allowed us to complete what could have easily been a years-long siege in a matter of months."

Micah flushed with pride. "Thank you, sir," he said. "It was our pleasure, sir."

General Hamazi shuffled some of the papers for a moment before he found the report he was looking for. "I have another mission for you."

"Name it, sir. The Night Birds are ready to serve."

"You are familiar with the mountain enclave, Patel's Rest?" General Hamazi asked.

"Yes, sir." Micah remembered the alpine village that he had tracked his brother to nearly a year before. It was a quaint town, well protected, that served as a key defensive position on the road across the Talia Mountains.

"Colonel Saranov will be leading a regiment to secure the community and the pass. We would like you to act as an advance team with the Night Birds. Infiltrate the town, identify any threats, sabotage defenses—you know what I mean."

Micah allowed himself a small grin. "Yes, sir! Do what the Night Birds do best. We won't let you down, sir. When do we leave?" Micah asked.

"You can leave as soon as you assemble your team. Keep it small enough to avoid notice. I hear they don't get many visitors up there. Colonel Saranov will follow with his regiment in three weeks."

"Yes, sir. Anything else?"

"No, Lieutenant. Good luck, son."

"Thank you, sir."

Micah surveyed his men. There were six sergeants in the Night

Birds, and he trusted every one of them with his life. "There will be six of us operating in pairs. Sergeant Einarsson, you will be in charge of the men while I'm away." Micah took a sip of his ale and glanced around the table.

"Of course," Joral responded. "Who are you taking?"

"I'll take Moab and Wang. Do you have any other recommendations?"

Moab raised his glass in salute. Sergeant Sasha gave Sergeant Wang a respectful nod and then punched him in the arm.

"That kid, Aslan, that joined us when we added replacements prior to the siege," Sergeant Yanov spoke up. "He did a great job running smash-and-grab missions. He can get into tight places and has a good head on his shoulders."

"Okay." Micah nodded. "Who else?"

"I've always liked Corporal Piccoli," Sergeant Garin said. "He's great with disguises and infiltration."

"You can't go wrong with Corporal Grigoriy," Sergeant Sasha added.

"Okay." Micah nodded again. "That works. Let your reports know. We'll meet here at dawn and head out."

"Yes, sir," the men echoed.

"Now, on to more serious matters," Moab said. "Can someone please help me seal the deal with that raven-haired barmaid before we go on the road again?"

"Like you have a snowball's chance in Saridon with her,"

Joral jested.

"I hear there's a goat in need of attention out back," Frederick added.

Micah stood and walked in the direction of his room, letting his men blow off a little steam without him.

Autumn — 35 A.E.

Chapter Seven

The Seafoam

Sweat rolled down Cordelia's back as she leaned into her horse's neck and dug her heels into the mare's flanks. Arrows rained down around them as the fleeing Magoran troops charged toward the open gates of Basara.

Their ride south had been endless. The first few days there was relative relief, presumably while General Hamazi had been securing Kasha Marka and the surrounding countryside. There were a few skirmishes, but the forces that pursued them in those early days were easily dealt with. After that, however, they could see the cloud of dust rising into the northern sky as thousands of horses began the pursuit. After a week, scouts had reported a pursuing army in the tens of thousands. The cavalry led the charge, but foot soldiers followed en masse.

They reached the walls of Kantibar, starving and exhausted.

General Hamazi's horsemen were only a day or two behind. The baroness and her brother took a calculated risk, and rather than stay to reinforce Kantibar, they completed a hasty resupply, swapped out their horses, and continued south. It took another ten days to reach Basara, and in that time, a detachment of imperial horse archers had caught up to them. The smaller horses with their lightly armored riders closed the gap more quickly than the slower heavy cavalry.

"Hurry!" Bedria Kess, Baroness of Magora, shouted. She too rode low on her horse. As she turned back to yell at Cordelia, her long black curls, usually so perfectly coifed, flailed wildly in the wind.

The lead soldiers with the fastest horses had already cleared the gates and were dismounting to join the defenders on the wall. The imperial horse archers that rained death down on the fleeing Magorans were out of range of the wall defenders, but they still tried.

Bedria's brother, Eshe, sat astride his horse at the gates shouting and waving his hand, beaconing them forward. His words were lost in the thunder of hooves, the sudden shouts of pain, and the rhythmic sound of arrows striking the ground around them. It reminded Cordelia of the sound a hailstorm would make striking the thatch roof of the home where she had raised her boys.

Cordelia galloped past the gate. Immediately, she reined her horse in and turned him to the side out of the way of her compatriots. She scanned the crowds of people entering the gate. She spied Anna on the opposite side of the throng. Kal was beside her and they occasionally exchanged words and pointed at the crowd.

"Are you all right, Mistress Cordelia?" Ander rode alongside her and checked her over with his eyes looking for wounds.

"I'm fine," Cordelia responded curtly. "Have you seen Lianna? I lost track of her in the final flight."

"No, ma'am. I haven't seen her."

Cordelia stood in her stirrups and continued to search the mob. Finally, she spotted the mousy brown hair of the teen a dozen paces away, sitting atop a dappled mare, wearing a yellow sundress. Cordelia forced her way through the crowd toward the young girl. Ander followed, shouting for people to make way. Kal and Anna must have seen them cutting across the current of people because they began making their way toward them.

"What now?" Anna asked once they had all regrouped in the center of the milling throng.

"I'm not sure," Cordelia admitted. She spotted Aisha Kess, the baroness's daughter, being guided through the crowd by a group of soldiers and angled her horse that way. "Come on."

The others fell in line and made the slow push through the crowd. The honor guard led Aisha down a side street where the crowd was lighter. Cordelia followed their example, and within a few moments, she was able to close the distance enough to shout.

"Aisha!"

The young woman turned at the sound of her name. She

recognized Cordelia and her companions. Aisha ordered her escort to stop.

"Cordelia, I'm so glad to see that you and your friends arrived safely."

"What are we supposed to do now?" Cordelia asked.

Aisha rubbed her chin and considered the question. "Well, Uncle Eshe will remain in Basara with most of the army to protect the port and create a last bastion where loyal Magorans may rally. He will coordinate with our cousin, Desta—pardon me…Admiral Haile—to defend the seas against imperial blockade and to reinforce partisan operations. I believe my brother, Kofi, plans to stay here as well and will command a regiment of Magoran soldiers."

"What about you and your mother?" Cordelia asked.

"Mother plans to lead a detachment east. There are a series of keeps along the Opal River, which forms the border between Magora and Merkar provinces. She will inspect their readiness and help the lords of the river valley to organize their bondsmen into a suitable defense of the border. The more they can slow the advance of the imperial army into Merkar, the better.

"As for me, Mother has booked me passage on *The Seafoam* bound for Ito. It will be my responsibility to coordinate with our allies in Yapon, Hurasham, and Aengal to plan a response. You and your companions are more than welcome to join me. Or I'm sure we can find you passage on another ship. I would not recommend remaining here for long, however. Uncle Eshe says it will only be a few days before the siege begins here, and after that, it will be more difficult to escape the city. Cousin Desta will keep the seas safe for as long as she can, but there are rumors that an imperial navy has rounded Cape Promontory and is headed this way."

"Are you sure we won't be in the way if we come with you?" Cordelia asked uncomfortably. The thought of staying in another city under siege after barely escaping the last terrified her. However, the Kesses had been so good to them so far, she didn't want to be presumptuous. Cordelia realized that she and her companions could offer little in the way of aid and would only add to Aisha's burden.

"Of course not, you will be welcome companions on the journey. It will take us more than a month to travel to Ito, if the winds are favorable, and I'm very likely to be the only woman on the ship if you don't join me." Aisha laughed.

Cordelia smiled. "Well, we wouldn't want you to have to endure that. We would be happy to join you. How much time do we have to clean up and resupply?"

Aisha shook her head. "None, I'm afraid. We are bound for the docks now. Don't worry about supplies…that will be taken care of. We'll reimburse you for your horses so you can replace them when we arrive at Ito. There won't be room for them on the ship, I'm afraid."

"Oh!" Cordelia exclaimed, surprised by the rapid departure. She turned to Kal and Anna. "You two should return to Isan with Ander. There is no need for you to take such a long journey. You should be with your family."

Kal and Ander looked genuinely hurt. Anna, on the other hand, showed nothing but resolute determination. "We will do no such thing. You are family, Cordelia, or soon will be, and you will have our support wherever you go."

Cordelia had always admired Anna's moxie. Even so, she was taken aback by the girl's show of loyalty and courage. She would not have blamed the girl if she wanted to find a way back to the safety of Isan to be with her mother and father. "Thank you, Anna."

"You're decided, then?" Aisha asked.

Cordelia nodded.

They continued through the twists and turns of side streets and alleys, avoiding the crowds and chaos. They emerged from a small thoroughfare between a collection of dockside ale houses. Cordelia got her first glimpse of *The Seafoam*. It was a small but sleek three-sail caravel. It was lightly armed with only a couple of heavy crossbows mounted to each side. She was definitely built for speed rather than defense. Aisha was not kidding when she'd said there would be no room for the horses. Cordelia wondered how there would even be room for the five of them and Aisha's entourage. She briefly reconsidered her decision to spend more than a month on the vessel, but then she straightened her back and put on an air of determination, not wishing to seem squeamish in front of the others.

"Okay," Anna said. Her face reflected Cordelia's own doubt.

"On to the next adventure then." She gave Cordelia a weak smile and turned her horse toward the gangplank.

Chapter Eight

Learning to Fight, Again

Darius moved through his weaponless forms with more confidence than he had the day before. Each day, he felt stronger and surer of himself. He knew that the months spent in the cramped wagon cell had taken its toll on his body, but it took him much longer to rebuild his strength and agility than he would have thought possible. He was finally starting to feel like himself again.

Several minutes into the exercise, Cheung Po lodged himself in one of Hamish Cherian's handcrafted chairs on the porch of the farmhouse. He sipped something from a steaming ceramic mug while he watched Darius. Antu, for his part, had contented himself with lying on the ground a few paces away. He appeared to mostly nap, but Darius noticed that Antu opened his eyes every so often to check and make sure he hadn't gone anywhere.

"That's better," Cheung Po called as Darius completed his fourth repetition of Striking Adder. "Can you feel the difference in where your hands or feet would strike an opponent without a sword?"

"Thanks," Darius called back and nodded in response to the question.

"Try it with this," Cheung Po said and tossed a dagger into the dust at Darius's feet.

Darius balked in his commencement of a fifth iteration of the familiar pattern. It felt odd to have a weapon in his hand again, but even odder to have something so short with such a limited reach. He moved through the form that he had just completed but it felt awkward. The motions seemed too long now. He started over and shortened the lunges and slashes slightly so that the dagger would strike where he imagined his foe would be standing.

Cheung Po nodded his approval. "Do you feel the moment at the end of the second lunge where there is a slight delay now that you are holding the knife?"

"I think so," Darius answered.

"Good, that is the perfect opportunity to turn the wrist like this." He demonstrated with a quick flick of his wrist. "The cut can be directed inside the upper arm, or if you lunge lower at the inside of the thigh to cut the arteries in either area. A smaller weapon can make more precise strikes at vulnerable spots and more easily slip past your opponent's guard."

Darius repeated the exercise again, adding the quick strike that Cheung Po had suggested.

"You have to retrain your brain to look for opportunities that fit the tool you are using. Heavy strikes with a sword or battle axe, precise strikes at veins or organs with the dagger or the sai, or hits to pressure points or joints with blunt weapons or with your hands and feet. Each tool will have a different reach and differing abilities to penetrate defensive postures. You adjust the flow and direction of your form to accommodate this. Do you understand?"

Darius nodded. He moved through the exercise several more times, getting used to the adjustments.

"Now, switch hands," Cheung Po said.

"What do you mean?"

"Hold the knife in your off hand. Feel the difference in the motions and look for different opportunities."

Darius knitted his brow, concentrating on yet another change to what was once a familiar form.

"I am curious about something," Cheung Po commented as he watched Darius practice.

"What's that?" Darius asked, seeing the chance for a counterstrike with the dagger as his feet retreated.

"What did Nasu Rabi tell you about me and our adventures together?"

Darius laughed. "Well, he didn't exactly describe it as adventures *together*. His description of the relationship was much more...adversarial."

Cheung Po shrugged again. "Fair enough. Tell me, what did he say?"

"Arthengal told me of a time when he was a young captain in

the imperial army. There was a group of raiders that was disrupting trade routes in the jungles of Hurasham. He was dispatched to protect traders and deal with the bandits."

"Hmm, interesting. Did he offer an explanation as to why the *bandits* were disrupting the imperial supply lines?" Cheung Po asked.

"No, not really."

"So, he didn't tell you that, at the time, Emperor Chen was demanding an unreasonable supply of fruits from the jungle and eel from the Hurasham shores and was paying a fraction of the market price for the goods? That after the caravanners and the merchants took their cut, the laborers that slaved all day in the humid jungle air or baked all day on the acrid shores didn't take home enough coin to buy a daily bowl of rice for their families?"

"Uh, no." Darius was beginning to feel uncomfortable.

"No mention of the fact that the raiders only liberated food from the trade caravans, which was then redistributed to those same families that worked themselves nearly to death to provide for the emperor's indulgences?"

Darius shook his head.

Cheung Po shrugged. "Okay, continue."

Darius hesitated before clearing his throat and starting again. "I'm sure he embellished the story a little, as he tended to do, but he told me stories of surprise raids on caravans, supplies disappearing in the night from way stations, and forays into the jungle to track down the bandits and bring them to justice. He did say that the more they engaged the brigands, the more he respected their ability to move undetected through the jungle and the fact that they rarely resorted to violence. Usually, they would sneak in, steal the goods, and disappear in the night. I think he respected them, at least for a while."

"What changed?" Cheung Po asked.

"Arthengal had a favorite lieutenant that served under him—a protégé of sorts. I don't recall the name, but—"

"Vasili Anoitos," Cheung Po interrupted.

"Yeah, I think that's right. How do you know that?" Darius asked.

"You tend to remember the name of the first man you kill," Cheung Po replied flatly.

"Right," Darius said, uncertain whether he should continue or not.

"What happened next? In Arthengal's version of the story, that is," Cheung Po asked.

"There was a late-night raid on a caravan that was being guarded by Lieutenant Anoitos. He took several men into the jungle after the bandits. Arthengal was leading a second caravan several leagues to the north when he heard news that Lieutenant Anoitos hadn't returned. He rode south to investigate. They scoured the jungle for days looking for the lost men, and he finally found an abandoned camp in the jungle. There were more than a dozen bodies littering the ground. Several were bandits but the rest belonged to Vasili and his men. No one from Lieutenant Anoitos's party had survived the battle."

"It was very unfortunate," Cheung Po said sadly. "They caught us by surprise and attacked before we could escape. We were left with no choice but to defend ourselves."

"After that," Darius continued. "Arthengal was relentless in his pursuit of the bandits."

"I would use the word merciless," said Cheung Po. "Merciless with a vengeance."

"He searched every town and village and rounded up any sympathizers," Darius added.

"He burned villages to the ground and executed anyone suspected of aiding us," Cheung Po corrected.

Darius was shocked at that description, and it took him a moment to gather his wits and continue. "He drove the bandits into the sea."

"Quite literally," Cheung Po said dryly.

"But they later regrouped under the leadership of Cheung Po the Pirate King, and Arthengal admitted that they were invaluable in the eventual civil war as they disrupted imperial supply lines and broke up blockades."

"At least we agree on that," Cheung Po said with a look of satisfaction. "Did he ever mention this?" He held out a small wooden disc painted black. It had a golden crown on one side and a silver-winged lion on the other.

Darius took the disc and turned it in his fingers, considering the question. "I think he mentioned something about a coin being left behind at every raid. It sort of became the trademark of the bandits."

"Not bandits. It's the symbol of *Sillu Aga*," Cheung Po corrected.

"Shadow Crown? What's that?" Darius asked.

"An ancient order founded centuries ago to balance the power of the emperors. We intervene occasionally to redirect events in the support of a healthier empire and to protect its citizens."

"Give me an example," Darius said.

"Well, for one, the order assassinated the previous Baron of Shalanum and placed the blame on imperial spies," Cheung Po explained.

"What!" Darius exclaimed. "That allowed Emperor Lao to invade from the north and take over Shalanum virtually unopposed. It led to the current siege on Magora and the current war."

Cheung Po nodded his agreement. "The outcome was not entirely as expected. The ministers in Kasha Amur took much longer to choose a successor than anticipated. The previous baron was a corrupt man concerned only with his personal wealth and the development of Kasha Amur. He neglected the rest of the province to the point of criminality. He allowed bandits to roam free in the northern territories and took no interest in governing the east at all. The result was a fragmented and disillusioned populace that struggled to survive."

"I don't remember it being that bad. We did okay in Koza when I was a kid," Darius protested.

"Really? You had your fill of fresh meat and produce? You had the tools that you needed to survive and the raw materials you needed to support a prosperous village?"

"Well, we hunted and fished. We gathered roots and wild grains. A few of the women in the village tended gardens with tomatoes, potatoes, and peppers. We took care of each other." Darius defended the small-town lifestyle but realized, even as he did that, compared to life in Eridu or Kasha Marka, it could be viewed as bleak.

"Yes, you took care of each other because there was no government or infrastructure to support you. The baron was a greedy and negligent man who cared nothing for the people he was supposed to lead."

"But it was better than living under imperial rule," Darius protested.

"Was it, though?" Cheung Po questioned. "I know you have reason to hate Emperor Lao, and I can't say that I fully support the tactics used by his officers, but I think you will find that with a stronger rule of law, life has improved in most of the smaller towns and villages over the past year."

"But life was great in Magora, and now they seek to take over there as well," Darius said angrily.

"Yes, well, that is the problem sometimes with trying to lead a rhinoceros with a string. It gets away from you, and you have to adjust your strategy," Cheung Po said.

"Hrmph," Darius grunted. "Better to just leave it well enough alone, if you ask me."

Cheung Po let the matter drop. "Why don't you try a defensive form like Wary Badger? See if you can find ways to adapt the form with and without the dagger."

Chapter Nine

Stolen Honor

Emperor Lao Jun Qiu relaxed in the luxury of his new traveling carriage. It had been a gift from some of the noblemen of Kasha Amur who were trying to buy his favor in hopes that they would maintain their positions of power. The coach was drawn by four horses. Inside, one end of the wagon was decorated with a comfortable bench and a small writing table. The other side held a down mattress adorned with an obscene collection of pillows. Emperor Lao lounged, half laying, half sitting across several pillows with his legs stretched out on the bed. He was surveying the latest reports from Kasha Marka as the carriage gently bumped along the road toward Eridu.

Prior to his departure from Kasha Amur, Lao Jun had heard that Arthengal's apprentice was captured at Kasha Marka and was being transported to Eridu. The boy and the retired general had created quite an uproar over a year ago when they had invaded the emperor's Northlands compound and set free several dozen farm workers. He found out later that the pair's true target had only been

Darius's mother, who was working at the camp at the time.

Emperor Lao ordered the recapture of all who had escaped as well as the two criminals who attacked his camp. The retaliatory strike against Arthengal's camp to fulfill that order had been a complete disaster. The escaped farm workers were mostly slaughtered, and Arthengal, otherwise known as Nasu Rabi, was killed. While the outcome could be spun as desirable, in reality, the old man, his apprentice, and a handful of farmhands had killed over fifty of the empire's best soldiers, including two officers. The apprentice, Darius, had escaped to the east with the handful of survivors.

To make matters worse, Darius had taken with him the reliquary of Chung Oku Mai, an ancient imperial artifact, which Emperor Lao could have used to solidify his claim to the empire. With the contents of the reliquary in hand, Emperor Lao could have leveraged tradition and superstition to convince several of the eastern provinces to join his cause without a fight.

The fortune of Antu had smiled on Emperor Lao in one sense, at least. He discovered after the botched attack that Darius's older brother, Micah, was a devoted member of the imperial army. Emperor Lao used this to his advantage and dispatched the soldier to track down his wayward brother and return the reliquary. The news of Darius's capture had been welcome, but Lao Jun Qiu had yet to hear any news of the reliquary or its contents. He was also anxious to hear the full story of events that led to the capture of Arthengal's apprentice.

There was a knock on the carriage door. Emperor Lao leaned forward to sweep the window curtains aside. Commander General Sharav rode alongside the wagon on his dappled mare.

"What is it, General?"

"Your Majesty. We will arrive at Eridu within the hour. I just wanted to give you time to prepare," General Sharav said.

"Thank you, General."

Emperor Lao let the curtains fall back into place and then rose from the comfort of his bed. He straightened his clothing, smoothing out a few wrinkles. He retrieved the tall, yellow cylindrical hat from where it rested on the writing table and placed it atop his balding head. A small silver mirror was mounted on the wall of the carriage. Emperor Lao looked in it now to make sure his long mustache and pointed beard were smooth. Satisfied with his final inspection he shifted his position to the cushioned bench and waited.

When he heard the clamor of a crowd beginning to form outside, he tied back the curtains on either side of the carriage so that he might be seen by the crowd as they passed. He examined the faces—many were soldiers, as was expected, lined up along the road to cheer enthusiastically as their emperor passed. The civilian faces were what interested Emperor Lao most. Some appeared intrigued. Many seemed bored or annoyed as if this was an inconvenient distraction from their day-to-day routine. Very few expressed the fascination or adoration that he had hoped to see, but nor were there

many who appeared outright hostile. He chose to take the lack of
hostility as a positive sign and an indication that a peaceful transition
of power was indeed possible.

The carriage clattered through the cobblestone streets on its
approach to the former magistrates' court, which had been converted
into imperial quarters and a headquarters for senior officers. General
Nowak waited on the steps of the building. General Sharav left
Nowak in charge of Eridu when they had ridden south with the army
to secure Kasha Amur and the rest of Shalanum Province. By all
appearances, General Nowak was doing an adequate job of guiding
the city in its transition from trade port to imperial outpost.

Emperor Lao exited the carriage once it stopped and
followed the normal pleasantries as General Nowak greeted him. He
then followed the general to the grand hall that had been converted
into a petitioners' hall. He took his seat in the high-backed leather
chair that sat atop a makeshift dais at the southern end of the room.

General Nowak had been prattling on about the condition of
the harbor, the increase in trade ships, the merchants and farmers
who had abandoned their shops and land, and the loyal imperial
citizens who had stepped in to fill their shoes. Lao Jun heard the
words but paid little attention. He would get more official reports
later from General Sharav once the commander general had the
chance to survey the condition of the army and the town.

Nowak moved on to a description of the improvements they
were making to the battlements when Emperor Lao finally

interrupted him.

"Very good, General Nowak. Your management of Eridu has been outstanding in our absence. Now, I would like to hear of the events that led to the capture of Arthengal's apprentice."

General Nowak faltered at the interruption and then looked uncomfortable at the change of topic.

"Well, General? Are you able to tell me the story or must we bring in someone else?"

"No, Majesty. I mean, of course, Majesty. I can tell you what I know." He cleared his throat awkwardly before continuing. "As I understand, the Night Birds had captured the apprentice's betrothed and held her in their camp."

"A rather unseemly course of action, is it not?" Emperor Lao interjected.

"Oh, no, it wasn't like that, Majesty. She was treated with honor…as a guest. She was there to help Lieutenant Kabir convince the apprentice to surrender without a fight and return peaceably for an audience with you."

"Uh-huh. And did it work?"

"Not exactly, Your Majesty. The apprentice staged a rescue attempt. He snuck into the Night Bird's camp in the heart of the encamped army and liberated her from her tent."

Emperor Lao laughed aloud. "Of course, he did. Brilliant! What happened next?" He found that he was leaning forward in anticipation of the story.

"The girl, Anna, was led away by the apprentice's allies—"

"You can call him Darius. That is his name, isn't it? You don't have to keep referring to him as *the apprentice*."

"Yes, Your Majesty. *Darius's* allies led Anna away while he created a distraction within the camp to give them time to escape. He slew several soldiers and led them on quite a chase through the camp. He was just about to escape into the woods himself when he was surrounded, and he surrendered."

"Amazing," Emperor Lao responded. "How many of our men did he kill?"

"Six or seven, I think."

"And how many of his allies did we capture or kill?"

"Uh, none, Your Majesty," General Nowak responded quietly, looking embarrassed.

Emperor Lao shook his head in appreciation. "Brilliant. I must meet this man. Please bring him to me immediately."

"We can't, Your Majesty...he escaped." General Nowak spoke very quietly and dropped his gaze to the floor.

"Excuse me?" Emperor Lao was sure he had heard incorrectly.

"He was rescued the night he arrived at Eridu. They left only this behind." General Nowak held out a black wooden disc.

General Sarav approached Nowak and retrieved the coin. He examined it, turning it over in his hand, before handing it to Emperor Lao.

Emperor Lao looked at the black disc in his palm. It bore a painted golden crown on one side and a white, winged lion on the other.

"Sillu Aga," Lao Jun cursed under his breath and closed his fist around the disc. "Of course, it would be them. I knew they had been quiet for too long, Sharav." He glanced at his commander general as he spoke.

"It would seem so, Your Majesty."

"We do have Darius's weapons, impounded from when he was captured," General Nowak said hopefully. "We believe they previously belonged to General Alamay himself, Your Majesty."

General Nowak waved at one of his subordinates, who scampered from the room only to return a few seconds later with a pair of swords wrapped in leather. Nowak unwrapped the blades and knelt before the dais, holding both weapons in his outstretched hands as an offering to the emperor.

Emperor Lao gave General Sharav a brief nod of his chin, and the general descended the steps to inspect the blades. He examined the scabbards and ran a finger over the etched likeness of a bear. He unsheathed one of the blades and looked at it closely. The appreciation for the craftsmanship was evident in his eyes.

"They are Arthengal's swords, Your Majesty," Sharav confirmed.

Emperor Lao nodded. *Stolen honor,* he thought, *taken without bloodshed to their owner. Surrendered in the darkness of night.* He hoped that his disappointment wasn't evident on his face.

"General Sharav, General Alamay has been a rival of yours since the earliest days of your career. It would be my honor to present you with his blades as a reward for your devotion and service."

General Sharav's eyes widened in shock. "Your Majesty," he said with awe. "It would be my honor. Thank you from the bottom of my heart." He bowed deeply, clutching the swords to his chest.

"The honor is mine, General," Emperor Lao said. *Apparently, Sharav doesn't share my concern about the dubious way the blades were acquired. Good for him, I hope they serve him well.*

Chapter Ten

Anbar Ur

Arnon burst into the kitchen. He was sweating and out of breath. Darius and half a dozen others lifted their heads from their morning meals and turned their attention to him. He bent over, hands on his knees, gasping for air. He extended a finger, indicating that they wait for a minute.

"Sorry...Ran...Eridu." He paused. "Emperor."

Backs straightened and ears perked at the last word.

Arnon took a final deep breath and stood. "The emperor just arrived in Eridu. I was visiting my wife, Gabriella, at her shop in town when the procession came through. They haven't announced anything yet, but I expect they will inspect the farms and surrounding area more closely now."

"Darius and his bear will certainly draw more attention," Cheung Po spoke from the entryway to the living room. He was leaning against the door jamb, sipping a steaming cup of tea.

"You as well, sir," Arnon said. "Many in the royal guard would recognize you, as would the commander general."

"Hmm," Cheung Po considered. "We'll need to find somewhere else it would seem. Somewhere that we have the privacy to organize a little more but still close enough to manage communications as we determine our next move."

"What about Anbar Ur?" Darius asked.

"Where is that?" Cheung Po asked, unfamiliar with the name.

"It's an abandoned city to the north," Arnon answered. "Arthengal had made his home nearby in the crater of an extinct volcano."

"That sounds perfect," Cheung Po said. "Can it be defended if necessary?"

"The gates are gone and the walls would have to be reinforced quite a bit," Darius said. "Winters are hard in the mountains, and they haven't been maintained. There arc only two roads into the city, from the south and west. The east and north are naturally protected by the mountains."

Cheung Po cockcd his head. "You know the city well."

"I've lived there for most of the past six years," Darius replied. "Rather, in the valley with Arthengal, but yes, I know the area well."

"What about supplies? How would we manage provisions into the city without drawing attention?"

"The road is serviceable between here and there," Darius replied. "But also, there are vast orchards south of the city, and it's probably not too late in the season to harvest some of the fruit. The river nearby is also flush with fish, and a pretty large herd of elk winters nearby. It won't be easy living—there will be a lot of snow in the winter, but it's close enough to communicate easily with Eridu."

"What about Arthengal's valley?" Arnon asked. "Winters are easier there."

Darius winced.

Cheung Po saw Darius's reaction and held a hand up to Arnon. "Maybe as an emergency. Arthengal is buried there, no?"

"And many others killed by the emperor's assassins," Darius replied glumly.

"Then we treat the valley like a sanctuary of sorts. We honor Arthengal and his sacrifice by leaving the valley to him and the ghosts."

Darius visibly relaxed. "He does have a cache of weapons and armor hidden in the valley. We could transport those to the city as well as any supplies that he and I had that would be useful."

Cheung Po nodded with a smile. "I like it. Is there any way for us to build up our supplies there, or will we have to bring things from Eridu?"

"The mines in the valley are barren. Arthengal kept the grain mill functional, although, after more than a year of neglect, it may need some attention. There is an old forge in the city where they used to build picks, axes, and shovels for the mine workers, but it's in pretty bad shape. And again, no raw metal to work with."

"And supplies to reinforce the walls and gates?" Cheung Po asked.

"There is plenty of stone and timber in the mountains. You would have to bring the tools to cut and shape it," Darius answered.

Cheung Po drummed his fingers against his cup, thinking. "On the surface, I like it. It sounds like the perfect place for a base of operations for Sillu Aga and may serve to shelter those who are not *fitting in* with their new imperial masters. Can we go and visit first to see if any other concerns come to mind?"

Darius shrugged. "Of course. We should go soon, though. Snow comes early in the mountains."

"Good enough," Cheung Po said. "Arnon, start outfitting a couple of wagons and ready eight or ten men to accompany us. As you said, Darius and I should make ourselves scarce as soon as possible. Load the wagons with as many tools and provisions as you can spare and still keep up appearances at the farm."

Arnon nodded and hurried out the back door.

Darius listened to the rhythmic crunch of the wagon wheels rolling over the frost-hardened ground. Ahead, he could see the breach where the alpine timbers gave way to the relative openness of the apple and pear orchards. Any hope of a late harvest was shattered as he saw that most of the fruit trees were bare of leaves. While there wasn't yet snow on the ground in the river valley, the surrounding peaks glistened white in the afternoon sun. He leaned down in his saddle to scratch Antu behind the ears. "How does it feel to be home, Antu?"

Antu turned an indifferent eye toward the valley and grunted. Then he maneuvered his head so that Darius was scratching a spot on the back of his neck.

"Why do you call him Antu?" Cheung Po asked curiously.

Darius gave Antu a final pat on the head and then straightened in his saddle. It was a question he had gotten many times before. "I believe that Antu, the Sky Father, imbued the bear with his spirit and has come to guide me on my path. Initially, it was to help me find my mother when she was captured by the imperials, but now I think he has other plans for me."

"Ah," the look of disbelief in Cheung Po's eyes was also something Darius was used to. "I see."

The road turned and started to slope up toward the city that was their destination. Their first view of the southern wall came as it peaked above the ridge at the top of the hill. It was a jagged line that looked like the broken teeth of some great monster. As they got closer, it was clear that much of the lower portion of the wall was still intact. The solid portions of the wall still stood taller than most men. A few areas, such as near the corner towers, still stood at their original height, and one could imagine what the wall would have looked like in its full glory.

They rolled through the wide gap in the wall that was once

home to massive timber gates. A century or more of weather and neglect had rotted the gates. Only the rusted metal hinges remained. The patchwork of stone foundations spread out like a moldy, dusty quilt in front of them. The once vast city, now defined more by the spider's web of cobblestone streets than by any buildings or landmarks, filled the space inside the crumbling walls. A stone fortress towered over the city from its perch to the north like an ancient skeleton keeping watch over a graveyard.

"It's beautiful," Cheung Po said with amazement.

Darius laughed. "If you say so."

"Tents can easily be assembled atop old foundations to provide dry, flat areas to sleep. The walls will provide a solid defense even without any work. I think the gates and the fortress should be our first priority. Come spring, there is plenty of arable land inside the walls to grow vegetables and grains to feed a couple hundred men." Cheung Po pointed to the terraced fields on the eastern side of the city.

Darius looked at the city with fresh eyes. He had never considered what it would take to make the ruins livable. He and Arthengal had lived a comfortable life in their valley east of the city. The volcanic soil was perfect for cultivating crops, and it was protected from the more extreme elements of nature.

"We can set up a stable over there." Cheung Po's voice became more excited as he spoke. "The grain mill looks okay. We'll need to fix that hole in the roof, but otherwise…there is enough cut stone lying around the city to build a couple of storehouses."

Darius watched with interest as the old pirate planned out the makings of a proper outpost.

"That space there can be cleared for a training ground. You said there were weapons in the valley, right?"

Darius nodded.

"Excellent. If we're going to shore up the walls, then we'll need men to defend them," Cheung Po said.

"Defend them against whom?" Darius asked. "If the imperials attack us here in force, those walls won't provide much defense."

"There are more dangers in the northern country than just the imperials," Cheung Po laughed.

"That's true." Darius itched the scar on his left eye, received from a bandit's blade when he was younger. Bandits were not uncommon in these parts, and there were wolves, bears, and other wild animals that the walls and a few guards could easily keep out. "I guess I'm just used to the defenses that we had in the valley and hadn't thought about securing the city itself."

"Understandable," Cheung Po said and then slapped Darius on the back. "I think this will work out very well. Okay, let's start unloading the wagons and getting tents set up."

Chapter Eleven

Antu and Kisha

Ullani sat on a pile of cushions inside the tent and methodically rubbed oil into her saddle and bags. The desert sun was brutal on the leather, and she needed to apply oil on a daily basis to keep it from cracking. It was a chore she hadn't thought of when she began her journey, and she thanked the gods that the desert nomads that she now traveled with had an ample supply. She slapped away the hands of the men and their wives who tried to do the task for her, insisting on caring for her own equipment.

While she appreciated the safety of the caravan and the company that it provided, he dismissed the silly notion that she was the new empress appointed by Antu, the sky father. However, she was happy to take advantage of their misplaced belief and accept the offerings of food, clothing, and shelter. Her own supplies ended up being completely inadequate for a journey across the Ziyandi Desert. If nothing else, this group would provide her with a safe escort to Kasha Haaki where she could slip away and complete her mission.

On the opposite side of the tent, Ullani's self-appointed

honor guard of eight Merkari nomads lounged against pillows of their own smoking shisha from an elaborately crafted glass hookah. The melon and apple-scented smoke hovered like a gray haze in the upper reaches of the large tent. The men passed the hose and mouthpiece between them, enjoying the relaxing effects of the tobacco and prattling endlessly about a broad range of topics that interested Ullani very little. Their voices passed over her while she focused on her task.

"But there are better grasses and shrubs for the goats if we turn north first," a man with a gloriously thick, dark mustache spoke. "The goats and camels must have food."

Ullani held in a giggle at the description of scattered clumps of sage, kapok bushes, and Launaea that these men considered good grazing land.

"We must hurry to get the empress to Kasha Haaki," a man with eyebrows as glorious as his friend's mustache challenged.

"The sky father will provide so that his Appointed One can reach her destination," a man Ullani only thought of as *Big Nose* spoke with confidence. "Antu will force Kisha to bring forth what we need from the earth to complete our journey."

Ullani grunted and laughed.

She glanced up when she noticed that the other side of the tent had fallen silent.

"What?" she spoke to the faces of the staring men.

"Have I offended you, Empress?" Big Nose asked. His eyes,

normally squinted slits in his leathery brown skin, were wide in horror.

"No, why would you say that?" Ullani asked.

"You laughed at me when I said that Antu would provide," Big Nose answered.

"No, I laughed because I thought it was arrogant to think that Antu had any power over Kisha and could make her do his will," Ullani explained.

"But Antu is the Sky Father. He rules over us all," Eyebrows spoke. He sounded offended at the insult to his religion but also a bit terrified at questioning the empress.

Ullani considered carefully how to explain to these men why she thought the idea was ridiculous. She could very easily upset her position here. She decided to start with a few simple questions. "What is your name?" *I really should learn their names if I'm going to travel with them.*

"Ahmad Hussain Khan Al-Saad," Eyebrows answered.

"Can I call you Ahmad?" Ullani asked.

"Of course, Empress, you may call me as you wish," Ahmad said and bowed his head in deference.

"Ahmad, let me ask you something. How often does it rain here?"

"I don't know," he shrugged. "Very little."

"And do the plants grow anyway?" Ullani asked.

"Yes, they grow in abundance in some places. More than

enough to feed our livestock."

"I see," Ullani said. "So, would you say that Antu provides for your needs with his abundance of rain or that Kisha provides for your needs by bringing forth grasses and shrubs for your goats?"

All of the men looked confused.

Ullani shook her head. "You, what is your name?" She pointed at Mustache.

"Muhammad ibn Abdullah, Your Grace," he answered.

"Muhammad, do you prepare all of your own meals?" Ullani asked.

The man laughed. "Of course not. I have wives to do that for me."

Ullani rolled her eyes. "And do your womenfolk rely on you to provide them instruction on how to season the meat, or milk the goats, or make the cheese?"

Muhammad glanced uncertainly at his companions. "No, of course not."

"Ah, then you make demands on them regarding when they should prepare the food and how it should be served."

"No," Muhammad said with more confidence. "My wives follow tradition and perform their duties well."

"Okay, then you tell your brother's wives how to prepare his food and feed his children?"

Muhammad glanced at Big Nose and laughed. "Of course not."

"Then what would make you think that Kisha needs any instruction from her brother, Antu, to provide for her children?"

The men stared at her blankly, then a growl came from behind the others. "Antu rules because he is the strongest."

Ullani leaned to the side slightly to see past Muhammad to the back of the group. A tall, muscle-bound man rose from the back. Ullani had rarely heard the man speak. She had seen him, though he preferred to let his fists speak for him and was too often seen ending arguments with a swift backhand. Ullani had watched on more than one occasion when he used this negotiation technique with his wives. She had nicknamed him Katili after a brutish monster from children's fairytales.

"Strength…you speak of strength." Ullani did not back down, but neither did she raise her voice. She had grown up around men like this her entire life. Men who thought with their hands—or other parts of their anatomy—rather than with their brains. They were thugs who tried to either join the Thieves' Guild or steal away territory. They rarely succeeded at either. "Let me ask you a question about strength."

The man smiled a wicked grin.

"Who is stronger? Antu, who bakes this land, steals the water, and cracks the soil? Antu, whose winds stir up the sand and dirt that will strip animals to their bones in deadly storms? Antu, who builds roiling thunderstorms to drench the land and cover it with flash floods that sweep away everything in their path, only to steal away the water again with his intense heat? Or is it Kisha, who endures all this abuse, and despite it, still manages to bring forth life to feed your goats and care for her children?"

Katili, who had been smiling through all the descriptions of Antu's might looked suddenly very confused.

Ullani recognized the look. She had led hard characters in The Red Shadow gang in Kasha Marka. Saria, her leader and mentor, had trusted her to guide and lead men twice her age, and the Merchants' Gate territory flourished under Ullani's leadership. The look she saw now was a dangerous crossroad, but her nature refused to let her stop now.

"Tell me, my friend," Ullani continued. "Does true strength come from an ability to destroy or to endure destruction and flourish despite it?"

"Are you saying that Kisha is stronger than Antu?" Katili growled.

"I'm saying that they are brother and sister, born from the same cataclysmic birth that formed the land and the sky from Nammu's eternal sea. I'm saying that they each have different strengths and that, together, they challenge, and nurture, and punish, and teach their children so that we might overcome adversity and thrive. I'm saying that they are equals."

"Blaspheme!" Katili moved fast for a man his size. He charged through his companions, pushing them aside as he pulled his curved sword from its scabbard.

In Ullani's short life of nineteen years, she had learned to endure and lead men like this. *And when neither of those worked...*

Her hands moved in a blur. Knives, hidden away in secret sheaths throughout her clothing or secured to her body, flew through the air. They struck Katili in the throat, chest, and face. His expression changed quickly from anger to fear, and finally, to the same confused, dumb look that had followed her first question. He hit the ground and skidded across the tent floor, stopping an arm's reach from her feet. His mouth moved uselessly like a fish suddenly thrown onto the riverbank.

...she had learned how to kill them.

The other men in the tent were frozen in awe. Some lay where they had been tossed aside by Katili. Some were halfway to their feet with their hands on undrawn weapons as if they could have done anything to protect her from the charging brute. The stories would grow in the upcoming weeks and months. It would change from a tale about how the empress fought the brute to the death to one of her striking him dead where he stood for speaking against her will. But for now, the stunned men clambered to kneeling positions, placed their hands on their hearts, and lowered their gazes to the floor as one spoke: "Long live the empress. Long live the empress. Long live Empress Ullani."

The following day, Ullani was interrupted by the sound of Ahmed's voice outside her tent. "May I enter, Empress?"

"Of course," Ullani said dismissively without looking up from the lightweight shawl that she was mending. She needed it to keep the sun off her arms and face, and she snagged it while dismounting that evening.

"Come, come," Ahmed said with a gesturing wave to someone outside. Four women entered the tent and stood quietly behind Ahmed with their eyes lowered to the ground.

Ullani looked up with a curious tilt of her head. "What's all this?"

"These are Qasim's wives," Ahmed explained.

Ullani shook her head, not understanding.

"The man you killed," Ahmed said simply—as if that would explain everything. Then, seeing that it didn't, he added, "They are yours now."

"What?" Ullani narrowed her gaze and her tone turned dark. "I will not take women as slaves. Now that they are safe from that brutal man's influence, they are free to do as they wish."

One of the women started sobbing.

"But where will they go?" Ahmed asked in general confusion. "Their parents are not from our tribe, and no other man is allowed to take them as wives until the year of mourning ends. They will starve without someone to care for them."

Realization finally dawned on Ullani. These women had no rights in this society. While they were not technically slaves, they depended on either their parents or their husbands to care for them. It also helped explain why they had endured Qasim's brutality.

Ullani's tone softened as she turned to the women. "Come in and make yourselves comfortable. Sit down. Help yourselves to some food and drink."

"What about our children?" one of the women cried in anguish.

"Bring them in too. You are all welcome," Ullani said, feeling the woman's pain at the uncertainty ahead of them. While she would certainly defend herself if she was put in the same position again, it was like a punch in the gut to see the very real consequences of her actions lined up in front of her. She vowed to make sure these women and their children were well looked after.

Ahmed pulled back the tent flap and waved someone else in. Ullani's eyes widened as, one by one, nine children ranging in age from three to about fourteen filed into the large tent.

She laughed uncomfortably as she surveyed the assembled group. *Well, I've stepped in it now!*

"Please." She gestured again. "Make yourself at home."

Chapter Twelve

Broken Refuge

The wind whipped through the pass, stirring up flurries from the light dusting of snow that had fallen the night before. The harvest season was still underway in the fertile valley that surrounded Kasha Marka, but here in the mountains, winter was in the air. The peaks were already capped with snow and the crunch of frosted earth was ever present as they marched.

Micah slapped a pair of wool-lined leather gloves against his leg several times to loosen the frozen fingers before pulling them onto his hands. He flexed the fingers until the leather moved easily. They were camped about a league from the eastern gatehouse that guarded Patel's Rest. Sergeant Wang and Corporal Piccoli had slipped into the cloistered valley the night before. They would have infiltrated the city by now and would be scouting targets of interest.

The rough sound of frozen earth breaking beneath hard-soled boots altered Micah to someone's approach.

"G'morning, boss," Moab spoke softly.

"How did you sleep?" Micah asked.

"Cold and restless, just like my dreams," Moab responded.

Micah chuckled.

"Are you and Corporal Grigoriy ready to move out at dusk?"

"Any time. We've stashed our excess gear in the cave behind that grove of pine trees."

"Are you clear on your targets?" Micah asked.

"Captain of the civil guard and the mayor."

Micah nodded.

"And you're going after the big guy himself," Moab said.

Micah nodded again. Quian MacCinidh had been Imperial Alchemist to Emperor Chen Bai Jian and his father before him. His genius had been responsible for the invention of the fireworks and explosives that the Zamani, or Lightning Bringers, used to light the night sky or rain hellfire down on enemy lines. During the early years of the civil war, MacCinidh had defected to the side of the rebels. His defection was a turning point in the war and had been disastrous for the empire.

Micah's mission was to eliminate the old man and any of his followers who served to stabilize and secure the mountain hamlet. In the wake of absent leadership, General Hamazi would send imperial troops to secure the pass and stabilize the town. Micah was ordered to keep his operation precise and inconspicuous. He was to leave no sign that imperial troops had been in the area or that anything untoward had occurred. The populace of the town must be left assuming that their leadership had merely abandoned them in the night. This was the type of mission that the Night Birds were trained for. They specialized in surgical strikes. Ultimately, they saved lives by preventing extended sieges or battles. Their work served to minimize civilian casualties and helped ensure a swift and stable transfer of power.

"Are you sure you're okay with the new kid?" Moab asked. "It's not too late to trade."

"No, I'll be fine. Aslan Tekin is a good soldier and he moves well in the shadows. I think he'll make a good corporal one day, and I'd like to assess his ability in the field."

Moab shrugged. The sun was starting to settle on the western horizon. "I'll see you back here once we're done then."

Micah gave a curt nod and extended his hand to clasp his friend's forearm. "Good luck."

"You too, boss."

Moab drifted back toward the tents, disappearing into the lengthening shadows.

Micah surveyed the hulking shape of the keep in the darkness. The three-story palace was a fortress. The windows were barred, and guards were posted at each of the doors. The heightened security must be a result of the siege on Kasha Marka. Such guards had not been present the last time Micah visited the valley. He assessed the six-story tower. The rough stones of the structure were not unlike the sea cliffs that Micah and Darius had grown up climbing.

"Can you climb?" Micah whispered to his companion, nodding his chin in the direction of the tower.

Doubt filled the young soldier's eyes. "I can try."

Micah shook his head. "That's not the type of climb you *try*. You either know you can do it, or you don't."

"I don't think I can." A pained look showed on Aslan's face as if he didn't like disappointing his commanding officer.

"It's okay," Micah reassured him. "You keep watch below and guard my back."

Micah moved quickly and silently through the garden that surrounded the tower. He used the hedges and low garden walls for cover. He waited for a guard to pass by on his patrol before sprinting the final distance to the tower. He pressed his back against the stone wall, hugging the shadows and listening. The only sound was his slightly labored breathing.

When he was sure that he had not alerted the guards, he turned to the wall and studied it. The rough surface of the tower had even more hand and footholds than he hoped. As children, Micah and Darius climbed the cliffs from the harbor to the town where they lived hundreds of times. This would be a breeze compared to the wet, slippery surface of the seawall from his youth.

He started slowly, sticking to the shadows and getting a sense of the texture of the wall and the strength of the stone. Micah picked up speed as his confidence grew. The stone blocks scraped his chest through his shirt as he glided from one hold to the next. He froze when he heard the scrape of boots against flagstone below him. He risked a glance below, but the owner of the boots was hidden from view. He breathed slowly and waited. Another sound, barely perceivable, betrayed a brief but fierce confrontation, and then he heard the muffled sound of dragging toward the hedgerows. Aslan gave a long low call that sounded like an owl, signaling that it was safe for him to proceed.

Hand over hand, he scaled the full height of the tower and paused before the pinnacle. He listened carefully to make sure no one was standing guard on the roof before pulling himself up and over the battlements. Organized piles of supplies and balls of metal and clay decorated the roof. Micah hadn't the slightest idea what any of it was for, nor did he care. He searched quickly until he located the trap door that led inside. He silently prayed that the door wasn't locked from the inside as he pulled on the handle and sighed with relief as the door lifted easily.

Micah slipped down the ladder and crouched on the floor while he allowed his eyes to adjust to the added darkness of the interior. He wound his way down the staircase until he found an entrance into the rest of the stronghold. Floor by floor, Micah drifted through the castle like a ghost. The bedchambers were all empty, as was the vast library. Micah found lamps burning in some sort of laboratory, a maze of tables with various experiments on each, but no sign of life. He was beginning to worry that the keep was vacant when he heard a clatter and a muffled voice from the kitchen.

"It's just me, Hudai," the voice said. "I was feeling a bit peckish and decided to make myself a sandwich."

Micah turned the corner and could see inside the kitchen. Two dark-skinned men were illuminated by the light of a single lamp. The speaker was smaller by comparison and much older. An array of meats and cheeses were spread out on the counter in front of him. He had been in the process of layering an assortment atop a thick slice of bread when he was interrupted.

"You don't need to worry," the speaker continued. "Or maybe you do." His eyes shifted to the dark doorway where Micah crouched. "You can come into the light, young man...there's no sense in hiding."

Micah was flabbergasted. He hesitated for a moment before stepping into the room and the flickering light. The second man, taller and heavily muscled, turned to face him.

"How did you..." Micah started to ask but stopped as the old man waved his hands to silence him.

"You are Darius's brother. I've heard of you."

Micah's jaw dropped and he started to speak but was interrupted again.

"Similar facial features," the old man explained. "And you have your mother's red hair. It would seem you've picked sides. It's a shame, really, that you haven't yet recognized the dangers of an autocracy. Even the best emperors struggle to balance the good of

the people with the good of the state, and the past few haven't even
tried. I've heard rumors that the new emperor is trying, but I've also
heard the horrors of what has been done in his name.

"You're here to kill me, of course," the old man continued.
His bodyguard, Hudai, stiffened at the revelation, and his large hand
edged toward the knife on the cutting board. "Hamazi is smart to
want to control all routes between Shalanum and Magora. Resistance
will be forming soon, and the more the imperials control all routes of
travel, the better—for them."

Micah loosened the long daggers in his belt and studied the
large man that stood between him and his target.

"Your mother had good things to say about you, Micah. I
think, under different circumstances, we could have become
friends."

Micah hesitated only for a moment at the mention of his
mother before duty and training took over. He leaped and placed a
hand on the counter, then propelled himself to the other side.
MacCinidh moved quickly for an old man and slipped behind his
companion. Hudai snatched the butcher knife off the counter and
turned to face Micah.

Micah feinted and then twisted to the right as Hudai slashed
to counter. MacCinidh slipped out of the kitchen and up a set of
stairs toward the servant's quarters. Micah tried to give chase, but
Hudai blocked his way again. Micah didn't have time for a
prolonged fight. He moved quickly, abandoning defense. His twin

knives cut quickly, slicing inside the larger man's thigh and thrusting up under the ribs. He was rewarded for his lack of caution with a piercing blow to his left shoulder. Micah had twisted expertly as his opponent's blow was delivered, accepting the knife but making sure to keep it clear of his heart or lungs. His shoulder throbbed, and he dared not pull the knife free until he could be sure he could staunch the bleeding, but the fight was over, and Hudai was dead before his massive body hit the floor.

Micah charged up the stairs. He saw a flickering light disappear behind a wooden panel at the end of the long hallway. He heard the click of a latch on the other side. Micah picked up speed and leaned his right shoulder into the hidden door as he reached the end of the hall. A burst of pain from his knife wound nearly caused him to lose consciousness. The lock shattered and the door burst open as Micah stumbled into the passageway beyond.

He heard a surprised yelp further down the passage, and the dancing light picked up speed. Another door stood ajar ahead, and more light crept through. Micah pushed it open and entered the laboratory. Across the room, MacCinidh was fiddling with a latch and lever. He looked over his shoulder as Micah entered the room, and his previously calm eyes looked panicked. He reached for a pair of glass bottles on a nearby table and threw them in Micah's direction. The contents of the two bottles mixed as they shattered on the stone floor, and a burst of purple flames erupted at Micah's feet. He recoiled and shaded his eyes. The fire burned out quickly, but it had served as enough of a distraction to allow MacCinidh time to move a section of the stone floor aside. He dropped into the space below, and the stone slab started to slide back into place.

Micah sprinted across the room and dove for the stone, trying to catch it before it settled. He heard a click and a whirring sound as the stone dropped. He clawed at the floor, but it was no use. He pulled on the levers and switches, trying to replicate what MacCinidh had done to no avail. Finally, he sunk to the floor with his back against the wall, staring at the stone square that had covered the old man's escape.

"Well, shit."

Winter – 35 A.E.

Chapter Thirteen

Ito

The deck of The Seafoam was quiet. The sails were furled and trussed to the mast so they wouldn't flap in the wind. Sailors sat on the deck in the shade of the rails. They were under orders of strict silence lest their voices carry across the water and attract unwanted attention.

The cove where the little ship was anchored was sheltered on three sides and wasn't visible from the open sea. It was risky. If their pursuers happened upon them, they could easily be pinned down in the cove and boarded. The captain thought the deception was worth the risk, however.

Cordelia sighed and watched gulls circling overhead, white specks floating in a sea of pale blue. Lianna sat next to her, leaning her head against Cordelia's shoulder. The journey was harrowing and had taken twice as long as expected, but they were so close to their final destination—Kashiko Island, only a day or so from Ito Harbor with favorable conditions. After months on the water, to be so close, one could feel the tension in the air from crew and passengers alike.

Kal sat down next to Cordelia and put his mouth close to her ear. "Has the captain told you his plan?" he whispered.

Cordelia turned to answer in a low voice. "He told Aisha and I overheard. We'll wait here until dusk and then make a break for it. He is hoping to put enough distance between the island and us under the cover of night that he will lose them for good this time."

"Is it the same ships that have chased us since the Sea of Whispers?" Kal asked.

"The same or similar," Cordelia answered. "They fly the same flag—the old imperial flag of the House of Hurasham. The captain has not heard news that Hurasham Province has joined Emperor Lao, so he thinks it must just be a few loyalist houses trying to make a name for themselves."

"I thought they were going to catch us after Cape Solitude," Kal whispered.

Cordelia nodded, remembering the event. They rounded the cape, and three ships had been waiting for them. The other two that had been chasing them since the Sea of Whispers were only a few hours behind. Captain Allister turned the ship toward land, trying to skirt around the ships ahead by sailing close to the treacherous Shadow Coast. It almost worked until one of the opposing captains angled behind a long sea spire and cut them off. Captain Allister was forced to reverse course quickly, and their pursuers had driven them out to sea. They'd given chase for two days, driving them further out every time the captain tried to angle north. The pursuit continued until an early winter storm had risen up before them.

Captain Allister wanted to surrender at that point rather than risk his ship in the storm, but Edwin Otieno, the captain of Aisha's honor guard, insisted that they prevent Aisha's capture at all costs. The argument had nearly come to blows before Captain Allister relented. The storm had battered the ship for three days, but when they came out the other side, there was no sign of the Hurasham ships. Until a week later, that was, when the same or a different group under the same flag gave chase as they were leaving Port Vago, where they had stopped to resupply. Instead of traveling north to Ito, they were forced to travel east to Kashiko.

"Do you think we'll make it this time?" Kal asked.

"I hope so," Cordelia sighed. "The captain says the seas are rough here in the winter, and we don't want to be out here any longer than we have to."

The sun began to set beyond the lush hills to the west. The captain roused his crew with hand signals, and they quietly went about the work of preparing the ship to move. As the western sky turned crimson, they hoisted the sails and raised the anchor. The ship drifted slowly around the corner of the rocky shoreline that separated the cove from the open water. All eyes were scanning the sea from horizon to horizon but there was no sign of the hostile ships.

Once they were clear of the island, the captain silently ordered his men to go to full sail. The wind picked up and they increased speed. The sky turned from crimson to violet, and finally, to black. Kashiko slipped from view behind them, and Captain Allister angled the ship north. They ran all night without lights. The only sound came from the slap of the waves against the hull and the creaking of ropes and pullies.

Cordelia's first view of Ito took her breath away. Before she could even see the coastal city, she saw the castle perched high up on a hill overlooking the valley below like a mythical guardian. The sun was setting, and dark-maroon clouds drifted through an orange sky. Purple mountains could be seen in the background. Standing in bold contrast to it all was the shining white castle. The last rays of the evening sun gave the illusion of a glittering white diamond perched atop a pedestal. Like many buildings of the imperial style, the castle was built in layers. The curved, elongated roofs at each level of the castle grew successively smaller, giving the structure as a whole a pyramidic shape. Two smaller structures of similar style rested on either side of the main structure and were set slightly further back on the hill.

Walls separated the hill into three layers. Unlike the bulky stone structures that surrounded Kasha Marka, the walls around Ito castle were as elaborately architected as the castle itself. The battlements looked like an undulating serpent wrapping itself around the hill. Stone dragons decorated the tops of the walls periodically, their open mouths ready to pour hot oil onto invading armies.

The ship docked. Cordelia and her companions followed Aisha Kess onto the docks. Captain Otieno and his men formed up around them. A delegation from the castle was waiting on the docks to greet them. At the front of the group was a handsome man, a few years younger than Cordelia, dressed in a green robe. Silver dragons were stenciled in the fabric, and an emerald sash was tied around his waist.

As Aisha approached, the man pressed his palms together at his heart and bowed slightly. "It is an honor to see you, my cousin."

Aisha gave a similar bow. "The honor is mine, Lao Ichiro. You honor my mother and our ancestors by granting us respite in your home."

Cordelia tensed involuntarily at the sound of the young lord's surname, but then dismissed it as silly. Lao was certain to be a common name in Yapon Province.

"You have brought other guests with you?" Lao Ichiro asked.

"Yes, this is my dear friend, Cordelia Kabir, from Shalanum. Her son, Darius, was apprenticed to *Nasu Rabi*, and she is an honored guest of my family. She is accompanied by her son's betrothed, Anna Cherian, and Anna's brother, Kal."

Lao Ichiro raised an eyebrow at the mention of Arthengal's

well-known alias and bowed to each in succession as they were introduced. "Arthengal Alamay was a beloved friend to my late uncle, Lao Cang Yu. You are most welcome."

"Finally," Aisha continued. "This is Kal's manservant, Ander, and Cordelia's ward, Lianna."

Ander nearly choked when she introduced him as Kal's manservant, which drew a raised eyebrow from several in Lao Ichiro's party.

"It is an honor to meet you all. Welcome to my home. Please let me accompany you to your rooms where you may refresh yourselves and rest."

"Thank you." Aisha bowed again, and they fell in step behind the delegation as they returned to the castle.

"Is he really your cousin?" Cordelia whispered to Aisha as they walked.

"We're distant relatives at best. My great-grandmother's sister was married to Ichiro's great-grandfather. Here, they refer to everyone with imperial blood as *cousin,*" Aisha answered.

"Ah, I see."

As they approached the gates to the lowest wall, the guards insisted that they surrender any weapons.

"Weapons are not allowed inside the castle," Lao Ichiro explained when Captain Otieno started to protest. "I assure you, no harm will come to the Honorable Aisha Kess and her companions while they are guests at the palace."

Captain Otieno started to protest again but reluctantly did as he was asked when Aisha signaled him to behave.

They continued beyond the gate and onto the road that encircled the hill. Cordelia saw, now that she was closer, that the walls that looked like a serpent from afar were, in fact, decorated like a dragon's back. Curved stone and metal scales protected the defenders on the wall from enemy arrows. Sharp spikes angled downward, away from the battlements, making it nearly impossible for invaders to scale the walls.

The road to the castle was paved with perfectly cut stones, and the side of the road was occupied by upscale shops of every sort.

"I would love to come back down here and do some shopping," Cordelia said as they passed a silversmith with magnificently designed broaches.

Lao Ichiro turned his head and smiled at the comment but didn't say anything.

When they passed the second set of gates marking the next level on the hill, the shops were replaced with elegant residences and fine inns.

It was here that Lao Ichiro paused. "I'm afraid that this is as far as most of your servants may travel. Captain Otieno is welcome to accompany you, but the rest of your soldiers must remain here, as must your companion's manservant. They will be boarded in the best accommodations and shall want for nothing, but it is the way of the palace. I'm sure you understand."

Aisha hesitated for a moment and then relented. "Of course." She bowed.

Cordelia's heart sank at Aisha's words. She had hoped for more of an objection. Ander felt like part of her family as much as the other three did. Besides, he was the only one of her companions who was her age, and she enjoyed his company and conversation. "Ander is not Kal's manservant…he's my fiancé," Cordelia blurted.

Aisha looked confused and embarrassed. Ander gave Cordelia a sidelong glance that was a mixture of shock and adulation.

"I apologize," Aisha said. "I had no idea. Well then, of course he must join us at the castle."

The others had the good sense to remain silent.

Lao Ichiro's eyes narrowed as he scanned the two women who were doing their best not to look flustered. It was obvious that he thought he was being duped but also didn't want to argue the point with his cousin in front of the soldiers and servants. He nodded his approval and then turned uphill.

Some of the soldiers had worried looks, but everyone did as they were directed. A contingent of Lao Ichiro's delegation led them in the opposite direction as Aisha, Cordelia, and the rest continued up the hill.

Once they passed the third gate, the buildings were the most elegant they had seen. Each home had property and gardens of its own. Each would have been a palace in its own right anywhere else but here, but they paled in comparison to the castle on the hill. This district was clearly where the nobles of Yapon lived.

"I thought Kasha Kyoshu was the capital of Yapon Province," Cordelia asked, confused.

"In name only," Aisha corrected. "The baron lives there and serves as ambassador to the other barons, but the true power in Yapon has always been in Ito. Our lifestyle has changed very little in the wake of the fall of Chungoku."

Cordelia nodded and then skipped a step when she saw the towering white gates that opened ahead of them. Golden dragons wrapped around the structure, staring down at anyone who dared to enter the palace grounds, judging them.

As a visiting dignitary, and more importantly, one descended from royal blood, Aisha and her immediate party would be given rooms in the palace. Cordelia realized now that by labeling her as "friend," Aisha had done Cordelia and her party a great honor. Otherwise, they would have likely been left in the residential quarter below.

Lao Ichiro escorted them to the eastern wing of the palace. He showed Aisha to her room first, although apartments would have been a better term. There was a main sitting area, two bedrooms, and a room with an elaborately tiled bath. Steam was already rising from the pool that Cordelia was sure must have taken days to fill. A hidden entrance led to a much smaller room with a bed and a wash basin where Captain Otieno would sleep.

Cordelia was shown to similar, if less elaborate, rooms where she, Anna, and Lianna would stay. Kal and Ander were given rooms separate from the women but nearly as ostentatious as the apartment that Cordelia and her companions would share.

Once Aisha nodded her approval at all three sets of accommodations, they were escorted back to her apartments. Most of Lao Ichiro's delegation bid farewell at this point, leaving only Ichiro and half a dozen guards.

"I hope you will be happy with your accommodations, cousin."

"They are beautiful, Ichiro, thank you," Aisha answered sincerely, some of the formality slipping now that the rest of the nobles were gone.

"Is there anything else that I can get for you, cousin?" Lao Ichiro asked.

Cordelia took a risk and spoke. "I would love to go shopping in the artisan's district that we passed."

"I'm afraid that won't be possible," Lao Ichiro said with genuine regret. Then he brightened. "I can have servants bring a sampling of wares to your rooms if you like. Tell them what you would like to see. They can bring you anything."

"Why can't my friend go shopping, Ichiro?" Aisha interjected, concern in her voice.

"It is best that you remain in the palace," he explained.

"But why? As guests of the palace, are we not free to come

and go as we please?" Cordelia asked.

"My father would prefer that you remain inside the castle walls. You are free to explore the grounds to your heart's content, however," Lao Ichiro said.

"You're not making any sense, Ichiro," Aisha said. "Why can't we leave?"

Lao Ichiro spread his hands in mute apology but didn't explain further.

"Are you saying we are prisoners here?" Captain Otieno asked.

"Of course not." Lao Ichiro seemed shocked. "You are our guests. Your every need will be attended to."

"We just can't leave." Aisha narrowed her eyes and her voice took on a harder tone.

"Correct. For now," Lao Ichiro said.

"For how long?" Aisha asked.

"Only until the hostilities between our families is at an end," Lao Ichiro said in a reassuring tone.

"Your father is siding with Emperor Lao, isn't he?" Aisha's tone was dangerous now.

Lao Ichiro shrugged. "I would not say that, exactly. But Emperor Lao is Lao Cang Yu's only son. Lao Cang Yu was a national hero and a martyr of the *Tyrant King*. My father is…considering his options. But please, there is no need to be concerned. You are guests of the palace and will be treated with the utmost respect. Please rest. Recover your energy from your trip. Servants will be by soon with your belongings from the ship and to bring you a hot meal and fresh clothes. Relax and enjoy your stay." With a final smile, Lao Ichiro backed out of the room and shut the doors. The sound of the latch clicking shut bore a finality that left a feeling of dread in the pit of Cordelia's stomach.

The sense of alarm was only momentary, however. As she turned to speak to Aisha, she jumped with surprise. Ander was standing very close. He reached to take her hand in his and looked up at her with puppy dog eyes. "Cordelia, I had no idea you had feelings for me. It would do me—"

Cordelia slapped his hand away gently and cut him off before he could finish the sentence. "Ander, dear friend, you are part of our family and I couldn't bear for you to be confined to the lower city with the servants and guards. It was the only thing I could think of that might work."

"Of course." Ander looked embarrassed and glanced quickly around the room at the others who were suddenly very interested in the elaborate decorations and artwork. "I knew that."

Cordelia caught Aisha's glance across the room. The other woman was covering her mouth to hide a smile.

Chapter Fourteen

Seeds of Rebellion

Visibility was non-existent. The wind had shifted to the south during the night, carrying with it clouds of fresh powdery snow from the mountain peaks. Even at midday, a sea of white still covered the valley south of the gate. Darius stood watch atop the newly repaired gate tower. Hunched over with his back to the driving wind, he scanned the valley as best as he could.

A runner had arrived in the middle of the night with news that the caravan of wagons with much-needed supplies had gotten snowed in a few leagues to the south. The drivers were trying to dig the wagons out but there was little hope that they would make it the remaining distance. The snow was simply too deep. Cheung Po had led a small band at first light with all the group's horses and mules to retrieve the supplies and rescue the drivers.

Arnon, who had been left in charge when Cheung Po left, was starting to get nervous. He had been considering sending a second party out after the first for over an hour. Darius convinced him to wait. He had dealt with these unexpected mountain storms before and knew that clearing a path through waist-deep snow was no simple task. Even a few leagues could take most of the day to travel back and forth.

The day dragged on. Arnon brought him a steaming mug that smelled of lemon and honey.

"What's this?" Darius asked.

"It's good for you…it will keep the chill off."

Darius laughed. "A little late for that." He raised the mug to his mouth. The strong smell of rum mixed with the citrus as the vapors hit his nose. He sipped and swallowed. Warmth spread throughout his chest. The sweet of the honey and the sour from the lemon masked the bitterness of the rum. The combination tasted much better than Darius had expected.

"What do you think?" Arnon asked.

"Mmm, this is good." Darius took another sip.

"This is actually Arthengal's recipe. I'm surprised you haven't had it before."

"He didn't usually keep spirits in the valley," Darius answered. "The only time we really drank alcohol was when we visited the Cherians, and Elsie only allowed ale and wine in her house. She said that men got too foolish when they drank whiskey or rum."

Arnon laughed. "Well, I can't argue with that."

Darius smiled. "Although some of Arthengal's funniest stories often involved one or the other."

"Yes, well, what men find funny, women often refer to as foolish," Arnon said.

A flicker of movement caught Darius's eye.

"What's that?" Arnon pointed south at the same time.

Ghostly, dark figures hovered inside the alabaster blanket that covered the landscape. The shadows slowly took shape, and the hard edges of men and horses formed. The men leaned into the necks of their mounts, protecting their faces against the driving snow.

Arnon and Darius rushed down the ladder. Antu rose and joined them at the foot of the ladder. The bear had not let Darius stray more than a few paces away since they had been reunited. Arnon shouted to others to spread the word and bring help, and then they hurried to meet the troop at the gate. Cheung Po passed through the gate first. Ice clung to the tips of his mustache and the fringes of his cloak. Men swarmed around the new arrivals and busied themselves unloading supplies and tending to the horses. Others helped the half-frozen riders dismount and escorted them to fires that blazed inside the makeshift shelters that were starting to form from the ruins of Anbar Ur.

Arnon, Darius, and Antu followed Cheung Po and another man back to the command tent. A blast of warmth greeted them when they opened the flaps. An iron brazier sat in the middle of the tent. Waves of heat could be seen rising from the glowing coals inside. Arnon had made sure to keep the fire burning, ready for Cheung Po's return.

Once they were inside and had shed the thick, wool riding cloaks, Cheung Po introduced his companion. "This is Claude. Claude, this is Darius, Arthengal's apprentice, and Arnon, my second."

"Nice to meet you both." Claude rubbed his hands over the heat of the fire.

"Claude has recently returned from Magora with reports of how things stand there. I thought you both would be interested in what he has to say."

Darius nodded enthusiastically.

"General Kess has mounted a solid defense around Basara, and as of a month ago, the imperials had yet to breach the walls. I can't guarantee that hasn't changed. Up to that point, the Magoran forces had maintained a steady stream of supplies through sea channels, but imperial blockades were forming up when I left.

"The baroness leads several bands of elite raiders from forests east of Kantibar."

"Wait, what do you mean the baroness *leads*?" Darius asked.

"She has established a secret base in the Obsidian Wood," Claude explained.

"I'm confused. Why is she not leading the army from Kasha Marka?"

All three men looked at Darius with confused expressions.

Arnon was the first to speak. "Kasha Marka fell months ago, and Kantibar soon after. Basara is the only major haven left in

Magora."

"What happened at Kasha Marka? What about Saria and Anna?" Panic edged Darius's voice.

"Eshe Kess, the commander general of the Magoran army, mounted a rescue during the summer. He managed to coordinate an attack with his sister, the baroness, and broke through the siege lines. They fled south with the bulk of their army," Cheung Po explained. "I thought you knew."

"No! I didn't know." Darius raised his voice, panic starting to set in. "How would I know? I was captured last spring, and I've been with you since. None of you told me anything."

Arnon shrugged helplessly. "Sorry."

"What about Anna? I was captured rescuing her. Did she make it back to Kasha Marka? Did she escape with the baroness?" Darius pleaded for information. His voice was on the edge of breaking.

The other two men looked at Claude, who held out his hands apologetically.

"I'm sorry. I don't know Anna. I only know that Eshe Kess and Bedria's son, Kofi, manage the defenses at Basara. Bedria is operating from a hidden outpost to the east. And Aisha Kess traveled to Ito via ship to establish relations there and lobby for additional support."

"What about Saria Oberman? I left Anna in her care," Darius asked.

"From what I gather, Sillu Mitu has slipped back into her role as the *Night Shadow*," Claude answered. "She is operating out of the shadows of Kasha Marka to funnel information to the baroness and General Kess. I've heard little of her other than what was contained in the reports she sent to Basara through her network."

"I have to go back and find Anna." Darius stood up with sudden determination. His mind flashed back to his childhood, and he felt the same sense of anxiety and helplessness that he had when his mother was taken by the same soldiers all those years before.

"And do what?" Cheung Po asked. "Wander around Magora until you hear word of her? Break through enemy lines at Basara and demand an accounting from the commander general? Track down Bedria Kess in the Obsidian Wood and plead for information?"

The sarcasm was not lost on Darius, but it did nothing to calm him. "I don't know. I have to do something. She could be in danger."

"And she could be fine," Cheung Po countered. "Just because we don't know anything, don't automatically assume the worst."

"Why is this damn empire so intent on tearing the people I love away from me?" Darius cried in desperation. "First my mother, then Arthengal, and now Anna. I hate this. I just want to live in peace with the people I care about." Darius collapsed into the pile of cushions, exhaustion suddenly overwhelming him.

"And you will," Cheung Po soothed. "Your place is here." He gave Arnon a quick, unreadable glance. "We've decided that the best thing for Sillu Aga to do is to mount a resistance force that can slow imperial progress and try to give the other provinces more time to decide what they will do. You are helping us raise the militia that will provide that resistance."

"What are you talking about?" Darius said glumly. "I'm not doing anything. I haven't been much help in rebuilding the city. I've brought in some meat from hunting, but other than that, what possible difference could I be making here?"

"How many men have joined us since we arrived here?" Cheung Po asked.

"I don't know—two or three hundred?" Darius answered.

Arnon nodded. "And more arrive every day."

"And?" Darius asked.

"Why do you think they're coming?" Arnon asked.

"To escape the empire. You said it yourself when we first arrived that there are those who don't *fit in* with their new imperial masters. We're providing them with a safe haven," Darius answered.

Cheung Po nodded, conceding the point. "True, but we've also put the word out that we plan to raise a resistance force, and more are coming because of that. Especially once we told them who would be leading them."

"You?" Darius asked.

Cheung Po laughed. "No. I'm just an old pirate. Nobody cares about me anymore. They are rallying around Arthengal's apprentice. The *adopted son* of the hero of the revolution. The sword master who stood side by side with his fallen mentor to drive the horde away from Anbar Ur and back to the Northlands. The notorious anti-hero whose image decorates posters on every tavern wall and city gate in Shalanum, and for whom the reward has risen to a thousand marks."

"What?" Darius drew the word out in disbelief.

He glanced around the tent. The other men's faces showed no sign of jest as they nodded their heads in confirmation.

Chapter Fifteen

Crossroads

Ullani closed her eyes, giving in to the gentle rocking of her horse and the soft sweeping sensation of the tall, yellow grass brushing against her calves. It was soothing and was starting to lull her to sleep. She felt her hands loosen on the reins, and her body started to lean to the right. She jerked awake suddenly and sat up taller in her saddle. She looked around, searching for something to distract her from the monotony of the journey. There was nothing. The steppes went on endlessly in every direction, a honey-colored sea of undulating boredom.

The desert had given way to the grasslands more than a week ago. She praised Kisha for the break from the heat. At least here the ground didn't reflect the temperature back up at them as intensely as the sun bore down. There was also plenty of food and water for the livestock, and the women had harvested late-season grains as they traveled, which they ground to flour in the evening and baked into fresh bread every morning.

Still, something about traveling through the desert stirred her soul. Living every day wondering if you would have enough to eat, dropping to your knees to thank Kisha when you happened upon an unexpected oasis just as the sun was reaching its zenith. Living with the constant threat of imminent death somehow made her feel more alive. Here, in the savanna, it was just…boring.

She roused from her mental musings and tried to entertain herself by thinking of other ways to describe the landscape. "Uninteresting. Dull. Tedious. Yellow."

"What was that, mistress?" Ahmed rode closer having not made out what she muttered under her breath.

"Nothing," Ullani replied. "Are we stopping soon? It's about time for dinner, isn't it?"

"No, Empress," Ahmed replied with a confused look on his face. "It is barely past mid-afternoon. We have only been riding for a couple of hours since the midday meal."

"Ugh!" She grunted in frustration.

Ahmed's face grew concerned. "If you are hungry, I will have something brought to you immediately. Or if you wish to stop for the day, I will order it."

"No." She waved a hand dismissively. They always took what she said so literally. She missed having someone she could just talk to or complain to without them falling over themselves to "fix" it. She missed having a real conversation with someone who just saw her as Ullani. She missed Darius. Even though he remained loyal to Anna and had not returned Ullani's overtures, she still missed his company.

"How much longer until Kasha Haaki?" she asked for what felt like the thousandth time.

To his credit, Ahmed didn't show the slightest sign of annoyance. "We will arrive at the crossroads by evening. From there, it is another week's journey to the capital. I do wish you would reconsider, your grace. Your rightful place is in Kasha Esharra. We should turn north at the crossroads and reclaim your rightful place in Chugoku."

He used the abbreviated form naming the province, but what he really meant was *Chungoku*, the country. He and the others saw Chugoku Province as the heart of the nation and Kasha Esharra, the old imperial capital, as its soul. They believed, and tried to convince her daily, that if she would only return to the true capital and bring it back to life, the spark would inspire the land, throngs of true believers would return, and they could restore *Chungoku*, the empire, to its prior glory.

"Uh-huh." She ignored the comment like she always did.

They rode in silence for a time. Ahmed started to allow his mount to drift further away from hers as if he were becoming uncomfortable being so near to her.

Ullani wasn't ready to ride in isolation again, so she pulled him back with a question. "Ahmed?"

"Yes, Your Highness?" His voice was hopeful. Ullani was sure he was hoping she was going to ask him to complete a task of some sort that would win him favor in her eyes.

"Let me ask you a question." His face was immediately crestfallen and maybe a little bit nervous. He could not refuse her, but her questions always vexed him. "We've had—what—a few hundred people join our caravan in the past month or so?"

"Five hundred, if you count the women and children," he said with pride.

"Oh, I do. Count them, that is. Which brings me to my question…dozens of you have appointed yourselves as my personal guard—"

"Imperial guard," Ahmed interrupted, then realizing what he'd done, attempted to apologize. "I'm sorry—"

She cut him off with a wave of her hand. "It's okay. Anyway, dozens of you are in the *imperial* guard. Maybe close to a hundred now."

"Yes, Your Grace."

"How come there are no women?"

Out of instinct, he started to smile at the thought of a *woman* serving as a guard. He relaxed for the briefest of seconds when he thought she was having a joke at his expense. Then he saw the expression on her face and realized that she was serious.

"Because, Your Highness, women—" He stopped when she tilted her head to the side, interested in what he was going to say about women. "That is to say that men—" She raised an eyebrow.

She continued to stare at him while his mouth worked, but no

words came out. She could see by his dancing eyes that he was
trying to think of an answer that would satisfy her but also would not
flip his culture and beliefs upside down. She was sure that more than
once his thoughts returned to the incident with Qasim.

Finally, she saw defeat on his face and then acceptance. "I
don't know, Your Grace," he said glumly. "I will make inquiries
immediately and see if there is interest from among the women."

"Wonderful," she said with a smile. "Thank you."

Normally, he perked up noticeably when she praised him, but
this time, he only gave her a half-hearted acknowledgment. She
wondered if she had pushed him too far this time. He started to turn
his horse away to begin his task when something in the distance
caught his attention. He stood in his stirrups, trying for a better look.

"What is it?" Ullani asked.

"I'm not sure, but I'd better take some men ahead to check."
He quickly rallied twenty from her personal guard and rode ahead of
the caravan.

Ullani watched with curiosity. It was several more minutes
before she started to see what had concerned him. They were
approaching the crossroads. Several permanent trading posts had
been established on the eastern side of the road both north and south
of the intersection. On the southern fork, there was an assemblage of
people, perhaps a hundred or more. As she drew closer, she could
see that they were armed and she caught the occasional glint of the
sun reflecting off iron breastplates.

The caravan slowed to a stop as others noticed the soldiers. Curiosity overcame many, and people spread out on either side of the road, trying to get a better look. Ullani continued forward as did the men who remained from her guard. She saw Ahmed arguing heatedly with an armored man wearing a plumed hat.

"What's the matter?" she asked Ahmed once she was close enough to speak without shouting.

"He says we cannot pass," Ahmed answered. "That Kasha Haaki is off limits to us."

"What seems to be the problem?" Ullani took in the soldier's uniform and an insignia that looked similar to what she was used to in Kasha Marka. "Captain, is it?"

"Yes, ma'am. Captain Bajwa, ma'am."

He was handsome and younger than most of the captains she knew in Kasha Marka, which meant he was also probably competent. *Or well connected*, she mentally corrected herself. He had dark skin, though lighter than her own, hawkish eyes, and a thick mustache. It made her wonder what Darius would look like with a mustache. *Not as good,* she thought. His hair was too light. A proper mustache needed to be dark like this one.

"What seems to be the problem, Captain Bajwa?" she repeated her question.

"Apologies, ma'am," he said politely. "We have been sent here to turn your caravan away, or at least north. The baron does not want the Cult of Kisha causing any trouble in Kasha Haaki."

"Cult of Kisha!" she exclaimed, and then laughed at the preposterous thought.

The captain looked uncomfortable. "Apologies, ma'am. You prefer a different name."

"No," she laughed. "I just hadn't heard the term. I assure you, Captain, we aren't a cult and don't mean any harm in Kasha Haaki. My name is Ullani Hailu, and I've actually been sent on a mission by Baroness Kess in Kasha Marka. I have important information to relay to Baron Aydin and then I need to secure passage to Ito."

Captain Bajwa's brow furrowed. He looked even more uncertain now.

"Here." Ullani dug through her saddlebags and produced a folded document with the seal of Magora at the bottom. The baroness had given her the writ in case she ran into any trouble seeing the baron once she arrived in Kasha Haaki. She handed the document to the captain, and he read it carefully.

Captain Bajwa studied her face and then the note again. "These men," he said hesitantly. "They are not from Kasha Marka."

"No," Ullani said. "I've met them along the way, and they have been kind enough to escort and protect me during the journey across the desert."

"Why?" Captain Bajwa asked with genuine curiosity. Ullani presumed from her experience with them that the nomads of the desert and steppe would not normally escort a stranger in this way and certainly wouldn't create a band as large as this to do it.

"Because she is Empress Ullani, appointed by the light of Antu to restore glory to *Chungoku*," Ahmed apparently couldn't take anyone questioning his devotion, so he blurted it out before Ullani could stop him.

She glanced sharply at Ahmed, and he fell silent.

"Empress, you say." Captain Bajwa folded the missive and handed it back to Ullani abruptly. "Interesting." The sarcasm and disdain were clear in his voice.

"Look," Ullani said, trying to recover the rapport she had been gaining before Ahmed ruined it with his pronouncement. "I really was sent here by Baroness Kess to deliver a message."

"No, you look." Captain Bajwa's voice took on a harder tone. "I don't know where you got that letter or what you did to the courier who bore it, but I've heard enough. I will ask you one more time to turn around."

"Yeah, get out of here, freaks. Nobody wants you in Kasha Haaki." The sound came from a crowd of people that Ullani just now realized had been forming. Forty or fifty merchants, travelers, and men-at-arms listened to Ullani's exchange with Captain Bajwa.

Captain Bajwa gave the crowd an angry look, but it was ignored, and others started shouting insults directed at the desert nomads.

"Captain," Ullani tried to reason with him. "It is very important that I relay my message. The fate of provinces may rely on it. What if I accompany you back to the capital by myself so that I might gain an audience with the baron without provoking any ill will?"

"That's not happening," Ahmed growled in rare defiance to her wishes.

Someone from the crowd threw a rock that struck Ahmed in the shoulder. He growled again and turned toward the onlookers with clenched fists. Captain Bajwa stuck out an arm and placed his hand on Ahmed's chest, stopping him from moving forward. Ahmed looked down at the captain's hand with fire in his eyes.

Another rock arched through the air, flying well over Ahmed's head. Too late, Ullani recognized the danger. There was an explosion of pain as the stone struck her in the side of the head, and her vision started to swim. She shook her head, trying to clear her thoughts. She felt weightless for a moment and then noticed how crimson the sky had become. With a jolt, her back hit the ground, and her shoulder wrenched violently. She realized that she had fallen out of her saddle. The throbbing in her head was now matched by the ache in her right shoulder.

She heard cries of rage. Then shrieks of panic. Captain Bajwa's voice blended with Ahmed's as they both shouted orders. She felt her shoulders lift off the ground. She floated in the air for a moment, her head was still spinning. Something warm ran down her cheek.

The air burst from her lungs and she cried out from the lance of pain that radiated from her injured shoulder down her back as she was thrown face-first over the back of a horse. She felt the warmth of someone's back against her side and then marveled at the swirls of dust that drifted amongst the stalks of grass on the side of the road. She coughed, partly from the clouds of dust that now reached her nose and partly from the rough bouncing on the back of the horse.

Ullani closed her eyes, trying not to vomit. She opened them again at the thunderous sound of hundreds of voices and watched as an ocean of pounding feet trampled the grass as it surged in the direction of the crossroads. Her head throbbed. She closed her eyes again. Then, without warning, the contents of her stomach erupted, flowing like a river into the air and the ground behind her. She groaned, coughed out the final remnants of her lunch, then closed her eyes and welcomed the throbbing darkness that enveloped her.

Chapter Sixteen

Sowing Rebellion

Despite the deepening snow in the Shahin Mountains, the city continued to fill. The ground froze around them, but construction continued to strengthen the walls and restore the gates. The bare limbs of the orchards were whipped about by winter winds sweeping down from the snow-capped peaks, but hunters braved the winter storms to bring back elk, deer, and trout to feed the growing masses.

Darius was amazed each day when he stepped out of the warmth of his tent into the bitter chill. Each morning when he awoke, the crowd of men, women, children, and livestock that sheltered inside the walls of Anbar Ur seemed to have grown. He stomped his feet and pulled a pair of fur-lined gloves over his fingers. He picked his way through the crowd, then up the hill to the courtyard in front of the skeletal keep. A circle in the center of the enclosure was bare, tramped clean from the hours that he practiced every morning. His strength had returned but his joints still felt stiff some days. The adaptations that Cheung Po introduced to the once familiar forms seemed endless. Every day, his eyes were opened to new possibilities. He had grown to realize the truth of Cheung Po's words so many months before that limiting his practice to the sword truly limited his potential.

Arnon Porter arrived midway through Darius's practice and took up a perch on the low wall that surrounded the courtyard.

"You seem to be getting the hang of it," Arnon commented when Darius finally took a break.

"Yeah." Darius hefted the pair of fighting sticks that Cheung Po had assigned him today. He gripped the wooden handles and spun the shafts deftly in a combination of moves. "It's different but the same. Do you know what I mean?"

Arnon shrugged. "Not really, but I'll take your word for it." He changed the subject. "They'll be putting the finishing touches on the wall and gates today."

"That's amazing," Darius said. "I can't believe how fast they were able to repair the defenses. And in the middle of winter, no less."

"Yeah, putting their backs into it for sure," Arnon said. "Men'll be getting bored now without the physical labor to keep them busy."

Darius scratched the three-day growth on his chin. "I suppose that's true. Is there anything else that needs to be done? More hunting, paddocks for the livestock, more shelters?"

"Aye, that will keep some busy but not all," Arnon answered.

"Near as I can tell, there will be three or four hundred men that'll have too much spare time on their hands. Got to be careful then. That's when the drinking and fighting will start if'n we don't keep them busy."

"Do you have any suggestions?" Darius asked.

"Aye, you should train them," Arnon suggested.

"Train them!" Darius exclaimed. "I've never trained anyone in my life. Train them in what?"

"The sword and the bow, of course," Arnon responded as if the answer was clear.

"Do we even have weapons to train that many men?"

"No, maybe a quarter as much, but weapons training won't take the full day. If they're going to be a decent fighting force, many of the men will need to build muscle and shed the bulk around their waists. There are others you could use to handle that portion of the training so you can focus on weapons training. Also, we have a lot of craftsmen in the city. They could start working on making bows and practice swords. We don't have the steel for real blades, but perhaps we'll find a way to get more."

"I suppose that's true," Darius considered. "Are you sure there are even enough men that are interested?"

Arnon shrugged. "Ask for volunteers."

"Okay." Darius set down his weapons and walked to the top of the stone staircase that led up to the courtyard. He looked at Arnon, uncertain how to proceed. The older man mimicked putting his hands to his mouth and shouting. Darius copied the gesture and raised his voice to shout across the city. "Excuse me. I'd like to make an announcement."

Heads lifted from those closest to the steps, and then a murmuring rose in the crowd. The murmur increased to a shout as the call to attention echoed across the city. Darius saw people abandoning their tasks to make their way toward the keep. The crowd grew at the base of the steps.

"Start by telling them how good they've all done," Arnon whispered in Darius's ear while the throng gathered.

Darius nodded.

As soon as it looked like everyone who was coming had arrived, Darius raised his voice. "I want to thank you all for the hard work you have put into restoring our defenses."

He saw a few smiles at the front of the crowd but mostly confused looks toward the middle and back. Darius took the hint when a couple of men near the back raised their hands to their ears.

He shouted at full strength, his voice bellowing across the yard. "I want to thank you all for your hard work. Our defenses are strong."

Claps and cheers rose from the crowd, and there were many more smiles. He saw people whispering in the ears of their comrades who still didn't hear.

Darius waited for the noise to die down. "But strong walls are only the first obstacle. We need strong backs and strong arms to buttress our defenses. I would like to start training those who are willing to use the bow and the sword. If you are not interested, do not worry—there are many important jobs to help our community grow. If you would like to join our…" Darius paused while he searched for the right word, "militia, please make your way up to the courtyard."

The crowd surged as people fought to be the first to clamber up the stairs. He saw more than one panicked expression in the crowd as people were starting to get crushed.

"Stop!" Darius bellowed.

The surge paused.

"Orderly. We do not want the first casualties of our militia to be our own people."

The crowd calmed and began to part to make way for the volunteers. Darius backed away from the low wall and into the courtyard as the first men arrived. He retreated to the broken doors of the keep and stood on the elevated landing while the group assembled. He was surprised by the number. Hundreds of men and women were gathering. Darius was taken aback by how many women were in the crowd. His instinct was to send them back to the city, but then he recalled how adept his mother was at the bow and how capable Ullani and Saria were, so he chose to remain silent.

Darius surveyed the mob once the trickle of volunteers had stopped. He guessed that there were upwards of five hundred. They nearly filled the courtyard to capacity. There would be too many to train here, so a much larger space was needed.

"Has anyone shot a bow before?" Darius asked.

Many hands went up, mostly men but more than a few women too. Darius nodded. About a third.

"Has anyone ever used a sword?" Darius asked.

Only a few hands went up, and those mostly belonged to grizzled veterans who had probably served in the civil war. There were a few younger men, former city guards or hired swords, perhaps. He searched the crowd, surveying the faces until his eyes fell on a gray-haired man missing his left eye and arm. There was an intelligence in his remaining eye, and he carried himself erect, demonstrating confidence and discipline.

"You, there," Darius pointed. "What is your name?"

It took a moment for the crowd to work out who he was pointing at, but the old man finally responded in a strong, raspy voice, "Karl Olson, Your Grace."

Darius choked back a laugh at the ridiculousness of the title. "Come forward, please."

Karl worked his way through the crowd to the front.

"You look like you've seen a bit of action in your day?"

"Yes, sir," Karl responded with a smile.

"Have you ever led men? Either in work or in battle?"

He shrugged and his chest puffed. "Was a foreman at the gristmill for almost twenty years after the war. Does that count?"

"Absolutely that counts," Darius said with a friendly smile.

"If I asked you to take a work group to clear some trees west of the city and build an archery range, do you think that's something you could handle?"

"Yes, sir."

"Excellent. How many men would you need?"

Karl shrugged. "Maybe twenty."

"Good enough. Pick your crew and see if you can find the supplies you need around the city."

Darius searched the crowd again until he found a tall man with broad shoulders and a square chin. He was perhaps thirty and had been one of the men who raised his hand when asked about handling a sword.

"You, there, in the back. The tall one. What's your name?"

The man glanced around before pointing to himself. When Darius nodded, he responded, "William Bratt, Your Grace."

"Darius is fine, William," Darius said. "We're all in this together, right?"

"Of course," William responded. Then he added awkwardly, "Darius."

Darius smiled. "Tell me about yourself, William. What is your weapons experience?"

"I served in the city guard at Eridu. Arnon helped a few of us escape after the city fell to the imperials."

"So, you're familiar with the sparring grounds in the city?" Darius asked.

"Yes, sir."

"Do you think you could build something similar south of the city?"

William looked uncertain. "I think so. Do you want me to build practice dummies too?"

Darius hadn't thought of that. He had never used dummies, but it could be a good idea. Especially since so many hadn't handled a sword before. "That's a great idea. We'll need a lot of practice swords as well."

William cringed. "The dummies won't be pretty."

Darius laughed. "They don't have to be, just functional. Why don't you take a couple dozen men to help and get started?"

William nodded. "Yes, sir."

Darius found a couple more volunteers to start rounding up equipment, bows, arrows, swords, knives, shields, and to start craftsmen on building more of what they could. Once that was finished, he addressed what remained of the assembled crowd. "The rest of you can continue to support final work on the wall and gates as well as gathering and preparation of food and shelter. As soon as we have areas to begin our training, I will reassemble everyone. Thank you again for volunteering. Your community will need you."

Darius let out a huge sigh once the crowd dispersed. Arnon clapped him on the back. "You did great, son."

"Thank you," Darius replied. "I was making half of it up as I went along. There were a lot more than I thought there would be.

I'm not sure I can handle this."

"You'll do fine, and I'm here to help. You have a good eye, too. Karl and William are both good men. They'll make excellent leaders."

Darius surveyed the newly constructed archery range. Karl had cleared out a wide swath from the forest. Some of the trees, he sent to William to use for the practice dummies, and the rest of the wood, he contributed to the community for building shelters and for firewood. His team had assembled forty targets, stuffing them with needles stripped from the trees and gathered from the forest floor. They had collected nearly one hundred bows and a dozen or more practice arrows per target. Lines had been painted on the ground at twenty-five, fifty, and a hundred paces.

Darius stood now at the line closest to the targets. He had already selected the first group of forty volunteers. The group looked nervous and excited. He decided that he would start with the very basics, even if more than a third of them already had experience from hunting or other endeavors.

"You will grip your bow here, near the center, just below the arrow rest." He held his bow aloft, showing them how he was holding it. "Everyone, grip your bow." He walked up and down the line, making sure their hands were positioned correctly.

"Don't grip the bow too hard. If you feel your knuckles

turning white or your fingers falling asleep, loosen your grip. Next, you will take an arrow. Place the shaft on the rest and nock the string."

"How do you nock the string?" someone from the crowd asked. Darius silenced the fits of laughter that followed and showed the young man who had asked how to properly nock the arrow. He noticed several others peering over his shoulder during the demonstration, probably too afraid to ask the question themselves.

"The shaft of the arrow should be parallel to the ground. You will place one finger above and two fingers below the nocking point." He turned to face the target and raised his voice to be heard. "Raise your arms together, draw the string back smoothly until your hand is near your ear, and then let your fingers slip gently from the string." He moved through the motions as he spoke. His arrow sailed through the air, striking the target in the center. "Now, you try. On my count."

He moved behind the line of archers and watched as each nocked an arrow.

"Ready," he called. Forty bows raised in a haphazard waterfall of motion down the line.

"Aim." He heard the stretch of the strings.

"Fire." Forty arrows flew in the general direction of the targets. Most fell well short of their goal. A few flew long or wide, but only one managed to find its home in the painted red circle at the center of the canvas. He glanced down the line to see a young woman, barely twenty, jumping up and down with excitement.

"Ready," he started the call sequence again. "Aim. Fire."

The smattering of shafts decorated the ground in front of the targets. All were closer, and two shooters managed to strike the outer red ring. The young woman gave a whoop as her second arrow hit the white, unpainted ring, just outside the center.

Darius repeated the sequence eight more times until each of the first group had fired ten times. Only half managed to hit their targets with any of their ten shots. Once everyone had retrieved their arrows, he separated them into three groups. Those who had missed entirely, those who had scored at least once, and those who had scored with at least half of their shots. There were only five in the last group. The young woman had hit the center two rings with all ten shots. Darius called her over.

"What's your name, miss?" Darius asked.

"Rose Thatcher, m'lord," she answered and tried to do a curtsy. Her red hair, which fell in waves across her shoulders and back, reminded Darius of his mother.

Darius waved the formality away. "That was very impressive shooting, Rose. How long have you been shooting?"

"Never—well, not really, I mean," she said excitedly. "I used to watch my dad and brothers practice, but he would never let me touch a bow." She leaned closer and added conspiratorially, "I would sneak off into the woods every now and then when they were out on the hunt to shoot at a few squirrels and whatnot."

Darius smiled. He knew from experience that squirrels and small game were a lot harder to hit with a bow than most people gave credit for. "Well, you're very good. I expect great things from you."

"Thank you, sir." She beamed and curtsied again before running off to join her friends.

Darius repeated the drill a dozen more times until everyone was given a chance. Some groups were better than others, but few, as it turned out, surpassed the first group of the day. It was well past midday by the time they finished. He dismissed them with his thanks and then called Arnon, Karl, and William over to discuss the results.

"Well, fifty at least demonstrated some skill," Darius said, trying to stay positive.

"Aye, and three hundred or more can't hit the broad side of a buffalo from twenty-five paces," Karl spat into the ground.

"Everyone can't be an archer, Karl," William reassured him. "At least we have a hundred and fifty or so that we can work with. That's a decent corp," he added hopefully.

"We'll let the rest try their hand with practice swords tomorrow and see how they fare," Darius said.

"It will be fewer than this lot," Karl commented. "Sword is a tricky weapon. Most won't take to it."

"What do we do with the rest?" Darius asked.

"Spear or javelin," William answered. "Simple weapons and easy to craft with what we have available. We'll need plenty of both if we ever need to defend the walls."

Darius nodded.

"Of course, if we ever need to defend the walls, we're sunk anyway because that means the imperials have found us and they could grind us up in this place in less than a fortnight," Karl grumbled.

"Well, don't tell them that," Arnon said under his breath, nodding toward the group of recruits.

"Ack!" Karl waved his hand. "I'm not daft. I know better than that."

Chapter Seventeen

Gilded Cage

Ullani's eyes opened slowly. The flickering light from lamps cast dancing shadows across the colorful silks that decorated the interior of her tent.

"She's awake," she heard someone say.

One of the women who had been placed in her care was kneeling beside her and was applying a cool, damp cloth to her forehead.

Ahmed's blurry face floated across her field of vision as he leaned down to look at her. Her head throbbed. Every pulse of blood felt like someone taking a hammer to her skull. She tried to speak but found that her throat was too dry to make words.

"Here." The woman offered a silver cup filled with water. "Drink slowly."

Ullani sipped, letting the cool liquid coat her throat. She tried again. "What happened?"

"The people of the crossroads attacked you and struck you down off your horse," Ahmed explained. His face came in and out of focus as he spoke, which made Ullani slightly nauseous. "Don't worry, though, mistress, we visited retribution upon them for the transgression."

"What do you mean?" Ullani croaked. Her head ached with the effort of speaking.

The woman raised the cup to her mouth again while Ahmed explained as casually as if he was discussing the weather. "We purged the crossroads of those who would dishonor the gods and their dually appointed empress."

Ullani let the full weight of his words settle on her for a moment. Was he saying that they massacred the citizens of the crossroads because someone hit her in the head with a rock?

"Survivors?" she managed to get out through searing pulses.

"Oh, don't worry, mistress," Ahmed said proudly. "We only lost a handful of men. It was their honor to give their lives for your honor."

"Crossroads?"

"In flames," Ahmed said joyfully. She shivered at the complete lack of remorse in his voice. He had, in his mind, participated in a horrific event that he could not conceive of as anything other than the admirable defense of his religion and his sovereign. She felt her stomach churn again, and she struggled to keep down the water she had just drunk.

The woman beside her saw the distress in Ullani's eyes. "Oh, you're cold, mistress. Let me fetch you a blanket. You, men, out of the tent for now. The empress needs her rest." She stood and shooed Ahmed and the others away.

"Not what I wanted," Ullani groaned.

The woman returned with a blanket and tucked it around Ullani. "Shh, mistress. Let's not worry about that now."

"No." Ullani struggled against the spasms of pain and pushed herself into a seated position. She paused for a second, fighting against the resulting nausea. "I didn't want a massacre in my name at the crossroads."

"I know," the woman said in a soothing voice. "Men do not always think before they act, and they are not used to consulting others. There is time to deal with them later. First, you must regain your strength."

Ullani nodded and sank back into the pillows. She gave the woman a curious look. "What is your name?"

"Randa, mistress." She bowed her head slightly as she spoke.

Ullani studied the woman more closely, truly *seeing* her for the first time. She was perhaps thirty. Her olive skin was darkened from the sun. Her brown eyes were sharp and intelligent, and her nose had been broken at least once, probably thanks to the kind treatment Qasim had shown his wives. She wore her hair wrapped in a colorful scarf, but Ullani could see a few loose strands of dark straight hair poking out the sides. Ullani placed her hand on the woman's arm. "Thank you, Randa."

Ullani let her eyes close and allowed the rhythmic throbbing of her head to lull her back to sleep.

Several days passed as Ullani convalesced under Randa's care. Her shoulder felt better—she was lucky not to have dislocated it. She finally felt well enough to confront Ahmed and the other men. She summoned Ahmed and waited for his arrival.

With Randa's help, Ullani sat up more comfortably. Randa took her place by Ullani's side in case she needed anything but kept her eyes lowered toward the floor as Ahmed entered the tent.

"I'm so happy to see that you are feeling better, Empress." Ahmed's thick eyebrows rose with the expression of joy on his face.

Ullani smiled sadly and spoke softly, projecting an air of motherly disappointment. "Ahmed, I need to talk to you and the others. Your response at the crossroads was extreme, and we need to discuss it."

A momentary flicker of confusion crossed Ahmed's face. Then he smiled, rose, and practically sprinted across the tent. He threw back the flaps and shouted to the men standing outside. "Assemble the council. The empress wishes to speak."

There's a council now? Ullani groaned. *I have got to nip this in the bud before it gets any further out of hand.*

Ahmed looked back at her, the smile still on his face. She ignored his expression and closed her eyes for a moment, settling back against the pillows arranged around her. The constant throbbing had subsided, but she did find that she was still more tired than usual. She must have drifted off because the next thing she was aware of was multiple voices arguing.

"You said she was awake, Ahmed," a deep voice growled. She didn't recognize it.

"Surely she would want us preparing for war rather than sitting here while she sleeps." She did recognize Muhammed's voice.

Her eyes flew open. *War!?*

"Kasha Haaki will burn for this!" another unfamiliar voice shouted.

Ullani sat up to her full height and glanced around. The tent was crowded with men. Many she recognized from her self-appointed honor guard, but others she did not. The newer members were all older. They wore their beards and their hair long. What little skin that was exposed on their faces was weathered and drawn. Their eyes were hard and their expressions severe.

"War is not what I want," she spoke as she tried to remain poised and keep her voice calm.

All eyes turned to her. They waited for her to speak again, and when she did not speak immediately, one of the older men sneered and pointed at her with disgust. A large, dark mole to the right of his nose seemed to glare at her like a third, disapproving eye. "You told us she was strong, Ahmed. A fierce warrioress appointed by the gods themselves to lead us out of the desert and restore the empire. All I see is a sickly *woman* too weak to get out of bed."

"She was bathed in the light of the Gods," Ahmed protested. "She is *the one*. She destroyed Qasim with a flick of her wrists."

The old man laughed, and the mole continued to glare at her even as he turned his eyes to Ahmed. "You have let your minds be clouded by her beauty and confused by her words. What you saw was likely the sun reflecting off the oasis pool, blinding you. And you have remained blind ever since."

"One thing is for sure…" the deep voice growled again. She picked his face out of the crowd. His temples and his beard were shot through with gray. "Kasha Haaki will not allow the attack at the crossroads to go unanswered. Whether it was the intention or not, there will be war. Your foolishness has surely led to the destruction of your people, Ahmed."

Ullani realized several things as she listened. Firstly, these new men were likely the elders and leaders of the various tribes that had joined them during their journey through the desert. She had thought that the younger men who called themselves her *guard* were, but this made more sense. Secondly, while the two older men blamed Ahmed now, the blame would surely shift to her before long. If she had learned anything about how these men regarded women, it was that she would not like the outcome once that happened. If she survived, she would either become a slave or someone's concubine, and neither option appealed to her. Finally, whether she had wished it so or not, the growly graybeard was correct. Kasha Haaki would not allow what they would see as armed rebellion to go unanswered. If Kasha Haaki justice demanded the right hand of anyone caught stealing, she shuddered to think how they would respond to this. Her mind raced looking for a way out—for a solution that would not only save her own neck but would prevent genocide.

Ullani decided that she needed to act before these old men took control of the situation and her fate was out of her hands. She came to her feet and rose to her full height. She was as tall as most of the men in the tent and taller than many of the older men. She adopted a severe expression while she gathered her emotions. Disappointment for failing to complete Saria and Bedria's simple task. Sadness that Darius would disapprove of what she was about to do. Anger at herself for allowing this ruse to reach this point of no return. Disgust at the old men arrayed before her and how little respect they had for women and their abilities.

"Apparently, you didn't hear me," her voice boomed. "That is not what I want."

Shock and anger played across the expressions of the two men who had been most vocal, but she didn't give them the opportunity to respond.

"War may come, but now is not the time. There is much to do before that bridge can be crossed. We will turn north." Greybeard opened his mouth to interrupt but she cut him off with a glance. "We will march to Kasha Esharra and restore the true capital."

Ahmed beamed at this pronouncement. She resisted the urge

to smile at him—it was his idea, after all. She didn't know what she was going to do, but she hoped this plan would give her the time to figure it out. It would also remove these people from the immediate threat from Kasha Haaki.

Dark Mole scoffed. "You don't command us, woman. We will decide what is best for our people—"

Ullani's hands moved in a flash. Small blades flew through the air, scoring deep cuts across each of the man's cheekbones before imbedding in wooden rafters of the tent.

"Outrageous!" Greybeard exclaimed as blood began to spill into his companion's beard.

Ullani's hands flickered again, and twin lacerations decorated his face as well. "You now bear the mark of Kisha," she bellowed. She was making this up as she went, but she knew she had to sound confident or it would likely backfire on her. "From this day forward, you will act as my servants, and you may only speak when I command it, or I will have your tongue cut out and nailed to a pole for the crows." *Nailed to a pole for the crows, what the hell, Ullani?*

Their mouths moved wordlessly for a moment. She could tell that they wanted to take command, but they saw the looks of fervor in the eyes of the younger men now that Ullani was asserting herself.

"Does anyone else wish to become my vassal?" *Vassal, seriously?*

The shock of what she was declaring settled onto the faces of the older men. They glanced amongst themselves, searching for a way out of this, for a way to regain control of the situation. She picked one out of the crowd who seemed on the verge of something. Sharp eyes over a hawklike nose were darting back and forth while they played out a scenario in his head. *Better watch that one, Ullani.*

Ullani's wrists flipped again, marking him. "I know what is in your heart, and I will not allow you to betray yourself or the others." Gasps echoed through the tent at this proclamation, and she knew that she had interpreted the man's expressions correctly. Many had probably been hoping that he would find a solution.

"You shall be known as Ubad Faran." She pointed to the man with the mole. She chose *Faran* because it was the word for mole in old Magoran. She chose *Ubad,* which meant *child* but also knew that it was very close in sound to the word for *slave* with the desert people. *No going back now. Might as well go all the way. If this doesn't work, they'll kill me—or worse, anyway.*

"You shall be called Ubad Cawlan." She pointed to the greybeard, *Cawlan* meaning just that. She chose *Dafo,* or hawk, for the last man. "And you shall be Ubad Dafo. Does anyone else wish to join Kisha's *children?*" She emphasized the diminutive status of the last word.

"Now, kneel!" she shouted.

The three men hesitated and then dropped to both knees. Shock and fear permeated the air. Wide eyes and baffled expressions decorated the faces of the older men. The eyes of the younger men gleamed as if redemption was within their grasp. She had to do something else for them.

"Ahmed," she declared.

"Yes, mistress." He dropped to a knee.

"You shall be my First Chancellor." *Holy shit, Ullani, what are you doing?*

"Yes, mistress." He pressed his forehead against the ground.

"Muhammed." She turned.

"Yes, majesty." He followed Ahmed's example.

"You shall be my second."

"You honor me, Empress."

"The two of you shall select five others from those most loyal to serve as my advisory council."

"Yes, Empress," they responded in unison.

"Now, clear my tent and alert the camps that we travel north at dawn."

"Yes, Empress." They stood and began escorting the others toward the exit.

"What about these three?" Ahmed asked once the tent was empty.

Ullani considered the question. In truth, she had no idea what to do with them. She knew it would be dangerous for her to relent now, but the impulsiveness of her actions hadn't given her time to consider the consequences. "For now, they can tend to the horses. I will think of something more befitting their new station later."

Ahmed bowed deeply. "Yes, majesty," He and Muhammed

dragged the other men to their feet and began moving toward the exit.

"And, Ahmed," Ullani said, having a final thought.

"Yes, mistress." Ahmed bowed.

"You will find me a dozen of the most capable women who wish to volunteer to be trained as my personal bodyguards. Present them tomorrow while we travel."

He swallowed hard. Ullani was sure he was hoping she had forgotten that part of their earlier conversation. "Yes, Empress."

After they left, Ullani collapsed into the pillows, her strength depleted. *By the Gods, Ullani. What the hell did you just do? You're in it now.*

"Well done, mistress," Randa spoke.

Ullani jumped at the sound of her voice. The other woman had remained so quiet, Ullani had forgotten she was there.

"Thank you, Randa. I'm not sure I made things better."

Randa shrugged. "You saved the people from what surely would have been a massacre. You are guiding them out of Merkar and away from the immediate threat. Give the Merkari time and they will forget about the incident at the Crossroads. They have greater concerns, I think."

Ullani's thoughts turned to the imperial siege on Kasha Marka and realized that Randa was probably correct. It also occurred to her that if she was going to be dancing this impossible line, then she needed to stay informed about what was going on in the other provinces. "Randa, aside from the four of you, are there other women in the camp who don't have the *protection* of a man?"

Randa gave a faint smile at Ullani's sarcastic pronunciation of the word protection. "A few, mistress."

"Bring them to me."

"Yes, mistress." Randa left the tent and returned a short time later with a dozen women in tow.

"How do your people communicate over long distances?" Ullani asked.

"We either use couriers or pigeons," Randa answered.

"Could we get a hold of a few dozen pigeons?" Ullani asked.

One of the other women laughed. "You are the empress...you can ask for whatever you want."

"Good." Ullani drummed her fingers on the pillow beside her. "How would you women like to travel to the other capitals and act as my eyes and ears to keep me alerted to what is going on? If I really can get anything I want, I'm sure I could come up with enough gold to pay for your expenses."

"Can we take our children with us?" one of the women asked.

"Of course!" Ullani said. "I wouldn't ask you to abandon your children."

The women glanced around the tent, and then one after the other, they shrugged. "We live to serve." Ullani could tell by the sardonic tone that they were reflecting more on their role in their society rather than Ullani's request.

Ullani smiled. "I'm hoping your efforts will go beyond servitude and will actually make a difference. If I'm going to do this"—she waved her hands around the tent—"then I'm going to have to make a few changes."

"The men aren't going to like that," Randa said.

"No, I don't expect they will," Ullani agreed.

Chapter Eighteen

Imperial Edicts

Snow covered the Dalaman Plains. Gently rolling hills that would be the mottled brown and green of fertile farmland in a few months looked instead like an undulating white sea as vast as the ocean itself. Emperor Lao Jun Qiu let his thoughts drift as his gaze passed over the bleak landscape. In the dead of winter, Magora was not unlike the Northern Wastes where Emperor Lao had spent most of his youth and bided his time while he built his army.

"We should be arriving at Kasha Marka in a few hours," Guo Wen, the emperor's uncle and closest advisor, broke the silence.

"Thank you, uncle," Lao Jun responded without shifting his gaze away from the hypnotic monotony outside the carriage.

"You seem lost in thought," Guo Wen prodded. "Is there anything you wish to discuss?"

Guo Wen had been instrumental in Lao Jun's upbringing. While Sengiin Sharav had always been present, his role had always been deferential, and he had focused most on protecting Lao Jun and helping the emperor build his army. Guo Wen had provided guidance and training regarding political and social concerns as well as helping to shape Lao Jun's worldview.

Since following his army south, Lao Jun had interacted more directly with the nobility of Shalanum. He was feeling more and more like Guo Wen had been playing a game of *wei-chi* but had only been showing Lao Jun half the board. Whether or not this was intentional or merely blindness created by Guo Wen's own political lens, Lao Jun was yet to determine.

"Nothing of note, uncle. I'm curious. What is your opinion of my edict in Shalanum to develop trade schools in Kasha Amur, Isan, and Eridu?"

The old man stroked his fingers along his jawline, pulling his beard to a point rhythmically while he thought. "I think that the planning and building of the institutions will draw the focus of the populace away from conflicts in other parts of the empire. I think the large number of workers needed to build the schools will engage many men and keep them focused on a task. Busy hands are less likely to pound plowshares into swords, as they say."

Guo Wen's eyes drifted up as if studying the ceiling of the carriage, and he pursed his lips. "Construction will be expensive and can be dragged out for several years. People will be more likely to pay taxes for public works that they think will benefit them or their children. Meanwhile, a portion of those taxes can be funneled to more important government tasks like the war effort. Overall, I think the development of the trade schools will be an excellent way to keep Shalanum distracted and will encourage stability in the region so we can focus on other areas."

Lao Jun sighed inwardly and mentally rolled his eyes, making sure to keep his outward expressions placid. "But what of the end result? Do you see the benefit in creating a mechanism for citizens to pursue trades that interest them or that they show an aptitude in rather than being stuck in the trades of their fathers, whether they are good at them or not? Do you see the benefit of being able to influence training programs that will fill labor gaps and improve the overall quality of trade goods?"

"I can see some benefits to trade," Guo Wen considered. "However, they will be expensive to maintain. I'm not sure how much the empire would benefit outside of the natural increase in taxes that would come from higher trade values." He pulled on the point of his beard again. "If we were to charge students to attend, the state could recoup some of the costs."

"But that would inevitably result in a different sort of caste system where only the wealthy could afford to send their children to the trade schools. It would exacerbate the class gap rather than eliminate it," Lao Jun countered. "If the opportunity were available to all, it would create more competition, inspire ingenuity, and improve the overall quality of all commodities and provide more incentive to trade outside the empire."

Guo Wen looked shocked at the idea. "Trade outside the empire? That sounds like an invitation for disaster. We have everything we need in Chungoku to sustain ourselves and prosper. To open our borders and encourage outside influence could introduce an ideology that runs contrary to that of the empire. It sounds very dangerous."

"Hmm, I understand your perspective," Lao Jun conceded. He could see that his uncle was not going to be dissuaded and open his mind to the possible benefits. He sighed again and then changed the subject. "What additional proposals do you think we should include in our negotiations with the nobility of Kasha Marka?"

Lao Jun's eye drifted back to the desolate white waves, half listening as Guo Wen presented his standard ideas—offer favorable trade deals to the wealthy, reintroduce conscription, and leverage the abundant crops that would be available in the spring and summer to support the army.

After several days of negotiations where Jun felt like he was walking the fine line between maintaining his uncle's support and trying to win the loyalty of the citizens of Kasha Marka, he found himself almost excited for his next engagement. He rearranged the placement of the bowls of stones next to the board and shifted his chair three or four times to find the ideal position for comfort and to study the board.

There was a knock at the door to his chamber.

"Enter," he called more loudly than intended.

The steward opened the door and bowed. "Lieutenant Micah Kabir, Your Majesty."

"Thank you, Li Bao."

The steward bowed again and then stepped aside to admit the young lieutenant. Micah bowed deeply and then stepped toward the table as Lao Jun waved him forward. Li Bao bowed again and then stepped backwards out of the room, pulling the door closed behind him.

"Please, sit, Lieutenant." Lao Jun indicated to the chair on the opposite side of the table.

Micah sat. "Thank you for inviting me, Your Majesty."

"Of course," Jun said dismissively. "It has been too long since we have played. You will have the honor of going first."

"Very kind, majesty, but the honor is yours. I insist." Lieutenant Kabir bowed his head.

Lao Jun smiled inwardly and reflected on Micah's complete lack of decorum during their first meeting. *His manners have improved.* "Very well." He reached for a black stone and placed it on the upper right corner star point.

Micah countered quickly with the standard opening response in the lower left corner star point. Lao Jun played lower right, and Micah completed the opening sequence by placing a white stone in the upper left.

"So, tell me about your most recent mission," Lao Jun opened the conversation.

Lieutenant Kabir's face turned red, and he lowered his eyes. "I was unable to complete my mission," he said uncomfortably. "Quian MacCinidh escaped."

"Don't be so hard on yourself," Lao Jun admonished. "Quian is a slippery fish who has eluded us for decades. My understanding from General Hamazi is that you were able to eliminate key senior officials in Patel's Rest, that you unseated MacCinidh who is on the run, and that the valley is primed for a regiment of imperial troops to establish order and secure the pass. I would argue that the mission was an overall success with a single minor setback."

"You are too kind, majesty." Micah still looked embarrassed.

As they spoke, the board began to take shape as they battled first for control of the lower left quadrant. Lao Jun had moved aggressively to overturn Micah's claims. Meanwhile, the right side of the board remained securely under Lao Jun's control.

"Have you heard any word of your brother?" Lao Jun asked, changing the subject.

"No, majesty. He captured me at Kasha Marka, and he was gone before I managed to escape. After that, I was very engaged between aiding in the siege and then traveling to Patel's Rest."

"Ah, so you haven't heard of his capture?"

The surprise was evident on Micah's face. "No, sir. I heard that they liberated his fiancé from the camps and that she fled south with my mother, but I did not hear what became of him."

"He was captured during the rescue and transported to

Eridu," Emperor Lao explained.

"So, he is in Eridu?" Micah asked.

"No, sadly." Lao Jun hid his own embarrassment with a nonchalance as if it didn't really matter. "Apparently, he had friends in Eridu who set him free shortly after his arrival. After that, he disappeared. I was hoping you had heard word. I would still very much like to meet with him to discuss his future. I think he would make a great asset to the empire if he can be convinced."

"I don't know if that's going to happen, majesty. He spent too long with the traitor, Arthengal, and I'm afraid he fell under his influence. Darius was at an impressionable age when he was left on his own, and General Alamay took advantage of that. They formed a strong bond, I'm afraid, and Darius blames the empire for Alamay's death."

"That is unfortunate," Lao Jun mused. "The empire does not need more enemies. I was hoping to bring him into the fold."

"If I know my brother," Micah said. "He is probably trying to find my mother and Anna. Have you heard any word about them, majesty? Last I heard, they had traveled to Basara with Bedria Kess, but I haven't heard anything since then."

Lao Jun shook his head as he studied the board. Micah had broken out, and stones now spread across the lower half of the board. Both of them now had territory that was at risk. "News from the front has been inconsistent with regard to the Kesses and their allies. The siege is still underway at Basara, and our ships have completed a blockade of the port. So, the city and most of the Magoran army are bottled up, but a sizable group of partisans led by the baroness herself continue to cause problems along the road to Kantibar. They use the woodlands south of the Meddian Plains to mask their movements and harass supply lines and patrols between here and Basara."

Micah nodded with a soldier's understanding that it would be impossible to tell if his mother was holed up behind the city walls, with Bedria Kess in the wilderness, or elsewhere. The maturity of his response reinforced Lao Jun's confidence that the young lieutenant was ready for what Lao Jun had planned for him.

They played in silence for a time as the game got more intense. Micah first locked up the northwest, pinning Emperor Lao's stones against the board's edge. Then play moved to the final open quadrant, and they maneuvered around each other in the northeast. Move followed countermove as they fought for control of the center of the board. Lao Jun placed a stone to link his territories in the north and south. Micah countered away, further securing the northwest quadrant. Micah then played several stones diagonally from the northwest to the center. Lao Jun realized his strategy too late, and a large block of his stones as well as the center of the board were suddenly placed in jeopardy. He searched the board for a way to recover but could find none. Stunned, he lifted his gaze to the young lieutenant. Micah was studying the board, carefully planning his next move. He didn't even realize yet that he had already won.

"Excellently played, Lieutenant Kabir. I resign." Emperor Lao gave the briefest of nods to acknowledge his opponent.

"Are you sure?" Micah studied the overall layout, counting points in his head. He straightened suddenly once he had calculated the outcome of the next dozen or so moves.

"You see it now?" Lao Jun asked.

"Yes, majesty. I'm sorry."

"Don't apologize. Never apologize when you outplay your opponent. It dishonors them and yourself. You did very well. Accept the victory with grace and humility."

"Yes, Your Majesty. Thank you for the game."

"Any time. It is my pleasure. I enjoy playing with an opponent who challenges me," Emperor Lao said. "There is one other matter that I wish to discuss with you."

"Yes, Your Majesty. I am at your command."

"I wish you to take command of the *amanu'dami* or *Blood Knives* as you may call them, as well as the *Shadow Order,* and *Silent Assassins* in addition to your *Night Birds*."

"Surely not, majesty! The Night Birds I understand—I've commanded them for some time now. But the rest would divide the Night Guard and weaken Captain Sobel's forces. Also, both Lieutenant Demir and Lieutenant Androv outrank me. Of those units, I only have seniority over Lieutenant Vesper."

"We will backfill Captain Sobel's *daku mitu* with new recruits. Your new company will be known as the *Sgarra'lamma*."

Micah tilted his head, his lack of fluency with the old tongue evident as his mouth sounded out the words.

"It roughly translates to *Avenging Angels*," Lao Jun explained.

"I'm honored, majesty. But there is still the matter of rank," Micah said.

"Hmm, yes. We don't want to create conflict within the ranks. I think the easiest solution is to promote you to captain."

Micah's jaw dropped.

"Captain Kabir, I would like you to take the *Sgarra'lamma* south and root out any resistance that you find in the forests south of the Meddian Plains. Your job is to ensure that our supply lines run smoothly and that Bedria Kess's partisans are routed."

Micah came sharply to attention and bowed at the waist. "Yes, Your Majesty. It is my honor."

"You must also name a new commander for the Night Birds. I suggest that you promote from within to maintain order within the ranks."

"Yes, majesty. I would recommend Joral Einarsson for the job. He is only a sergeant, but he has been invaluable in—"

Emperor Lao cut Micah off with a wave of his hand. "I leave that to your judgment. Send any recommendations for promotion through the proper channels, and I will see that they are approved. I expect good things from you, Captain Kabir. Do not disappoint."

"Of course, majesty."

"And if there is time, I would love the opportunity to redeem myself with another game before you leave the city."

"It would be my pleasure, majesty."

Spring – 36 A.E.

Chapter Nineteen

Growing Rebellion

"Thrust. Parry. Retreat. Lunge." William Bratt called the movements of Striking Adder while Darius walked slowly through the group of forty men and women, watching their form. Occasionally, he had to use his staff to raise an elbow that had dropped or move a foot into the correct position, but overall, the students were doing well.

Sixty students learned much more slowly than one. At first, Darius was frustrated by their lack of progress. He had known a dozen forms by this point in his training. The recruits had been training all winter and only knew four. Several times, he considered abandoning the idea of training anyone in the sword. He had already sent more than twenty of the original recruits to either train with Arnon Porter's spears or Jenna Allister's javelin.

Jenna was a lucky find. She had come from Sidia with her

father, Rhys. Jenna's mother died in childbirth. Rhys claimed he "knew nothing about rearing girls and had raised Jenna as he would a son." He'd taught her to farm, fish, hunt, and throw javelin. It turned out she had a natural affinity for the weapon, and he began entering her in contests at tournaments and fairs at an early age. Eventually, they were making more from her prize money than he ever did farming potatoes and onions, so he abandoned his tenant farm and took on the task of training her full-time. Between the two of them, they had raised a solid corps of a hundred or so javelin.

William called for a break and Darius wandered over to where Antu was watching the proceedings with a bored look on his face. Darius dropped to the ground next to the gigantic beast and leaned against the creature's side.

"How you doing, old man?" Darius asked the bear.

Antu raised his head and looked at Darius. Darius could tell from the look on his face that Antu would rather be hunting rabbits, but he had not let Darius out of his sight since they had been reunited at the Cherian farmstead. Darius scratched the bear behind his ears, which earned him a satisfied growl.

"I promise I'll take you hunting as soon as we are done here." That seemed to placate Antu, and he lowered his head back to the ground. Darius continued to stroke the bear's fur and Antu's eyes started to close, a contented smirk on his massive muzzle.

"Form up!" William shouted.

The men and women abandoned their water skins and hurried

to retrieve their practice weapons. They arranged themselves into orderly columns six rows deep behind the squad leaders that William had appointed to each of the ten groups.

"Find your practice dummies and begin attack drills," William ordered.

Darius walked through the practice field, surveying each squad as they rotated through their turn with the dummy. Arthengal had never forced Darius to participate in this type of practice, opting instead to spar. Darius saw the advantage with their raw recruits. While Arthengal had been confident in his ability to block Darius's attacks and encouraged Darius to attack with full force and speed, such a tactic here would have resulted in many injuries. It was better for them to practice all-out attacks against an opponent made of wood and straw than one of flesh and bone that might not be skilled enough to counter the blows.

It was midafternoon before William called for a halt. Sweat was pouring off of the trainees, and they collapsed with relief next to their gear.

William allowed them a brief respite before calling his next order. "On your feet! It's time to run."

The collective groan was palpable, but they struggled to their feet, nonetheless.

Darius touched William on the shoulder to stop him for a moment before he took his position at the front of the line. "I'm going to take Antu out and see if we can't rustle up something for dinner."

William nodded and then called for the recruits to follow his lead as he broke into a light jog in the direction of the orchards to the south.

Darius trudged back up the hill with Antu at his side and a string with four rabbits slung over his shoulder. The rain was a light drizzle. Darius had the hood of his leather cloak pulled over his head to keep the water out of his eyes. Arnon was leaning against the gate waiting for them.

"How was it?" Arnon called.

"Good," Darius answered. "The snow is mostly gone from the valley. It's a bit muddy in parts, but it made it easy to track. Antu caught five and I managed to shoot these four."

Arnon raised his eyebrows in appreciation. "Not bad indeed."

"You should come out with us sometime," Darius invited.

"Thanks, maybe I will." Arnon smiled and then changed the subject. "Cheung Po has called a council meeting, and we would like to talk to you about something."

"Lead the way." Darius waved his arm.

Darius and Antu followed Arnon through the city in the direction of the keep. Most of the foundation stones from the old buildings had been scavenged to rebuild the wall. Lean-tos, tents, and makeshift market stalls now flanked either side of the main

throughfare. The paving stones had been left in place, thankfully—
otherwise, the road would be ankle-deep in mud this time of year.

The area in front of the decrepit stronghold had been
converted into a command center of sorts. Several large pole tents
were erected in the main courtyard of the keep. Each had a cooking
fire surrounded by a hodge-podge of seating assembled from the
remnants of the timber that was cleared to reinforce the walls and
gates. Darius shared one such tent area with Cheung Po, Arnon, Karl
Olsen, William Bratt, and the Allisters. They often stayed up late
into the night sharing stories and planning training activities for their
growing band of rebels.

The other five were already waiting under the tent. They
broke their conversation and turned in his direction as Darius
approached. Antu immediately plopped to the ground in his reserved
spot, and steam began rising from his soaked fur, warmed by the
crackling fire. Darius unstrung his bow and wiped it down, drying
the string as best as he could and then stowed his weapons in his
sleeping tent at the back of the courtyard. Cheung Po waved
someone over from one of the other tents to relieve Darius of the
rabbits and have them cleaned and cooked for dinner.

Finally, Darius sat on a block of oak near the fire and
extended his hands to warm them. He looked at the others
expectantly.

"The weather is improving," William started.

Darius thought he was joking. It had rained every afternoon

for the past week. "Yeah, it's great," he laughed.

"I think what he means is that the snows have stopped, and most of the snow has melted in the lower elevations," Arnon added.

"That's true. Are you suggesting that it might be time to send people south for more supplies?" Darius asked.

"Sort of," Cheung Po said with a smile.

"The troops are getting antsy," Karl said bluntly.

"The troops?" Darius said, raising an eyebrow.

"Aye." Karl spat into the fire. "We've been training all winter. They've been working hard. They need to do something."

"What are you proposing?" Darius asked warily.

"A raid," Jenna said, barely containing her excitement.

"On Eridu?" Darius exclaimed.

"No, nothing so grand as that," Cheung Po said. "There are regular caravans between Shalanum and Magora. The iron mines in the Talai Mountains have been operating at maximum capacity all winter, and there is a steady stream of new armor and weapons moving from Isan to both Kasha Marka and Eridu. There are also supply convoys moving grain and other foodstuffs from Kasha Amur to Kasha Marka to replenish what was lost during the siege."

"That seems inefficient. Why don't they just ship the goods?" Darius asked.

"Basara is still held by Eshe Kess, and Magoran river pirates raid any ships that try to make the trip upriver to Kantibar. The overland route is the most secure. We're hoping to change that,"

Cheung Po answered.

"Won't it hurt our cause to starve the residents of Kasha Marka?" Darius asked.

"Nobody is going to starve," Cheung Po assured him. "But if we force them to tighten their belts a bit, it will raise doubt in the emperor's ability to provide for his people. It will also help us provide for our own needs."

"Are you sure we're ready for this?" Darius asked.

"Ready enough," Arnon said. "We can start small—a dozen or so archers, a handful of your best swords, and some of Jenna's javelin."

William dragged a table near the fire and rolled out a map. "We were thinking here. It's near the intersection between the roads from Eridu and Isan and close enough to the river that we can transport any goods that we get quickly downstream to escape. And it's far enough away from here not to draw attention to our camp."

Darius got to his feet and studied the map where William pointed. It was near the northern point of the Talia Mountains. The river that flowed through the valley at Anbar Ur turned north a few dozen leagues from the crossroads.

"How would we transport anything we captured across the Taspin Plains?" Darius asked. "Wagons aren't going to travel quickly across those hills."

"Horseback," Arnon answered. "Twenty to thirty raiders all on horseback, plus another ten or twenty transport horses. Hit the wagon train and carry whatever you can cross country to the riverbend where you would meet rafts to transport everything downriver to here."

"Then what do we do with the horses?" Darius asked.

"Separate groups," Karl grunted as if the answer was obvious. "We've got plenty of people who can steer rafts. The raiders would drop off and then turn north to hide out in the plains. It's vast, hilly country, plenty of hiding spots."

Darius clasped his hands together and rested his chin on his thumbs while he leaned on the table and studied the map.

"We'd need rafts," Darius said.

"Boats aren't a problem," Arnon laughed. He pointed a thumb at Cheung Po and himself. "We know a couple of old sailors with a few contacts."

"You think it would produce enough to supply us?" Darius asked.

"Maybe, maybe not," Cheung Po answered. "It would supplement our supplies and, more importantly, would be a thorn in the side of the empire. I would slow down their supply chain, force them to assign more men to guard the wagons, and create enough of a distraction that it might give the other factions time to organize."

"I thought the *Shadow Crown* wanted this war," Darius stated.

"As I've explained before," Cheung Po said with a sigh. "War wasn't our end goal. Neither is it our goal for the empire to win. A strong, healthy, united empire…that's what we're after."

"And the baronies didn't provide that?" Darius asked.

Arnon laughed, but Cheung Po held up a hand to cut him off. "Fragmented and disinterested at best, corrupt and neglectful at their worst. We have replaced a homicidal narcissist with a group of self-serving isolationists. Trade is minimal, cooperation is nearly nonexistent. It won't be long before nine provinces become nine separate nations, and then the infighting and territorial battling will start and rip the nation apart. Chung Oku Mai's empire will be at an end, and the Sillu Aga will have failed in our mission."

"And you think we can fix it with a few raids?" Darius studied the map again. "It seems like you're trying to push an elephant with a mouse."

"We don't plan on changing the course of the war ourselves," Cheung Po explained. "Only to give those who can have an impact the time they need."

Darius shrugged. "I can't say I understand your end goal, but I agree that it would be a potential source of supplies and would give the men the "

"And women," Jenna interrupted.

"Give the Sillu Aga soldiers," Darius corrected himself, "the opportunity to test and improve their skills. When are you thinking?"

"Now," Cheung Po said. "It will take you a few weeks to travel upriver and establish a base camp for your raiders. During that time, Arnon and I can get enough craft and navigators together to meet you upriver."

"Me? You want me to lead the raids?" It finally registered what they expected Darius to do, and uncertainty crept into his mind. He was used to operating on his own or following Arthengal's instructions. He had never led people into battle, and he wasn't sure he could do it. "What about training?"

"Karl, William, and Rhys will stay here with me to continue training," Arnon said. "You will take Jenna and Rose with you to command the raiders."

"Wait, how did Rose get involved in this?" Darius asked.

"She's the best archer we have, next to you," Karl grunted. "Who better to lead the bows?"

Darius turned and glanced over at Jenna, who had an expectant smile on her face.

"What do you think, Antu? Are you ready to get out of the city and back into the wilderness?" Darius asked the bear. Antu raised his head and perked his ears. The expression on his face was all the convincing Darius needed. "Okay, let's do it."

"Huzzah," Jenna clapped.

"Here." Cheung Po jogged to his sleeping tent and returned with a wrapped bundle. "You'll need these."

Darius took the proffered gift and began unwrapping the canvas coverings. Inside were two swords. They had simple, unadorned pommels. He unsheathed one of them and inspected the blade. It was straight, well-fashioned, sharp, and free of knicks or dents. The weapon wasn't fancy, but it was functional and well-balanced.

"I think you are ready to reclaim your crutch." Cheung Po smiled.

Darius had not touched a sword—other than the wooden practice blades he used for training—since he made the promise to Cheung Po.

"Just don't forget what you have learned and fall into old habits too quickly," Cheung Po cautioned.

"Don't worry, I won't." Darius grinned as he strapped the belts around his waist.

Darius watched the five wagons approaching on the road from Isan. Even with reinforced axles, they rode low. Whatever they were carrying was heavy. This was also the first convoy that they had seen that had a full escort of imperial soldiers. The caravans that they raided previously were run by merchants and guarded by hired swords. They had been transporting grain and beef and surrendered their goods quickly without much of a fight once Darius and his raiders had emerged from cover.

"What do you think they're carrying?" Jenna whispered.

They both lay on their bellies hidden in the undergrowth several paces away from the main road.

"I bet it's weapons and armor," Rose whispered from

Darius's other side.

"Or gold," Jenna speculated. "Look how low the wagons are riding."

"I'm less concerned about their cargo than I am the twenty mounted soldiers guarding it," Darius responded.

"We outnumber them three to one," Jenna said defensively.

"Maybe, but facing trained soldiers is different than hired guards," Darius said. "There is a small bluff a few leagues to the north. I'd feel better if the archers and javelins attacked from an elevated position. The rest of us can ride in from the west and try to keep them pinned against the bluff face."

Jenna nodded. "Smart."

They returned to their camp and led their troops north. They discussed the details of their plan while they rode. They easily outpaced the slow-moving wagons and arrived at the bluff well ahead of the convoy. Jenna and Rose took positions on top of the hill and Darius led his swordsmen into the shelter of the trees on the other side of the road. They knelt in cover, waiting for Jenna's signal.

Darius heard the strained creaking of the wagons before he saw the column. They moved slowly, but that was to be expected with heavily laden transports. The soldiers looked bored. Their weapons were sheathed and they carried their shields on their backs. If Jenna and Rose were lucky, they may be able to cut the imperial numbers in half with the first surprise attack.

Darius heard the call from Jenna's horn and a cry from the hillside as the archers and javelins attacked. He signaled his raiders to their feet, and they moved forward in a crouched position to the edge of the trees. Darius could see half a dozen soldiers on the ground, but the rest had shields raised and were easily defending against the second attack while their officer ordered them into position to counterattack.

Darius gave a second silent signal as they reached the edge of the woods and then broke into a full run as he exited the trees. He bellowed a war cry as he ran, which was echoed by the men and women of his group. Several imperial soldiers turned their horses to face the charge.

The sight of the mounted soldiers clad in their black leather armor brought back a vision of his mother being ridden down and captured all those years ago. He recalled the helplessness he had felt then, and rage boiled inside him. He picked up his pace and was soon running ahead of the rest of his raiders. Two imperials turned their horses toward him and charged on either side of him. Before he could be caught between them, he dove out of the way and rolled, springing back to his feet next to Antu.

He lunged as the closest horseman spun. He pierced the man's calf, but more importantly, stabbed into the side of the horse, which caused it to rear in surprise and pain. Neither wound was fatal, but it created enough of a distraction that the rider almost lost his seat. Darius danced out of the way of the kicking hooves as the soldier settled his mount, then he thrust his sword upward at an angle, catching the man in the side just below the edge of his leather breastplate.

The rider's companion had circled around and prepared to strike Darius, who quickly drew his second sword and met the downward attack with crossed blades. He spun inward at the apex of the soldier's attack, locking the blades in place, and pulled downward. He had intended only to jerk the blade from the man's grasp, but the soldier had an iron grip. Instead, the momentum of the move pulled the soldier out of the saddle. He crashed to the ground, and Antu pounced on him, making sure he didn't rise again.

Darius checked the first soldier, but he was holding his side and guiding his horse away from the battle. Darius turned back to the center of the convoy. Several of the soldiers had dismounted so they could engage the raiders behind the shelter of the wagons to protect themselves from Jenna and Rose's attacks. Other horsemen were navigating their horses up the gentler southern slope to try to reach the archers.

Darius saw the imperial lieutenant and a small contingent of imperial troops fighting against a dozen raiders. As the officer struck one raider down, Darius flashed back to the valley battle where his mentor, Arthengal, was mortally wounded by an imperial officer. Darius's vision turned red and he charged the young officer.

The surprised raiders jumped out of the way as Darius and Antu thundered past them. Darius drove the lieutenant back with

Boulder Crashes Down Mountain while Antu batted the other imperials away like flies. In his mind, Darius saw himself coming to Arthengal's aid and striking the enemy officer down. He turned from the bloodied shape on the ground and saw the wreckage that Antu had created around him. Then he spied another dismounted imperial and narrowed his eyes to focus on the new target.

His own men backed away as Darius let his rage guide him from one opponent to the next until, finally, he frantically searched from one side to the next and could no longer find any black-clad targets for his anger.

He put his hands on his knees, breathing heavily. Antu let out a satisfied growl by his side. Darius draped an arm over the bear's thick neck and leaned against his body for support while he caught his breath.

Rose and Jenna organized the wagons for transport back to their rally point while Darius rested.

"So, that was different," Rose said when she finally thought it was safe to approach him.

"What?" Darius asked, he gave a final deep sigh and then stood erect.

"You went a little battle rage-y back there. Sort of like the old tales of northern berserkers. We weren't sure you were going to come back to us."

"Sorry." Darius blushed.

"It's okay. I get it. You have some unresolved issues with the empire. I'm not complaining. You saved more than a few of our swordsmen, and your battle frenzy caused the riders to abandon their attempt to take the hill in order to turn back and deal with you."

"Really?" Darius said. He searched his mind and honestly couldn't recall the details of the battle. His mind flashed back to other battles—in the valley, rescuing Anna, his mother's capture, his own capture—but here and now was a blank.

"How about we get this gear back to the boats?" Rose changed the subject. "Weapons and armor, by the way, in case you were interested. Loads of it."

Prince Kamal Sayyid was bored. He sighed as he glanced out the window of his elegant coach at the dreary gray skies and ever-present rain. He missed the sun and splendor of Kasha Nisir. He longed for the sunbaked bricks of the city walls and the alabaster white of the city buildings.

Every step of his voyage was worse than the prior. He had been miserable on the ship to Kasha Haaki, spending half of his time vomiting into the chamber pot next to his bed and the other half trying to choke oat cakes and too-salty fish, which, in the end, just led to more vomiting.

The river boats from Kasha Haaki to Magora had not been as turbulent and had at least been warm, but traveling through a landscape of sand and scrub was almost as tortuous as the muddy snow and overcast skies of Magora. Kasha Marka had been the only bright spot in the journey. The city was not as beautiful as Kasha Nisir, of course, but it had a certain elegance. His meeting with Emperor Lao had gone well but he was disappointed when the emperor decided to appoint him as Hurasham's ambassador to Shalanum instead of Magora. It would mean another arduous journey from Kasha Marka to Kasha Amur.

Prince Sayyid had at least hoped for some adventure on this leg of the trip. He had heard rumors of raiders hitting imperial convoys on this road since early spring. This fact caused Emperor Lao to double the number of imperial troops that escorted his coach. The undisciplined brigands would be no match for well-trained imperial troops, and he wished to witness the rabble getting their comeuppance. It seemed that it was not to be, however. He sighed deeply again.

"Are you okay, highness?" his manservant, Paal, addressed him across the coach. Kamal forgave the break in protocol because he could tell Paal was just concerned for his wellbeing.

"Yes, I'm just ready for this journey to be over," Kamal complained.

"Of course, highness. Can I make you some tea?" Paal asked.

"No," Kamal sighed.

"It was lucky that the emperor had a supply convoy ready to escort us to Eridu, no?"

Now Paal was pressing his luck by engaging Kamal in idle

conversation. He ignored the question and turned his face back to the window. A flicker of movement caught his eye. Dark figures rose from the rain-soaked hills and a barrage of arrows arched through the air. He heard shouts of alarm from the soldiers escorting the caravan. Black banshees raced from the trees beside the road, cloaks trailing behind them in the wind and rain. They launched javelins at the nearest riders. He heard a cry from his driver outside and saw his limp body fall from the side of the carriage.

"We're being attacked!" Paal said in a panic.

"I can see that," Kamal responded. *Finally! Some excitement.* "Are you just going to sit there or are you going to do something?

Paal was shaken from his stupor by the admonishment. The coach was still moving forward but slowly. Paal dropped to the ground outside and climbed into the driver's seat. He whipped the reins and yelled at the horses. The beasts whinnied with fright and took off at a gallop. The carriage bounced uncomfortably, and Kamal was tossed from side to side, making it impossible for him to get a good view of the battle outside. There was an incredible jolt, and Kamal was thrown to the floor. He heard a cry outside. The idiot, Paal, must have run someone over.

Kamal heard hooves thundering on the road outside, but from his position on the floor, he couldn't see the riders. There was another jolt as something large hit the coach. It rocked precariously onto two wheels and started to settle before something hit them again. Kamal was weightless for a moment as the carriage tilted and overturned. He heard Paal cry out as he was thrown from his seat. Kamal hit the wall with a painful thump and then was sprayed with water and mud as the horses continued to drag their burden forward. The arched roof slats began to snap with the stress. Leather and silk were torn away. Grass, rocks, and mud pelted Kamal until the horses were brought under control and the wagon stopped.

The young prince scrambled through the holes in the roof into the driving rain. His eyes fell on Paal a few paces away. Blood seeped from his head where it had struck a rock, and his neck was at an odd angle. Around him was chaos. Soldiers and horses lay dead beside the road. His was not the only wagon that had been overturned. The dark spirits raced through the convoy, striking down anything that moved with either a javelin or sword.

Fear suddenly overtook him, and he regretted his desire for *excitement*. Kamal struggled to his feet and ran. He saw a small stand of fir trees near the road and sprinted for their cover. He dodged around a wagon tilted sideways on a broken wheel and collided with a wall of wet fur. The impact threw him to the ground and knocked the air out of him.

He wiped mud from his eyes and stared up in terror as a bear the size of a mountain rose onto two legs above him. The roar that emanated from the beast was deafening. Kamal watched as a specter with its dark flapping cloak seemed to separate from the monster to stand over Kamal.

The figure assessed him, lying in the mud with his opulent

robes torn and stained with mud. Then it spoke. "Leave him alone, Antu. This one is harmless." The tall spirit placed an outstretched hand on the monster's flanks, and the bear settled to all fours. "There, Antu. Those soldiers are escaping." The bear turned to where the figure pointed and charged in that direction.

The tall black figure crouched, settling a sword dripping with blood across its knees. It leaned forward so that Kamal could see its white skin as its thin, serious lips whispered the word, "Run."

Kamal screamed and scrambled to his feet. He ran, screaming in the direction of the trees, but he didn't stop. He continued to run until his legs could carry him no further, and he collapsed near a field of boulders. He crawled next to one of the larger stones and huddled in his tattered robes, sobbing.

"Antu spared me," he muttered. "Antu spared me. The Sky Father spared me." The beast could have come straight off of one of the terrifying murals in Kasha Nisir that depicted the Sky Father, assuming the form of a bear to decimate his enemies on the battlefield. Kamal could picture clearly in his mind one mural in particular, which depicted fire raining from the heavens. Antu stood in the forefront, every bit the terrifying monster that had loomed over Kamal. On all sides, Antu was surrounded by an army of shades who swept across the land, laying waste to the god's enemies. The mural was called the "Hand of the Shadow."

Chapter Twenty

Blood Spring

"Cousin, why are you so glum? The sun is shining, the Festival of Flowers starts tonight. It is a time for celebration!" Lao Ichiro was in an exuberant mood.

Cordelia looked up from where she had been mindlessly pushing a raspberry around her bowl of porridge with her spoon. She glanced across the table at Aisha. The baroness's daughter had an agitated look on her face. Aisha's eyes narrowed, and she gave Lao Ichiro a sidelong glance but held her tongue.

"Join me tonight. We are planning a glorious ball. There will be music and dancing and more cherry blossom cookies than we can possibly eat. It is a time of renewal. Please come…it will lift your spirits," Lao Ichiro pleaded.

"Lift my spirits?" Aisha's tone was acidic.

Cordelia stopped stirring her porridge and watched the other two in anticipation. She could feel the tension in the air like a thousand invisible fireworks going off around them. She felt her heart racing as she watched Aisha's complexion darken.

"Lift my spirits, you say. And what, pray tell, do I have to celebrate, cousin?" She spat the last word like it tasted foul on her tongue. "My brother and uncle are being starved out in Basara. The trade ships that would bring them aid are either sunk by Hurasham pirates or are stopped by imperial blockades. The new *emperor* sits on my mother's throne. I haven't heard from my mother in weeks, and the last missive that did arrive spoke of a new threat that was pursuing her and her followers relentlessly, driving them eastward toward the border of Merkar. And I am trapped here, helpless to assist them in any manner, imprisoned by our *allies* in Ito. So, tell me, *cousin*, what should I celebrate?"

Lao Ichiro looked crestfallen at the accusations.

At least he has the grace to look remorseful, Cordelia thought.

"We do have some word regarding your mother," Lao Ichiro said. "It is not much, but it may be welcome news."

Aisha looked surprised—or was it irritated? "What is it?" she asked. The tension in her voice told Cordelia that Aisha was definitely annoyed. It was a bit rude, Cordelia thought, not to lead the conversation with this information.

"There are rumors. We have yet to confirm," Lao Ichiro started. "But it is said that a fleet of Merkari river boats took on several hundred passengers fleeing from the forests of Magora. It is further rumored that your mother was among them. It is said that they are rallying in Kasha Haaki and that more refugees arrive by the day."

"Why didn't you tell me this before?" Aisha accused.

"As I said, cousin, it's all rumor at this point. We haven't received any official word, but I thought it might give you hope."

"Hope," Aisha whispered. If possible, she looked even more depressed. "If that is true, then Magora has truly fallen. It is only a matter of time before Basara falls, and my mother is now a refugee." Tears welled in her eyes.

"Aisha." Cordelia rose and walked to the other side of the table to place her arms around the girl's shoulders. "I am sorry. I'm sure your mother is fine. At least you can take comfort in the fact that she is alive and safe behind the walls of the Merkari capital."

Aisha turned in her chair to bury her face in Cordelia's shoulder and started sobbing. Lao Ichiro looked very uncomfortable. He fidgeted for a few moments before backing awkwardly out of the room. Cordelia stroked the girl's hair, whispering comforting words while she cried.

Eshe Kess pulled his cloak tighter around him as the cool night breeze buffeted him on his perch on the city walls. Campfires and torches spread out across the plains in all directions like a thousand stars. He heard Kofi's approach before he saw him.

"What news do you bring?" Eshe asked when his nephew emerged from the darkness.

"Ten ships ran the blockade. A collection of merchantmen from Merkar and Aengal. Only three made it to the port. The others were either captured or sunk by the imperial navy."

"What did they bring?" Eshe asked, trying to focus on the positive.

"Food mostly. Much-needed, of course, but not much help in bolstering our defenses. The sailors have little hope of breaking the blockade again, so they have joined our cause. I've already deployed them to help defend the port."

"Thank you, Kofi. You have been a great help."

"Of course, uncle. It is my duty and my pleasure."

Eshe turned once again to survey the constellations that decorated the plains. "I fear that our cause may be lost."

"Take heart, uncle. Our allies will come through. They always do. Surely, Aisha has reached Ito by now, and they are rallying behind her. I know there have not been as many reports lately of mother's activities, but she is strong, and they will continue to harass the supply lines as long as they can."

"I appreciate your optimism, Kofi." Eshe smiled. "I pray that it is not misplaced. We have heard no word from Aengal other than the occasional merchant ship. Ito too has been silent, and every report that we hear would indicate that Hurasham either refuses to take sides or has joined the emperor outright."

"What of Orlyk and Chungoku?" Kofi asked.

Eshe shrugged. "I wouldn't expect much in the way of aid

from either of them. Kasha Ekur is the only major city in Orlyk, and they are probably more worried about Rusticar getting involved than they are in our plight a thousand leagues to the south. The rest of Orlyk is much like Merkar—scattered tribes and very little resources. As for Chungoku, it never fully recovered from the civil war. There is a government of sorts in Kasha Libbu, and they are good for trade for silver, copper, and tin, but not much else. Of course, the imperials would be diverting any overland trade across the Dalaman Plains to Kasha Marka. I doubt the nobles of Kasha Libbu care much where their gold is coming from as long as they're getting paid for their goods."

"At least Rusticar has remained silent," Kofi said.

"For now," Eshe agreed. "It would be unwise for them to do anything foolish at this juncture, trapped as they are between Orlyk and Aengal. No, I'm afraid that if Yapon or Merkar do not come to our aid soon, then we will have little choice but to surrender."

Waves lapped against the riverbank. An owl called from the darkness. Bedria Kess crouched, moving forward into the trees silently. Behind her, soldiers continued disembarking from the river boats. Lord Misrak approached to kneel beside her.

"Captain Shehu's unit should be about an hour northwest of here," Misrak whispered.

Bedria nodded and scanned the darkness.

"We'll need to move quickly and quietly to rendezvous with them and escort them back here to the boats. The Merkari captains will hide their boats near the opposite shore and wait for our signal."

"Let's move then," Bedria ordered. "I have a bad feeling."

Lord Misrak sent scouts ahead into the night as they marched silently through the woodlands. An hour before midnight, they received confirmation of Shehu's camp and made their way there.

Captain Shehu was surprised to see the Baroness. "We heard you had escaped to Kasha Haaki."

"We did," Bedria confirmed. "And we've managed to evacuate a dozen more units. You're next, Captain."

Captain Shehu nodded with understanding. "Give me an hour to break camp and get everyone moving."

Bedria peered westward, beyond the light of the perimeter torches into the darkness beyond. The hairs on the back of her neck had been at attention since they entered the camp. "I'm not sure we have that long."

"Well, hurry," Shehu assured her. "We can't just abandon all of our supplies."

A flicker of motion caught Bedria's attention, black moving on black. "Too late," she groaned in frustration. "Full retreat now. Lord Misrak, guard their retreat."

As if on cue, arrows rained down on the camp out of the night. Shouts of alarm echoed across the camp.

"Retreat!" Captain Shehu ordered, and soldiers began

D.L. Roley

scrambling out of their tents. Weapons were hurriedly snatched up from their racks, but armor and other supplies were left where they lay.

Hooded shapes clothed in dark clothing emerged from the woods around the camp as the Magoran soldiers surged toward Bedria. More fell as a second wave of arrows pelted them.

Bedria and Shehu urged the camp soldiers into the woods behind them as Lord Misrak formed a defensive line with the hundred or so guards that had traveled with them. The invaders clashed with Misrak's line, and torchlight flickered off of their black leather armor. Misrak held his ground until the last of Shehu's men were safely out of the camp, and then he organized an orderly retreat. As soon as they entered the darkness of the trees, he ordered a full retreat, and the rout was on.

Bedria ran, dodging the hulking shapes of trees. A dozen or more guards surrounded her. Every so often, a black leather figure would attack from the side and two or three of her guards would peel away to engage them, but their spots were quickly taken up by others to keep her safe.

The fighting was eerie, and it made Bedria's skin crawl. Occasionally, she would hear cries of terror or shouts of pain from her own men, but their attackers didn't make a sound. They emerged from the night as silent as ghosts to attack and then either faded back into the blackness or died as silently as they had arrived.

Several of Misrak's scouts appeared at the river ahead of

them to signal the Merkari and the riverboats were waiting for them. Lord Misrak formed another defensive line along the shore as the boats filled. As soon as one boat was full, it would push off and begin its voyage downstream only to be replaced with another.

Lord Misrak fought for as long as he could while stragglers continued to reach the river and climb aboard. When it became clear that he and his men were about to be overrun, they retreated to the remaining boats and rowed quickly away under a hail of arrows.

The boats regrouped about a league downstream and Bedria was able to count their successes and their losses. Of the hundred and fifty that had accompanied her, half remained. The losses were worse for Captain Shehu. There were five hundred in his camp when Bedria's party arrived, but less than two hundred made it to the boats. Others may yet survive, but if they did, they were on their own now. Bedria reluctantly admitted that this would be the last of her rescue missions. The *Sgarra'lamma* would surely be waiting for them wherever they tried to land in the future.

Chapter Twenty-One

Empire of Ashes

The walls of Kasha Esharra were magnificent. They made the fortifications at Kasha Marka look like a backwoods outpost. Even where they were blackened and scarred from siege and battle, they looked impressive. Ullani marveled at them as they approached the city. *How did Nasu Rabi breach these walls?* she wondered and realized even as she did that, treachery from within the walls would have been the only way. The stories had not been told that way, of course. Nasu Rabi had stormed the city, scaled the walls, and defeated Emperor Chen in a glorious battle that lasted two days. She realized now, looking at these walls, that would have been impossible.

Inside the walls was a different story. She guided her horse slowly through the destruction. Buildings had been gutted by fire, statues were toppled, and everything of value had been looted. Ullani even saw where some buildings had been carefully disassembled, presumably to reuse the stone or timbers elsewhere.

"Nasu Rabi did all this?" Ullani asked and shivered.

Ubad Cawlan glanced around. "No, the city was relatively intact when he left. The people of Chugoku did this. Rage and sorrow ran rampant the first few years after *the fall*. They took their anger out on the greatest remaining symbol of Emperor Chen's rule and, in doing so, destroyed thousands of years of history and culture." His voice cracked as he spoke.

"I thought your people didn't like cities and preferred the nomadic life," Ullani said.

Ubad Cawlan shrugged. "We do, but we still have a deep appreciation for our history and the history of our empire."

"So, you don't think the empire should have been overthrown?" she asked.

"Emperor Chen was an evil and selfish man, but there were other evil and shellfish men that the empire withstood and flourished in the wake of their demise. The destruction of an empire that had lasted more than three thousand years solely for the actions of one man breaks my heart," Ubad Cawlan said sadly.

"But the empire isn't really gone, just reformed under the barons," Ullani said.

"If you believe that, then you are a bigger fool than I thought," Ubad Cawlan spoke, clearly *without* thinking, and then caught himself. "Apologies, mistress."

Ullani narrowed her eyes. These old men continued to be a thorn in her side. They challenged her authority, belittled her, and had to be reminded repeatedly that they no longer led their people.

Reluctantly though, she had to admit they possessed knowledge and insight that she lacked. Their experience was valuable to her, however it was obtained.

She set her pride aside and then waved him on to continue. *I'll just have him beat later.* She consoled herself with the thought. She was kidding, of course, but the more they challenged her, the more she considered actually following through with it.

"If you put all the barons in one room, they wouldn't be able to agree on the best way to take a shit. In a mere thirty years, the laws of each province have started to diverge. How long before each barony breaks apart into smaller fiefdoms? Some say it was already happening in Shalanum before the new emperor arrived. Once that happens, the continent will descend into endless wars and petty squabbles over borders. Warlords will rule the weak, and the strong will bicker over lines on a map. The empire united us under one ruler, under one code of law. For three thousand years it endured, and it would take less than a century for the *barons* to destroy it completely."

"So, you would follow the new emperor?" Ullani asked.

Ahmed, who had been riding close, eavesdropping, eyed the old graybeard with suspicion.

"No, of course not. We follow you, Empress." Ubad Cawlan was unable to hide the sarcasm in his voice. Ullani chose to ignore it.

"And what would your counsel be?"

"Show to the people that you are the true ruler appointed by

the gods and unite Chungoku under your dominion. First the capital,
then the empire."

"And what of your *new emperor?*" It was Ullani's turn for
sarcasm.

Ubad Cawlan cleared his throat. "Make him bow at your feet
and wipe your sandals on his cloak."

"Or marry him and unite the empire under your combined
rule," Ubad Dafo, who had also been listening, added. The others
looked at him in shock. The old man just shrugged his shoulders.
"What?"

"We have arrived at the palace, Your Eminence."
Muhammad rode up beside them, unaware of the sudden tension.

Ullani took the opportunity to change the subject. "Show
me."

The group dismounted, and they ascended the stairs. The
broad, arched steps ended at what some may have called a courtyard
but what, in truth, was a thoroughfare long and wide enough to host
a parade. The actual palace was still some distance ahead. A second
set of walls surrounded the citadel where the emperor saw petitioners
and a larger keep, which was home to the private residences. The
gold and other adornments had been stripped from the buildings, but
otherwise, they remained surprisingly intact.

Ullani noted that grass and tree roots had wrecked the smooth
surface of the inner courtyard, and ivy had taken over the southern-
facing wall of the stronghold. Spring flowers bloomed in unkempt

gardens. Cherry blossoms abounded in the orchards on the eastern side of the palace grounds. A covered walkway between the citadel and the keep had broken and crumbled from neglect.

"It's amazingly well kept," Ullani said. "Especially when compared to the rest of the city."

"Even the disgruntled masses would not dare defile the palace for fear of angering the gods. The looting was bad enough, but I guess they make a distinction between the accoutrements of power and the holy site itself," Ubad Cawlan said before snorting.

The inside of the throne hall was bare. All artwork, furniture, and decorations had been stolen away. Even empty, Ullani could feel opulence emanating from the room. She tried very hard not to gape at the murals carved into the walls and columns and painted on the ceiling. Once they had finished exploring the citadel, they moved on to the rest of the palace. Again, Ullani was barely able to restrain her awe as bare rooms and empty hallways failed to belie the elegance of the palace.

"I guess this will do," she said, obviously kidding, but all of the men around her seemed to breathe a collective sigh of relief as if she was serious. *I really need women in my personal guard. It's definitely time to press the issue again if we are settling here.*

"Excellent, Your Highness," said Ahmed. "Please make yourself at home, and we will do our best to furnish rooms for you before nightfall. Might I suggest a walk in the gardens? I hear they are most spectacular."

Ullani rolled her eyes. "Thank you, Ahmed. I think I might." She turned to Randa, who had been following silently in their wake. "Join me, won't you?"

Randa nodded and fell in beside Ullani. Once they were out of earshot of the men, Ullani whispered, "Any word from the Watching Widows?"

Randa had come up with the name for Ullani's group of displaced women.

"Most are settling in nicely. It will be easier to coordinate communications now that we aren't on the move anymore," Randa said. "I'm working with one of Muhammad's wives to set up a pigeon roost on the roof of the palace. Once the birds have established themselves, we'll start shipping them out to the widows. Aside from that, there is no real news of import yet. Soon, though, mistress. Soon."

Ullani nodded. It would be comforting to receive regular communications about the state of the nation that weren't filtered through Ahmed's reports or delivered with the acridity of the Ubads's sermons.

PART II

Drumbeats stir the soul and trumpets cry.
Soldiers shout for blood as banners fly.
Storm clouds soar above in darkened sky.
The time is nearly on us, war is nigh.

Hoofbeats stir the ground to clouds of dust,
armor and weapons gleam free from rust.
In their leader's judgment, soldiers trust,
tyranny's end is near—long live the just.

Heartbeats race as enemies approach.
Arrows fly, antagonists encroach.
Malice reigns that Antu sets abroach,
bravery and honor, beyond reproach.

Drumbeats stir the soul and mothers cry.
Anguish fills the night as soldiers die.
Emperors give commands from on high.
In the sweet embrace of darkness, we lie.

– "The 'Honor' of War"
General Lao Wen – Third Dynasty

Summer – 36 A.E.

Chapter Twenty-Two

Fruits of Rebellion

The verdant green fields that stretched in every direction as far as the eye could see took Darius's breath away. The landscape was broken only by the occasional smudge of pink, lavender, or coral of wildflowers that had survived into early summer. During the spring, the plains had been alive with color. His eyes and nose had been bombarded with scents and scenes that stimulated the mind and invigorated the soul. But now, staring at league upon league of dark green brought Darius a sense of peace that he had never before experienced. The sun hovered quietly above the horizon to the east. The bees had hushed now that most of the flowers were gone, and even the birds were quiet. It was like all of the world had just taken a deep breath and was holding it before letting out a long, satisfying sigh.

Darius reminisced about the peaceful summer he had spent at

Eban Malik's farm near Isan. He remembered the simple tasks of tending livestock and working on the ranch. He smiled as he thought of picnics with Anna, and his heart ached to return to a time when they could lie together on the grass and watch the clouds drift lazily overhead. He longed to feel her touch on his face and feel her lips against his.

"There is a large convoy headed up from Isan," Rose Thatcher's voice broke the silence of the morning.

Darius closed his eyes, regretting the end of the serene moment—precious and far too rare. He opened his eyes and turned. "How far out? Any idea of its cargo?"

"It will reach the crossroads by late afternoon. We'll need to leave soon if we want to beat them there and have time to set up. I'm betting it's arms, but Jenna thinks beef."

"The veal would be excellent this time of year," Darius answered before he started walking back toward camp. Rose fell in beside him. "What size is the contingent guarding them?"

"One hundred imperial soldiers and assorted hired swords. There are about twenty cargo wagons in all," Rose answered.

"That's a lot. Even with the newest batch of recruits, I don't like those odds." Darius ran his fingers through his long blond hair. He hadn't tied it into a ponytail yet for the day, and he enjoyed the feeling of his hands running through his thick locks.

"I've thought about that," Rose said. "What if we wear them down with a series of hit and runs?"

Darius flexed his back and rotated his shoulders in their sockets to loosen up the muscles. "Tell me more."

"Well," Rose explained. "I was thinking we could break the archers into four or five groups with twenty or so in each. We hit them quickly from both sides with one or two volleys and then disperse. If the soldiers respond like they have in the past, they'll circle the wagons and set up defensive lines both inside and outside the circle in anticipation of an attack that will never come."

"Okay, and then what?" Darius asked.

"Then nothing. We ride away in different directions and rally near the crossroads. If they do give chase, they won't catch but a few of us, but I'm guessing they won't. They will wait until they realize no attack is coming and then start moving again. The next group will hit them a league or so further on. If we can hit ten soldiers or guards with each attack, we can cut their numbers in half by the time they intersect with the road from Eridu," Rose explained.

Darius was starting to catch on. "So, then, we bombard them again when they do reach the crossroads. After five attacks, they will be haggard. Their defensive lines will be looser. They won't expect the actual attack when it does come."

"Exactly," Rose said with a smile.

"It's a good plan. Good job, Rose," Darius said.

Her smile broadened further, and she stood a little straighter. "Thank you, sir."

"Divide your archers as you see fit and appoint unit leaders that you trust to organize each ambush. Jenna and I will head to the crossroads with the javelins and the swords. Your attacks will have the added advantage of delaying their arrival and will give us more time to set up a couple of more surprises."

Darius looked up from where he was digging a shallow pit trap when he heard the riders approaching. He counted twenty riders in all, most of what would have been in the first ambush party. "How did it go?" Darius asked the leader when they were close enough to hear.

"Perfectly." He was beaming. "We fired three volleys and then took off. They had the wagons circled by then and a shield wall in place. It would have been a waste of arrows to stay longer. I was surprised at how fast the leader of the soldiers got their defenses in place. They were very well trained."

"How many do you think you hit?" Darius asked.

"Best as we could tell, ten or twenty. Not all the wounds were fatal, but it will slow them down in a fight."

"Any casualties on our side?"

"None, sir. They didn't even give chase, just like Commander Thatcher said."

"Excellent. Good work. Grab a shovel. We're trying to build a dozen or so pit traps on either side of the road. Knee-deep at most. Just enough to trip up a charge or possibly break a leg if someone steps wrong."

Darius was staking down a leather tarp over one of the pits and placing sod and grass to disguise it when the second set of riders approached. This group was slightly smaller than the first and looked a little more haggard. Darius folded his arms across his chest and waited.

"Jesop Bergstrom reporting, sir," the lead rider said as he pulled his horse to a stop.

"How did it go?" Darius asked warily.

"Okay, I guess. We got off two good volleys. We should have stopped at that point, I suppose, but I got greedy. The imperial captain rallied the soldiers around the wagons, but he sent the hired guards out to chase us down. The third attack was disrupted, and we had to scramble to get on our horses ahead of them."

"How many of them did you get?" Darius asked.

"Maybe ten or so. The imperial soldiers were riding with their shields facing out, and many of our shots were deflected."

"Any casualties on our side?"

"We were twenty when we deployed and there are five of us missing still. I don't know if they were taken or killed. I'm hoping they escaped and are just taking longer to get here."

"Thank you, Jesop. Can you and your men start helping Jenna? We're creating taller walls of grass that we can lay behind and, hopefully, add an element of surprise."

Darius checked the sun again. It had been a long time since the second group had arrived, and it was at least an hour past when he had expected the third ambush group to join them. Finally, he saw dust rising to the west. A group of riders was moving fast.

Rose reined in her horse, breathing heavily. "Well, that didn't go well."

"What happened?" Darius asked.

"We never saw the wagon train at the third rally point. The imperial captain had deployed wings of scouts on either side of the road ahead of the wagons. They ousted us from our hiding spots before we even got the chance to fire. We rode quickly away, and I joined up with the fourth group.

"We redeployed and tried a different tactic. When we saw the scouts approaching, half a dozen of us would ride in and fire a couple of shots. When they turned to engage us, a different group would come from the other direction and fire at them. We took out ten or fifteen before they adjusted and organized a counterattack.

"We lost a couple of groups before we broke ranks and fled. We didn't want them to follow us to the next ambush point, so we rode west to escape."

Just as Rose was finishing her report, Darius saw another horseman riding fast from the south.

"They're right behind me," he was shouting.

"Archers ready," Darius called out. Darius strung his own bow quickly and readied an arrow.

Twenty or thirty soldiers wearing breastplates and carrying shields rode into view. They saw Darius's line of archers and quickly realized they were outnumbered. They wheeled their horses around just out of range.

"Fire," Darius called anyway, hoping for the best.

Most of the arrows hit the ground several paces short of the riders. Only Rose and Darius struck targets. Both men wobbled in their saddles but neither fell.

"Okay, redeploy!" Darius shouted. "Archers, along that rise over there. We have horsemen hidden in a hollow just behind it. Jenna, move your javelin in closer to the pits. The element of surprise is gone so we want you to be within range of the road. The rest of you, come with me."

Darius led his small group of swords and quickly erected a collapsible barricade that they had constructed. They moved the pieces into place. It was built from broken wagon parts and barrels taken from previous raids. The barricade looked stronger than it was, but the idea wasn't to stop the imperial soldiers but rather to redirect them toward the pits on either side of the road. He placed two fingers in his mouth and gave a shrill whistle. Antu raised his head from where he had been rolling in the dirt to scratch his back. The bear loped to Darius's side and settled behind the wall.

Within minutes, a full wedge of imperial horsemen rode into

view. They took up the entire road, and as soon as they saw Darius and his makeshift barricade, they charged. Arrows and javelins flew at the cavalry from either side, but most either bounced harmlessly off of armor or shields or struck the thick padding that protected the flanks of the horses. The riders split just before the obstructions to circle around and strike Darius from the sides. As planned, the first file of horses were tripped up by the pits. The second file easily corrected and leaped the pits or navigated around the tangled forms of their companions. It succeeded in breaking the momentum of the charge, and Darius's swords moved quickly to attack the broken flanks while they reorganized. Meanwhile, projectiles pelted the riders from the sides.

Too late, Darius noticed a second rank of horsemen riding from the south on either side of the road. They were about to box in Darius's forces between two converging lines of cavalry.

Thankfully, Rose saw this from her perch on the rise to the west. She waved a flag to signal the mounted rebels behind her as well as the archers opposite her position. A second flag began waving from the second hill, and the thunder of hooves increased as Darius's troops moved to join the fray.

Darius and Jenna were trapped between two arcs of riders. They rallied and formed a square on the road in front of the barricade. Javelins were not as useful against horsemen as spears would have been, but Jenna and her troops did their best. Darius and his men formed a shield wall and defended with their shorter weapons while the javelins were thrust or thrown from behind the line.

Darius's horsemen finally arrived and hit the imperials at an angle. Darius and Jenna took advantage of the momentary confusion to reposition themselves. They used the pits alongside the road and the makeshift barrier to slow the cavalry attacks. The added security was short-lived, however.

The wagons appeared on the road and were driving fast to the north. Twenty or so hired swords rode tightly on either side of the wagons, protecting them. Darius could tell the wagons had no intention of slowing. He ordered his troops off the road, and they were forced to clash with the imperial horsemen on the other side of the pits.

Darius dodged a plunging lance and then pivoted to thrust his sword up under the rider's left armpit. Blood flowed freely down Darius's blade, and the soldier collapsed. Darius jumped out of the way quickly before he was crushed by the fallen rider. He took advantage of the momentary break and waved at Rose. She signaled with the flag to indicate that she saw him, and he pointed at the cargo train.

She understood his intention and began giving orders to the archers. They quickly abandoned their positions on the hill and mounted their own horses. They rode toward the wagons as they drove toward their escape. Then, finally, luck was on their side. The first wagon crashed through the barricade, and a piece of timber became tangled in one of the wheels. Several of the spokes snapped, and the wheel came close to breaking free from the axel. The wagon train was forced to stop while several of the guards helped pull the wagon and its team of oxen off to the side out of the way. The delay gave Rose's group the time they needed to close the distance.

Darius heard an agitated roar from his right. Antu was surrounded by half a dozen mounted soldiers who were attacking him with swords and lances. Blood was flowing from several wounds on Antu's thick hide. Antu swiped at the horses and weapons, but he wasn't able to hold them off.

"Antu!" Darius shouted, feeling the now familiar rage begin to boil. He let it take him and charged toward the melee.

A rider moved to cut Darius off. With a series of moves that looked like Dancing Lights in aerial execution, he knocked the thrusting lance out of the way. He lunged at a second soldier approaching from the ground on the left. Darius's sword slipped above the collar of the breastplate, and the man gave a surprised gurgle. His opponent dropped to his knees, clutching his throat, and Darius leaped, placing a foot on the armored shoulder and launching himself through the air toward the rider. A sweeping cut separated the rider from his head as Darius landed on the saddle behind him. He pushed the dead soldier to the ground and grabbed the reins.

The horse resisted at first, but Darius dug a heel into its left flank and pulled the reins in that direction. The horse turned, and Darius charged to Antu's rescue. He attacked with the blind ferocity he had become known for over the past few months and then leaped from the horse once Antu's attackers were dispatched and knelt by the bear's side.

Antu groaned and licked Darius's hand before struggling to his feet.

"Go," Darius said. "You need to get out of here."

Either the bear truly didn't understand, or the embodiment of the Sky Father was too stubborn to abandon his allies. In either case, Antu limped in the direction of a group of javelins being pinned down near the pits.

Darius followed and fought side by side with the reinvigorated bear.

With their support, the javelins were able to regroup to counterattack. Rose finished off the handful of guards that had been escorting the wagons and began providing support by shooting at the back lines of imperial troops.

Slowly, Darius's troops pressed forward. The imperial lines bent and then broke. Their discipline collapsed at that point, and they began a full retreat. The remaining imperial officers rallied the remaining soldiers at the far end of the field. The delay gave Darius time to reorganize their defenses as well.

Darius could see the imperial commanders discussing the situation. Both sides had suffered devastating losses, but the corps of Sillu Aga archers was relatively intact, and their uncanny accuracy must have dissuaded the imperials from a second attack. Darius gave a sigh of relief when he saw the opposing commander give the signal for retreat and the soldiers back into the trees to the south.

When the battle was finally over, Darius glanced around. The green grass was stained red a dozen paces on either side of the road. Moans rose from fallen soldiers—both those wearing the hardened black leather armor and those clad in dark cloaks over stolen chain mail shirts.

Darius ordered Rose to position her archers so they could stand watch against a counterattack while others tended to the wounded and prisoners.

Darius called for someone to bring medical kits, and he led Antu to a clean patch of grass to clean and bind his wounds. Jenna regrouped their men and inspected the wagons as well as secured the prisoners.

Rose joined him as he was finishing his work. Her expression was severe.

"Well?" Darius asked.

"Jenna's men were decimated," Rose said sadly. "Only twenty of her one hundred and fifty remain healthy. Many are wounded and may yet survive, but they need to get back to Anbar Ur for recovery as soon as possible. Your swords fared better, but you still lost fifteen and another ten were injured."

Darius groaned. That was half of his smaller force. "And the archers?" he asked.

"Other than those lost at the ambush sites, we are okay. We

still number over one hundred. But archers can't take guarded supply trains by themselves. I fear we may need to regroup and lick our wounds after this one. We'll need more reserves from Anbar Ur."

Darius nodded. "What about the wagons?"

"That's the only bit of good news. Two are loaded with weapons from the forges of Isan and leather armor. The weapons are mostly spearheads and arrows, but there are a couple of crates of good swords as well. It's all good steel wrought from the iron in the Talia Mountains. The armor is breastplates and greaves like these soldiers are wearing. The rest of the wagons are loaded with cases of beef packed in salt. There is enough meat there to feed all of Anbar Ur for a couple of months. There is also an entire wagon filled with barrels of beef in brine that could be stored until winter if we get them someplace cool."

"Good," Darius said. He surveyed the carnage around them. "I can't say it was worth the cost but maybe some good will come from it. Okay, start organizing transport. With the number of wounded we have, I don't think we have any choice but to use the wagons. They'll be able to track us easily overland if we do, but I don't think it can be helped."

"Yes, sir." Rose nodded somberly. "How is Antu?"

"He'll be okay after a little rest." Darius patted the shoulder of the massive beast and was rewarded with a satisfied grunt and a lick that coated his hand in saliva.

Chapter Twenty-Three

The Prophet

Emperor Lao watched from his carriage as they inched through the crowded market square. He focused on breathing slow, controlled breaths to soothe his impatience and reminded himself that he had agreed to this meeting and that it would go a long way toward smoothing relations with the nobles of Kasha Marka.

Lord Neberu had invited the emperor to dinner at his extravagant home on the southern side of the city. It was nobody's fault that it happened to coincide with a particularly busy day in the market. The first early summer harvests were starting to pour in. The sun was shining after more than a week of rain and the people—his people—were happy and excited to be out enjoying the beautiful weather and the fresh produce.

"Busy day," Guo Wen said, possibly sensing his nephew's tension.

"It is good, though," Jun said with a weak smile. "The harvests are good, the sun is shining, the people are happy." He replayed the thoughts that had just gone through his head, hoping that saying them out loud would help convince him.

"It is good," Guo Wen confirmed. "It demonstrates growing contentment. You were smart to make sure that the transition of power did little to disrupt the lives of the common folk. The markets are thriving; the harvests are good. That is all most people care about. Prosperous times also help them forget slightly higher taxes needed to fund the war effort."

"Prosperous times," Jun laughed. "You know we got lucky with that. As depleted as the city storehouses were following the siege, we needed a good harvest."

"Bah." Guo Wen waved a dismissive hand. "Further proof that the gods support your rise to power."

The crowd was growing denser as they approached *La Dame d'Miracles*. There was a commotion near the fountain and people were pressing closer to get a better look.

"What's going on over there?" Jun asked.

Guo Wen shrugged. "Who knows what petty entertainments distract the masses these days?"

"I want to get closer to take a look," Jun said.

Guo Wen sighed and then banged on the ceiling of the coach. "Get us closer to the fountain. Emperor Lao wants to investigate."

The carriage turned slowly, easing toward the fountain. A voice could be heard over the noise of the crowd. "He is coming! Repent! For the end days are upon us."

They passed a row of vegetable carts, and the break in the

throng allowed Jun to see a man standing on the edge of the fountain. He wore disheveled and dirty clothing, but the cut and color of the garments showed the elegance they once reflected. The man's beard was long and dark and in much need of grooming. His hair wasn't much better. The cart lurched forward again, and the man passed from view, but Jun could still hear him.

"Antu and the Hand of the Shadow are upon us! He is coming for us all!"

"What is he carrying on about?" Jun asked.

"Who knows?" Guo Wen scoffed. "He's clearly a lunatic."

Jun craned his neck to see through gaps in the crowd. The man looked oddly familiar. "That looks like Prince Sayyid."

"Surely not," Guo Wen laughed. "You sent him to Kasha Amur, didn't you?"

"Yes, but the speaker bears an uncanny resemblance. And his clothes are much too fine for a pauper."

Guo Wen finally decided to take a greater interest in the crier. "I guess I can see some similarities. We should investigate to make sure that Kasha Haaki isn't sending agents up to sow unrest."

"Oh, I'm sure they are, but this would be a very unusual tactic for them," Jun said. "I could see the Aengals trying something as gauche as this, but it doesn't seem like the style of the principality. No, I think he is authentic, if crazy. We should investigate, though."

The carriage finally broke through the crowd and was able to move more freely. In short order, they arrived at Lord Neberu's manor. They exited the coach and were greeted by their host and a full assemblage of his household staff all dressed in their finest livery.

"Emperor Lao, you honor us." Neberu bowed deeply. "Allow me to show you to the gardens where we might take refreshments before dinner."

Jun followed and decided to raise the question about the town crier as they walked.

"They call him The Prophet, m'lord," Neberu said. "He arrived with the first produce carts from the countryside a week ago. Apparently, he has been moving from farmstead to hamlet across the Meddian Plains all spring, spouting his messages of doom. I wouldn't worry about him, Your Eminence. The people will grow bored of his ravings, and he will move on, I'm sure. Now, the Cult of Kisha...they are more of a concern, in my opinion."

"The what now?" This was the first time Jun had heard the term.

"The Cult of Kisha. It's a new band of religious zealots that has risen out of the nomadic tribes of Merkar. Apparently, there was a clash with Merkari regulars near the Ziyandi Crossroads. Nasty business."

"What happened?" Jun asked.

"They were trying to travel to Kasha Haaki. For what, I don't know. Those people rarely leave their desert. Anyway, the way I heard it was a company of infantry was dispatched to turn them away at the crossroads. There was a fight, or rather a slaughter. The Merkari troops were decimated, and then The Cult fled north in the direction of Kasha Libbu. You haven't heard of this?"

"No." Jun gave a particularly dissatisfied glare at Guo Wen. "I haven't."

Guo Wen had the grace to look embarrassed. "I'll send people to look into it at once, Your Highness."

"Now," Lord Neberu said. "Enough about zealots and malcontents. Let us speak of the future of Magora and our shared prosperity. I hope you don't mind, my lord, but I invited a few others from the noble houses that are friendly to your cause."

"Of course," Jun said and waved Lord Neberu forward.

Jun sat behind the large oak desk in his study, pouring over the reports that Guo Wen had gathered on the Cult of Kisha. They were concerning indeed. The rumors of an "empress who was bathed in the light of the god" were particularly troublesome given that they were yet to determine what had become of the reliquary of Chung Oku Mai following the siege.

It wasn't hard to deduce that it was someone from Bedria Kess's household. She must have spirited the reliquary away during the confusion prior to the siege. But he couldn't work out who it would be. Bedria herself was causing trouble along the Merkari border. According to reports, Bedria's daughter, Aisha, was safely tucked away in Ito. There were rampant rumors about the troublesome Saria Oberman returning to her alter ego as *Sillu Mitu* and causing trouble all over the city. He had men on perpetual patrol for her and her agents. So, who could this be? He mused. *Surely no one not of royal blood would dare to don the crown.*

To make matters worse, it seemed that this Cult of Kisha had grown to be a substantial size and had embedded themselves in the old capital of Kasha Eshara. In addition, it seemed that Baron Harmenos of Chugoku, the very definition of corruption, had let them waltz in without any confrontation.

There was a knock on the door. "Enter," he called somewhat more abruptly than he intended.

Guo Wen entered and bowed. "We have him, Your Highness."

"Good, good." Jun got up from his desk and walked across the room to a sitting area that was more appropriate for receiving guests. He sat in a padded mahogany chair with ornately carved arms. In front of the chair, a safe distance away, was an ornate rug where supplicants could kneel comfortably to present their petitions.

Two burly guards escorted the bedraggled man into the room. His eyes danced around the study, taking everything in. Unlike most, though, he didn't seem interested in the priceless artwork or other trappings of power. His eyes seemed almost frantic as if he expected someone, or something, to jump out from behind the furniture and grab him.

He settled once the guards led him to the carpet. He knelt, and with proper decorum, said, "Your Highness."

Upon closer inspection, Jun was sure now. "You are Prince Sayyid."

"That is who I was, Your Highness. That man is no more. I am but a humble servant of Antu spared by the god himself to spread word of his return and to encourage people to return to the true path of discipleship."

"Tell me," Jun said.

Sayyid retold the story of how their caravan had been attacked. He told of the darkness, and the rain, and of wraiths that swept through the night, killing all in their path. When he got to the part about Antu standing above him, Jun raised his hand and he paused.

"You say there was a giant bear and a cloaked spirit carrying a sword?"

"Yes, Your Majesty. Antu himself appeared before me and screamed at me with the wrath of the heavens. I knew in that moment that my life had been measured and that he was unhappy with what I had wrought."

Jun gave Guo Wen a knowing glance and stroked his pointed beard. At least now they knew who had been raiding their supply lines in upper Shalanum. "Continue."

"Antu's spirit guardian whispered into the ear of Sky Father, and he agreed to forestall my judgment. The god's avatar then ran off to render his judgment on others and the guardian spirit knelt at my side."

"What did it say?" Jun asked with feigned fascination.

"It told me to tell others what I had seen there that day. I knew from that moment forward that I was chosen to spread the word of Antu's return," Sayyid explained.

At that moment, they were interrupted by an enthusiastic knocking at the door of the study. Jun sighed and then nodded at Guo Wen to answer.

"Your Highness. Emissary Guo." An out-of-breath runner dropped to his knees as soon as the door was opened. He pressed his forehead to the floor and held up a missive with an extended arm.

Guo Wen took the message and read it. A smile slowly crept across his normally serious face. "You may go," he instructed the soldier.

"What is it?" Jun asked.

"A combined fleet of Magoran, Aengal, and Merkari ships ran the blockade at Basara in a late evening effort to *flee* the city," Guo Wen read. "Several of the escaping ships were sunk and a few others were captured. The remaining ships, numbering twenty, were making for open water, and our forces were in pursuit when I penned this message. Basaran defenses have fallen, and the city has been brought back into the fold of the empire."

Guo Wen finished reading and looked up. "It's signed by

General Hamazi himself."

Jun could not help but smile. "That is good news." *And it couldn't have come at a better time.*

The original plan was to send General Hamazi to Orlyk Province to secure Kasha Ekur once he had finished in Basara, but now, Kasha Esharra sat in between them with a new threat in the way. While the Cult of Kisha might not be an actual threat, it could slow them down, and an extended siege in the middle of Chugoku Province would put the army at risk of being attacked by Merkar in the south and Aengal or Yapon in the east. While Yapon was sitting out for now, he couldn't rely on that remaining the case if he set them up with a nice tasty treat. Hurasham had a brilliant navy but would be little help on the ground. Rusticar would provide much-needed infantry forces but only if they could be safely linked through Orlyk. Jun drummed his fingers on the arm of his chair while he thought. The center of the board was out of play, it would seem. A flanking maneuver seemed best.

Jun's eyes refocused on Prince Sayyid. *Maybe he could be of use in Kasha Esharra.* "Apologies for the disruption, Prince Sayyid."

Sayyid started to protest.

"I'm sorry, you said you no longer go by that name. If I can't call you Sayyid, how shall I address you?"

"I am no longer worthy of a name, majesty," Sayyid responded. "But some have taken to calling me Antu's Prophet."

"Hmm, a bit of a mouthful." Jun considered. "How about I

call you Süba?"

Süba was one of the many words in the old tongue for priest or prophet, if not the most flattering variation. It translated more precisely to "one who licks the boots of the gods."

Prince Sayyid recognized the word but seemed not to know the subtleties of the translation. He brightened at the title. "Thank you, Your Highness. I would be honored by the title."

"As I was saying, Süba, thank you for telling me your story. As Antu's rightfully appointed ruler in this realm, I do, of course, want to make sure I am following his precepts. Your words serve as a reminder to remain vigilant."

Süba blushed at the compliment and pressed his forehead to the mat briefly.

"There are those who would dishonor his name, however, and are in great need of atonement," Jun said.

"Yes, Your Majesty. I have been trying to seek those out and encourage repentance before the wrath of Antu is visited upon them."

"Quite so," Jun said. "I wonder, have you heard of the Cult of Kisha?"

"No, majesty."

"They are a cult of heretics that have established themselves in the holy city of Kasha Esharra. They seek to raise Kisha above her brother and install an empress of their own in my place."

"Sacrilege!" Süba exclaimed.

"My thoughts exactly. It's like trying to lift the earth above the sky. Pure lunacy. But I fear that they are good, Antu-fearing men and women who have been led astray by this false empress. I wonder if you might be convinced to travel to Kasha Esharra to proselytize to them."

Süba gasped and tears filled his eyes. "You honor me again, Emperor Lao. To be Antu's emissary to the east is more than I could have asked. I do not know what to say. It is as though Antu has made my path clear through your words."

Jun resisted the urge to roll his eyes. "Yes, my good servant. You can further the mission of Antu and his duly appointed monarch by fulfilling this holy quest. Please, my men here will see that you have everything you need for your journey."

"Thank you, Your Highness." Süba rose and backed out of the room, bowing and repeating his thanks with every step.

Jun noticed that Guo Wen was covering his mouth with a hand, doing his best to maintain a serious expression until the doors were closed before letting out a laugh. "Brilliantly played, nephew."

"Thank you, uncle."

"Now what shall we do about Arthengal's apprentice and that bear of his?" Guo Wen asked. "Should I send orders to recall Captain Kabir?"

"No, I think not this time. He still has work to finish in the south," Jun responded. "Darius is in Shalanum—let the problem belong to Shalanum. Send word to Commander General Sharav regarding what we have learned and leave it to him to respond accordingly. I wonder if they might not have established an outpost near *Nasu Rabi's* old abode near the ruins of Anbar Ur. It's a bit far from where the raids are happening but worth investigating just the same. Tell him to send scouts."

"Of course. And General Hamazi? Events in Kasha Esharra would make it difficult to travel the easy road to Kasha Ekur."

"I was thinking the same, but we must establish the link to Rusticar. He'll have to go the long way around, across the Dalaman Plains north of the Saridon Desert."

"They won't make that trip before winter," Guo Wen said cautiously.

"I understand," Jun said. "But I don't see an alternative. But sometimes there are advantages to the slower play. Let us see where we can turn this delay to our advantage to further strengthen our holds on Shalanum and Magora."

"As you wish, highness." Guo Wen bowed and exited the room to distribute the new orders.

Chapter Twenty-Four

Beauty from Ashes

Ullani walked casually from one vendor's cart to another. Muhammad walked beside her on the right, and Fatemah, the new girl, walked on her left a step or two behind Ronda. Fatemah was Ahmed's conciliatory female guard. She was tall and muscular. Her nose had been broken at one point, and her hands were heavily calloused from years of manual labor. This was Ahmed's interpretation of what a woman who could defend the empress must look like. Ullani had the feeling, however, that if the opportunity arose, it was more likely that she would be defending Fatemah. Ahmed had given the woman a small sword, but it was obvious that she had no idea how to use it.

Fatemah could be really nice, but Ullani wouldn't know since the woman never talked other than to answer direct questions, and even then, with the fewest syllables possible.

"Fatemah, did you see that a shipment of mangos came in from the Paradaisu Islands?" Ullani asked.

"Yes, Empress."

"Have you ever had a mango, Fatemah?"

"No, Empress."

"You really must try one. Muhammad, go and buy us a couple of mangos so that Fatemah can try one," Ullani ordered.

Muhammad gave a bow of his head and then ordered one of the servants from the entourage that followed her constantly to complete the task. Soon enough, the servant returned with an armful of mangos. Ullani rolled her eyes at the overabundance and picked two that looked the juiciest, doing her best not to upset the rest of the load.

"You paid for these, right?" she asked the servant, who responded by giving Muhammad a confused look.

"Pay them." Ullani shifted her gaze to Muhammad and looked him directly in the eye. "The merchants are not our slaves, Muhammad. They depend on commerce for their livelihood. We can't simply take what we want without reimbursement."

"But it is their honor to serve, Empress," Muhammad argued.

Ullani shifted her expression to one that Saria had often used with newer members of *The Guild*. More experienced members referred to it as "the look." It was a hard-eyed, thin-lipped, no-nonsense expression that Ullani remembered literally gave her shivers when it was directed at her.

"Pay them. Now," Ullani said through clenched teeth to complete the look.

Muhammad actually gulped. "Yes, Empress."

She turned back to Fatemah with a smile and handed her one of the fruits. Fatemah raised it to her mouth and started to take a bite. Ullani quickly grasped Fatemah's wrist to stop her.

"No, no. It's better if you peel it first." A knife appeared in Ullani's hands, and she sectioned her mango and peeled off the skin. Juice dripped from her fingers as she handed Fatemah a slice.

Fatemah took a cautious bite, uncertainty in her eyes. As soon as the flavor reached her tongue, her eyes widened, and a smile almost touched her lips. Almost. She popped the rest of the slice in her mouth and chewed loudly.

"Good, right?" Ullani asked.

"Yes, Empress," Fatemah mumbled with a full mouth and gladly took the next slice that Ullani offered.

Ullani rolled her eyes again and took the second mango from Fatemah. She nodded to the servant to hand out the rest of the fruit to Ronda and the rest of the entourage that trailed behind. Ullani began walking again and began cutting the rind to expose the juicy yellow fruit underneath. Fatemah tripped and almost fell, walking and eating apparently being a challenge. Ullani restrained a sigh. *Alright, time to take matters into my own hands.*

"Muhammad." She turned to her second chancellor with a smile. "I would like to tour the camps."

The camps referred to the section of Kasha Esharra, which had not yet been rebuilt. Or basically, everything in the city outside of the three-block radius surrounding the palace. Ahmed had organized work crews when they arrived at the palace, the walls being top priority. Ullani had been amazed at how quickly the palace came together. Repairs were made, the grounds were revitalized, and rooms were furnished. In a few short months, it had gone from being a broken-down reminder of a fallen empire to a beautiful symbol of rising power. Ahmed had expanded improvement efforts outward from the palace. However, most of the city's growing population still lived in tents or ruined buildings.

Muhammad gave her a hesitant look, "But, Empress, the camps…"

"Are filled with your people, Muhammad."

"Not *my* people," Muhammad objected. "The Ziya tribe is either in the palace district or out gathering supplies to fund rebuilding the city."

Ullani gave him *the look* again. "Let me rephrase. *My* people live in the camps." Ullani hated using the term, but it seemed the only way to get through to Muhammad and Ahmed sometimes. They seemed intent on using their closeness to her to improve the lot of their own relatives and tribe members but did very little to improve the conditions of the thousands of other people who had been flocking to the city since they arrived. Ullani felt trapped by her current situation, but she also felt responsible for the throngs that were arriving in her name. It was getting out of control, but she couldn't see a way out of it.

"Yes, Empress."

They left the pristine streets of the palace district, and her entourage tightened around her. This section of the city was still filled with buildings falling in on themselves following decades of neglect. It wasn't as bad as Ullani had expected, however. The streets had been cleared of debris. The residents had taken it upon themselves to improve their conditions as much as possible. Tents filled market squares and parks. Buildings that could be repaired were in various stages of improvement and others were being disassembled for building supplies. Food and clean water seemed to be the most critical resources needed. Ullani made a mental note to start working on a solution for that immediately.

An inflated goat's bladder rolled across the road and stopped at Ullani's feet. A little girl chased it, oblivious to Ullani and the others. One of the guardsmen started to move forward to clear the girl out of the way, but Ullani stopped him and knelt down. She picked up the ball and held it out for the girl.

"What's your name?" Ullani asked.

"Sara," the girl said shyly.

The name reminded Ullani of her mentor, Saria. She smiled and waved the servant who was still carrying a few mangos over. She plucked a mango from the pile and held it out to the girl. "Would you like a mango?"

The girl's face brightened, and she snatched the fruit away.

"What do you say, Sara?" a voice came from the side of the street. It was a young woman, not much older than Ullani, leaning against a walking staff. She was dressed simply and wore her flowing dark hair to her shoulders.

"Thank you," Sara said demurely and then ran away with her ball to rejoin a group of other children at a nearby park.

Ullani straightened and looked at the woman who had spoken. "Is she yours?"

The woman smiled. "No, I'm just watching the children. Her father is tending flocks outside the city, and her mother is busy all day trying to keep them fed, clothed, and the rain off their heads."

"That's kind of you," Ullani said. "You don't have children of your own?"

"No, this is my flock," the woman joked. "I help keep the wolves away." She winked and then twirled her staff menacingly.

Ullani laughed. "I'm Ullani. And you are?"

"I know who you are, mistress," the woman answered. "I'm Ava."

Ullani smiled. *Finally, someone who doesn't rush to kiss my hems.* Then she had a thought. "Were you joking? Or can you really handle yourself with that thing?" She pointed to the staff.

"I do alright," Ava answered with a shrug.

"Show me," Ullani said.

Ava moved through a series of steps, swinging the staff with a practiced hand. It reminded Ullani of watching Darius practice with Lord Misrak. Ava's movements weren't as refined as Darius's, but there was a certain elegance and surety to her actions.

"Very nice. Think you could do that against an armed opponent?"

"I suppose. Why?" Ava said warily.

"Humor me," Ullani said. She signaled to one of the guards that she knew was less than an expert with his sword. "Spar with her."

The guard unsheathed his blade and moved forward. Ava moved into the street where she had more room. The guard took a half-hearted swipe at the girl, and Ava struck the blade firmly with her staff and knocked it from his hand. It clattered across the street.

"Seriously?" Ullani looked at the guard with disappointment.

Embarrassed, he ran across the road and retrieved his weapon. He attacked again, this time with a series of aggressive moves meant to redeem himself. Ava knocked aside the first two easily, dodged the third, and then swept her staff below the guard's knees, knocking him off his feet. He landed hard on his back, and again, his sword rattled out of his grasp. He sprung to his feet with rage in his eyes.

"Thank you, Jahan. That will be enough," Ullani said. His head whipped around in anger, which dissolved instantly when he saw Ullani's hard look and the knife that she idly tapped against the fingers of her hand.

Jahan retrieved his blade, sheathed it, and took his place near the back of the column of guardsmen.

"How would you like to join the Red Shadow?" Another

impulse, Ullani had just then decided to name her band of women bodyguards after her old gang in Kasha Marka.

"What's that?" Ava asked curiously.

"It will be an elite band of women guards that I'm forming."

"Empress," Muhammad said under his breath, "Ahmed isn't going to like this."

"I'm sorry, Muhammad. Who is the empress here?" *If I'm going to play the part, I'm going to play it my way.*

"But she—" Muhammad looked Ava up and down, barely concealing the disgust in his eyes, "—is *Kujab*."

"I have no idea what that means, Muhammad, but as I seem to find myself reminding you constantly, everyone that gathers in this city under *my* name will be afforded the same considerations. Old prejudices *must* die."

"But, Empress," he said meaningfully.

Ullani leaned in and spoke so that only he could hear. "Old prejudices *will* die. Or I will *kill* them. Am I clear?"

Muhammad took an involuntary step back. "Yes, Empress."

"So, what do you say, Ava?" Ullani asked.

"What does it pay?" Ava responded.

This was followed by a gasp, not only from Muhammad but from several others in the group.

"Those that guard the empress are volunteers," Muhammad spoke indignantly.

"Two drachs a month," Ullani spoke over the top of him.

And then looking at Muhammad, added, "Starting now. Anyone who is responsible for guarding my person shall receive two drachs a month."

Whispers spread through the group. She had not known until Muhammad voiced it that her guards were unpaid. That wouldn't do. Loyalties were too easily bought among all but the most fervent.

"Understood, Your Highness," Muhammad replied. "Ahmed is *really* not going to be happy."

"Then *Ahmed* can take it up with me," Ullani said, putting an end to the argument.

"Yeah, I suppose I could do that," Ava said casually. "I'll have to find someone else to watch the children."

"Of course," Ullani said. Then a thought occurred to her. "Do you have any friends? You know, who can handle themselves in a scrap?"

Ava smiled. "I might know a couple of girls who could use the money and know how to keep a man's hands from wandering too far."

Muhammad looked indignant.

"Perfect. I'm going to continue my inspection of this district. Meet me back here in say, two hours," Ullani said.

Ava nodded. "Thank you."

When Ullani returned a couple of hours later, her head full of ideas for improving conditions in the camps, Ava waited with a group of twenty or so women. Their ages ranged from twenty to thirty. Some of them were armed with knives or staves but most were not. The women represented a cross-section of the camp. Some were dark-complected like Ava, but others were as blond and fair-skinned as Darius. They all looked like they would have fit in perfectly with the Red Shadow in Kasha Marka. They had a bearing about them that spoke of a missing childhood, growing up on the streets or in the slums learning to take care of themselves when they couldn't depend on anyone else to do so.

"Perfect," Ullani said with a smile.

Muhammad could barely contain his disgust but had at least decided to hold his tongue, for now.

"Let's get you all back to the palace," Ullani ordered. "Food, baths, and clothing first. Then let's see if any of you have skill enough to be part of the Red Shadow."

Autumn – 36 A.E.

Chapter Twenty-Five

Vengeful Eagle

The golden eagle of Magora flew on every ship in the fleet. The Aengals and Merkari had mounted it below their own flags, but it was still displayed as a symbol of solidarity. Eshe had escaped Basara with fifteen ships and reunited with Bedria in Kasha Haaki. The Merkari had added their twenty largest vessels to the fleet. The rest they held back to protect their own ports and to patrol the rivers. As Bedria gazed out from the stern of the Magoran flagship at the small navy arrayed behind them, she wasn't sure whether to feel pride or cry.

On the one hand, their defeat had not been complete. There were enough here to rally if Aengal and Yapon joined them. However, it was clear now that Hurasham stood with the new emperor, and their armada was not to be trifled with. Add to that the hundred or more ships that the imperials managed to reclaim from the remnants of the Shalanum navy, merchant vessels, and their own vessels that they had brought from the Northern Wastes. It was clear that this war would not be won on the sea.

"We're not out of the fight yet, sister." Eshe approached from behind, and his words echoed her own thoughts.

Bedria tilted her head to look at him. "No, but the road will not be easy."

"When is it ever?" he asked.

She couldn't help but smile. Even in the worst of times, Eshe managed to keep a positive attitude and look for a path to victory.

"We'll be arriving at Ito soon. You should be ready," Eshe said.

Eshe was right. Ito was grounded in tradition. It would be expected that she would arrive in full regalia. Her current state, wearing torn and stained battle leathers with her hair bedraggled and her face smudged with grime, would be unacceptable and would be viewed as a lack of respect.

Bedria nodded. "You have the helm then, brother."

It took her some time to round up a few maids to help her with her hair and to don the multiple layers of ceremonial splendor, but by the time she emerged from her cabin, she was a vision of grandeur. She wore a long black dress stitched with white flowers along the sleeves, bodice, and hems. Diamonds sparkled from the center of each flower and a belt of silk and diamonds wrapped around her corseted waist. She wore matching diamond earrings set in gold that hung along the nape of her neck. The front of her black hair had been set into tight cornrows, and a resplendent cascade of curly locks flowed over her neck and shoulders. Diamonds, emeralds, and sapphires had been painstakingly applied to strands. A headband made of three strands of luminescent pearls completed the outfit with a carved mother-of-pearl pendant depicting an eagle in flight resting on her forehead.

The port of Ito was just coming into view when Bedria rejoined her brother. He too had changed into the blue and black satin dress uniform of the Magoran Commander General with a large golden eagle covering the back of his flowing cobalt blue cape.

They were met with full pomp and circumstance. Soldiers in dress uniform lined the dock, and a band played as Eshe took Bedria's elbow and guided her down the gangplank. Lao Ichiro waited for them at the end of the pier.

"It's unusual that his father isn't here," Bedria whispered to Eshe.

"Indeed, and far too many soldiers for a formal reception," Eshe whispered back.

Bedria's eyes scanned the shoreline and quay. Eshe was right—dozens of soldiers stood guard around Lao Ichiro and guarded other approaches to shore.

"Do you think he misinterpreted our intent?" Bedria whispered.

"Or maybe we have misinterpreted his," Eshe returned. "I

think we should proceed with caution."

"Aisha isn't here either," Bedria noticed. "That is a significant break from tradition."

"Agreed." Eshe put his other hand behind his back and Bedria could feel the subtle movements of his hand. She was aware of one of the commanders who marched behind them breaking off from the procession to return to the ship.

"What was that?" Bedria asked.

"Just a precaution," Eshe answered, but he didn't have time to explain more as they neared Lao Ichiro's entourage.

"Cousin," Lao Ichiro bowed deeply. "Welcome to Ito. It is our honor to receive you."

"The honor is mine, Lao Ichiro." She bowed her head slightly. "The prestige of your reception demonstrates tribute beyond all expectation. You are truly a credit to your house."

"Thank you, cousin." Lao Ichiro bowed again. "And you, General Kess. We are further glorified by your presence."

"Thank you, Lao Ichiro," Eshe acknowledged.

"I am curious, though…why was Aisha not able to join you in welcoming us?" Bedria asked.

Lao Ichiro's pause almost wasn't there, but Bedria noted it just the same. "She has taken ill and wasn't able to join us, I'm afraid."

"Oh?" Bedria allowed the correct amount of concern in her tone. "Nothing serious, I hope."

"No, something she ate, I am sure," Lao Ichiro replied.

"But surely she would have sent someone to stand in for her so as not to break tradition," Bedria said.

There's that pause again, Bedria thought.

"I don't think there was time," Lao Ichiro said.

"Time to prepare all of this." Bedria waved her hand at the procession around them. "But not time for my daughter to appoint a surrogate? I must have a word with her about the importance of protocol."

"Of course." Lao Ichiro seemed unsure.

Something definitely isn't right here, Bedria thought. "And your father...did he also eat something that didn't agree with him?"

"I believe so, yes," Lao Ichiro responded. "Oysters were served last night. It is possible some had turned."

"Lucky that you were able to escape their effects," Bedria added.

"Yes, well, I have an allergy to mollusks and don't normally partake," Lao Ichiro commented, embarrassed by the personal nature of his response.

"Lucky indeed, then." Bedria smiled.

"Shall we adjourn to the palace?" Lao Ichiro asked. "Our kitchen staff are preparing a spectacular meal. I'm sure you must be famished after your long journey."

"Yes, of course," Bedria answered, and Lao Ichiro started to turn. "As soon as Kofi joins us. He is overseeing the final protocols of arrival."

Lao Ichiro's reaction was subtle, but Bedria saw his annoyance. "Surely the ship's captain would do that."

"Yes, but Kofi must learn," Bedria responded. "And this seemed like the perfect opportunity."

"I see." Lao Ichiro said with a tense smile.

"While we wait, perhaps you could settle an argument between Eshe and me?"

"It would be my pleasure to try," Lao Ichiro nodded.

"The white crane on the standards of Yapon, what does it symbolize?"

"Honor and strength." Lao Ichiro seemed offended at the question.

"Of course, everyone knows that, but what else?" Bedria asked.

"Loyalty," Lao Ichiro added.

"Ah—loyalty, of course." Eshe made a show of slapping his forehead at his ignorance. "I thought it was integrity."

"I think you must be thinking of the symbolism in the Aengal standard," Lao Ichiro said, clearly offended further by the comparison.

"Of course, I apologize," Eshe said. "I wonder, do you know the significance of the golden eagle?"

Lao Ichiro didn't actually roll his eyes, but the tone was certainly in his voice. "Honesty, courage, and strength," he replied.

"And the field of red?" Bedria asked with a thin smile that didn't reach her eyes. "What does that symbolize?"

Lao Ichiro was caught off guard by the question and then cleared his throat when the significance of the conversation finally came to him. He chose to ignore the implication in his answer, though. "The traditional meaning is passion, strength, and love."

"Yes, and the historical meaning?" Bedria narrowed her eyes.

Lao Ichiro seemed to pale. "It signifies the fields that will be bathed in blood by those who betray Magora."

"Exactly," Bedria smiled. "Very good." Then her tone became dangerous. "Now, where is my daughter?"

Lao Ichiro's face lost all expression, and then he raised his hand. The soldiers along the quay began to move in their direction. Eshe similarly raised his hand. There was a twang from the ship, and a ballista bolt buried itself in the stone-covered ground a few paces in front of the troop captain, who immediately stopped.

Bedria clasped her hands in front of her, and her face became hard. "Think very hard before you act, *cousin*."

Lao Ichiro scanned the harbor. The navy was not large, but he seemed to take note of the Aengal ships in particular. Finally, he sighed. "We do not wish to become entangled in this dispute."

"Does your uncle feel the same?" Bedria meant the baron who resided in Kasha Kyoshu and Lao Ichiro understood that.

Ito was unlike the other provinces. While Kasha Kyoshu was the seat of civil power and the baron served as ambassador to the other provinces, the military power, and indeed the true power of Yapon, had always been controlled by Ito, and more specifically, the Lao family.

Lao Ichiro shrugged. "We haven't discussed the issue." Which implied that he also didn't really care.

"And your father?" Bedria asked.

"Truly is ill and has taken to bed," Lao Ichiro explained.

So, Ichiro is regent until his father dies and he becomes head of the house, Bedria thought. "I see."

"Lao Jun Qiu represents an opportunity for your family that you have not had since the fourth dynasty," Eshe added.

Lao Ichiro blushed at the accusation but didn't protest.

"I see," Bedria said. "So, you are with Hurasham?"

"Absolutely not!" The thought seemed to offend Lao Ichiro more than being compared to Aengal. "Your mother and the other barons rallied to our cause when Emperor Chen assassinated my uncle Lao Cang Yu, who was one of the most revered fathers of our nation. We respect and appreciate you for that. But we cannot take up arms against Lao Cang Yu's son."

His words spoke volumes, most importantly, of how Yapon saw themselves as a sovereign nation, apart from the rest of Chungoku. This was a well-known, if rarely spoken, attitude that most dignitaries were aware of. But for Lao Ichiro to actually voice the words was significant.

"Honor dictates that we shall not betray your prior support by allying against you," Lao Ichiro continued. "But neither can we join you in this fight. Ito must remain neutral."

Bedria considered his position. "This is disappointing, of course, but I do understand. You *will* return my daughter and her companions to me, and we will be on our way."

Lao Ichiro paused again.

"Or you will have chosen a side and must bear the consequences of that decision," Bedria added.

"Of course," Lao Ichiro said finally. "I will make arrangements at once."

"You have an hour," Bedria said sternly.

Lao Ichiro bowed again and signaled for his entourage and accompaniment of soldiers to follow him back to the palace.

Bedria and Eshe returned to the ship.

"Well, that was an inauspicious turn of events," Bedria spoke softly to Eshe as they walked.

"Kasha Kyoshu may still stand with us." Eshe tried to console her with his eternal optimism.

"A few thousand militia and city guards at best," Bedria said darkly. "Merkar, Aengal, Orlyk, and what we have left against the growing legions of Emperor Lao. I do not like our odds."

"What of Rusticar and Chugoku?" Eshe asked hopefully.

"Come on now," Bedria said. "Even your optimism can't go that far. You know how Rusticar will ally, and Chugoku is a den of corruption and narcissism under Elias Harmenos's rule."

"So, what, then? We surrender?" Eshe asked.

"Of course not. We continue to fight. For the dignity of the people and freedom from imperial rule."

Chapter Twenty-Six

Sgarra'lamma

The energy of the city was different. Micah and his men had arrived late the previous night so had not noticed. Bone-weary from weeks of travel, the Sgarra'lamma had marched to their assigned barracks near the Wadi Gate and collapsed in their bunks. A summons from the emperor had woken Micah earlier than he would have preferred, but such was the life of a soldier.

He noticed the difference almost immediately on his trek from the barracks to the palace. The city was bustling. Kasha Marka was always busy, even when it was under siege, but this was different. There was a sort of nervous energy that seemed to permeate everyone. People hurried by, barely looking at each other as they passed. The traditional friendly morning greetings were replaced with quick sidelong glances and maybe the hint of a smile or the nod of a head.

When he arrived at the palace, it was worse. Pages and military aides were practically running, or as close to it as they could without looking undignified. Micah had been looking forward to a relaxing game of *wei-chi* with Emperor Lao. However, when he arrived, he was directed to the Great Hall rather than the emperor's apartments. It looked more like this was going to be an official summons.

He arrived at the emperor's antechamber and stood at attention. A haggard-looking Captain Vasiliev rushed out and waved a half-hearted greeting to Micah as he passed.

"Captain Kabir," the emperor's aide addressed him. He held the door open without waiting for a response. "Emperor Lao will see you now."

Micah marched into the hall to stand before the emperor's throne and bowed deeply, as was tradition, and held the position while he waited for acknowledgment. The door closed and Micah was left alone with Emperor Lao.

"Ah, Captain Kabir, so good to see you," Emperor Lao spoke, and Micah rose. "I regret that we cannot share a game of stones this morning, but it is a busy morning."

"Yes, majesty," Micah responded.

"You arrived last night, yes?" the emperor asked.

"Yes, majesty."

"I've read your reports. It would seem that you and your men have performed admirably."

"Thank you, majesty." Micah felt pride at the compliment. The Sgarra'lamma had spent the past eight months wandering the wilderness of southern Magora, rooting out the remnants of Bedria

Kess's rebel forces. Even after General Hamazi had marched north with the bulk of the army, Micah and his men had remained to enforce the *emperor's peace*. It was harrowing work, but he was proud of his men and his officers. It was reaffirming to hear that Emperor Lao shared his view.

"How much do you know of the rest of the war effort?"

"Only the occasional rumor, majesty. We have been somewhat isolated from events," Micah responded.

"Yes, of course. Where to start?" The emperor pondered the question for a moment. "Shalanum is settling in with good order. There is the nasty business of supply raids in the north, but Commander General Sharav is dealing with that. General Hamazi has crossed the Beiji River and is reassembling the army on the Dalaman Plains—"

"Dalaman Plains?" Micah interrupted before he could stop himself. "Apologies, majesty," he said quickly.

"Quite alright. Please, if you have questions, don't hesitate to ask. Your counsel is valuable." The emperor waved a hand to dismiss the apology.

"I'm just curious about why they would cross the White River to the Dalaman Plains rather than take the road to Kasha Libbu. My understanding was that General Hamazi was to invade Orlyk. It seems like such an indirect route."

"Excellent question, and you are quite right. Normally, that would be the preferred route, but events in Chugoku Province prevent that at present."

"What events?" Micah asked.

"We'll get to that…it is related to why I've called you here today. But I want to make sure you understand the whole picture before I explain your next mission."

"Yes, of course, majesty." Micah nodded.

"General Hamazi hopes to cross the Dalaman Plains before winter. They will cross the Temny River at Zymova and then camp there in the relative safety between the Temny and the Pusteli until spring."

The emperor was using the names of places that Micah had never heard of before, but he tried to follow and resolved to find a map once their conversation was over. He knew the White River, or rather the Beiji River as the emperor had called it, but the rest of northern Magora and all of Orlyk was a mystery to him. His only exposure to the history of Orlyk was his mother's stories about the famous Sisuma horse soldiers, and her tales tended to be light on geography.

"Any questions so far?" Emperor Lao asked.

"No, majesty." *So many questions, but I won't embarrass myself now by asking.* "Please continue."

"Very well. Admiral Kasumi will work with our allies in Hurasham to cordon off the Sea of Whispers. That should effectively isolate Merkar and limit their ability to cause trouble."

"Very wise, majesty. The Merkari riverboats caused a lot of

trouble for us in our campaign. Cutting them off from the east will limit their resources and access to aid. It would effectively make them a *dame*." Micah used the wei-chi term for a neutral territory with little benefit to either player.

"Not entirely," Emperor Lao corrected. "They could still be dangerous in their own right, but it will limit their effectiveness."

"What of the eastern provinces?" Micah asked.

"There is still much undetermined there," the emperor said. "Largely due to the concerns arising in Chogoku Province. And that is where you come in."

"How so?"

"There is a group that is building power in Kasha Esharra."

"The old capital?" Micah asked.

"Yes. They call themselves the Cult of Kisha. They are led by a heretic who claims to be the new empress appointed by the gods," Emperor Lao explained.

"Empress? It is a woman?"

"Yes. I assume it is related to why they claim kinship to Kisha rather than Antu, but our intelligence is limited. It is most likely an overly ambitious warlord from the Ziyandi desert that is trying to take advantage of the current turmoil to carve out a position of power. There is undoubtedly another power behind the pretender, and they are using her as a symbol of Kisha's allegiance. However, they are enough of a concern that we didn't want to risk sending General Hamazi that route to Kasha Ekur."

"What would you have me do?" Micah asked.

"I want you to take the Sgarra'lamma east to Kasha Libbu and Kasha Esharra. Find out where Baron Harmenos's loyalties lie. If you think he could be trouble, then eliminate him. We don't need two forces working against us in Chugoku. Then infiltrate the Cult of Kisha. Send back whatever intelligence you can gather. I want weekly reports once you arrive."

"Kasha Esharra? That has got to be more than five hundred leagues away." Micah sounded concerned.

"Closer to seven hundred and fifty, actually," Emperor Lao corrected.

Micah looked at the ceiling while he seemed to do some calculations in his head. "That would take nearly a month for my messages to reach you, and that's only if I set up regular waypoints along the way so that riders can relay the missives without stopping."

"I am hoping you can improve on that time," Emperor Lao said hopefully. "We will provide you with the fastest horses at our disposal, breeds that are more favorable to the desert climate. In either case, late intelligence is better than no intelligence. We will also send you with a couple dozen communications pigeons. Once you reach Kasha Esharra, set up a discreet outpost outside the city where you can house the pigeons. With the established roost, we should be able to communicate back and forth much more quickly."

"Of course, majesty," Micah replied.

"You will be operating mostly in isolation. I trust your judgment, and I know that you will make decisions for the betterment of the empire."

"Yes, majesty." Micah blushed at the compliment. He fully understood the gravity of what Emperor Lao was asking. He was being sent deep into unknown territory with little to no support and no advanced intelligence. He would be operating in the dark and would need to make decisions based on what he discovered. Add to that the fact that if he was going to set up waypoints for riders, he would need to station Sgarra'lamma forces across vast distances, at least until the carrier roost was built. His men would be isolated and spread thin. This was going to be his most difficult mission yet and possibly his most important, depending on what he found in Kasha Esharra. "I won't let you down, Your Highness."

"I know you won't, Captain Kabir," the emperor said with confidence. "Take a few days to let your men rest and resupply. I would like you to leave by the end of the week."

"Yes, Your Majesty."

"That is all, Captain Kabir."

Micah bowed and turned toward the door.

"And…Micah."

Micah turned back to the emperor, surprised by the familiar use of his name.

"May Antu guide your journey," Emperor Lao said.

"Thank you, majesty."

Chapter Twenty-Seven

Doubt

The three Ubads watched from the shadows, barely concealed scowls hidden beneath thick beards. The twenty women who were the object of their loathing moved in a carefully orchestrated dance. It would have been beautiful to watch had the women been clothed in veils instead of tight leather armor and wielding zills instead of long serpentine daggers.

"Fatemah, get lower to the ground when you squat-lunge. Ava would have taken your eye with that thrust, and you want to make sure you get under her guard when you lunge." Ullani called instructions as she circled between the sparring women.

The old men winced at the coarseness of the language. Women should not be speaking that way—it was vulgar.

"This is getting out of hand," Ubad Faran whispered. "It was one thing when Ahmed and Muhammad had her under control, but this goes beyond sacrilege."

"What are we to do?" Ubad Dafo whispered back.

"I have an idea," Ubad Cawlan growled under his breath.

Faran rolled his eyes. "And make a martyr of her? I think not."

"Then what?" Dafo asked. "The people fall farther and farther under her bewitchment. She doesn't even promise them riches or glory, she just demands *equal justice* and insists that the kujab and behani be treated the same as the ziyanib. It saddens me that the young are so willing to throw away centuries of tradition to follow this whore."

"It's not just the young," Faran corrected. "Women of all ages across the clans, and of course, many of the kujab and behani men see it as an opportunity to rise above their station."

"Even within the ziyanib, there are others," Cawlan said.

Dafo scoffed loudly. "The outcasts and the ibne. She won't even let us mutilate the ibne for their sexual depravity. They are coming out of the shadows under her protection and spreading their debauchery like a virus. Just last week, my nephew's son canceled his engagement to Alura Shebai and admitted to the entire family that he was *in love* with the kujab man who tended their horses." He spat on the ground.

Faran and Cawlan turned their faces from him so as not to call greater awareness to his shame.

"In my day, both men would have been staked in the desert with the mark of *Hanbi* carved into their chests and left for the jackals," Cawlan said.

The other two nodded their agreement.

"Uban Dafo!" Ullani's voice called across the courtyard.

"Yes, mistress." Dafo put on a countenance of enthusiastic servitude.

"The women of the Red Shadow are thirsty. Fetch them some water, please," Ullani ordered.

"Yes, of course, mistress," Dafo called. "Something must be done," he growled under his breath to his companions without breaking his smile.

"Repent! Or the wrath of Antu will be visited upon you."

Ullani turned at the sound of the bellow across the market square. "Who is that?" she asked Ava curiously.

"He showed up a few days ago ranting about the return of Antu. He calls himself The Prophet," Ava said dismissively. "He's a lunatic from the desert. Don't worry, mistress. Nobody listens to him."

Ullani shrugged and started to turn when The Prophet spoke again.

"Antu appeared to me in the form of a great bear accompanied by a host of shadow warriors. The visage was missing an eye, plucked out to keep him from seeing the depravity of this world."

Ullani paused and turned back. *A great bear missing an eye?*

"His attendant urged the Sky Father to spare me that I might spread their message of redemption."

Ullani tilted her head, listening. She felt her heartbeat quicken in anticipation.

"The shadow warrior was a giant, clothed in darkness, but as he knelt by my side, his features transformed into that of a man with a jagged scar across his left eye as a symbol of solidarity with his deity. He spoke to me and ordered me to save Antu's people before the Sky Father's wrath caused fire to rain from the sky."

"Darius!" Ullani exclaimed. "He's talking about Darius." Excitement willed her forward.

"Who?" Ava asked.

"Darius! He's a man I knew in Magora," Ullani explained somewhat dismissively, focused more on pushing her way through the crowd than Ava's question. "He always talked about his pet bear. It has to be him!"

"Pet *bear*, mistress?" Ava sounded shocked, but hearing it voiced aloud, Ullani couldn't blame her.

"Yes, it's a long story." Ullani's pace quickened as she spoke, and her attendants struggled to keep up. "But he named the bear Antu in honor of the god. Well, sort of…he actually thinks that the bear is Antu come to this plane to guide him."

"So, The Prophet isn't just a raving lunatic?" Ava asked.

"I didn't say that," Ullani laughed. "He must have come across Darius and Antu somewhere. I have to find out where."

Ava tried to grab her arm. "Mistress, no."

Ullani shrugged off the hand and continued forward.

Ava hurried to catch up. "Mistress, if you acknowledge him, people might start to pay more attention to his ranting. Especially if you confirm some part of his story might be true," she whispered urgently.

Ullani broke through the crowd to the center of the square. The Prophet was standing on the edge of a decrepit fountain, calling out over the crowd. The people had mostly been giving him a wide berth, which left the area immediately surrounding the fountain clear. As Ullani approached, some of the people who had been ignoring The Prophet before stopped to watch the confrontation. They must have thought Ullani was going to strike him down or something.

"Tell me your story," she said to him.

He looked down at her in surprise. Now that he had an audience, he seemed suddenly dumbstruck.

"Go on. Where did you encounter this man and bear?"

"Not a man. A spirit warrior," The Prophet claimed.

"Eh, let's call it a man for now. Tell me your story…where did you meet them?"

The Prophet continued eagerly now, encouraged that someone was listening. "I was sent as an envoy from the palace at Kasha Nisir to meet with the new emperor and to bring gifts of support from the princes of Hurasham. Emperor Lao, honored by my presence, sent me to spread word of the alliance to the lords of

Kasha Amur and to act as his liaison between the two provinces."

"Okay," Ullani said uncertainly. The bedraggled man before her definitely didn't look like any sort of *honored* diplomat.

"I was traveling with an armed escort when the Hand of the Shadow beset upon us," The Prophet continued.

"Hand of the Shadow?" Ullani asked curiously.

"Yes, Antu's army of shadow warriors created by the hand of The God himself to visit his retribution upon this world when our sins become too great."

"Ah, of course." Ullani suppressed a smile and looked at Ava, but she saw concern on Ava's face. She glanced around the crowd and noticed that others were paying attention now too.

"Then what happened?" Ullani asked.

"The Hand of the Shadow slaughtered all of the emperor's soldiers and destroyed the wagons in our convoy. I was fighting to defend myself and my wards when the avatar of Antu appeared before me. The beast stood on its hind legs. The monster stood at least forty hands. I am not ashamed to say that I fell to the ground at his feet in terror. He let out an awful roar that deafened me and smote my companions.

"I was sure the beast was going to devour me whole, but the shadow of a titan materialized beside him and placed a hand on Antu's shoulder. The specter urged the divinity to spare me, and Antu agreed, moving off to visit his vengeance upon others. The specter knelt by my side and whispered in my ear. He told me to travel in haste to every corner of the kingdom to announce Antu's return and to urge those devoted to Antu to abandon their sinful ways and return to the true path of discipleship."

"Huh, what is Darius doing in Shalanum?" Ullani said half to herself.

"You know the phantom by name?" The Prophet asked.

"It is no phantom, you fool. It's a man. An impressive man, to be sure, but still a man," Ullani explained. "He has traveled with the bear since he was young. An odd companion, no doubt, but it is just a bear."

"Blaspheme!" The Prophet shouted.

Ullani was taken aback. She had grown accustomed to deference, and the verbal assault surprised her. "Excuse me?"

"Sinners! Repent!" The Prophet pointed at her.

Ava stepped in front of Ullani. "Watch your tongue, heretic, before I cut it out. You are in the presence of Empress Ullani, duly appointed monarch raised by the gods themselves to lead us to salvation."

Ullani was surprised by Ava's outburst. She hadn't thought that the woman bought in so thoroughly to the masquerade, but apparently, she did, or at least pretended to in front of the masses.

The Prophet's eyes went wide. "You are Kisha's whore!"

"Alright, that's enough." Ullani was angry now. Pretender or not, nobody called her a whore. She nearly killed him on the spot, but she resisted because she wanted to find out what else the man knew about Darius. "Take him to the dungeon in the palace," she ordered Ava.

Half a dozen members of the Red Shadow stepped forward and physically removed the man from his perch on the fountain. He continued shouting obscenities at her as they dragged him away toward the palace. His ranting grew louder until one of the women pulled a kerchief from a pouch at her side and stuffed it into his mouth.

The gathering dispersed slowly. Ullani was aware of several sidelong glances and hushed muttering from the crowd.

"Why didn't you kill him?" Ava whispered.

"I'm not done with him yet," Ullani growled. She felt her fingernails digging into the palms of her clenched fists and willed herself to relax her hands. Her breathing came in loud puffs, and she could tell by the averted gazes around her that her face reflected her fury. *Kisha's whore. How dare he!*

"Ah, I see, you'll torture him first. He deserves it." Ava nodded with satisfaction.

"What? No," Ullani said, the surprise at Ava's response jolted her from her rage. She saw doubt creep into Ava's eyes and quickly thought up a more appropriate response. "I will interrogate him to find out more about Darius and how far his ravings have spread. We can't simply execute him without further understanding. We don't need a martyr on our hands."

The answer seemed to appease Ava and the other guards who

were listening in silence.

"She might be her own undoing," Cawlan said hopefully. The three Dafos had gathered again in a shaded alcove on palace grounds. They spoke in whispers in case anyone happened to pass by.

"Yes, had she executed him on the spot, the matter would be ended, and her power solidified," Dafo agreed.

"Instead, she gave credence to his claims by validating the existence of this boy and his bear," Faran added.

"We can use this," Cawlan said. "The spark of doubt must have been ignited in some of the witnesses at the fountain. We must fan the flames and see what we can make of it."

"Agreed," Faran said. "But quietly. At least until we are sure we have enough support to act."

Chapter Twenty-Eight

Scattered Rebellion

"You're back," Arnon said with surprise as Darius and Jenna stepped off the first of the longboats.

Darius nodded. "They've rerouted most of their supply caravans. The guards that we captured most recently said that most actual supplies are being driven over the pass at Patel's Reach or shipped and delivered through Basara."

"It seems like shipping would be more expensive, and the mountain route will only be a viable option for a few more weeks."

Darius shrugged. "I guess we were causing enough trouble to make the shipping route more cost-effective. The larger convoys that we've encountered during the past month have been traps with wagons full of soldiers rather than supplies. We've managed to avoid most of them, but we've had a couple of harried retreats."

"So, what happens now?" Arnon asked.

"I'm not sure," Darius answered. "That's the main reason we came back. We aren't doing much good out there anymore, and we decided it was time to come up with a new strategy."

"Do you want me to gather Cheung Po and the rest of the council?" Arnon asked.

"Yes, I have a few ideas, but I'd like to hear what you all have to say as well," Darius said.

"Sure, take some time to get cleaned up from your trip and grab something to eat. I'll finish overseeing the unloading of everything here. We can meet in, say, an hour?" Arnon said.

"Make it two," Darius confirmed. "I think I'm going to head into the valley and take a hot bath in the pool that Arthengal constructed near the hot springs."

"That sounds amazing. Mind if I join you?" Rose asked as she disembarked from the second raft.

Darius considered. He had a momentary flashback to the last time he had bathed with a woman.

His uncertainty must have shown on his face because Rose dismissed his concerns with a laugh and a wave of her hand. "Oh, please," she said. "Nobody wants in the middle of the little love triangle you've got going on."

"What?" Darius blurted.

"Talking about Anna and Ullani?" Jenna asked, having heard the tail end of the conversation as she approached.

"Yes," Rose said. "Darius is going into the valley to take a bath."

"Oh, count me in too," Jenna interrupted. "Wait, what does that have to do with Anna and Ullani?"

"When I asked if I could join, he got a weird look on his face like I was asking him for a midnight rendezvous," Rose explained.

"Oh, got it," Jenna said as if she understood completely.

Darius watched the exchange and finally decided to defend himself. "There is not a love triangle between me, Anna, and Ullani. Ullani is just a friend."

"Right," both women said together sarcastically.

"There's not!" Darius's voice came out as a squeak.

"Darius," Jenna said with exaggerated kindness. "We have just spent more than six months with you in the field. When it is time to relax around the fire at night, you have three topics of conversation."

"Arthengal the hero, Ullani the thief, and Anna the maiden," Rose finished the thought with a laugh.

"And let's be honest," Jenna said. "You talk way more about Ullani and Anna than you do Arthengal."

"And like I said," Rose added. "Nobody wants in the middle of that. So, can we join you? I can't remember the last time I had a proper bath, and the way you've described Arthengal's grotto, it sounds divine."

Darius lowered his head in defeat. "Yeah, sure."

"Excellent," the two women shouted. "Give us a minute, and we'll meet you at the edge of town."

Darius guided the two women down the narrow canyon that led to the valley. As they reached the end and broke out onto the viewpoint at the head of the trail, Jenna gasped.

"Oh, my goodness, this view is amazing!" She stopped to study the jagged peaks that surrounded the mountain valley.

"I have never seen water that color," Rose said, commenting on the blue-green of the volcanic lake.

Darius smiled, glad that he could share this with them. After months in the field, the beauty of the valley was a bit of a respite. He led them down the winding path. Both women exclaimed in delight again when they got their first view of the waterfall that cascaded into the valley and the crystal blue stream that fed the lake.

"Where does all the water go?" Jenna asked.

Darius shrugged. "That's something I've always wondered. There are still active vents under the water—you can see the steam rising above them." He pointed out several places on the lake. "So, I assume some of the water just evaporates. But the rest must escape through underwater fissures and feed streams on the other side of the mountain. The depth of the lake fluctuates with the winter rains and the spring thaw, but for the most part, it stays about the same."

They stopped briefly at the cabin where Darius retrieved brushes and cloths for washing along with towels and extra clothes. Then he led them along the shoreline trail to the far end of the lake.

"That is incredible," Rose said when she saw the natural bath that Arthengal had constructed near the edge of the lake. "How long did it take to build that?"

Darius studied the carefully fitted and polished stones that lined the edge and inside of the chest-deep pool, the smooth underwater benches, and the hand-crafted conduits that fed hot water from the springs in the lake to the bath. "I don't know. Arthengal had built it all long before I arrived. Years, I would guess."

Both women started peeling off their clothing in a rush. The sight of their nubile, athletic bodies made Darius blush and he turned away. He heard exclamations of pure delight as they stepped into the water and settled onto the submerged benches.

"Aren't you getting in?" Jenna asked.

Darius risked a glance at the pool and saw the water lapping around both women's shoulders.

"I, uh—" Darius sputtered.

"Are you embarrassed?" Rose asked.

Jenna rose, exposing her breasts, and pointed to a scar along her lower ribs. "Darius, you stitched this up for me. You've seen us at our worst and most vulnerable."

"You've watched us bleed and puke and relieve ourselves in the woods, and *this* embarrasses you?" Rose stood as well and waved her hands to indicate her youthful body. Then she scoffed. "Get over yourself. We've already told you we're not interested in you in that way, and even if we were, now when we're covered from head to toe in dirt and our hair is thick with weeks of mud and oil would not be the time. Now, quit being an idiot and get in the bath."

Sufficiently chastised, Darius slowly began to remove his clothing. Jenna and Rose were talking to each other and barely noticed when he slipped into the water. He forgot all about his discomfort as the relief of the water overtook him and he laid his head back with a satisfied sigh.

Darius stretched his feet toward the fire. The sun still hovered on the horizon, but the evenings in the mountains were much cooler than they had been on the plains. He felt like himself again. The bath had done him wonders and a fresh set of clothes that didn't stick to his skin made him feel like a new man.

Cheung Po approached and handed Darius a pint of ale before settling into one of the chairs on the opposite side of the fire. "You had a productive summer."

"Yeah." Darius took a long pull from the drink. "Not as much in the fall. Once Basara fell and they started rerouting shipments, our spoils quickly faded."

"Not unexpected," Cheung Po said and took a drink from his own mug.

Rhys Allister and Karl Olson joined them at the fire.

"Volunteers are up, and training is improving," Karl commented.

"Except with the swords," William Bratt said as he joined them. "I do the best I can, but without your expertise to guide them, the recruits take longer to come along."

Jenna and Rose joined them, looking as refreshed as Darius felt. Jenna's blond hair shined, and Rose's auburn curls bounced rather than matting to her head. He subconsciously drew his fingers through his own blond locks. Their hair had taken on the same dingy brown as his did after months on the road. He had forgotten what their natural color even looked like.

Arnon finally joined them to complete their circle, and Cheung Po raised the same question that Arnon had asked earlier. "So, what do we do now?"

"I don't want to give up just because the raids stopped being productive," Darius said. "I think we were having a real impact, and I'd like to build on that momentum."

"I agree," Cheung Po said. "What did you have in mind?"

"Our reach is limited here. The imperials have very few outposts in the north, and with the supply lines drying up, I'm not sure what else we can do. We don't have the strength for a direct assault on Eridu or Isan, and the southern cities are too far."

"So, you want to leave here?" William asked with skepticism in his voice. "But we have such a good thing going."

"I'm not sure," Darius admitted. "That's why I wanted to speak to all of you—to see what ideas we could come up with as a group."

"There isn't another safe haven for a group this large anywhere south of Eridu," Arnon said. "The camp is more than ten thousand souls. It would be impossible for us to all move without attracting attention."

"What?" Darius said with surprise. The camp definitely seemed larger than when they had left in the spring, but he would have never guessed that many. He studied the crowds now with more interest.

He saw that men and women stood guard atop the city walls every few paces. From their elevated position near the keep, he could also see larger groups than before in the sparring and target grounds. Many of the ramshackle buildings near the center of town had also been replaced with proper two-story buildings that could easily house a dozen people each. The edges of the camp too had expanded up the hill and along the ridge to the east.

"Men and women have been arriving all summer and fall to join the cause. Those who come to fight bring their families with them. Nearly two-thirds of the camp are children, parents beyond their fighting years, or spouses that came to show their support but haven't made the leap to take up arms themselves."

"That's still a sizeable force," Darius said. "More than I would have thought."

"Yes, but most are undertrained," Rhys said. "And we will lack equipment for all of them."

"What if we deployed multiple raiding groups across Shalanum?" Jenna asked. "Rose and I both have the experience now to lead our own units."

"But where?" Darius asked. "And how would we concentrate our gains to support the rest? The river made it easy to transport goods from the Taspin Plains to here."

"Maybe we worry less about the units shipping supplies back to a central location and worry more about making them independent and self-sufficient," Rose suggested, building on Jenna's plan.

"With winter coming, we'll need the influx of supplies here to provide for the civilians," William said. "We can't just cut Anbar Ur entirely out of the plan. We've made a home for ourselves here, and the people feel safe."

"Okay, so say we went with Jenna's plan," Darius said. "Where would be the best places to have the greatest impact?"

"The woodlands south of Eridu," Karl offered. "There are plenty of places to hide that are within striking distance of the roads east to Isan and south to Kasha Amur. And if supply lines are limited, the forest is flush with game."

Darius nodded. "Okay, what else?"

"Pirates off the Morbush Peninsula to harass shipping lanes," Cheung Po said. "Arnon and I could take charge of that, and there are enough old sea dogs out in the city to man half a dozen ships."

"Where do we get the ships?" Darius asked.

Cheung Po grinned at Arnon, who smiled back. "Oh, just leave that to us. I'm sure we could come up with something."

"What if someone took a group farther east?" Arnon suggested. "Rumors are that General Hamazi is marching across the

Dalaman Plains to position themselves for an attack on Orlyk in the spring. There should be supply lines running northeast out of Kasha Marka that we can raid."

"West of Sidia would be another good place," Rhys suggested. "What they don't carry overland from Isan, they would surely ship via the waterways to Kasha Amur and ports to the south."

"Okay, okay," Darius said. "All solid ideas, but—"

"General Kabir!" A soldier sprinted into the courtyard.

"What did you call me?" Darius said with a laugh. He looked between the other council members, half expecting them to join in on his mirth. Instead, he was met with serious or expectant gazes.

Cheung Po shrugged. "What else would you have them call you?"

Darius stumbled over a response and the soldier looked confused. *A debate for another day,* Darius thought.

"What is it?" Arnon saved the awkward situation from further disaster.

"We captured an imperial spy outside the western gate."

That got everyone's attention. Darius was the first to his feet and the others quickly followed.

"Take me there," Darius ordered.

"Yes, sir." The guard bowed.

"Where did you find him?" Darius asked as they walked.

"He was hiding in the trees outside the walls," the soldier

answered.

"And how do you know he's an imperial?"

"He's dressed like an imperial scout, and he admitted as much after we captured him," the guard explained.

Fair. Darius shrugged and nodded his head.

The group followed the guard to the western wall. They found the soldier in question bound and gagged inside a small guard house near the gate.

Darius pulled down the gag. "What's your name?"

The imperial soldier spat at Darius's feet.

Darius raised an eyebrow. "I think he wants to meet our chief interrogator."

The others glanced among themselves but didn't respond.

"Bring him outside," Darius ordered.

The guards dragged the prisoner to his feet and out near the wall.

Darius put his hands to his mouth and shouted, "Antu!"

Understanding passed between the members of the council, and Cheung Po suppressed a smile.

"Your gods won't help you," the prisoner laughed and spat again.

A clamor arose from the gathering darkness in the northern part of the city. The prisoner looked confused as the sound of something large moving in their direction became more distinct.

Antu arrived, breathing hard, and glanced around the group,

looking for whatever threatened Darius.

All color drained from the imperial soldier's face.

"Antu," Darius said gently. "We have captured a spy, and he isn't being very forthcoming." Darius pointed to the soldier, and the bear swiveled his enormous head in that direction. "Would you mind seeing if you can convince him to talk?"

Antu lumbered toward the man, who started trying to scamper backward through the dirt. Antu leaned forward and sniffed the man, then turned back to Darius.

"Go on. Say hello," Darius instructed.

Antu swung his head back, opened his jaws, and let out a massive roar inches from the prisoner's face. Darius watched as the front of the man's pants became discolored and wet.

"Corporal Ennis," the man sputtered frantically. "My name is Corporal Ennis."

"And what are you doing here, Corporal Ennis?" Darius asked politely.

"General Sharav sent scouts out in all of the surrounding areas, looking for the base of operations for the Hand of the Shadow."

"The what?" Darius asked.

"The Hand of the Shadow. The rebels that have been raiding our supply lines," the prisoner said.

"I like that," Cheung Po said. "It has a certain ring to it."

"And you're the unlucky one who found our camp?" Darius

asked.

"No, there were six of us, the others have already headed back to Eridu. You'll never catch them. It's too late for you. You're doomed. As soon as General Sharav learns where you are, he'll send a legion here to wipe you out."

"Why did you stay?" Darius asked. He was sure he already knew the answer, but he wanted to hear the man say it.

"To gather more detailed intelligence."

Darius nodded as he heard the expected response. "You drew the short straw."

The spy's cheeks colored, and then he puffed his chest in an attempt at bravado. "No! I volunteered."

"Sure you did," Darius said sarcastically before turning back to the others. Darius ran his fingers through his hair, scratching the back of his head while he thought. "Well, that changes things a bit."

"I'd say," Cheung Po said.

"Send scouts out to try to intercept as many of the spies as we can," Darius said. "It may be pointless, but we have to try."

"What do we do with him?" Karl asked.

"An excellent question," Darius said. "Tie him up for now and keep him under guard. I'll think of something. We should continue our meeting with this new information in mind."

They reconvened around the campfire.

"What do we do?" William asked, perturbed. "Where can we go? We have to protect the families that have entrusted their safety to us."

"We could go north," Darius suggested. "Most of the imperial camps in the Northern Wastes would be abandoned but many would still be in good shape."

Nobody seemed excited about that idea.

"What about Koza?" Karl asked.

Darius was shocked at the mention of his hometown. "Koza? It was abandoned years ago. There are no defenses, and most of the buildings have probably fallen in on themselves from neglect."

"Not exactly," Karl said. "After it was abandoned, a group of brigands moved in."

Darius touched the scar on his eye, remembering the fateful encounter with bandits who said they had been staying in Koza.

"Why haven't I heard of that?" Darius asked.

"Because it's Koza," Karl said as if it was obvious. "How many even know it exists? In any case, they've been thriving the past few years and have built up quite a settlement. They even put up a palisade of sorts."

"How do you know this?" Darius asked.

Karl shrugged. "I've had a few dealings with them over the years. They're good at getting things that you can't find on the open market. Should you need them."

Darius held up a hand. "I don't want to know."

Karl shrugged.

"The fishing isn't great in the winter," Darius said. "But

probably enough to supplement the supplies we already have and any venison we can harvest from the surrounding forests."

"Plenty of sheltered coves up on that part of the coastline where we could hide ships," Cheung Po added.

"It would be a decent place to ship supplies once we start raiding again," Rhys said.

"We'd be back to tents for most of us. Even if the bandits have built up the town, it wouldn't be enough to house all of us here," Arnon said. "We'd be starting over in the spring with harvesting trees for housing and defenses."

"Yeah, but winter isn't as bad there as it is here," Darius said.

"How do you know that?" Rose asked.

"Oh, you don't know?" Cheung Po asked. "Koza is where Darius is originally from."

Darius was a bit surprised that even Cheung Po knew that, but he let the comment slide.

"We'd have to break camp and start moving right away. It will take us a week, at least, to mobilize everyone," William said.

"We should send groups to Imbros and Larissa until we can secure Koza," Karl said. "They can trade for supplies while they are there."

"We'll need our best trackers to go back over our passing and mask our travel. A group this large is going to leave a trail that even Rose could follow," Darius added.

"Hey!" Rose chirped.

"What do we do about the bandits?" William asked.

Most of the others smiled at the question.

"Oh, I think we'll be fine in that regard," Darius said. "Jenna, Rose, and I will leave in the morning with enough of our men to get the job done quickly and quietly."

"So, winter in Koza," Arnon said. "Sounds like a treat."

"What are you complaining about?" Cheung Po said. "You'll be too busy all winter helping me equip a navy."

Arnon winced. "Winter in the Sea of Tears. I think I'd rather take my chances in Koza."

The others laughed.

"So, we're agreed?" Darius asked. He glanced around the group, and everyone nodded.

The flurry of activity that followed was more organized than Darius would have anticipated. The residents of Anbar Ur seemed to take the news of their discovery in stride, almost as if they were expecting it. Karl and Rhys organized groups with several dozen families in each.

Darius got a few hours of sleep, and before he, Jenna, and Rose were ready to leave, caravans were already on their way out of the gates destined for Imbros, Larissa, and the handful of other small villages that stretched out across the wilderness of the Dechora Plains.

Cheung Po and Arnon bid farewell and headed south with a couple hundred former sailors. By the time Darius and his captains were ready to leave with their soldiers at mid-morning, the city was already half deserted.

"What do we do with the spy?" the gate guards asked as Darius prepared to exit the western gate.

Darius paused. He had actually forgotten about the captured soldier who had started this. "Once everyone has evacuated, lock him in one of the more secure buildings with a week's food and water. I'm sure Sharav will be here by then."

The guard gave Darius a conflicted look. Apparently, he had expected a more severe punishment.

"We're not monsters," Darius explained. "We don't execute our prisoners."

The guard nodded his understanding and then stepped out of the way to let Darius pass.

Chapter Twenty-Nine

Koza

Darius knelt behind the clump of bushes at the edge of the forest. The trees had been cleared for several hundred paces around the town of Koza to provide timber for new buildings and the wall that surrounded his childhood home. It had been seven years since he'd fled the small village to track down the raiders who captured his mother. Darius barely recognized the booming, fortified town that Koza had become. He couldn't see any of the stone and thatch huts where they used to live. If they still existed, they were obscured by the palisades. The only building he recognized was the tall community gathering hall. It had once been the center of town, but now it was set off at the southern end of the new settlement.

The gates were closed, and he could see a handful of guards patrolling the walls. The message was clear—outsiders were not welcome. Darius realized that the second advantage of clearing the forests around the town was that it gave the sentries plenty of warning if someone approached. If they were friends, there would be time to open the gates. If the visitors were unknown, there would be time to summon more guards to the wall.

Jenna gave a low whistle by his side. "This isn't going to be as easy as I thought."

"The distance is too great for my archers to take out the wall sentries quietly," Rose added.

The bulk of their forces were camped a couple of leagues northwest of the coastal hamlet. Darius, Jenna, Rose, and a small force of scouts had snuck through the forest to get a better look at their objective.

One of their scouts returned from his mission with unwelcome news: "The wall goes all the way to the cliff wall on the west and then angles back inside the town. Spiked chains and wire have been dropped from the edge of the wall down to the water to prevent anyone from scaling the cliffs around the end. There are archers posted at the corner, and a large iron cauldron is poised to dump something nasty on anyone who tries."

"I'm sure it will be the same on the eastern side," Darius said.

"We could lay a siege," one of the other scouts suggested.

"No." Darius dismissed the idea. "Without ships to guard the water's edge, those trapped inside would have an endless supply of food, and there are enough wells in the town that fresh water wouldn't be a concern. Besides, it would be more likely to draw the attention of the imperials."

"We don't even know how many we're dealing with," Jenna

said.

"Exactly," Darius agreed. "I have to get inside for a better look."

"But how?" Rose asked.

Darius winked. "That won't be a problem. There's a trail that goes down to the water just east of here. The terns use the cliffs there for nesting, and it was a great source of fresh eggs during the spring. I can swim from there to the path that leads up to the village."

"Won't the water be freezing?" Rose asked.

"Nah, it will be fine," Darius answered.

"I'm coming with you," Jenna blurted.

"I'm not sure that's a good idea," Darius said. "I know the cliff trails like the back of my hand. It won't be as easy for you."

"I'm coming," Jenna said firmly. "You'll need backup in case something goes wrong."

The group dropped further back into the woods and then cut east, following Darius's lead.

"I thought you said there was a trail?" Jenna said when they reached their destination.

Darius studied the rocky cliff that sloped steeply to the water's edge. Rock ferns and aster had grown over much of the trail, but he could still make it out. "It's there still, just a little overgrown. Watch your footing, and when we get lower, make sure to hug the rocks."

Darius removed all of his gear, stripping down to pants and a light shirt. He started down a dirt path barely wider than his foot. It sloped steeply toward an outcropping with several large bushes. He could still see the remnants of last season's nests hidden beneath. Terns circled overhead, ignoring them. Without nests to guard, the sea birds were more interested in scanning the water below for shoals of herring.

The path turned back at the ledge and angled downward at an even steeper slant. Darius turned to face the cliff wall and used his hands to steady himself as he shuffled down the trail. The angles and crevices felt small against the skin of his hands and feet. Muscle memory attempted to take over, but everything was in the wrong place. He moved slowly to avoid any missteps. He heard Jenna gasp as she made the turn. "You okay back there?"

"Yep, fine," she squeaked.

Darius continued inching along the path until it widened into a flat recess large enough for two people to sit side by side. He squatted there and waited for Jenna. She clung desperately to the roots and rocks as her bare feet scooted along the narrow track.

"We're almost halfway, but this next part is a bit tricky," Darius said as Jenna sank gratefully to the ground by his side.

Her eyes widened, but she didn't protest.

"You'll need to scoot right up to the edge on your belly and drape your legs over. There is another ledge below us, but you can't really see it from here. You should be able to reach it with your toes. A slab of granite sort of juts out there, and we can edge along it to the next part of the trail."

Jenna looked over the edge doubtfully. "And you've done this before?"

"Yeah, hundreds of times. It's not too bad, I promise," Darius reassured her.

He laid down and swung his legs over the edge, probing for the ledge with his feet. It was higher up than he remembered. Once his feet were planted and he stood, the bench where Jenna still sat hit him midthigh.

She gave him a quizzical look, and he shrugged. "I guess I'm taller now."

He scooted sideways to make room for her, and she followed suit.

"Keep the rock in the center of your foot for balance. Once we cross this, the rest of the trail is wider down to the ocean."

Darius's feet had grown too. His toes were wedged against the hard cliff wall as he navigated the sharp outcrop. Once he reached the end, the dirt path was more visible, and there was enough space to turn sideways. It switched back one more time before reaching the water's edge, but Jenna didn't have any trouble with the final turn.

"We'll have to swim from here," he said and lowered himself into the water.

Jenna gasped as she followed him. "I thought you said it wouldn't be cold. It's freezing."

"You'll be fine." Darius gave her an unconcerned look. "It's not that cold, and you'll warm up as you swim." With that, he pushed away from the cliff face and started swimming with long breaststrokes.

Jenna was a strong swimmer and had no problem keeping pace with him. He should have known. She had the strong back and shoulders of an expert javelin thrower and she spent her childhood in the river country of southern Shalanum. It was actually Darius who needed to rest first, and he angled back to the cliff, hanging on to a jutting rock to catch his breath while he bobbed in the gentle waves.

"Okay," he gasped. He was surprised by how quickly he had gotten winded. He and Micah used to swim for hours without getting tired. "Just around that next cliff, there is the path up to Koza."

"*Path?*" Jenna asked mockingly. "You mean like the last *path?*"

"No," Darius laughed. "It's a little better than that."

They rounded the rocks and Darius's jaw dropped. A large pier had been secured to the cliffs with a long, flexible gangway that could rise and fall with the tide. A couple of unused fishing boats were tied to one side of the dock. The broader side of the landing was taken up by a pair of longboats. What was once a narrow fisherman's trail had been expanded. The brigands that took over Koza had dug a road wide enough to accommodate the handcarts that sat on the dock next to the ships.

"You weren't kidding," Jenna said. "That's a much better

trail."

Darius stammered, "Uh, yeah," and continued to stare at the expanded port that bore no resemblance to the humble fisherman's wharf of his youth.

"Come on. The docks are empty. Let's go," Jenna urged him forward.

They swam the rest of the way and pulled themselves out of the water. Barrels and crates had been unloaded from the longboats and were waiting to be transported up to the town. Darius could tell from the smell that the barrels were mostly full of pickled herring and salt pork, but a fair number had tap holes and were probably ale or spirits. The crates were painted with labels identifying them as raw goods like linen, leather, iron, and grain.

Jenna ignored the cargo and headed toward the path. Darius quickly followed. They were near the top of the trail when they heard voices approaching from the direction of town.

"Come on," Darius whispered. "This way."

He edged off the path and scampered sideways along the cliff, his hands finding the familiar hand and footholds more easily now. Jenna followed with more difficulty, carefully watching where he placed his hands and feet. A few paces from the pathway, Darius slipped into a crack in the cliff face. He edged further back to make room for Jenna and then held a finger to his lips.

As the voices approached, he could hear them more clearly.

"Can't believe Hadley didn't get more ale. What are we

going to do with fifteen barrels of herring?"

"*Captain* Breeden did the best he could," growled another voice. "And you'll be praising the fish come late winter once all the venison and pork are gone."

"Bah," cursed the first man. "Who needs food when you have plenty of drink?"

A third man laughed uproariously at the comment.

"Lighten up, Braddock," the first voice said in a reconciliatory tone. "I'm only jesting. You know we appreciate everything that you and Captain Breeden do for the town."

The voices came level with Darius and Jenna and then began to fade in and out again as they wound their way down the road.

"Besides," a fourth man added. "Without your lot, who would bring in the girls from Lenwall?"

This brought a round of laughs from all.

"True, true. Ale may warm the body on cold winter nights but it does nothing for the bed."

"It doesn't seem fair, though," another man with a thick brogue complained. "We work all summer to steal that hard-earned coin, and then the girls sail away with it in the spring."

Another round of guffaws erupted as the men passed out of earshot.

"Come on." Darius pulled Jenna further back into the cleft.

It soon widened, and the ground they were walking on became firmer. Before long, they entered the maze of gullies and crevices that dominated the clifftop west of town. Darius's mind drifted back to the frantic chase through these trenches all those years ago when he and Micah had tried to escape the raiders who attacked the village. In the end, Darius was the only one to make it out by slipping down a rockslide into a hidden cave below.

They reached a point where Darius knew they would have a good view of the village and carefully raised their heads above the lip of the ravine. Surprise and sadness overtook Darius as he surveyed the scene. Most of the old buildings that had once been their homes were knocked down and built over with log cabins and a few larger stone buildings. The only remnant from old Koza was the gathering hall near the southern end of town. Marku's blacksmith's hut had been expanded into a full-fledged forge. What had once been open fields and croplands was now dominated by pubs, small shops, and a brothel or two. The streets were busy with men rushing to and fro, occasionally stopping to wave up at one of the women who called out to them from the balconies of the bordellos.

"There's got to be almost a thousand people here," Jenna whispered with concern in her voice. "This is no small bandit camp."

Darius nodded. The majority that he saw were civilians and went about unarmed. Still, they looked like a rough lot.

They studied the scene for several more minutes before Jenna abruptly pulled Darius down. "Okay, let's go. I know what we have to do."

"What?" Darius asked.

"I'll fill you in when we get back to the others."

Jenna's plan was simple, it turned out. She and Rose were to ride up to the gates with three wagons loaded full of ale and whisky. They would be accompanied by two dozen women from the ranks of Darius's forces dressed in the least appropriate attire they could find. They would con their way through the gates with the promises of drunken escapades that were sure to make any brigand or pirate's blood boil. Then, late at night, once the town had either taken to their beds or whatever comfortable patch of gutter they could find, Jenna and her team would subdue the guards on the wall and open the gates for Darius and the rest to enter.

Darius gaped at her once she finished explaining the plan. "I don't know..."

Several of the other men in the group looked uncomfortable and wouldn't meet Jenna's eyes.

"You have a better idea, I suppose?" Jenna asked.

"No, I just—" Darius started.

"Don't trust us to get the job done?" Rose finished his sentence.

"No, it's not that." Darius searched for a better way to explain.

"You think we need you men to keep us safe and protected?" Jenna cocked her head and narrowed her eyes. Several other women in the group crossed their arms over their chests.

"No, you're more than capable," Darius said.

"Oh, so you think this level of deception and guile is beyond us then?" Rose nodded as if understanding.

"No, it's just that—" Darius knew that everything she was saying was true. Jenna, Rose, and the others had proven themselves over and over again during the spring and summer raids. They were as capable as any one of the men in their group. He also knew, deep down, they were right. Something in the back of his mind spurred him to protect them from unnecessary risk. He also knew that if it was a group of men proposing a similar operation, he wouldn't question it. Finally, he sighed, pushing aside his inner struggle and deciding to trust the women who had fought beside him for months. "It's a good plan. How can we help?"

Chapter Thirty

New Home

Jenna guided the oxen that were pulling the wagon at a relaxed pace as they approached the gates. It had taken several days to find the provisions that they were looking for and arrange the transport.

"Whoa," she called and pulled the team to a stop at the signal from the pair of guards that manned the wall above the gate.

"State your business," one of the archers called down.

"Hey, boys!" Jenna called. "Just your friendly neighborhood maids of leisure hoping to brighten your day. It's gotten so boring and stuffy in Eridu lately that me and the girls thought we might take a little trip to the country."

The two guards looked at each other suspiciously and then surveyed the group of women loaded into the second and third wagons.

"I don't know," one of the guards said. "We're pretty set. We've got an agreement with some of the houses in Lenwall, and we wouldn't want to get into trouble."

"Oh, come on," Jenna pouted. "We brought our own libations." She gave the closest barrel behind her a friendly pat.

She could practically see the second guard's mouth start to water as he took in the ten barrels packed and stacked in the bed of the wagon. The first guard started to protest again but was cut off with a sharp elbow to the ribs from his companion.

"What are you doing, Sheffield?" the guard muttered under his breath. "Look at all that ale."

"Yeah, Sheffield, please," Jenna batted her eyes. "And it's not just ale." She lowered her voice confidentially. "Four of those barrels are good lowlands whiskey."

The second guard didn't even give Sheffield the chance to respond. He shouted down inside the wall. "Open the gates."

There was a clatter of activity on the other side of the gate, and then the big oak doors started to swing outward. Jenna snapped the reins, and the oxen moved forward again. She flashed a smile at the young man who was holding the gates open.

"Ma'am," he said with a tip of his hat.

"Oh, aren't you the cutest. I will definitely save a pint of Eridu's finest for you," Jenna said with a seductive smile.

The gate guard blushed and averted his eyes.

The activity had drawn the attention of others from the town. Jenna saw a tall, well-dressed man with a waxed mustache and a sword at his belt approaching with a determined look on his face.

"Sorry, ladies," he said. "You'll have to turn it around.

We've got agreements with Lenwall."

"Oh, come now, Captain," Jenna whined. "Surely there's enough fun to go around. And besides, we're practically paying our own way." She waved to the wagonload of barrels.

"It's not *Captain*. It's Isaiah Livingston, and I'm afraid the answer is no. Eridu had its chance a couple of years ago, but we weren't worth your time then. Now we have a nice relationship with Lenwall, and we don't want to jeopardize that."

"Yeah, but that was before," Jenna smiled. "Now, those damn imperials have taken all the fun out of the Eridu nightlife, if you know what I mean."

Isaiah spread his hands in apology.

Jenna's smile faded, then her face brightened with a new idea. "What if you let me talk to the woman in charge of the girls from Lenwall? We could make sure they get their fair share of any coin we make, and like I said, we brought plenty of drink to share."

He hesitated.

"Come on, Mr. Livingston, surely there are enough drachs to go around."

"Drachs! Surely you mean pennies," Isaiah answered, balking further.

Jenna leaned down to speak to him in a lowered voice, "I mean, yeah, pennies are fine for those Lenwall girls, but you can see who I've brought with me, right?" Besides herself and Rose, Jenna had selected twenty of the comeliest members of their fighting force to accompany her. They were competent fighters all, but Jenna had wanted to make sure the window dressing got them in the door. One of the women, with a particularly large bosom, leaned forward from the second wagon, giving Isaiah a wink and blowing him a kiss.

"Well, I guess if the Lenwall group are okay with it, then—"

Isaiah cut short as a staunch woman in a red dress approached the group from the direction of the brothel. Her expression was severe. "What's going on here, Isaiah? I thought we had a deal?" the woman addressed the leader of the brigands.

"We do," Isaiah assured her. "Miss…"

"Reddy," Jenna said sweetly with a wink.

"Miss Reddy, here." He coughed when he caught the euphemism. "Miss Reddy here has a proposition for you, Esther."

The madam's eyes narrowed, but Jenna beckoned her forward and leaned over farther so she could speak to the woman without any of the men hearing. "We've got ten barrels of ale and whiskey. I can guarantee the coin will flow freely for the next couple of days. Then when the drink is all gone, we'll be out of your hair and back to Eridu. Plus, we'll give you ten percent of anything we earn."

Esther considered the proposal. "Thirty percent," she countered.

Jenna knew better than to accept right away as it would be suspicious. Instead, she looked aghast. "Esther, you wound me." Jenna placed a hand to her heart. "Fifteen."

"Twenty-five," Esther said with a smile, seeming to enjoy the banter.

"Twenty," Jenna proposed.

"Done," Esther said and extended a hand.

"Brilliant!" Jenna exclaimed and took the madam's hand. "Well, it's got to be fourth bell somewhere. What say we tap one of these barrels or three and get the evening's festivities started early?"

Esther threw a glance at Isaiah, who shrugged in response.

"Welcome to Koza," Esther said with a smile.

The moon was a narrow crescent in the sky. Darius had watched with discomfort as Jenna played out her masquerade and was admitted into the city. That was hours ago. The afternoon slipped into evening and the revelry in the small town increased. Music, shouting, and laughing had drifted across the open space between the walls and the trees in waves that set Darius's nerves on edge as he worried about the women and how their mission was going.

Now it was full dark and the festivities in the town were winding down. The music had diminished to a single mandolin playing soulfully in the night. The occasional whoop or holler would break the otherwise quiet night.

Darius watched with anticipation until he saw dark shadows moving along the wall. The shapes of the guards leaning heavily on their spears began to disappear from their posts one by one. Soon, the wall was vacant, and Darius saw one of the gate doors edge open ever so slightly. He signaled to the rest of his troops, and they poured silently out of the cover of the forest. They moved in a crouched run across the field. Antu loped easily beside Darius.

When they were halfway across the expanse, Darius heard a cry of surprise from inside the gates followed by angry shouts. There was the clash of steel on steel, and his heart skipped a beat. He gave another signal, and the warriors doubled their effort. They were no longer concerned with stealth and ran at full speed toward the gate before it could be closed on them.

Darius burst through the door into flickering torchlight. The sudden brightness made it difficult for a moment to make sense of the scene in the courtyard. Two women were engaged in a fight with a burly man near the gatehouse. He swung a sword wildly at them, and they worked together to counter his attacks. Angry drunken brigands were emerging from the surrounding buildings drawn by the noise. As they saw Darius and his men, additional shouts went up. The collective groan from the town was palpable as men dragged themselves, bleary-eyed and inebriated, from their cots.

A pair of arrows came in quick succession to drop the man fighting near the gatehouse. Darius glanced up and saw Rose already lining up her next shot on one of the approaching bandits.

A war cry rose from Darius's throat as he unsheathed his blade and charged the oncoming men. His soldiers followed suit, and their cries were answered by shouts of surprise and anger from the other side. Somewhere in the darkness beyond, the pace of the mandolin picked up, and instead of playing emotional tunes, it began to play an energetic melody that reflected the scene in the courtyard.

Darius met his first two attackers head-on, quickly countering their awkward blows. He dropped the first with a quick strike to the temple with the pommel of his sword as he passed. The second he hit in the back of the head with the flat of his blade as he spun. More archers joined Rose on the wall, and the single twang of a bow became a symphony. Meanwhile, a lute joined the mandolin in a dueling ballad that reflected the fighting that had moved from the courtyard to the houses.

Horns sounded, and the brigands and pirates fell back to the southern end of town where they regrouped. Darius and his men followed, emerging onto the flat stretch between the houses and the cliffs.

The pirate captain and the leader of the brigands quickly organized their men into a defensive line. Darius held up a fist, and his troops slowed and regrouped around him. The archers repositioned from the walls to a line behind the swords, and Jenna's javelins took positions on the wings.

The music from the mandolin and now a pair of lutes switched to an ominous dirge that reflected the tension and anticipation on the plateau.

The townsfolk still outnumbered Darius's group on the whole, but most cowered behind the thin line of pirates and brigands that guarded them. Darius could tell the defenders were suffering the effects of a night of passionate revelry.

The music switched to a jaunty march, and without thinking, Darius and his line took a step forward. Antu pushed through the line to stand by Darius's side, and he saw fear in the eyes of the opposing leaders. At the music's prompting, the warriors of the Hand of the Shadow moved forward again, and the defensive line took a step back. Only a few paces separated the brigands from the edge of the cliffs.

The two bandit leaders looked at each other and assessed the situation quickly. They called commands to their men, and all set their weapons on the grass in front of them one after the other and then held their hands high above their heads.

The music turned sad and reflective, with a hint of disappointment, at the surrender. Darius finally found the musicians in the flickering light of a nearby fire and shot them a look that needed no interpretation. The music stopped.

The bandit leaders crossed the field to approach Darius. They stopped several paces away and one of them spoke. "I'm Isaiah Livingston, leader of the town, and this is Captain Breeden, commander of the ships docked in the bay below. We offer our surrender and appeal to your mercy."

Darius considered the two men. "It's trying times, Mr. Livingston, Captain Breeden. The imperials have seen to that."

Livingston spat at the mention of the empire. "We have no

love for them, young man."

Darius considered his next words carefully. "We are responsible for the safety of a large group of freedom fighters and an even larger group of refugees. I grew up here, in Koza." He waved a hand toward the town. "We would like to winter here out of the watchful eye of the empire."

The two men looked at each other uncertain where Darius was going with this.

"Cheung Po leads our naval forces," Darius mentioned casually.

Captain Breeden turned white at the mention of the legendary name, and Isaiah gulped.

"I lead our ground forces," Darius continued. "We can always use more good fighting men and women, but secrecy is of utmost importance. If you are willing to join us, we can let bygones be bygones, although a few things would need to change about the town."

"And if we don't?" Livingston asked.

"We are not murderers, Mr. Livingston, but neither can we have you running off to tell the imperials that a large armed group moved into Koza. We would build a stockade outside of town to house you and your men. You would be under guard but would be cared for through the winter months. After that, we would let you go."

"I, for one, would be honored to serve under Cheung Po. I

can only imagine what he has in store for imperial shipping lines once the winter storms have passed," Captain Breeden said with a laugh.

Livingston pursed his lips, considering the thought.

"There will be plenty of raids on imperial supply lines come spring and plenty of spoils to share with you and your men, Mr. Livingston," Darius said. "However, there could be no more attacks on the common folk of Shalanum, and your *lively* lifestyle would need to be tamed a little bit. We'll have families here, after all."

Livingston scratched his head. "We could probably come to an accord. I'm not sure I can convince all of my men to buy into the idea, though."

"The stockade will remain an option for anyone we can't trust, and you will be held responsible for the actions of your men, including any current residents of the town."

"And the women from Lenwall," Jenna added.

Livingston nodded his head and held out a hand to Darius. "Agreed. Very well played, young man."

Later, as they were gathering discarded weapons and separating the pirates and brigands into small groups that could be watched until Livingston and Breeden had the chance to relay the terms, Darius found Jenna. She was talking to Rose and organizing a defense of the walls.

"Uh, Jenna," Darius started.

"Yes," she answered.

"Earlier, when you all came in. I mean, during the celebration. None of you had to, you know. I mean, you didn't. Or rather, none of the brigands…"

Jenna took pity on him and met his gaze with a firm look. "Darius, we can take care of ourselves. Men are easy to manipulate, and I can promise you that nobody took part in anything untoward."

"Unless they wanted to," Rose shouted from behind.

"Well, yes, unless they wanted to, of course," Jenna said with a smile and a wink.

Darius blushed, and he couldn't tell if she was joking or not, so he decided to let the subject drop.

Winter – 36 A.E.

Chapter Thirty-One
Kasha Esharra

Micah entered the city of Kasha Esharra through the south gate. He and his men weren't even questioned. So many travelers were on a pilgrimage to the old capital to follow the rumors of the new empress that ten more barely stood out. His men, the Sgarra'lamma, the Avenging Angels, were spread out in groups of three or four across the nearly eight hundred leagues between here and Kasha Marka. No more than fifteen leagues separated each of the fifty-five stations that they had established along the route. Riders each had two mounts, which they would rotate every few leagues. They would switch horses at every station and switch riders at every other. Still, the round trip to relay messages took more than a month. They had started immediately after the first posting and sent a new message at each new stop. So, responses were coming back every other day. However, the information was often old and irrelevant.

"Not much to look at, is it?" Moab asked.

"You're not wrong," Micah answered. He had been expecting a grand city like Kasha Marka, but the reality was much different. Tents were packed tightly in city squares, burned-out buildings, and wherever else there was room. The people looked beyond poor and filthy—bedraggled children roved the streets and alleyways in packs like feral dogs. "Mind your purses if you want to hold on to your coin. First, let's find lodging, and then we'll need to reconnoiter the surrounding area and find a good place to set up the pigeon loft."

They led their horses carefully through the throngs toward the center of the city. They moved past pop-up vendors on nearly every street corner selling a pitiful array of wares. Suddenly, they crossed a street, and it was like stepping into another world. On one side was the crumbling ruins of a fallen empire, and on the other side was the majesty of a proper imperial capital.

"Now this is more like it," Moab smiled. "The streets are clean, the buildings are amazing, there are proper shops, and the people don't look like they haven't bathed in three weeks."

Micah looked at Moab in surprise. He wasn't known for his regular grooming habits. "You're one to talk."

"I'm a reformed man. As soon as we find a decent inn, I'm taking a bath." He scratched the back of his neck furiously. "I think those urchins might have given me fleas."

"I'm pretty sure the fleas were already there," Joral responded.

Micah itched his upper lip to hide a smile.

"How about that place?" Moab said, ignoring Joral's comment. "The Shining Rose, sounds nice."

"You wait here," Micah ordered. "I'll see if they have rooms."

Micah stepped into the ornately decorated building. He could tell by the size and the layout that it had probably been some sort of residence for nobility in the past, but the current resident had converted it into an opulent boarding house. The foyer was dominated by a grand staircase, which led to the upper two levels. To the right, the walls had been taken down to open up the space and create a pub of sorts. The tables were well-spaced for privacy, which seemed unnecessary since there were only a handful of patrons. A woman sat on a stool at the front of the room plucking a lyre. It was hard to tell if she was attractive. Her colorful robes flowed around her, obscuring her form, and she wore a scarf covering her head and face. The outfit drew Micah's attention to her soft brown eyes, long lashes, and a penetrating gaze.

"Welcome, welcome." The proprietor approached with his hands spread in greeting. He was dressed in a white kaftan robe buttoned up the front. His beard was neatly trimmed, and he wore a red and white head scarf held in place with a black headband.

"Good day," Micah greeted him. "Do you have any rooms?

My companions and I are looking for someplace to stay for an extended period."

"Of course, of course. Two drachs a night, and you will be treated to all of the luxuries that the Shining Rose has to offer— comfortable room, delectable food, the harmonies of my sister's lyre to soothe your soul, and a newly tiled public bath to soak away your troubles. It truly is an experience in luxury worthy of the empress."

Micah's eyes bulged. "Two drachs," he coughed. "Per room?"

"Yes, sir," the innkeeper responded with an unflinching smile.

"Do you have stables for our horses?" Micah asked.

"Of course, of course. Your beasts will be cared for by well-trained grooms. They will be brushed daily and fed only the finest grains from Orlyk."

"And that's included in the price?"

"Sadly no," the man frowned. "One drach per week."

"What if we paid for five rooms and boarding for twenty horses up front for a month?"

The owner tapped his fingers and his lips moved as he calculated the cost. "Seventy-two marks for a month," he finally responded with his perpetual grin.

Micah had already done the math by the time the innkeeper responded. Two drachs a night per room and one drach a week per horse was, in fact, seventy-two marks and not a penny less. *I guess they don't provide a discount for extended stays.* Micah was not very adept at bargaining. In lands held by the emperor, his soldiers were generally given a quarter with very little quarrel and only a few pennies in recompense for food and supplies. He had enough coin in the coffer secured to his saddle, but it would significantly reduce their resources during the stay.

He would have to request additional funds from the emperor to stay beyond the second month. He pinched the bridge of his nose. He was tired and hungry and had a week's worth of dust. He was sure it would take several baths to feel clean again, and he didn't feel like wandering the city to look for alternatives.

"Why don't we call it seventy marks for the month for an even number?" Micah countered.

A sad smile appeared on the owner's face as if he was disappointed at Micah's offer. For a moment, Micah wondered if he had countered too low, but when the owner nodded his acceptance, he realized that the opposite was probably true. The proprietor had probably been looking forward to a lively bargaining session, but Micah had never had the talent for haggling and found it easier to just pay what was asked.

"Can my men unload while I fetch my funds?" Micah asked.

"Of course," the man replied. "I will fetch the boys to care for your horses while we settle up in my office." He waved his hand toward a closed door to the left. "Then I will have someone show you and your men to their rooms."

Ullani dodged under the slashing knife. It was a curved blade and nearly two spans long. It was practically a sickle. The assailant gripped the oak handle firmly and moved in for another slash. His overlapping robes flowed with the movement, creating a distraction. Ullani fell backwards as the blade swept over her, barely missing her chest. She rolled out of the way and sprang to her feet as she let loose another throwing dagger. His wrist twitched and he knocked the blade out of the air as easily as he had the first.

"Ava!" Ullani shouted again. *Where is she?*

Ullani threw three daggers in quick succession as the man charged. He dodged the first and knocked the second out of the air, but the third caught him with a glancing blow just above his face cover. Blood welled from a deep cut below his right eye.

The assassin produced another blade, like the first, as he ran and attacked her with a double strike, cutting down to form an *X* with his arms and then quickly slashing again as he lunged. Ullani dropped to the floor. The man was off balance and his chest was exposed for a brief moment at the end of his attack. Ullani took advantage and thrust a foot upward, striking him just below the ribs. The air rushed out of him and he stumbled back, gasping for breath.

She spun, grabbing a vase off a nearby table and throwing it at him. He punched the vase and it shattered, but she used the distraction to run toward the door. She pulled the door open with a jerk and was confronted by a second man identical to the first. Ullani fell backwards. The man let out a choking gurgle as Ava's long serpentine dagger jutted out from his chest, piercing his heart from behind. He started to fall on her and Ullani rolled out of the way.

The first attacker had recovered and was closing quickly. A flurry of daggers flew through the air over Ava's shoulders, catching the killer by surprise. He staggered back with wide eyes, three smooth hilts protruding from his chest. He sank to his knees and his weapons fell from his hands as he toppled over—dead.

Ava and the other women who had been standing guard outside the room poured in from the hallway.

"Empress, are you okay?"

"We're so sorry, Empress."

"They were attacking us from all sides."

Ava held up one hand to silence the chatter and extended the other to help Ullani to her feet.

Ullani smoothed the front of her dress and took a couple of breaths to steady herself. Blood flowed from a couple of wounds on her arms. She examined them. Now that the adrenaline rush was passing, they were starting to throb. "I'm fine. Just a couple of scratches."

"I'll send for the healer to tend to them immediately," Ava said and gave a signal to one of the other women. "Let's sit you down and make sure we're not missing anything more serious."

Ullani let Ava lead her to a padded chair at the side of the room and sat with a grunt. Ava carefully checked her over, looking for additional wounds.

Ahmed burst into the room, followed closely by the doctor.

"He looks angry," Ullani whispered to Ava.

"Empress, this is unacceptable!" Ahmed exclaimed. "This is the third attempt on your life this month."

"What would you have me do, Ahmed?" Ullani asked calmly.

"Increase security around the palace, for one," Ahmed said as if it was the most obvious thing in the world. "Supplement your personal guard with men, for another. I know that you are more comfortable with your Red Shadow, but it is obvious that they aren't up to the task."

"We dispatched six attackers with barely an injury to ourselves," Ava countered. "You think you could have done better?"

"And yet one still slipped through and nearly killed the empress," Ahmed answered condescendingly.

"Fine, Ahmed. You can assign a handful of guards to the hallway outside my rooms, but Ava is in charge, and they are not allowed inside," Ullani relented.

Ahmed saw an opening to push his other favorite issue. "I also think you need to make a display to solidify the faith of your followers. If they could only see you bathed in the light of the gods, it could only strengthen their devotion."

Not this again, Ullani thought.

She winced as the doctor applied a salve to her cuts and wrapped them in bandages. "I've told you, Ahmed, I don't feel comfortable doing that."

"But, Empress," he pleaded. "The faithful are faltering. Support is wavering. There are stirrings in the camps, and your opposition is growing bolder." He gestured at the dead bodies as evidence.

"I don't want to anger Kisha by abusing her power. It is not the faithful who ask for signs and wonders." She used the same argument that she always did, but in truth, it felt like a greater deception that she was currently taking part in, and it made her feel guilty. She had not opened the reliquary since that day at the oasis. She was grateful at the time for the accompaniment and added safety for her trip across the desert, but with each step of this journey, she found herself sinking deeper and deeper into the lie. If she let herself don them again, she would be embracing the deceit to its fullest, and any hope of escaping this mess would be lost.

"I think Kisha would understand," Ava added.

Not you too! Ullani groaned and rubbed her temples with her thumbs.

"Empress, the agents of Antu will continue to come. You barely survived this attack. Next time, you may not be so lucky. What will become of your supporters if they succeed? Without your protection, they would be set upon by Antu's followers." Ahmed was not giving up.

"All the good you have done would be lost," Ava spoke softly.

"Argh!" Ullani screamed. "Fine! I'll do it, but only this once."

Ahmed let out a deep breath as if the world had just been lifted from his shoulders. "Thank you, Empress." His voice was calm again, all of his anger gone with the sudden great sense of relief. "I will make the arrangements."

Micah followed the crowd into the palace courtyard. Bodies pressed together uncomfortably. The wealthy and the poor were jammed together in an inescapable mob. He pulled Moab to the left, circling to the back of the square. His men followed, and they found relative reprieve in a small alcove between two buildings.

The noise was deafening as the throngs speculated about what Empress Ullani was going to say. It was her first public address.

An awed hush passed over the crowd as a retinue of guards filed onto the high balcony that overlooked the crowd. Six women took up positions on the right and six men on the left. A man in his early thirties, dressed in colorful kaftan robes, approached the edge and raised his hands to silence the crowd.

"That's Ahmed Al-Saad," Joral whispered. "Her first minister."

Micah nodded and watched.

"He's younger than I thought he'd be," Moab said.

"Oh, faithful," Ahmed started to speak. "Blessed followers of
Empress Ullani, the duly appointed representative of the gods and
the embodiment of the Goddess Kisha in our terrestrial realm. We
gather here today to hear the words of the goddess empress that our
faith may be renewed and our hearts stripped of doubt and despair.
We come to have our souls lifted as one to honor Kisha in all of her
glory and to pay homage to Empress Ullani, who is her
representative among us."

"Wow, he's really laying it on thick," Moab whispered.

A tall, dark-skinned woman joined Ahmed on the balcony.
She was dressed in flowing yellow robes decorated with patterns of
red and white that sparkled in the sun and wore a gem-encrusted
crown. The golden staff that she carried was topped with a prismatic
globe that flashed rainbows across the crowd as she walked.

"Close your mouth, Moab, before flies land in it," Joral said.

"She's beautiful," was all Moab said in response as he
continued to gape.

"Thank you all for coming," the woman spoke softly but with
a voice that carried across the crowd. "I am honored by your
presence and by the faith you have shown in me as we work together
to restore this once-great city. You have shown me true love and
grace by accepting me here as your leader and by bearing with me as
I try to follow the guidance of Kisha to bring peace and equality

among our people. I know the journey has been hard, and change has not been easy. I am convinced that we are on the right path, and I am here today to ask for a sign of confirmation from the Goddess Kisha that she approves of our efforts here."

Once spoken, the woman raised the staff into the air. As the globe caught the full light of the sun, there was a flash of light. The crowd gasped and averted their eyes from the sudden brightness. Micah turned his gaze back to the balcony as his eyes adjusted to the light and saw Empress Ullani bathed in light that seemed to dance and flow around her body. The light enveloped her, and as she turned to face the different sections of the crowd, it seemed to lift her off the balcony to float on a cloud of brilliance. Micah noticed that the elevation of her head did not change and surmised that the effect must be a trick of the light. But he could not deny the brilliance of the display.

First in ones and twos, and then in large groups, the people in the crowd began dropping to their knees and averting their gaze. A light humming rose from the crowd and bodies rocked in time with the rhythm.

Moab gave a low whistle. "Well, that's not something you see every day," he whispered. "Are you sure we're following the right guy?"

Micah gave him a sharp glance, and Moab raised his hands in defense. "Kidding, kidding."

"This definitely changes everything," Joral admitted.

"Agreed," Micah said. "We need to get word to Emperor Lao immediately."

Chapter Thirty-Two

Missing Hand

"What do you mean disappeared?" Emperor Lao let his composure slip and yelled at General Kalin.

The general took a step back, and his eyes danced about the room, involuntarily looking for an escape route.

"I'm sorry, Emperor Lao. General Sharav didn't provide much in the way of details, other than what I've already relayed. It seems that a couple of months ago, a group of scouts found the rebel camp in the ruins of Anbar Ur. By the time Commander General assembled a force large enough to eliminate them and marched north, the city had been abandoned. There was evidence of multiple large groups moving away in multiple directions, but they dispersed and became impossible to track once they reached main roads. General Sharav has canvased the area surrounding Anbar Ur as well and the countryside to the north and west. There is no sign of the Hand of the Shadow or the Shadow Crown."

Jun drummed his fingers on the arm of the chair. "And did they check the mountain valley where Nasu Rabi had been hiding?"

"Yes, Your Majesty. General Alamay's camp was searched as well, but there is little evidence that anyone has been there since Alamay's death," General Kalin answered.

"But there is some evidence?" Jun asked.

"There were a handful of towels hanging from a line outside the cabin that indicated someone may have stayed there recently. They also discovered the remnants of a large weapons cache, but the crates and barrels were all empty and no real way of telling when they were taken."

"The boy, Arthengal's apprentice. He was from Koza. Has anyone checked there?" Emperor Lao asked.

"Koza, majesty? No, not that I'm aware of, but the town was taken over by brigands shortly after we liberated its residents. They're an annoyance, but mostly a harmless lot. Small time— attacks against farmers and merchants but no real threat to the empire."

Jun sighed. "Send someone to investigate anyway, just in case. Could they have disappeared into the Northern Wastes? The boy would have been familiar with several of our established camps based on what we were able to deduce following the raid on the imperial compound and the rescue of his mother."

General Kalin held his hands out helplessly. "It's possible. We could send resources to investigate, but as you know, The Wastes are vast. We managed to hide the size of our armies and influence from the barons for decades."

Jun shook his head in frustration. "Send a couple of dozen scouts to investigate and look for signs of activity."

"Of course. Anything else, majesty?"

"No." Jun rubbed his forehead. "Keep me posted on any new developments."

"Of course, Your Majesty."

After General Kalin left, Emperor Lao paced the room. "I must understand this enemy better," he muttered to himself. "The Shadow Crown has been a thorn in my side for long enough."

Jun paused in his pacing as a thought struck him. Long ago, prior to Chen Bai Jian's rule, the Kesses had served in the office of imperial historian. *I wonder if anything was recorded about the Sillu Aga. I wonder if anything remains in the archives below the castle.*

He summoned an attendant to ask about the location, who, in turn, fetched an old archivist with a long white beard.

"Yes, majesty, there may be some remnants of older historical documents in the storerooms below the library," the old man spoke slowly, considering each word as he stroked his beard.

"Show me," Jun demanded.

A retinue of guards fell in behind him as he followed the ancient librarian down the hall into a room lined from floor to ceiling with bookshelves stacked with leather-bound tombs. They wound their way through the stacks until they came to an old oak door with a rusted iron ring for a handle. The old man pulled heavily on the ring, but the door didn't budge.

Lao Jun nodded for one of the guards to help, and together, the guard and the librarian managed to pull the door open a bit. The hinges groaned and popped as the door opened more until there was a gap wide enough to squeeze through.

"This way, majesty." The archivist retrieved a lantern from a nearby table and led the way down a set of stone stairs.

Below the library, they found a maze of hallways and storerooms. A second stairway led more deeply into the castle. Finally, the old man stopped at a room lined with triangular-shaped cubbies. It reminded Lao Jun of a wine cellar, but instead of bottles, each of the alcoves held worn, dusty leather cases. Inside each case were carefully rolled parchment scrolls. Lao Jun inspected a few. Despite best efforts to preserve them, many of the scrolls were dry and fragile. Descriptions of the documents inside were etched into the sides of the leather cases.

"Thank you." Lao Jun addressed the librarian. "That will be all."

Captain Sobol, commander of the legionnaires at Eridu, reined in his horse outside the gates of Koza. The company of men behind him drew to a halt.

"Good morning, Captain," a pleasant-looking woman with wavy red hair called down from the gates. "How can I help you?"

"We've heard reports of bandits operating out of this village, and we've been sent to investigate," Captain Sobol called up to the woman.

"Oh, we ran that lot off months ago. Nothing but trouble. You're welcome to look around if you'd like to satisfy your duty."

"Thank you, ma'am. We would appreciate that."

"Open the gates!" the woman called down, and the gates began to swing open.

Captain Sobol guided his horse onto the main thoroughfare and rode slowly through town. They drew curious looks from the townsfolk, but nothing seemed to be out of order. Blacksmiths working the forges, fishermen mending nets, women washing clothes and preparing evening meals, and children kicking an inflated pig's bladder around in a field on the south side of town.

The city was larger than he had expected. It didn't rival Eridu in its size, but it was still impressive. The small fishing village that he helped to liberate nearly five years ago had grown into a proper city. But there was no sign of bandits or pirates as the rumors had alleged. The residents were typical country families. The only people carrying any sort of weapons were the archers posted on the walls— a wise precaution this far from the protection of the empire.

Captain Sobol remembered a rat's warren of tunnels and ravines close to the cliffs from when they had raided the village years ago. "You three, go and investigate the canyons southeast of town."

"I think you mean southwest, Captain," a nearby villager

called out helpfully. "Nothing southeast but tern nests and blackberry briars."

"Uh—yes, southwest…that's what I meant. Thank you," Sobol responded, giving the man a cursory glance. He was one of the blacksmiths. A bulky lad in his twenties with blond hair and a scar on his left eye, probably caught a stray bit of metal that he hammered the wrong way.

"Anything to help. Long live the emperor," the villager said with a smile.

Captain Sobol guided his horse back toward the gate and dismounted. He climbed the narrow staircase that ran parallel to the wall and surveyed the surrounding landscape. Nothing moved except the occasional wild bird and a small cluster of deer at the forest's edge to the north. He spotted something outside the western wall, hidden from view from the road. "What's that?" he asked the woman who had first greeted them.

"Stockade," she replied. "We put it up after we ran the good-for-nothings off to discourage any more antisocial behavior. Mostly used now when the menfolk get too deep in their cups."

Captain Sobol grunted. He saw his men returning from their survey of the ravines. The lieutenant in front caught his eye and shook his head. "Alright, let's wrap it up."

His men reassembled near the gate. "Okay, back to Eridu. Just another false lead. There's nothing here, just another boring little town on the edge of nowhere."

"Just the way we like it, Captain," the woman called down from the wall as they passed under.

Captain Sobol turned his horse onto the road headed southeast and heard the woman call out, "Close the gates!"

Chapter Thirty-Three

War Council

"Rusticar is the most obvious threat," a stout man with a thick red beard spoke with a heavy accent. "We should prepare to land a first strike in Artyomovsk while the ground is still frozen, and we can establish a winter base there and block access to the river port."

"I disagree," countered Bedria. She had been having this same argument with Chief Dobhailein for the past week. "Hurasham has already mobilized. They are setting up active blockades and isolating us from the rest of the continent. We need to break their land defenses and secure their seat of power. If they have nowhere to resupply, their navy will be at a disadvantage."

There were a dozen clan chiefs from the province of Aengal present at the council, and they were split in their opinions between that of Dobhailein and her own. Chan Haitao, the baron of Yapon Province, had remained mostly silent, contenting himself with listening to both sides of the argument without inserting his opinion.

"But with Ito between us and them. An invasion into

Hurasham is too risky," Chief Dobhailein spoke again.

"I understand your concern, Chief Dobhailein, but Ito is neutral," Bedria said.

"For now, but how long will that last?" Dobhailein asked. "The last thing we need is to establish a battle line with Hurasham only to have those damned Laos hit us in the rear. You know there are reliable reports that General Hamazi has already traveled north. Come spring, Orlyk will be crushed between Hamazi and the Rusticarian forces unless we do something to help."

"Kasha Ekur is nearly impenetrable," Bedria argued. "They can hold out. If we can gain control of Kasha Nisir, then we can minimize the threat that Hurasham poses on the seas, and we have a chance to reinforce Merkar and take back Magora."

Chief Dobhailein shook his head sadly. "Bedria, I understand your desire and motives, but Magora is lost. You have to let it go and move forward. The only thing an attack on Kasha Nisir will accomplish is to stretch our forces thin and eliminate any support that we can lend to Kasha Ekur. Yes, the fortress is strong, but no one can hold out forever. By focusing our efforts on the north, we are able to keep our forces consolidated and we can strike with force in many directions. We remain nimbler. If we remove Rusticar as a threat, then it will be General Hamazi who is forced to support long supply lines with little to no support."

Bedria could feel herself losing ground in the argument, and she threw a lifeline toward Baron Chan. "Baron Chan, do you have any thoughts on the discussion?" Bedria asked.

Baron Chan was old, nearly eighty, and he was content to let the younger leaders bluster. However, now, when confronted with a direct question, he paused to consider. "I think that we will not prevail in this conflict without allies. Those are few and far between at the moment. Merkar is strong. Hurasham will not move against them until the imperials are ready to do so. Orlyk, on the other hand, is weak. They have had little strength since Emperor Chen destroyed the Sisuma. Kasha Ekur is a strong mountain fortress. As you say, nearly impregnable. But even a great city such as her cannot withstand the focused might of both the imperial army and Rusticar."

"That's what I've been saying," Dobhailein interrupted.

"I am agreeing with you, Chief Dobhailein," Baron Chan said patiently. "We must try to protect every ally that we have in this war. Our greatest chance at doing so is to eliminate the threat of Rusticar. If we can take Kasha Muscava and scatter the Rusticarian army, then Orlyk Province may have a chance. If not, then it will be us who is caught between the hammer and the anvil next."

Bedria groaned and leaned her forehead into the crook between her thumb and forefinger knowing that she had lost. With Baron Chan's endorsement, enough of the other clan leaders would shift their votes to support Dobhailein's plan. She inhaled deeply and let the breath out slowly. To argue further at this point would only create unnecessary division. They needed to be unified.

She raised her head slowly and stared deeply into Dobhailein's brilliant green eyes. "Fine. How can the Magoran forces help?"

A warm smile spread across Chief Dobhailein's face. He wasn't one to gloat in his victory. He respected Bedria and the force with which she had argued her point. He gave her a brief nod of appreciation and then turned to the map spread out on the table between them.

"Neither clans nor Aengal nor the limited forces of Kasha Kyoshu have a navy to speak of. Our long boats are meant for exploring the open seas."

"And the occasional raids on our neighbors across the North Sea to the east," one of the other clan chiefs added.

Chief Dobhailein grinned but didn't comment directly. "In either case, our ships are not built for war. Rusticar, on the other hand, has several vessels that rival those of Hurasham. Where Magora can help most is by making sure they are occupied and cannot play a significant role in the defense of Rusticar or any counter-offensives to Aengal or Kasha Kyoshu."

Bedria glanced at her brother, Eshe, who nodded. They didn't have many ships left, but it would be enough to keep the Rusticari busy.

"Meanwhile," Chief Dobhailein continued. "We can lead forces in a pronged attack against Kasha Muscava. The rivers will still be frozen, as will the plains, and travel will be easier before spring. We can position forces here to the west, on the road between Kasha Deira and Kasha Muscava, and here along the border to the southeast." He points to the map, indicating the three locations.

"Kasha Kyoshu can hold their forces in reserve at Kasha Deira where they can be deployed where the need is greatest." Chief Dobhailein glanced at Baron Chan, who nodded his support.

"And what of Kasha Esharra?" Bedria asked. "There are uncomfortable rumors of that cult, which is gaining power in Chugoku. What if they move against us?"

Chief Dobhailein shrugged. "It will be much easier to disengage Rusticar and return to defend Aengal or Kasha Kyoshu from there than it would be if we were spread out along the easter provinces between here and Kasha Nisir. I'm not saying my plan is without risk, but there is *less* to risk and *more* to gain, in my opinion."

Bedria studied the map. Now that she had made the decision to support his plan, she could see some obvious benefits. It made her heart ache to think of abandoning Magora entirely, but she also knew that there was nothing she could do without the combined support of Aengal and Kasha Kyoshu.

Finally, she nodded. "Magora has more forces remaining than we will need for a naval operation. We can deploy scouts along the borders of Chugoku to serve as an early warning if they do decide to move this way."

Chief Dobhailein smiled. "That's a good idea and much

appreciated."

Bedria glanced across the table at her brother. "Anything we're not considering?" she asked.

Eshe shook his head. "No, I think it's a good plan. I'll send word for our ship captains to make ready as soon as the winter storms have died down."

"Anyone else?" Chief Dobhailein glanced around the table. He received shrugs and shaking heads in response. "Excellent! Then tomorrow we return to our clans and begin organizing our forces. We will gather in Kasha Deira in one month's time."

Spring – 37 A.E.

Chapter Thirty-Four

Auspice

Kasha Esharra was a city transformed. The residents worked like a people possessed. Previously, Ahmed had struggled to find enough workers to rebuild one or two buildings at a time. Since Ullani's *presentation*, there were more volunteers than he could manage, and independent work crews had sprung up all over the city.

"It's amazing, Empress," Ahmed said ecstatically. He stood by Ullani's side on the high balcony, surveying the magnificence of the city.

"I suppose," Ullani said doubtfully. "The city is beautiful, but people are neglecting their own needs. Children are starving in the camps, and the winter drained our stores."

"There are no more camps, Empress," Ahmed said, confused. "Stone is coming in from the quarries faster than we can use it. The walls have been repaired and the buildings have been rebuilt. The people are safe and have roofs over their heads. They are no longer sleeping in the streets and plazas."

"But a dry home and a warm hearth are both worthless if the pot over the fire is empty," Ullani said, growing annoyed with Ahmed's optimism.

"There is plenty of food to be had in Chugoku, and the storehouses are full in Kasha Libbu," Ahmed said, dismissing her concerns.

"And yet we have no gold or resources to trade," Ullani said. "We have used everything we had over the winter to pay workers and buy building supplies."

"Trade?" Ahmed seemed legitimately confused by the prospect.

"What are you saying, Ahmed?" Ullani asked.

"I'm saying...look at what we have accomplished." He waved a hand at the city. "If this doesn't prove that we have the will of Kisha behind us, then what does? It is time to bring the rest of Chugoku into the fold."

It was Ullani's turn to look confused. "We have avoided any conflict with Kasha Libbu by *not* expanding our influence beyond the walls of Kasha Esharra and by paying him a lot of money."

"Exactly, and it's time to take that money back. Baron Harmenos should be bowing to you, not the other way around." Ahmed pounded a fist into his palm to enunciate his point.

"Ahmed, we don't have an army. Baron Harmenos commands trained soldiers. Not as many as the other provinces perhaps, but still…" Ullani tried to make him see reason.

"We don't need an army when we have Kisha on our side. Besides, there are plenty of fighters among the Ziyanib. Look at what we accomplished at the battle of the crossroads."

Ullani crossed her arms. "Do you mean the slaughter of innocent civilians or the *honorable* defeat of a single squad of Merkari soldiers?"

Ahmed looked wounded at the accusation and Ullani felt guilty. Even though the outcome was unfortunate, Ahmed and the rest had done what they did to protect her and save her from what they perceived as danger.

"Look, Ahmed. I appreciate what you are trying to do. But we need a better plan to feed our people than just leading hasty raids on the good people of Chugoku. That is more likely to make them rise against us than join us."

"An auspice campaign." Both Ahmed and Ullani jumped at the sound of Ubad Dafo's voice.

"Where did you come from?" Ullani asked in annoyance.

Ubad Dafo waved away the question. "The best way to win over support from greater Chugoku and spread the good works of Kisha is through mutual support and aid."

"What do you mean by that?" Ullani asked.

Ubad Dafo shrugged. "Organize the people by their

strengths. Deploy those who are good with physical labor to help the people of Chugoku with the spring planting. While doing so, they can spread word of Empress Ullani's benevolence and ask for small donations of food or coin to help spread Kisha's will and your good grace beyond the walls of Kasha Eshara. Send those who are good orators and savvy traders to negotiate with the nobles of Chugoku. Show them that there is a better way than to continue to follow the corrupt ways of Baron Harmenos. At the same time, you undermine his authority and win powerful allies. Finally, send those with skill in battle to police the lands. Root out bandits and corruption. Make the roads safe to travel and the towns free of the immorality that keeps the people of Chugoku from thriving."

Ullani narrowed her eyes. "That sounds an awful lot like a caste system."

"Not at all," Dafo said. "Merely allowing the people to recognize their full potential by letting them pursue their strengths."

"And what if we find that there are strong warriors among the Behani or strong laborers among the Ziyanib?" Ullani asked the old man suspiciously.

Ubad Dafo cringed but quickly recovered. "Then they join the efforts where they can contribute the most."

Ullani considered his plan. It made sense on the surface but something in her gut made her feel uneasy. Even though the old men had not openly defied her since she demoted them, they also had not been very forthcoming with their aid unless it benefited them.

"Ahmed, what do you think?"

The first chancellor shrugged. "I think his plan has merit. Shall I start asking for volunteers?"

"Sure, start with the laborers first. Spring planting has already begun. It is the perfect time to offer our assistance, and maybe the landowners can be convinced to trade food stores for labor that can be used to feed others."

"I will see to it immediately," Ahmed said.

"I would humbly like to offer my services to negotiate terms with the landowners," Ubad Dafo said respectfully.

"Very well, but make sure you document the agreements and bring them to me to approve. I don't want you taking advantage of this situation to generate profit for yourself."

Ubad Dafo gasped. "Empress, you wound me."

Ullani narrowed her eyes again and then said with an exasperated moan, "Fine, get started."

Chapter Thirty-Five

Harvest

Lao Jun looked at the bedraggled captain expectantly. He had just arrived from Shalanum—one of the few survivors from an attack against an imperial supply convoy. "Tell me what happened," Emperor Lao commanded.

The captain swallowed several times while he searched for the words. "We were escorting a caravan of merchants and imperial supply wagons from Isan, Your Majesty. We had camped for the night near the crossroads from Eridu. The night was uneventful, but as we were packing up the wagons and preparing to leave in the morning, dozens of riders emerged from the fog. There must have been a hundred of them.

"What did the riders look like?" Lao Jun asked.

The soldier scratched his head, considering the question. "Just like normal people, I guess. I mean…like men and women who you would see in any village in Shalanum. A few of them wore chain shirts and some had patched together leather armor, but mostly, they just looked like everyday citizens.

"But they were very organized," the captain added. "As organized as any military regiment we've faced. Their leader called out signals, and they quickly assembled into a flying wedge that shattered our defenses. After that, they broke into two columns that attacked and disabled the wagons on either end of the train."

"What did their leader look like?" Lao Jun asked.

"He was tall, blond, and had a scar on his left eye," the soldier described his attacker.

"And was there a bear?" Emperor Lao asked.

"By the gods, yes. I had almost forgotten about the bear. It was attacking the other end of the caravan from where I was, but it was monstrous."

"Then what happened?"

"It didn't take them long to bring us to heel," the captain continued. "They outnumbered us two to one and had the advantage of being mounted. They dispatched more than half my men in short order, and I surrendered," he said the last with a shamed look on his face.

Emperor Lao sighed. "Did they leave any sort of message?"

"Yes, majesty." The soldier nodded his head. "Once they disarmed and bound us, the leader of the group dropped this coin at my feet." He held out the coin, and one of the emperor's attendants retrieved it.

Lao Jun didn't need to look at the disc to know that it was painted black with a crown on one side and a winged lion on the other.

"When he handed me the coin," the soldier continued. "He said, 'Make sure you let your superiors know that the Hand of the Shadow is back, and we won't stop until Shalanum is free from imperial rule.'"

So, they are abandoning any pretense that the Hand of the Shadow and Sillu Aga are not one in the same, Lao Jun thought.

"Thank you, Captain. I appreciate you bringing this to me as soon as you arrived. Please get cleaned up and see to the welfare of your men," Lao Jun said.

"Majesty." The captain gave a quick bow and exited the room.

Lao Jun turned to Guo Wen after the officer had left. "I knew it was too much to hope that we had seen the last of them."

"It would seem so," Guo Wen responded. "They must have gone to ground for the winter and are now looking to resume the same harassment from last year."

Lao Jun shook his head with an exasperated sigh. "Very well, send a report to General Sharav and have him start organizing regular patrols in the Taspin Plains. We can't allow them to disrupt our supply lines with the same unchecked success that we saw last summer."

A few days later, General Kalin brought a similar report of Sillu Aga activity.

"Another convoy raid in the Taspin Plains?" Lao Jun asked.

"No, majesty. This time, they attacked a nobleman and his retinue on the road between Isan and Eridu. They blocked the road with a fallen tree, and then a group of archers emerged from the trees to attack the coach and its guards. The battle was short and very one-sided. They did leave the hallmark wooden disk of Sillu Aga, however, and a message for the nobleman and his wife to 'Make sure to tell all your friends that any imperial collaborators will be subject to the judgment of Sillu Aga and the Hand of the Shadow.'"

The news took Emperor Lao by surprise. The previous year, Sillu Aga's activities had been limited to mostly trade and military targets along the road to Kasha Marka. The fact that they were expanding their activities to other areas and targets was concerning.

"Was anyone harmed in the attack?" Emperor Lao asked.

"One of the nobleman's knights tried to resist, and he was wounded badly, but otherwise, no, majesty."

"Anything else?" Emperor Lao asked.

"Yes, majesty. There was also a report of bandit activity along the river channels near Sidia. We have not recovered anything that specifically points to Sillu Aga yet, but their tactics are similar, and the outcome is the same. They take the supplies and leave the merchants and guards who don't resist bound and disarmed, but otherwise, in good health."

Lao Jun bit the inside of his lip in an effort to control his anger. When he was sure of his composure, he spoke. "Send additional orders to General Sharav to increase military support for trade routes to southern Shalanum. We need those supplies to reach Basara. Also, send a message to Captain Sobol at Eridu and order him to offer military escorts to any of the aristocracy that should wish it. We don't want our allies in Shalanum to start thinking we can't keep the roads safe for them."

"What is this?" Emperor Lao demanded the following week as he surveyed the most recent report that General Kalin brought him.

"Pirates, majesty," General Kalin said simply. Then, seeing the anger in Lao Jun's eyes, he expanded on the explanation. "It seems that there are several dozen incidences over the past few weeks of pirates molesting the merchant traffic in the Sea of Tears."

"And we're just hearing about it now?" Lao Jun was losing his patience.

"It was just a few isolated reports at first, nothing too unusual for this time of year," General Kalin explained. "But then it started to happen more frequently, and most recently, one of the merchant captains reported that the pirate captain left him with a crown and lion coin and a message that the 'Pirate King' was in charge of the seas once again and that 'Shadow Crown' was making the calls."

"Why!" Emperor Lao shouted. He had been learning bits and pieces about Sillu Aga from the documents he retrieved from the archives below the city. There was nothing to indicate thus far that Sillu Aga was an overtly hostile organization. Ancient and covert for sure, but never in the history that he had uncovered had they directly challenged an emperor. "What do they have against me? I'm trying to help reunite the empire. I'm not the villain here!"

"Of course not, majesty." General Kalin seemed flustered and uncertain about how to respond to Lao Jun's outburst.

"Thank you, General," Emperor Lao said shortly. "That will be all."

Emperor Lao threw the report onto the table with half a dozen more just like it. "What is Sengiin doing over there?"

General Kalin winced. It was unlike the emperor to break protocol and call the Commander General by his given name, much less in the presence of lower-ranking officers. General Kalin glanced around and saw a room full of lowered eyes.

"Emperor Lao," General Kalin spoke quietly. "Might I speak with you privately?"

The emperor regained his composure and realized the audience present in the war room.

"Of course, General Kalin." The acid was still in his tone. "Clear the room and let's speak. This activity cannot be allowed to continue. It is costing us more than just the value of the stolen coin and cargo. It is creating doubt amongst the Shalanum nobility, and it is starting to have a real impact on our ability to keep General Hamazi adequately supplied."

The junior officers quickly filed from the room. A few gave General Kalin unenviable glances on their way out. Once the room was empty and the doors were closed, General Kalin spoke again. "Emperor Lao, how would you like to handle this situation?"

"I want them eliminated!" Emperor Lao raged. "Knocked from the board entirely."

"There are tactics we haven't used that could facilitate that, but we have avoided them because you previously indicated a desire not to use them."

Emperor Lao looked up and met the general's eyes. "You mean torture."

"We prefer the term 'interrogation,' Your Majesty." General Kalin shrugged. "Currently, the residents of Shalanum, aside from the merchants and nobles, of course, largely support the actions of The Hand and have been unwilling to provide any information regarding their whereabouts or membership. If you allowed Commander General Sharav the latitude to explore more extreme measures, then that might change."

Emperor Lao shook his head as he considered. "You know General Hamazi would not appreciate your proposal any more than I do."

General Kalin shrugged again. "That's true. There are lines that General Hamazi refuses to cross in the interest of *honorable* battle tactics. But…General Sharav and I have spoken on the matter and agree that while such tactics shouldn't be the norm, there are certainly situations, such as this one, where they may be necessary to reach the desired ends."

"General, one of the reasons that I deplore such tactics is because, in the end, it makes management of the rest of the empire more difficult. If rumors arose that we were willing to torture our citizenry to track down rebels, then we will be greeted with terror and doubt rather than welcomed, or at the very least, greeted with a sense of apathy as most don't really care who their rulers are. If we allow ourselves to slip down the road my cousin followed, dread will eventually lead to revolt, and we will have much bigger problems on our hands than a few rebel raiders."

"We can be very discreet, majesty. The rumors need not spread," Kalin responded.

"It's a slippery slope, General Kalin. And rumors always spread. There were plenty of rumors about Emperor Chen before he lost his mind entirely and began to truly believe himself a god beyond the laws of mortal men. It did not make for good diplomatic relations, and eventually, cost those, like my father, who were willing to stand up to him, their lives." Emperor Lao shook his head again. "No, I'm not ready to follow the path you suggest. Find another way."

"As you say, majesty." General Kalin bowed and then let himself out.

Chapter Thirty-Six

Orlyk

"Second and third infantry battalions will cross the Temny River here." General Hamazi stabbed at the map in northwest Orlyk. "There shouldn't be much in the way of resistance, but make sure the commanders know that they are to secure the northern settlements and welcome them into the new empire with as little bloodshed as possible. We need a good relationship with them if we are to ensure a steady supply of horses and cattle for the army."

"And if they do meet resistance?" General Volkov asked.

"They are to favor diplomacy over force, but they can defend themselves, of course," General Hamazi answered. "The rest of the army will cross the Pusteli River here." He pointed to a ford northeast of Zymova. "We'll traverse the Jeminy Plains, and then we'll take the bridge at Atasu and reform on the other side."

"And what about the Rusticari army? We will need the *Gora Voin* to successfully take Kasha Ekur without an extended siege," General Malik said.

"While we make our way across the breadth of Orlyk, they

will travel through the mountain passes east of Kasha Muscava. They will meet us after we take Atasu. Once we redeploy and move south, their mountain warriors will scale the peaks surrounding Kasha Ekur to secure the roads to the south and block any aid that might come from Kasha Libbu or Kasha Deira. Without relief and supplies from the south, we should be able to wear them down before the winter snows set in."

"And if we don't? Wear them down, that is," General Volkov asked.

"Then we'll lead a full assault," Hamazi answered.

"That would be suicide!" General Volkov exclaimed before regaining his composure. "What I mean is that the mountain fortress has never been breached, and it would be very costly to try."

"I understand," General Hamazi answered calmly. "And let's hope it doesn't come to that. But the security of that city will be critical to our plans to control the eastern provinces of Chungoku."

"It's a beautiful plan," General Volkov joked. "I can't wait to see what actually happens."

"You know what they say, General," Hamazi smiled back. "'In preparing for battle, plans are useless, but planning is indispensable.' If we encounter challenges, we'll change the plan. Any other questions before we prepare to break camp?"

"No, General," General Malik responded. "The snows have receded enough to travel. The men are anxious to get started."

General Hamazi groaned as he looked at the swollen banks of the Pusteli. It had started raining three days after they left Zymova and hadn't stopped. Now, standing in the drizzling remnants of the spring storm, he saw what the tempest had wrought. The river was dark brown and frothing rapids were choked with debris. Reluctantly, he signaled his column to move south. The next closest crossing would take them well out of their way, but he saw little choice.

A pair of messengers waited for them when they rejoined the main road. Two weeks marching across less-developed trails had worn the men out.

"Set camp here," General Hamazi ordered. "We'll rest for a few days while the rest of the army catches up. Erect the command tent on that hillock over there and join me there with the messengers once it's done."

Hamazi summoned the quartermaster, and together, they moved through the camp while he waited. He sought out battalion commanders to offer words of encouragement and check on the state of the men. The quartermaster made notes of what supplies they needed—new boots seemed to be the greatest demand but other supplies like tents and tack had been worn or damaged during the detour across rough terrain.

"We're going to have some trouble filling some of these demands, General," the quartermaster said in confidence after one such inspection.

"I understand," Hamazi answered. "Do the best you can. Prioritize the greatest needs, and once the craftsmen catch up, see how much of the reclaimed supplies can be refurbished. We may be able to stretch things while we wait for the spring supply caravans to get up to speed."

Once Hamazi had completed his inspection, he met the other generals in the command tent and the messengers were summoned. The first messenger bore letters from the first and second battalions reporting on first interactions with the northern horsemen as well as a short missive from Kasha Marka.

"Sir, Captain Zima reports that the Sisuma may be gone, but their stubborn attitude has not left their descendants. He also states that the clan leaders have said, quote, 'Emperor or barons, the leadership of the southern provinces means nothing to them, and they do not wish to become involved in yet another dispute between their irritable cousins to the south.' End quote."

"Are you sure Captain Zima was the best choice to lead that group?" General Volkov asked.

"He's a rule follower and will make sure the others stay in line. The real resource there is Captain Zowalski from the diplomatic corps. What does he have to report?"

The messenger reviewed the missive before handing it to General Hamazi. "Captain Zowalski reports that the leaders are rightfully distrustful of imperial forces. He is trying to get them to understand that Emperor Lao is not like Emperor Chen and that he wants to bring peace and prosperity to the land. Some of them are willing to trade horses and beef, but so far, what they are asking in return is beyond exorbitant. He is working with them to come up with more reasonable concessions and favorable trade terms."

"Well, that's not terrible news then," General Malik said.

"It's not like we expected them to welcome us with open arms," General Volkov agreed.

"What word is there from the emperor?" General Malik asked, indicating the final message.

General Hamazi scanned the note and frowned. "It seems that the raiders who were harassing supply lines last summer are back. General Kalin ensures us not to worry, that General Sharav will soon have things under control, but our first resupply may be slightly delayed."

"Delayed by how long?" General Volkov asked.

"It doesn't say," General Hamazi answered while flipping the note over to make sure he hadn't missed anything. "We'll just have to make do for a little longer with what we have. We have plenty of provisions. It's gear that I worry more about. Start gathering things up in your divisions that aren't being used so we can redistribute it where there is a greater need."

The assembled generals nodded.

"And you," General Hamazi addressed the second messenger. "What news do you bring?"

"Sir, Corporal Sirdov from Rusticar Provice. Commander General Antoli reports that 'The Aengal army is on the move,' sir." The young man saluted when he was finished.

"That's unfortunate," General Volkov said sardonically.

"But not unexpected," General Hamazi reminded him. "Tell us what you know, Corporal."

"They started moving troops into position in late winter while the ground was still frozen," Corporal Sirdov explained. "They didn't cross our borders, so it was difficult to tell whether or not they were just securing their borders or if they had hostile intentions. However, three weeks ago, a small fleet of Magoran vessels began harassing our supply lines and attacking our naval vessels. At the same time, the Aengals crossed the border, moving in three directions toward Kasha Muscava."

"I see," Hamazi said. Inside, he was seething. He supposed it was too much to have asked that the Aengals stay out of the conflict given their historical animosity toward Rusticar, but he had remained hopeful. "There is nothing we can do about it from here. We must trust our allies to manage their own borders."

General Hamazi watched from atop his horse while the men, ankle-deep in mud, levered a metal bar against the banded wagon wheel to pry it free from the muck. The first few weeks across the Jeminy Plains had been easy to travel. Cold nights ensured that the ground remained firm. Now, as the rains increased and the weather warmed, the soil became increasingly sodden. Long stretches of mud in the road had become more and more common as they traveled.

"General, the rest of the army is continuing its march around this section of road while we work to clear it."

"Thank you, Captain," Hamazi responded without even looking up at the man. Between the extended hike to find a good crossing point on the Pusteli and now this, they were falling behind schedule. It was already mid-spring, and he had hoped they would reach Atasu before summer.

"General." General Volkov rode up beside him. "We have another message from Rusticar."

Hamazi accepted the sealed letter. He broke the wax and read the words twice before crumpling the paper and stuffing it in his pocket. He resisted the urge to shout curses at the top of his lungs. Instead, he clenched his jaw and tried to hide how much his hands were shaking with rage.

"What did it say?" Volkov asked.

"The Rusticari are falling back to the safety of Kasha Muscava. The Aengal army has been reinforced from Kasha Kyoshu, and the Magorans have blockaded the harbor," Hamazi explained.

"So, in short, our allies are as stuffed as a turkey at winter solstice." General Volkov winced. "Has the baron at least dispatched the Gora Voin to meet us in Orlyk?"

"No, he says they are needed to keep the Aengal army from sweeping to the west to take the mountain passes. He will send them as soon as they have 'the blasted Aengals locked down.'"

"I see," said General Volkov, looking more than a little worried. "And has there been any word on supplies yet?"

General Hamazi shook his head. "The latest promise from General Kalin is that they will reroute supplies from Kantibar and Basara."

"Provisions are starting to run low. We only have about three weeks of rations left and less of grains for the animals," Volkov said.

"Graze the horses and oxen at night to preserve feed and assign herd guards since we won't be able to picket the horses. Send out scouts to see if the surrounding villages have food reserves they can sell," Hamazi ordered.

General Volkov looked doubtful. "The towns around here are small. They won't have enough reserves to make a difference for an army our size, and they'll charge a premium for the shriveled potatoes and limp carrots that they do have."

Hamazi sighed. "I understand, but it's the best we can do for now."

Riders approached from the west—at least a dozen. Hamazi squinted into the setting sun and revised his estimate. Only two riders, leading another ten horses.

"What's this?" Hamazi asked as the riders pulled to a stop.

"A good faith offering," one of the men panted. "Captain Zowalski is making progress with his negotiations, and a few of the clan leaders have presented these mounts in exchange for fifty stone of grain seed from Kasha Marka."

Hamazi rolled his eyes. A steep price for ten horses, but at least it was a step forward. Another rider approached from the head of the line. *What now?* Hamazi groaned internally.

"General," the rider spoke. "Another village up ahead is refusing to trade, and a few villagers have spoken obscenities at the officers in charge there."

General Hamazi sighed. "Post a garrison outside of town, enough to maintain order and to protect our supply lines."

"Yes, sir." The rider saluted and then returned in the direction he had come.

"Emperor Lao was right to place you in charge of the forward army instead of General Sharav," General Malik spoke in a low tone.

"How so?" Hamazi asked curiously.

"These people have a long memory. General Sharav would have had a price on his head the second he stepped into Orlyk, and we would have been dealing with outright revolt rather than a few malcontents and stubborn village leaders."

General Volkov nodded in agreement, "And knowing Sengiin's temper, he would have left a string of burned-out villages instead of a handful of armed garrisons designed to maintain the peace. You're doing very well, General."

"Thank you for saying so," General Hamazi said. "It doesn't feel like it. We are behind schedule, our supplies are stretched thin, and we are not supplementing it as much as I hoped we would from the townships in Orlyk."

At the mention of supplies, one of the riders spoke up. "We passed a sizeable supply caravan from Kasha Marka a couple of days back. They were having some trouble with the roads, but they should be along soon."

"Well, that's good news at least," General Volkov said. "Should I dispatch riders to help them?"

Hamazi nodded. "And order relay squads to start transporting provisions back and forth ahead of the convoy. At least an injection of fresh food might help raise morale. Things might be starting to look up, gentlemen."

Chapter Thirty-Seven

Assassins

Micah studied the note with pursed lips. It was a simple enough command. Three words: "Eliminate the threat."

"What does it say?" Moab asked.

Micah passed him the note, and Moab let out a low whistle as he read. He passed it to Joral when he was done.

"More easily said than done," Joral said. "Especially with only ten of us."

"We have our orders," Micah said with a confidence that belied his inner emotion. "We are the Sgarra'lamma. We will get it done."

"Did you practice that in front of a mirror?" Joral asked, hiding a smile.

"Did you see the way he stuck out his chin a little to show that extra confidence?" Moab asked Joral.

"Yeah, it was a nice touch," Joral answered.

"All right, all right—that's enough," Micah said. He should have known better than to project false confidence to these two.

They knew him as well as he knew himself. "We have work to do. We'll scout the palace tonight."

"Of course," Moab said, puffing his chest a little. "We are the Sgarra'lamma. We will get it done."

Joral covered his mouth to stifle a laugh.

The men sat if they could find room or leaned against the walls if they couldn't. Micah's room was the largest of the five, so it made the most sense for them to meet here.

"We've scouted the palace. Getting in and out shouldn't be an issue," Micah started.

"There are plenty of servants' access corridors and other means to gain entrance," Joral added.

"The wing that houses the pretender's quarters is the most secure. There are regular patrols and a permanent guard of twenty stationed outside her room," Micah continued.

"I asked around about that," Moab interjected. "It seems that there were some earlier attempts on her life, so they increased palace security around her rooms significantly."

"What about her personal balcony? Can we come in via the roof?" one of the men asked.

"Secured and barred from the inside," Micah answered. "We could break the glass, but that would likely raise the attention of the guards outside the room."

"So, we're outnumbered two to one against the hallway guard," another soldier interjected. "Those don't seem like bad odds. We could eliminate close to half of them before they even knew we were there and dispatch the rest before they could raise the alarm."

"I like your confidence, Stefan," Micah said. He'd made a point early on in his command to make it clear that, during these planning meetings, anyone could offer ideas and ask questions. "I'd like to see if we can't tip those odds a bit more in our favor, though."

"Also, half of the guards are women," Moab added.

"Women?" Several questions went up at once.

"I've seen her walking through the city with women guards. I assumed they were honorary. You know, since she's an empress," Stefan said. "I wouldn't have expected them to be guarding her door. So, the odds are already in our favor."

"That remains to be seen," Micah said. "It's an unknown at best. We ran into plenty of capable interference from the women under Sillu Mitu's command when we were working the siege at Kasha Marka."

"Yeah, but most of the women don't even have swords, just staves and those *S*-shaped knives," Moab said.

"Can we lure a few of them away from the door?" Stefan asked.

"That's what I was thinking. I'm just not sure how to do that without raising a general alarm. If they see or hear something suspicious, they may just summon additional guards to intervene."

"How do they do that?" Adam Piccoli asked.

"There is a gong at the end of the hallway," Micah answered. "My assumption is that if they ring it, then it will be heard throughout that wing of the palace and more guards will come."

"Got it," Piccoli said. "So, we have to keep them away from the gong."

"What about smoke bombs?" Stefan asked.

"That might work if we had any," Micah said.

"I can make them," Stefan said. "If I can find the right ingredients."

"How?" Moab asked.

"You drill holes in either end of an eggshell and blow out the contents," Stefan explained. "And then you fill the dried eggshell with a powder similar to what the Zamani use in their flash bombs, except instead of creating a flash of light, it creates smoke. It just has different ingredients in the powder. Then you seal the ends up with wax."

"Where did you learn how to do it?" Micah asked.

"I was studying to join the Zamani when I was assigned to your squad before Eridu." Stefan shrugged. "I played around with different combinations of minerals to see what results I could get. One day, I accidentally filled the entire Zamani quarters with smoke. Actually, it was right after that that I was reassigned to your team."

Micah gave Moab and Joral a quick look. The revelation certainly explained a lot. Stefan was not a bad soldier, but neither was he the most focused of Micah's corporals. He was a bit of a dreamer. Micah nodded seriously at Stefan. "You don't say."

"Anyway, I'm sure I could replicate the formula and create smoke bombs. We'd have to test a few out first, but it shouldn't take too long," Stefan said.

"Where can you find the materials you need?" Micah asked.

"Any alchemy shop should have what I need. They're pretty common ingredients."

Micah looked around the group to see if there were any other questions and then shrugged. "Let's give it a try. How much time do you need?"

"If you can spare the coin for the supplies, I can probably come up with something in a couple of days," Stefan said.

"I can do that. But maybe test your prototypes outside of town so you don't draw any unwelcome attention," Micah said.

They hid in the shadows down the hallway from the guarded room. Stefan was with Micah, and he had given two of the eggshell bombs to Moab, who were more than happy to try them out.

"Moment of truth," Micah whispered.

Stefan nodded, holding the eggs carefully. He nodded across the hall to Moab and then directed a slow three count. Both men tossed the eggs in the direction of the guards. They worked brilliantly. As soon as the eggs hit the wall or floor, they broke.

There was a muffled bang and then acrid smoke filled the hallway.

Micah and his men sprinted the ten paces and engaged the male guards before they could react. There was a clash of blades and the sound of steel slipping through leather. It was Micah's job to make his way through the chaos and secure the gong. He danced his way through the smoke using his ears and his hands to guide his way. He ducked under the swish of a blade behind him. Turned as he felt a body encroaching from the side. Jumped as someone stumbled and fell in front of him. As quickly as he had entered, he was free of the smoke.

One of the female guards was ahead of him in the hallway and had nearly reached the gong. He unsheathed his sword and, gripping it with both hands, threw it at her back. It struck with a force that both penetrated the protection of her armor and sent her sprawling on the ornate rug.

She tried to scramble to her feet, but her legs weren't working correctly. Micah closed the distance, and as she drew her serpentine blade, he turned it on her and thrust it into her chest. Then he pulled his sword free and turned to face the battle in the hallway. The smoke was already starting to thin, and he could see the dark shapes moving clearly.

The smoke cleared further, and he could tell that two of his men were down but so were most of the male guards. Joral was engaged with the last swordsman. Moab and the others were fighting with the women who were doing remarkably well at holding off his men's attacks with their staves.

One of the women, wearing epitaphs on her collar, turned toward Micah. "Fatemah!" she cried out. She charged down the hall toward Micah.

Hearing the cry, the other women switched from defense to offense. They fought in pairs, one defending with the staff and the other attacking with her knife. Joral still fought the guard captain. The other eight fought the remaining six men in Micah's party. *Make that five.* Micah cringed as he saw one of the wicked-looking blades pierce Adam Piccoli's neck.

The woman attacked Micah with a ferocity he had rarely encountered. Before he knew it, he had been driven several steps down the hallway toward the gong. He analyzed her movements and was able to select an attack sequence that returned the advantage to him. Fox Dances with Dandelions stymied her attack and forced her to take a step back. He followed up with a series of powerful slashing overhead strikes that drove her to her one knee. Micah thrust quickly, which she parried easily, but then he reversed his grip and countered with a hard strike, which disabused her of her weapon. Before he could take advantage, she had two of the twisting knives in her hands and was using them to counter his sword strokes.

Out of the corner of his eye, he saw Joral finish his opponent but also noticed that Moab and Stefan fought alone against five women. Joral quickly joined them, leveling the odds. Just then, the door to the inner chamber flew open. The beautiful woman they had seen from afar so many weeks earlier stood in the doorway. She was wearing a flowing blue evening gown, and the shape of her body was outlined by the lantern light beyond. She surveyed the scene efficiently, and then her hands flashed in opposite directions.

Micah saw the dagger flipping end over end toward the gong but could do nothing to stop it. The sound that it made when the butt of the dagger struck it echoed through the hallways. The second dagger caught Stefan on the side of his head, taking part of his ear with it as it ricocheted away. The momentary distraction gave his opponent the opportunity she needed to bury her knife up to its hilt in his ribs. He staggered back and collided with the wall. He sank to the ground, gasping for breath as bubbles of blood began to form around the edges of his mouth.

"That's enough!" the dark woman shouted. "Drop your weapons."

Micah made a final desperate lunge at her with his sword. The pommel strike on the side of the head took him by surprise and darkness overtook him before his body hit the floor.

Micah's head pounded. He heard voices far off in the distance. Or at least it seemed that way over the echoing pound of his heartbeat.

"Who sent you?" The words drifted through the darkness again.

Micah opened his eyes slowly, the dizzying patterns of light nearly making him vomit.

"We're not telling you anything." Micah heard Moab's voice.

Micah realized that his cheek was cold. He forced his eyes to focus, and the stone floor that he was lying on crystalized into view.

"Was it Ubad Dafo or Ubad Cawlan?" The question came in a more conspiratorial tone.

Micah leveraged himself up on his elbow with a groan.

"He lives!" The voice was directed at him now.

He shifted his gaze, searching for the speaker. He was inside a stone cell. Joral and Moab were with him, but there was no sign of Stefan. Iron bars separated them and the speaker. It was the same woman, he realized—the beautiful dark-skinned woman who had been bathed in the light of the gods. He shook his head, willing the memory away. "Empress Ullani." His voice sounded weak and far away.

"That's right," she answered. "And who might you be?"

"The pretender," he finished his thought.

"You're the pretender?" She seemed legitimately confused.

"No, you." Micah struggled with the words. "Empress Ullani, the pretender."

The woman standing next to Ullani raised her staff to strike Micah through the bars, but Ullani stopped her with a gentle touch of her hand. "No, Ava."

Ullani laughed and knelt so that she was at eye level with Micah. "Oh, so you're one of those. One of the zealots that refuse to let go of the old ways."

"No," Micah shook his head and immediately regretted it. "Micah…" he started to say and then was cut off by Moab.

"Captain Kabir, don't tell her anything."

Ullani stood in surprise. "Micah Kabir. Your name is Micah Kabir?"

"Why?" he asked. "Does that name mean something to you?"

"Oh, yes, it does," Ullani said simply. "I know all about you. You're an imperial officer in the service of Emperor Lao. I admit that I didn't know you were a captain, surprising if I'm honest, for one so young. You grew up in a small coastal village. Your mother was a seamstress, and your father was a hunter…until he was killed."

The words were all true, but they made no sense coming from this woman.

"Witch!" Moab pointed at her in shock. "That's how you did the magic on your balcony to fool everyone."

Ullani laughed. "No, I'm not a witch, but I am very good friends with Captain Kabir's brother, Darius."

Chapter Thirty-Eight

State of Affairs

Ullani sat comfortably in an overstuffed chair in her sitting room. This was her favorite room. The decorations were understated, and aside from the chair she currently occupied and a small reading table next to it, the only furniture was a narrow coffee table with a pair of padded, whicker settees set on either side for when she wanted to meet someone in a more casual setting.

The rest of her apartments had been decorated by Randa, who, in Ullani's opinion, had gone over the top with adornments that were "fitting of an Empress." Ahmed and Muhammad had taken charge of the décor elsewhere in the palace with the help of their wives, and the result was an opulent mix of nomadic culture and traditional imperial furnishings.

There was a knock on the door.

"Come in!" Ullani called across the room.

Ava escorted Micah through the door. His hands and feet were bound in iron shackles connected by a short chain that allowed only the minimum necessary movement. It had been a couple of weeks since the failed assassination attempt. Ullani had meant to meet with Micah earlier, but other matters of state prevented the opportunity. He seemed to have recovered from his injuries and his alert eyes darted around the room, taking note of the furniture and exits before coming to rest on Ullani.

"You can take the irons off, Ava," Ullani said.

"Empress?" Ava asked with concern in her voice.

"I'll be fine," Ullani assured her.

Micah looked offended. "What makes you think I won't try to complete my mission once I'm free?" he asked.

"It would be an unfortunate mistake if you tried," Ullani said. "However, I think you'll hear me out. Darius described a man who was loyal and headstrong but also curious and kind. He may not have used such flattering words, but I could read between the lines when he told me stories of your childhood."

Micah gave her an unreadable look.

"Ava." Ullani gestured at the shackles.

Ava reluctantly removed the chains and then took a guard position near Ullani's chair.

Micah didn't move. Ullani studied him for a few seconds before standing herself.

She smoothed out the wrinkles on her ankle-length lavender-colored gown. The chiffon style was belted at the waist and gathered at the bosom to emphasize her decolletage. She had worn the outfit for several reasons. The loose-flowing skirt would allow her to move quickly and freely if the need arose, but she also wanted to see if Micah was the type of man who was easily distracted, and potentially manipulated, by exposing a little collarbone and cleavage.

"Micah, make yourself comfortable." She pointed to the small couch near the table as she took a seat on the opposite side. "Ava, could you leave the two of us alone for a while? I would like to speak to Emperor Lao's representative about matters of state."

"Empress!" Ava's tone was shocked and pleading.

"Please, Ava." Ullani soothed her guard captain's nerves. "You can wait right outside. I'll shout if I need anything, but I promise you, I'll be fine."

Ava sulked as she plodded toward the door and slammed it behind her.

Micah sat stiffly on the edge of the sofa. "What is this all about?" Micah asked. To his credit, he met her gaze resolutely and didn't allow his eyes to wander.

Ullani paused, gathering her thoughts. "Do you know who I was before all of this?" She waved a hand indicating the palace itself more than the subdued sitting room.

Micah shook his head.

"I was a thief. I served under Saria Oberman in the guild in Kasha Marka."

"What? How did you meet my brother then?" Curiosity broke him out of his shell a little bit. "Unless he's changed more than I thought, I can't see him running around with thieves."

"The relationship between the palace and the guild is a…complicated one, in Kasha Marka," Ullani explained. "Saria, you may know her as *Sillu Mitu*, was an esteemed scout and spy during the last war. She established the guild under the direction and guidance of Nyala Kess, the former baroness. They both realized that there was no way to *stop* criminal activity in a city the size of Kasha Marka, so they sought instead to *control* it."

"I don't understand," Micah said. He seemed genuinely curious. His shoulders relaxed ever so slightly.

"Saria rules the underworld with an iron fist. It's impossible, of course, to prevent crimes of passion or to keep men from beating each other to a pulp when they've had too much drink. But the rest— robbery, embezzlement, graft, smuggling, prostitution—it's all controlled by the guild. Activities without guild sanction are strictly forbidden and are met with swift and strong consequences. In this way, Saria is aware of everything that is going on in the dark underbelly of the city, and she relays that information to the baroness who uses it to her advantage to guide the actions of the nobles and to decide which social programs will have the greatest benefit."

"I guess that makes sense in a certain way," Micah said doubtfully. "Did it work?"

"For the most part." Ullani shrugged. "Saria would use the guild to recruit orphans and runaways. She treated us like her children. She raised us with a respect for duty and hard work but also with discipline and a respect for authority. She taught us how to protect ourselves, and she made sure we were educated."

"How very kind of her," Micah said sarcastically. His back stiffened again as though he found the idea repulsive.

"I know that you're being sardonic but think it through. I know you're bright. Emperor Lao wouldn't have promoted you to such a high rank at such a young age if you weren't. What would happen to the abandoned children in a city the size of Kasha Marka without someone like Saria stepping in and taking us in hand, teaching us skills and a trade, of sorts?"

"I guess you either wouldn't have survived long or you would have become criminals anyway," Micah shrugged.

"Exactly," Ullani agreed. "Except, we would have been the worst kind of criminals—brutal, self-serving, relying only on ourselves, and without a care for consequences of our actions. Saria taught us to be deliberate with our actions. She also taught us to think on our feet and analyze a situation from all sides before acting. And to make sure that we understood and could live with the consequences."

"So, why are you telling me this? I already know you're a fraud—this only proves my point," Micah said. He crossed his arms and leaned back slightly. He turned his head a fraction and narrowed his eyes as he asked the question.

"Saria sent me on a mission. To deliver a box to Kasha Haaki for safekeeping."

"The reliquary of Chung Oku Mai," Micah said. "Emperor Lao sent me on a similar mission to retrieve the box. My understanding was that it was in my brother's care. How did you come to possess it?"

Ullani chose to ignore his question but made a mental note to probe what he knew of the box later. "Yes, but I didn't understand that at the time. I had the keys, and I couldn't resist opening the box to take a peek during my journey. The crown and the orb were beautiful. I was traveling by myself, and I didn't think there was any harm in trying the crown on. I was admiring my reflection in the pond, and then I raised the orb to look at it in the light. The sun reflected through the prism and hit the jewels in the crown, bathing me in light. Others at the oasis saw the burst of light and came to investigate. They saw me shimmering like an immortal being sent from the heavens and immediately seized on the legend of the crown, that it was 'created by the gods to make clear to the mortals of this realm who their appointed ruler would be.'"

"I was in the palace square. I saw you on the balcony. I have to admit, it was a pretty powerful display," Micah said.

"Exactly, and for an impoverished people wandering the desert, it was a sign from the gods that their savior had been sent to them."

"So...superstition put you in a position where you could take advantage and beguile these poor people into setting you up in a life of luxury." Micah curled a lip in distaste.

"Not exactly," Ullani said. "It is true that I took advantage of the situation, but I had only intended to use it to secure safe passage across the desert. I figured, at the time, that traveling with a larger group would keep me free from bandits and other dangers. I had intended to deliver the box to the baron at Kasha Haaki."

"So, what happened?" Micah asked.

Ullani sighed. "There was a series of incidences that made it more and more difficult for me to leave. And the longer I stayed, the more I began to realize that I could use the opportunity to improve the lives of some of these people, especially the women. Now it has reached the point where I don't think I could leave even if I wanted to."

Micah nodded, finally understanding. "You are in a gilded cage. You can't leave, or they would follow you. You can't admit what you've done, or they would kill you. You can't trust anyone with the truth, or they might use that knowledge to manipulate you and grab power for themselves. Even if I were to kill you, it would only create a martyr, and then we'd have a holy war on our hands."

"I knew you were smart," Ullani said with a smile.

"So, why tell me?" Micah asked.

"That's an excellent question," Ullani said. "First, you are a foreigner and a *spy* for Antu's emperor. No one would believe you if you tried to tell them the truth. They would just see it as propaganda meant to undermine me."

Micah shrugged and nodded. "And second?"

"Because you are Darius's brother." Ullani shrugged. "I trust him, and based on what I've heard about you, I trust you to be...*predictable*...and loyal to who you are."

"And who is that?" Micah asked.

"An intelligent, ingenious leader who is loyal to Emperor Lao but also loyal to his family and the nation of Chugoku as a whole," Ullani said.

Micah laughed. "You've gathered all of that from a few stories about me?"

"Some of it," Ullani admitted. "But mostly from stories that your brother told about you. He was very angry with you when I knew him, and he spoke about you more than I think he realized. I know who you *were,* and I can intuit who you have become based on your exploits."

"It's a big risk if you're wrong," Micah said.

"Maybe," Ullani agreed. "Look, the world is a mess right now. The empire has invaded Orlyk. The Aengals have invaded Rusticar. Hurasham rules the seas and Merkar rules the deserts. The empire is holding on to a tenuous grasp of Shalanum and Magora, and your brother is rallying the people to do everything he can to break that grasp. I even know a little bit about your exploits in the south of Magora."

Micah looked shocked. "How do you know all of that?"

"I told you...Saria trained us to analyze the situation from all sides. If I'm going to be stuck in this position, then I'm going to make sure that I know what's going on around me. I created a network early on to keep me informed. It has served me well," she explained.

"Smart," Micah said.

Ullani laughed. "Was that a compliment?"

Micah shrugged again. He was becoming more relaxed. She still wasn't sure she could depend on his help but decided to risk the next step.

"Look," Ullani said. "Everything that is going on are like pieces of a puzzle."

"Or stones on a board," Micah responded.

"Sure." She gave him a curious look. "I still believe there is a way out of all of this, but I can't see it. I can't share my thoughts or plans with my advisors. So, I'm hoping you can help me. With your wit and your knowledge of the inner workings of the empire, you might be able to help me understand the pieces that don't fit."

"I won't betray the emperor," Micah said firmly.

"I wouldn't ask you to," Ullani assured him.

"And if I agree?" Micah asked.

"Then there is one other person I want you to meet. Now, he's a bit crazy, following an unfortunate encounter with your brother, but I still think he can be useful, both for his knowledge of Hurasham and for his ties to the emperor."

"Okay, you've piqued my interest. I'll hear you out, but I won't make any promises," Micah said.

"Fair enough," Ullani said. Then she raised her voice. "Ava!"

The guardswoman burst through the door with knives in hand. She relaxed when she saw the two of them lounging in the chairs.

"Fetch The Prophet," Ullani said.

"Empress?"

"Oh, and clean him up a bit first. He's been in that tower without a bath for weeks."

"Yes, Empress." Ava bowed and retreated.

"What shall we do while we wait?" Ullani asked.

"Have you ever played wei-chi?" Micah asked.

Micah watched the bedraggled man with interest. The wei-chi board had been pushed aside after the man was brought in. The beggar prostrated himself on the ground near Ullani's feet. He hadn't moved from the position since he entered and groveled across the floor. *It must be very uncomfortable on the knees*, Micah thought.

"Prince Sayyid is originally from Hurasham," Ullani explained. "Your brother's raiders attacked his convoy on his way to Kasha Amur, and he had a life-changing encounter with Antu."

"The god?" Micah laughed.

"No," Ullani explained. "Darius's bear."

"Ah." Micah nodded his understanding. "I haven't had the pleasure."

"Me neither," Ullani said. "But from the stories I've heard, an encounter with him on a dark and stormy night during a pitched battle could change anyone's perspective on life." She nodded toward Sayyid. "Following this encounter, he made it his personal mission to spread word of Antu's return and the retribution of the Hand of the Shadow for the sinners of the world."

"Like from the children's story?" Micah asked.

"Exactly," Ullani confirmed. "Emperor Lao found him and renamed him Süba, one of the Old Tongue words for prophet. Then Lao sent him here to undermine the Cult of Kisha."

"He doesn't seem to be doing a very good job," Micah said.

"I imprisoned him shortly after his arrival because I wanted to find out what he knew of Darius's work. Not much, as it turned out. After that, it seemed better to keep him in the care of the state than let him continue to wander about causing trouble," Ullani explained. "He was in the prison tower the day of my *demonstration* and saw everything through the bars. He's been like this ever since."

"How do you think he can help?" Micah asked.

Ullani shrugged. "He's very loyal. And he has detailed knowledge of the inner workings of the Hurasham principalities. So far, however, his only meaningful contribution to a solution is that I marry Emperor Lao."

"The houses of Antu and Kisha joined again to bear the fruit of a glorious empire." Süba raised his head as he spoke and then quickly lowered it again when Ullani gave him a sidelong glance.

"It's not the worst idea," Micah said.

Ullani waved the thought away. "I think we can do better. Anyway, think on it. I'll have Ava show you back to your cell and see that you and your men get a good meal and more comfortable cots."

"You could always give us rooms in the palace," Micah suggested.

Ullani laughed. "I think not. You are still assassins, after all. I'll make the accommodations as comfortable as I can, but your men won't leave that cell, and you'll stay with them when we are not in discussions."

Micah nodded his understanding. "It was worth a try."

Micah followed Ava up the corridor to Ullani's personal rooms. It was their sixth meeting in as many days. A porter opened the door as they arrived. Ullani was lounging on a chaise, reading a book when he entered. Today, she was wearing a luxurious orange satin dress that was split at the knees and flowed evenly over her outstretched legs.

Micah caught his breath when he saw her. She was truly magnificent. Each of her outfits had seemed designed to accentuate one or more of her physical qualities, today it was her legs. He wasn't sure if she was doing it for his benefit or if it was just how she dressed. It was a test of his discipline to focus on her eyes and mouth when she talked and to remain engaged in the conversation.

"Micah, welcome," Ullani said with a smile as she rose and set her book aside. "Can I have tea brought?"

"I would love some, thank you," Micah said politely.

"Please, sit." She waved a hand toward the couches where they normally had their discussions.

"No Süba today?" Micah asked.

"No," Ullani said. "He's a bit of a distraction, and until we have an actual plan, I think it's best that he stays in his room."

"So, we've ruled out war, and marriage, and outright surrender. What should we discuss today?" Micah said.

"Right down to business," Ullani laughed. "Let's take a break for a bit. We'll enjoy some tea and biscuits. You can teach me a little more about your game of stones, maybe something will come to us through the strategy of the game."

They played several games over the course of the morning and afternoon. Ullani was a fast learner, and she quickly picked up the basic mechanics of the game. The strategy came more slowly, but it came. He beat her by almost two hundred points in the first game, but by the fifth, she had cut that lead in half.

"Another good game," Ullani said. "I think I'm getting better."

"You are," Micah admitted.

Ullani reached her arms high above her head, stretching the muscles of her back and shoulders. The orange dress clung to her curves as she did so, and Micah caught himself staring. He darted his eyes up to her face to see if she had noticed. Her eyes were closed, and he breathed an inner sigh of relief.

Ullani opened her eyes and tilted her head, first to one side and then to the other. Then she reached up and kneaded the junction between her neck and shoulder. "I think I've been too tense during the game. My shoulders are stiff. Do you mind?" She pointed to where she had been massaging.

"No, of course not." Micah rose and circled behind Ullani's chair. The cut of her dress left her neck and shoulders exposed. As he placed his hands on her skin, he was surprised by its warmth. He rubbed the skin gently, working the tight muscles back and forth.

"Oh, come on," Ullani chided. "You're a strong man—you can do better than that."

Micah increased the pressure and dug his thumbs into the knotted tissue, rubbing in tight circles across her flesh.

"Mmm," Ullani groaned. "That's better."

He continued to work the knots out of the tops of her shoulders and the upper, exposed portion of her back. His mind was drifting as the sensual feel of her skin stirred more carnal sensations. He kept forcing his thoughts back to the task at hand, convincing himself that she surely considered this a servile duty.

After several minutes, Ullani flexed her shoulders again and seemed satisfied. "Thank you, that's much better."

Her pragmatic response reinforced his idea that, for her, the shoulder massage was a practical service and nothing more.

She stood and walked toward the door. "Well, I think that's enough for today. You've given me a lot to think on. Tomorrow then?"

Micah hurriedly wiped his hands on his pants, fearing they had become sweaty. "But we didn't even discuss anything?"

"Didn't we?" Ullani tilted her head. She pointed to the board. "You helped me realize that my current position is weak compared to the strength of the empire and other forces. I would be easily surrounded and dispatched if I tried to take too aggressive a stance. I would be overwhelmed, eventually, if I tried to take a defensive posture. I need to work harder to understand the strengths and weaknesses of my adversaries and find ways to exploit them without giving too much up myself."

Micah gaped. Not only were his thoughts still in disarray from the feel of his fingers on her skin, but he found her ability to transfer the tactical lessons of the game to her real-life situation impressive.

"Isn't that the point of the game?" Ullani asked innocently.

Micah nodded appreciatively. "It is."

"Good, then I'll see you tomorrow." She held the door open for him to leave, and Ava waited in the hallway to escort him back to his cell.

PART III

And in the morn', the cock did crow
with the ravens' shill reply.
The smell of blood is in the air,
the din of war gone silent.

A shattered fence, a broken blade,
the field an eerie quiet.
Trampled earth, green grass stained crimson
as the mist slowly rises.

Man's passage marked upon the land,
fatal gathering ended.
And in its wake, the scene reclaimed,
creation's ruin mended.

The scavengers that live for death:
Vultures fly, coyotes howl,
joining to scour the landscape clean,
nature overcoming man.

– Nature's Victory
General Lao Wen – Third Dynasty

Summer – 37 A.E.

Chapter Thirty-Nine

Countermoves

"What news do you have this morning?" Emperor Lao asked General Kalin. Lao Jun had barely looked up from the parchment spread out on the table before him. Lead weights secured the corners of the document. The language was old—third or fourth dynasty, a predecessor to the current imperial language, which itself was often referred to as the *Old Tongue*. Lao Jun had been struggling with the translation for several hours.

"Quite a lot, Your Majesty. Not all of it is good, I'm afraid," General Kalin answered.

"Is it ever these days?" Emperor Lao straightened to face the general, then crossed the room to a large map table.

"The Cult of Kisha is continuing to make large expansive moves. Their strategy of winning hearts and minds seems to be accomplishing its goal throughout Chugoku. As of yet, they have not expanded beyond the provinces' borders, but there are indications that they soon may."

"Move additional forces to reinforce the northern border of Merkar. We don't want them threatening our supply lines across the Dalaman Plains." Emperor Lao picked up a metal rod and moved two figurines of foot soldiers from near Kasha Marka to the spot indicated on the map.

"Which brings us to our next point," General Kalin said. "The Hand of the Shadow—"

"Sillu Aga," Emperor Lao corrected. "Call them what they are."

"Apologies, Emperor. Sillu Aga is moving more fully into Magora. Recent raids are on this side of the Talai Mountains, in addition to continued actions in the Sea of Tears and the southern river valleys."

"Is there any word from General Sharav?" Emperor Lao's frustration was clear in his voice.

"Yes, Emperor. The road between Eridu and Isan, at least, has been made safe. His soldiers have driven the last of the bandits from the surrounding forests, and there hasn't been any activity there in recent weeks."

"Good. Have him focus his attention next on protecting our supply lines. Move additional battalions from Shalanum to protect all river crossings along the Beiji River." Emperor Lao repositioned a horse figure and two additional soldier figurines. "I want him to bring an end to this threat once and for all. We cannot have our supply lines pinched between Sillu Aga and the Cult of Kisha. General Hamazi's success depends on it."

"As you say, Your Majesty." General Kalin nodded.

"What news is there from Hurasham?" Emperor Lao asked.

"They caught three more Merkar vessels this week attempting to ship supplies to the Aengal front. Their efforts to stop any reinforcement efforts continue to be successful. Ito remains neutral despite our efforts to persuade them to join our cause."

"And Rusticar? Are they holding their own?" Emperor Lao asked.

"It would not seem so, majesty. The siege at Kasha Muscava is not going our way. They do continue to hold the mountain passes to protect General Hamazi's flanks, but I don't know how long that will last. The most recent reports received via courier pigeon from Rusticar have been cautiously optimistic, which I interpret to be a bad sign."

"Anything else?"

"No, majesty. General Hamazi continues to make progress toward Atasu but is not ready to engage. All communications from Captain Kabir have stopped, which is concerning," General Kabir finished his report.

"Thank you, General. You may go."

Emperor Lao turned toward the shadows, to the secret alcove where Guo Wen had been observing. "You heard all of that?"

"Yes." Guo Wen stepped into view. "The fact that the Cult of Kisha continues to expand and that we have no news from Captain Kabir would seem to indicate that his mission failed."

"I would agree," Emperor Lao said and then studied his mentor. Guo Wen looked thinner and paler than usual. "Are you feeling okay, uncle?"

As if in response, the older man began coughing. He held a kerchief to his mouth as he did. The cough sounded wet and indicated congestion deep in the old man's chest. "Yes, I'm fine. Just a summer cold. I'm sure I'll be over it in a few days."

"Hmm, see the physician just the same. He may have a tincture that can aid with your recovery." It didn't sound like a summer cold, and Jun didn't like the way Guo Wen had hurriedly stuffed the handkerchief into a pocket once the spasms had stopped.

"Is there anything else you think we should be doing?" Jun asked as he turned back to the map.

"No, as in the game of wei-chi, you are showing your fighting spirit or *kiai* by aggressively countering your opponent's moves. I would suggest invading Chugoku to stop the spread of the Cult of Kisha, but Merkar would undoubtedly see that as a sign of hostility and would move to counter our efforts. It's better to see how Merkar deals with the threat of the cult as they expand into their borders."

Jun nodded. "I am starting to feel like the lion with jackals nipping at my heels. These problems with Sillu Aga and the cult are an unwanted distraction from our objectives."

Chapter Forty

Atasu

Rain. Unrelenting, driving, bone-chilling rain. General Hamazi pulled the hood of his cloak forward more to provide additional shelter for his face. The early summer storms were well into their second week. Every step of this journey had been a grind, it seemed. Hamazi struggled to maintain a positive attitude for the sake of his subordinates, but the string of constant setbacks was starting to wear on his mental state. After supplies had started to arrive again, he hoped for a change of luck but the summer rains were worse than the spring, if that was even possible.

"It's no wonder Saridon is a desert," General Volkov shouted over the constant drumming. "Antu leaves all the water in Orlyk."

Hamazi grunted an unintelligible response. The storm was moving out of the northeast, and it certainly seemed that way. The clouds seemed intent on relocating every ounce of water from the North Sea directly on top of their heads.

"You okay, General?" Volkov asked.

"Yes, sorry." Hamazi tried to shake off his foul mood.

"Scouts reported this morning that the Zloy River near Atasu had blown her banks," Volkov continued.

"Is the bridge still intact?" General Hamazi asked, suddenly concerned that this news could cause yet another delay.

"It was," Volkov answered. "We'll know soon enough, though. The front ranks should reach the western edge of the city by nightfall."

"Good," General Hamazi said. "They can start organizing the siege while the rest of the army catches up."

"Whenever that will be," Volkov glanced over his shoulder. The army was spread out over at least fifty leagues. The muddy roads and boggy land had seen to that. "It could be next spring before they join us."

"Gods, I hope not," General Hamazi said. "But the rate we're going, it wouldn't surprise me."

"Cheer up, General." Volkov slapped him on the shoulder. "With Antu making the getting there so difficult, surely he'll hand Kasha Ekur over to us with hardly a fight."

"Right," Hamazi grumbled. "Because that's what the gods do. They give us a pat on the back and a hearty reward for our perseverance. It's better to hope that they lose interest in us entirely and let us be on our way."

General Volkov laughed. "Well said."

The next morning, as the sky turned from black to steel gray, General Hamazi got his first view of the city. The river had indeed overflowed its banks near where it passed under the fortifications that surrounded the city. Water surged around the western wall to the city, sweeping the farmland clear in a roiling, brown tumult. Townsfolk rushed about outside the wall, stacking burlap sacks filled with sand around the bottom edge of the wall to keep the flood from undermining the wall's foundations. They cast wary eyes in the direction of the army that continued to pour into the river valley.

"That wall's not going to hold," Volkov said.

"We'll see," Hamazi answered half to himself as he watched the efforts to reinforce the wall.

"It's a shame we can't make this work to our advantage, but if we try to cross now, we'd lose as many men to the flood waters as we would the wall's defenses," General Volkov said.

Hamazi nodded. Volkov was right, of course. The raging river that swept around the outside of the city was more than waist-deep and was moving fast. Horses would have a hard time swimming it let alone foot soldiers. They would just have to wait and watch until after the storm finally passed.

The sound that woke him was the cross between thunder and an avalanche. General Hamazi pulled on his coat and boots in a hurry and rushed out of his tent. In the dim evening light, he could see immediately the source of the calamity. The northwestern portion of the wall had completely collapsed. Even as he watched, stone and mortar were carried away. Additional sections began to fall. Archers atop the wall scrambled to safety.

General Hamazi looked to his left as General Volkov exited his own tent. "It seems you were right."

General Volkov gave a low whistle. "The breach has to be forty paces at least."

"And likely to grow," Hamazi said as he pointed. "The waters are already pounding the exposed portions of the wall and flooding the town."

By the end of the week, the rains had stopped. Slowly, the flood waters began to recede. In another two days, it would be safe to cross.

"What do you think?" General Hamazi asked the officers assembled around him.

"I think we should send them terms," General Malik said.

"You don't think they'll still resist?" General Hamazi looked at the gaping hole in the wall.

General Malik shrugged. "I don't see that it would do them much good."

"We can offer to leave them a company of sappers to repair the wall and the river channel if they let the rest of the army pass unmolested," General Volkov suggested.

"Not just sappers, though. Orlyk's Twilight Battalion is stationed in Atasu," Malik said. "If we only leave a couple of hundred engineers, they might get it in their heads to hit us from behind once we're trapped between them and Kasha Ekur."

"We'll have to disarm them," General Volkov nodded.

"We could take their officers with us as prisoners," General Soliman offered in a rare contribution.

General Hamazi raised an eyebrow. It was a good suggestion. Without weapons or officers to lead them, the rest of the soldiers might be easier to keep in line and could be convinced to focus on repairs to the town. "I think a company of light infantry could help to maintain order."

The others nodded in agreement.

General Hamazi held his hands in open invitation. "Any other ideas?" When the question was greeted with silence, he turned to General Malik. "Write up the terms and have them delivered." Finally, it seemed, Orlyk's cursed weather had dealt them a winning hand, of sorts.

"See!" General Volkov wrapped an arm around Hamazi's shoulder. "Antu decided to smile on us after all."

Chapter Forty-One

Crusade

Ahmed waited nervously outside the empress's chambers. He fumbled with the reports in his hands. As he read the first report in the stack, his hands began to tremble. The guard woman, Ava, opened the door and waved a hand for him to enter. They were not high on ceremony, these ones, and it made Ahmed cringe internally.

"Empress," he said as he entered. He bent at the waist in a low bow and waited for her acknowledgment.

"What is it, Ahmed?" Her tone seemed on edge, and as he rose, he could see that she was eyeing him suspiciously.

He shuffled through the reports, finding one that was better news. "We have reports in from the eastern territories. The early harvests have been incredible. Donations of fruits and vegetables are already starting to arrive for distribution to the people. The grain harvests look promising as well. With our help, the farmers were able to double the amount of land they were able to plant, and we should recognize even more of a bounty in the fall."

"That's good," she smiled weakly in anticipation of bad

news.

He shuffled through the papers again, looking for more promising news. "And we have reports out of Rusticar. The capital has fallen, and the Aengals are driving the rest of the Rusticari army into the mountains."

"That's bad for the imperial forces and good for Kasha Ekur, but I'm not sure how that helps us. Aren't you afraid that we may draw the attention of the provincial forces if they try to march through our lands to lend aid to Orlyk?" Ullani asked.

"Well, um...I guess I hadn't thought of that. I suppose it's a possibility, but they will still be engaged in fighting for a while as they secure the passes." Ahmed blushed.

"Ahmed," Ullani stopped him as he started rifling through the pages again. "Why do I get the feeling that you are avoiding something you don't want to tell me?"

"Well, there was some troubling news from the Hurasham border. Skirmishes are breaking out with Hurasham regulars as our influence starts to expand south. There have been some deaths among the warriors and the workers."

Ullani bit her lip. "And?"

"Well, they have burned the few villages."

"Who has?" Ullani asked with concern in her voice.

"The Hurasham army. But our people are offering aid and preparing defenses to protect the people. Many of the common folk are grateful for our aid, though others blame us for the troubles in the first place."

"Okay, I guess that's understandable. Is that why you seem so nervous? Or is there something else?" Ullani asked.

"Well…" He drew the word out. "There was a small riot in Kasha Libbu."

"How small?" Ullani narrowed her eyes. She was starting to get annoyed by the fact that he seemed to be intentionally underplaying the severity of the news. His demeanor was cagey, and it was making her more and more suspicious as he talked.

"Um, well, it started small. Some of the city guards were harassing our followers, who were trying to spread your teaching. There was some armed conflict. Some of the citizenry got involved, speaking out against the corruption in city leadership. More soldiers were called in, and it got a bit out of hand."

"How out of hand?" Ullani growled through clenched teeth. She wished he would just get to the point.

"An armed group of followers and disgruntled citizens stormed the palace, killed Baron Harmenos and several of the nobles, burned the palace to the ground, and placed the heads of the former leaders on pikes outside the palace gates," Ahmed blurted it all out in a rush.

"What!" Ullani rose from her chair. Anger rose in a flood of red to her cheeks. "That is not what I would call a *small* riot, Ahmed." She began pacing back and forth.

"This is bad," Ullani mumbled to herself as she paced. After a moment, she realized that Ahmed had not moved and still clenched the reports with white knuckles. "There's more!"

"Empress." His voice squeaked. He cleared his throat and then continued. "Ubad Faran was leading a trade expedition to some of the wealthier nobles south of Kasha Libbu. They refused to trade and were very stubborn about coming to terms. So…" he faded off.

"What did he do?"

"He ordered their execution and seized their lands and assets in the name of Empress Ullani and the Goddess Kisha. He also issued a proclamation in your name that all who do not join Kisha's cause shall be struck down by her vengeance."

Ullani sank back into her chair and rested her head in her hand. When she looked up again, she spoke very quietly. "Have Ubad Faran brought to me at once."

"Yes, Empress. I can send for him, but he is several days—"

"At once!" she shouted.

Ullani's mood had not improved in the intervening days. Especially since more reports of armed conflicts between the followers of Kisha and the nobility of Chugoku began to pour in.

Ubad Faran marched into the room and gave a cursory bow. "Empress."

"What in the name of all that is holy do you think you are doing, Faran?" Ullani raged. "We are not at war with the nobility of

Chugoku. Our goal is to win allies and bring them to our side—not slaughter them."

Uban Faran's expression was composed. "With all due respect, Empress. I was told to root out corruption and free the good people of Chugoku from its hold. The noblemen of the southern districts were corrupt to the core. If we do not deal with the oppression when we are faced with it, then we will look weak and hypocritical in the eyes of the common folk who we wish to follow the way of Kisha."

"If that's the case, then you bring them here for investigation and trial. You do not summarily massacre them in their homes. You are not judge, jury, and executioner, Faran."

"Forgive me if I overstepped, Empress," he answered, still calm. "We have liberated the lands and turned them over to the peasants and slaves that the so-called *nobles* had toiling in their fields. Their abundance of wealth has been given to the people who need it, and a small portion was liberated for the expenses of the empire. Now, instead of an immoral aristocracy resisting your cause and hurting the people, we have strong allies and a countryside filled with devoted worshipers."

"I am not inclined to spread terror and strife among those who will not follow us, Faran. Our goal is to spread grace and equality to win the hearts and minds of people to our side."

"Quite so, Empress. Equality will be impossible to deliver as long as the land barons continue to oppress the people. We have freed the southern counties, and now equality is free to grow," Faran said, undeterred.

There was a light knock on the door, and Ava entered. "Empress, Captain Kabir is here for the discussion you wished to have."

Ullani glared at Ubad Faran. "This conversation is not over, Faran."

"As you say, Empress." He gave another half bow and turned on his heels to leave. His attitude did not seem any less arrogant than it had when he arrived. She got the distinct impression that he was trying to goad her into an impulsive response. *Breathe, Ullani.* She calmed herself. *Think it through before you decide how to respond.*

Chapter Forty-Two

Course Correction

The older man shouldered roughly past Micah. "Excuse me," Micah said politely, and the man looked him up and down with an unmasked gaze of disgust before marching down the hall.

"Captain Kabir, if you please." Ava held the door open for him. She maintained an air of confidence and formality. If he didn't know better, he would have thought that she was presenting a mask, afraid to show her true self for fear of being judged. But he had seen her in action and knew better. She was a truly competent warrior and was devoted to her empress.

"Micah, it's good to see you again." Empress Ullani welcomed him with a smile as he entered the throne room. Ullani was already stepping down from the elevated platform where she had been sitting in an ornately carved throne with purple cushions.

"Empress." He nodded his head briefly in greeting and then pointed a thumb in the direction that he'd come. "What was that about?"

Ullani waved a dismissive hand. "Posturing. I'll fill you in while we play." She walked to the side of the room and pulled a hidden lever that opened a door to an adjoining room.

The construction of the door matched the surrounding wall, and Micah would never have known there was a door there. He followed her into a small room decorated with ornate tapestries depicting the history of the empire. In the center of the room was a round table surrounded by several straight-backed chairs. The wei-chi board was already set up in the center of the table. Ullani sat, and Micah chose a chair opposite her.

As they placed their opening stones, Ullani retold the encounter with Ubad Faran.

"He is setting you up," Micah said once Ullani finished explaining. "He's trying to convince you that he is creating a position of strength when, really, he is weakening your position."

"Well, I know that," Ullani said with an overly patient tone that told Micah he didn't need to explain the obvious to her. "My conflict is, how do I continue to use the power and influence of the elders, who clearly disapprove of me, while also advancing egalitarian changes to an inherently patriarchal society. If I can't use this position that I find myself stuck in to make real, meaningful changes, then what's the point?"

Micah smiled, again impressed with her grasp on political intricacies. Her mentor, Sillu Aga, truly had prepared her for a position of leadership even if the intention was not this one. Although he had to admit that dealing with underworld leaders probably wasn't that much different than dealing with political opponents. "I don't know," he said finally.

"Hmm, oh, well. I'll figure something out." She turned her attention back to the board.

"I'm sure you will," he said with confidence.

They completed the game in contemplative silence. She had started with a very unusual strategy of trying to dominate the center of the board while allowing him free reign over the edges. The tactic had not worked in her favor, and he beat her by eighty-five points.

Ullani rolled her shoulders uncomfortably. "This position really isn't the best for my poor back. Would you mind terribly?"

"Of course not," Micah said. A mid-game or post-game massage break had become somewhat of a standard during their encounters. Her gown was plum-colored with a high collar and pleats that ran down the front and a wide belt to accentuate her waist. However, when he circled around behind her, he discovered that it was open-backed, and her dark, luxurious skin was exposed from the collar to the belt. He started with her shoulders and neck, massaging the tight muscles there.

"Do you mind working a little lower?" she asked. "Between my shoulder blades is particularly stiff."

Micah spread his fingers laterally and worked his thumbs into the solid muscles of her back. Her skin felt like silk beneath his fingers, but the smoothness belied the firm strength beneath. His fingers drifted along her ribs as his thumbs reached the base of her shoulder blades.

"Oh, yeah—right there." Ullani arched her back as he reached a knotted muscle along her spine. She continued to study the board and the outcome of the game while he worked.

Micah aligned his fingers parallel to her spine and worked in a kneading motion from the middle of her back down to the edge of her wide belt. Then he turned his hands sideways and pressed firmly with his thumbs while his fingers drifted lightly up her sides. He felt the swell of flesh as his fingertips passed up and under her armpits.

Ullani turned her head, "Getting a bit cheeky, are we?"

Micah jerked his hands back. "Sorry, I didn't mean—"

"It's fine, don't worry about it," she assured him. "My back feels better. Why don't you come around? I've noticed something, and I want your opinion."

Micah's cheeks burned as he resumed his seat opposite Ullani. Over the years, he had watched Moab's many successes and failures with women and had admired his resilience in the face of rejection. Micah, however, never had time for any of that. In the training camps, there had not been any women, and following his sudden promotion after their first campaign, he was more concerned with not letting Emperor Lao down. So, he'd focused his attention on his career rather than his personal life.

His interactions with Ullani over the past month had stimulated feelings that he wasn't sure how to deal with. On one hand, she was intelligent, charismatic, and beautiful. He enjoyed spending time with her. They had a similar determination to succeed, but he also found it easy to talk to her about things that weren't directly related to politics or wei-chi. On the other hand, her interests were in direct conflict with Emperor Lao's, which tore at his loyalties.

"I'm here." She pointed to the black stones in the center of the board. "Even given the advantage of going first, I have no way to overcome an advance from all sides if I let you control the edges."

"Right, you give up your advantage by accepting a weakened position," Micah agreed.

"But if you replace your stones in the east with another color, say purple, as well as this group there to the south, then I've actually played you to a tie around the rest of the board," Ullani said.

Micah laughed. "I suppose so, but the game doesn't work that way."

"It does if there are three players," Ullani affirmed.

"But we don't have three players…it's just the two of us." Micah wasn't following her train of thought.

"Ah, but we do. We have me in the center, Emperor Lao and his allies to the north, west, and south, and the remnants of the baronies to the east. I can't win against all sides, but if I play for a tie against the empire, then it writes a different story. Individually, we are each stronger than the east, and together, we dominate the board."

Micah studied the map and overlaid the current geopolitical

structure in his mind. "So, are you suggesting an alliance with Emperor Lao?"

"Hmm, I'm not sure that's the right word," Ullani said. "But I think you are on the right track. I'd like to bring in Süba to get his opinion."

Ava held open the door as an armed guard arrived, escorting the ragged-looking man in chains.

"Empress!" he exclaimed as soon as he saw her and dropped to his knees. He crawled across the floor, keeping his head lowered until he reached her feet and then he took the hem of her skirt in his hands and began kissing it.

Micah rolled his eyes. He had observed the same behavior from The Prophet during each of their prior meetings with him. Between what Süba had experienced with Darius and Antu and the observation of Ullani's *ascendence*, the man's mind had broken. Micah didn't know what sort of man Süba had been before, but he had a hard time imagining a circumstance that he could be so overwhelmed by superstition to fall to The Prophet's current state. Micah pitied the man but also felt uncomfortable when he was around.

"Empress?" Ava said, letting the unasked question hang in the air.

"I'm fine, Ava. Thank you." She dismissed the guard captain

before turning to the groveling man. "Okay, that's enough, Süba." She pushed him away with a foot.

Süba shuffled away from her and knelt on the floor an arm's length away and pressed his forehead to the ground.

"Süba," Ullani addressed the man softly. "Captain Kabir and I were just discussing the possibility of an accord of sorts with Emperor Lao. Do you think Hurasham would endorse such a thing if it were to happen?"

"Kisha and Antu! Together as one!" Süba shouted. "As it was in the beginning. As it was always meant to be."

"No." Ullani shook her head. "Not as one, as two. A mutually beneficial agreement of some kind."

Süba looked confused.

"If both Emperor Lao and I agreed to set aside our differences and create an alliance, would Hurasham endorse it?"

What she was proposing seemed to penetrate his fanatical mind. His eyes cleared briefly, and he appeared to give the idea serious consideration. Finally, he nodded. "Yes," he stated. "Ours is not to question the will of the gods. If they are to reach an agreement, who are we to disagree?"

"Okay, but what makes you think that Emperor Lao would accept such a proposal?" Micah asked. "In his mind, all of the white stones are his. He controls the position of strength, and it is only a matter of time before your *purple* stones become white."

"Except for the troubles that your brother is causing and the fact that he doesn't control Merkar or the east yet," she interjected.

"Even so, from what you've told me, Darius's actions have been an inconvenience at best. There are multiple routes that the empire can transport supplies, and he hasn't done significant damage to either their forces or their holdings in the province," Micah said.

"He's sure making them look bad, though," Ullani laughed.

"Maybe." He shrugged. "But reputation damage aside, his efforts are superficial. Aside from that, the imperial forces control all of the major towns and cities in Magora, and I eliminated the last vestiges of Baroness Kess's resistance before I came here. General Hamazi controls the bulk of Orlyk and will soon take Kasha Ekur."

"Your confidence in the general is admirable, but I wouldn't count Kasha Ekur out just yet. Rusticar has all but fallen, and he will be hard-pressed to take the city without their aid," Ullani countered. Micah was continuously impressed with how well-informed she seemed to be.

"Be that as it may, Emperor Lao controls nearly three-quarters of the continent. More if you count Hurasham. No offense, Empress, but you control the smallest province, and you are surrounded on all sides by enemies. I'm not sure what you have to offer him."

"The unification of Antu and Kisha!" Süba blurted. His eyes were wide as he glanced nervously back and forth between the two of them. When they didn't respond immediately, he lowered his head in a pout.

"I do have the reliquary," Ullani reminded Micah. "Surely that's something."

"True, but what's to stop him from just coming to reclaim it once Orlyk falls?" Micah asked.

"*If* Orlyk falls," Ullani corrected him.

He rolled his eyes but conceded the point.

Ullani tapped her fingers in a rapid drumming pattern while she considered. "Resources? Manpower?"

Micah couldn't help but laugh. "Empress, you are only just gathering enough to feed your own people and have not yet established significant enough control here to offer anything the province may offer in trade. And besides, Emperor Lao has the vast resources of Shalanum and Magora at his disposal. As far as manpower—again, no offense—what you offer is an undisciplined rabble of fanatics."

"What do you suggest then?" Ullani asked.

"Send me back to Kasha Marka," Micah started. "Give me the reliquary to offer in trade along with your peaceful surrender and let Emperor Lao claim dominion in Chugoku. He may let you maintain your role as provincial leader instead of Baron Harmenos."

"Baron Harmenos is dead," Ullani said.

Micah was shocked at the news but recovered quickly. "All the more reason for him to allow you to stay to provide stability to the region until he can complete the re-establishment of his power elsewhere. I'm sure he would welcome your support, but as a subservient, not as an equal."

Ullani shook her head. "I understand what you're saying, but if I can be honest, I don't think my followers would accept that, and I'm not sure I could control their reactions."

"Undisciplined fanatics," Micah emphasized his previous point.

She opened her hands helplessly. "It's the position we find ourselves in. I may not like it any more than you, but it makes simple surrender impossible. Might I remind you…we've already dismissed it as a possibility."

Micah looked down at The Prophet for a moment, considering him. "You know, I know you've already said no, but he does have a point," Micah suggested. "Emperor Lao is unmarried. We may want to consider—"

"Ew, gross." Ullani's composure broke as she wrinkled her nose. "Isn't he like fifty years old?"

"Forty-something. It's not uncommon for an older man to marry a younger woman, especially among the nobility," Micah explained.

"Oh, I know. I saw plenty of it in Kasha Marka," Ullani said. "That doesn't mean I want to marry an old man."

"Even if it brings about the peace you're hoping for?" Micah asked.

"I don't know." Ullani shook her head. "I rarely saw those relationships work to the benefit of the woman. Some, maybe, but I have no interest in becoming either a trophy or a progenitor. I mean, I may want children someday, but I don't want my only purpose in life to be providing an heir to the throne."

"But—" Micah started.

"If you are about to say, 'you are a woman,' I might just cut your tongue out," Ullani warned.

Micah clamped his mouth shut.

"I've seen how women are treated in Kasha Marka and here among the Merkari. Saria raised me as an equal with my male counterparts, and I have no desire for less," Ullani explained.

Micah sighed. "I'm just not sure what I'm supposed to propose to Emperor Lao. He will be hard to convince that you have anything of value to offer."

"Excuse me!" Ullani exclaimed.

"No, that's not what I meant," Micah backpedaled. "I mean, from a strictly political and military perspective, he has the upper hand, and he knows it."

"Maybe I need to speak to him myself," Ullani grumped.

"He'll never come here!" Micah exclaimed.

"Maybe somewhere else then?" Ullani considered. "Not Kasha Marka…he would have even more advantage there. Somewhere neutral."

Micah shrugged. "I could try to convince him. If you were to let me and my men return to Kasha Marka, I could—"

"You, maybe," Ullani interrupted. "Not your men."

"Why not?" Micah asked.

"Uh, because they tried to assassinate me!"

"We were just following orders," Micah protested.

"Uh-huh, and unless I'm mistaken, those orders still stand. I trust you. I do not trust your men."

"They will do as I say," Micah assured her.

"No. They stay. If nothing else, it will motivate you." Ullani's jaw was firmly set. "Don't worry, they are in no danger, and they will be well cared for."

Micah nodded his understanding. "So, when can I leave?"

Ullani laughed. "In a hurry to give up my hospitality so soon?"

"Such that it is," Micah smiled. "I think I would rather sleep on the open ground than in a closed cell. I understand enough about your interests to discuss with Emperor Lao and present the idea of a rendezvous."

"Ew, that sounds dirty." Ullani wrinkled her nose again. "Perhaps a *convention*."

"That makes it sound like others would attend," Micah said.

"Maybe they should," Ullani suggested. "Maybe we should try to bring an end to all of this mess at the same time with representatives from the baronies, myself, and Emperor Lao."

"It's worth a try," Micah said. "I can't promise anything."

"No one is asking you to," Ullani said.

Ullani watched Micah leave. She had to admit she would

miss his company. It was nice to have someone she could speak frankly with. She squeezed the junction between her neck and shoulder, massaging the tight muscles there. *I'll also miss his strong hands*, she thought with a smile. It may have also been interesting to see how far she could guide those cheeky impulses of his for a little fun.

Autumn – 37 A.E.

Chapter Forty-Three

Reckoning

Darius dug his heels into the flanks of his mare, willing her to move faster. He leaned forward as she burst through a pair of juniper trees. The rough branches scraped his arms as they passed. He ventured a glance over his shoulder. Antu was keeping pace casily, doing a better job of dodging the trees and rocks than Darius was. Behind them, his men were spread out across the hillside driving south.

Smoke rose from the plains behind them in roiling gray billows. The fire was spreading quickly, and he knew that it would chase them uphill faster than they could move once it reached the slope. They had to reach the ridge before the fire caught them.

Darius pulled on the reins to guide the horse around a boulder, only to be slapped in the face by an overhanging branch on the other side. He chastised himself silently. He should have known that the convoy was too good to be true. Twenty wagons, lightly guarded. *Stupid, stupid,* he thought over and over.

Hubris had led him directly into the imperials' trap. As soon as Darius and his men attacked, enemy soldiers had risen up from hidden pits north of the camp and set fire to the dry grasslands behind them and on either side. Their only route for escape was the steep hillside to the south.

Darius was the first to reach the ridge, and he charged over it. He leaned back suddenly and pulled on the reins to slow his horse so that she didn't topple over on the sudden decline. Several riders behind him were not as cautious, and he heard cries of distress as horse and rider somersaulted down the hill or as riders were thrown when the horses made their own decision to slow and the men weren't prepared.

He angled past a stand of fir trees. As he did, he was given the first clear view of the narrow valley that rested between this and the next ridge. Horsemen were marching in an orderly fashion out of the trees on the far side, several hundred in all. His heart jumped.

How did our scouts miss a force that size? he thought.

He surveyed the landscape. The imperials couldn't have picked a better spot for an ambush. The ridge he had just crossed angled southeast, joining the rim of the other at a point half a league to the east. The hill opposite was just as steep and covered with debris as the one he had just climbed, but there was little chance to reach it before the imperial riders reached them.

To the west, the valley widened and afforded more room to maneuver, but the woods on the western end were dense. He judged the distance. It was no better than the ride to the ridge, but it would be better than being cornered in a box canyon or trying to climb a hill while imperial archers picked them off at leisure.

Making a decision, he angled west. Not so much that his horse would have difficulty running sideways along the slope but enough that he would be even with the midpoint of the imperial lines once he reached the valley floor. He glanced nervously at the numbers of imperial horsemen that continued to enter the valley and kicked his heels, urging more speed from his mount.

Darius risked another glance behind him and saw that half the riders were trying to remount their horses or were traveling on foot. The other half had changed direction to follow him. Antu was slightly uphill and loping along easily.

The imperial lines had formed up in the center of the valley and were making a slow, steady march forward, lances held at rest. Once Darius reached the flatter ground, he angled parallel to the hill. The imperial horsemen increased speed to a canter. His heart hammered in his chest as he dug into the horse's flanks, encouraging her to a gallop.

As more of Darius's men joined him at the foot of the hill, Darius heard a trumpet sound. The horsemen lowered their lances and charged. Darius slowed slightly as he held his right hand high above his head and gripped his reins with his left. He could only hope that his troops would be able to follow his lead in time.

Darius judged the speed and distance of the approaching riders. *Wait for it*, he mentally told himself. Then he thrust his arm to the side, pointing uphill, and then pulled right on the reins and pressed his knee firmly into the side of his mount. The horse jerked slightly but then thundered up the hill back toward the smoke.

Darius breathed a sigh of relief when the lance struck the hillside a few paces below him and showered him and his horse with sprays of dirt. The unprepared rider was jerked abruptly from the saddle. He heard a few cries of surprise as other imperial riders did the same, but he heard just as many cries of anguish as lances struck his men. Those who had shields at the ready fared better but just barely as the force of the perpendicular attack pushed them from their saddles.

An arrow flew past Darius to strike another rider, and he looked uphill. Rose waved at him. She had rejoined him more than a month before when her position along the road to Isan became untenable. The added force of her archers allowed them to be more ambitious with their raids.

More archers, who had mostly been on foot, were starting to arrive at the top of the ridge. Smoke and the light of the fire covered the skyline behind them like the macabre painted backdrop of some tragic traveling play.

The imperials regrouped and began following Darius and his men up the hill. Lances were discarded in place of swords. Darius and his men drew their weapons and prepared to defend themselves as they fled. More arrows began to fill the air. Most struck the ground harmlessly, but those who found home easily penetrated the hardened black leather armor of the imperial soldiers.

The archers moved downhill and west between each shot, closing the range and putting more distance between themselves and the fire. Darius could see the first flames licking the lower branches of trees along the ridge. He signaled to his men to reform as he turned his horse back to the east. Thirty riders were able to group together in a tight defensive formation around him. He signaled an advance, and they attacked, using their elevation to their advantage. He pressed toward the right flank of the emperor's soldiers, trying to break the line to clear a path to the relative safety of the forest.

A second group of riders started to assemble uphill to the west. As Darius and his group finished their attack, the second group charged at the same side. Darius circled his men back up the slope to regroup farther west. The archers focused their fire on the back lines of the same side, trying to weaken the flank.

Following the second such attack, Darius's forces were reduced enough that they had to join into a single defending force. The tree line was in sight, however, and another strong push would see them into cover. Once they were in the forest, the imperial troops would no longer be able to form into strong attack lines, but neither would Darius's archers be able to provide cover fire.

Darius pressed forward, driving his sword through the leather breastplate of a cavalry officer in front of him. The sound of steel on steel and steel on flesh echoed around him. He pressed forward again, his men following, and suddenly, the line broke. They charged through the gap, making for the woods.

The archers lined up a final, deadly volley at the center of the imperial lines and then began running along the slope in the same direction.

Darius dodged around a tree and slashed down on the arm of a black-clad rider. He turned his horse again to pierce the back of a second soldier. He charged through a narrow glen and then circled back to attack the side of another soldier who was attacking one of his men. It was impossible to see how many of his troops had made it into the woods. He also could no longer see what had become of his bowmen. Imperial riders were everywhere. Darius would dodge, and strike, heel his horse to add distance, only to be cut off by another rider.

Then, as suddenly as they had entered the forest, they burst free on the other side into a wide-open plain. Darius groaned. He had been hoping to take advantage of the cover for longer. As he exited the trees, he saw another rider exit several paces away. The rider's sword was slick with blood, and he was dressed in the finery of an imperial general.

On impulse, Darius turned his horse and charged. There was a momentary look of surprise on the officer's face before he wheeled his horse to respond. They were approaching on the sword side.

Darius studied the way the soldier sat upon the horse and how he held his sword. He saw an opening and prepared to exploit it when, suddenly, the general pulled his reins to the right, switching to shield side at the last moment. Darius didn't have a shield and had to adjust quickly and awkwardly to block the blow. He nearly fell from his saddle as he twisted.

Both men turned their horses and began a second charge. Darius was aware of more soldiers, both imperial and Shadow Crown, emerging from the woods. They didn't immediately engage each other as their eyes were drawn to the battle between the two generals in the center of the field.

They charged sword-side again, and Darius prepared for the last-minute change, but instead, the general attacked with two quick strikes from his blade. The first knocked Darius's sword to the side just enough to create an opening, and the second scored a glancing blow on his right shoulder. The second attack didn't have much force behind it, but Darius felt warmth spreading from the point of impact and could tell that he was bleeding.

I have to get him on the ground, Darius thought. *He outmatches me mounted.*

As they rode at each other again, Darius turned his horse to block the path of the other horse. The general's mount pulled to a stop before the collision. His opponent tried to maneuver his horse free, but Darius kept them close together so that he could strike at close range rather than on the charge. The older soldier had both sword and shield, so he was able to easily block Darius's attacks, but Darius had the advantage of youth and size, and his blows were starting to wear the other man down.

Finally, a forceful blow against his shield unbalanced his enemy, and Darius was able to follow up with two quick strikes that caused the imperial to start to slip in the saddle. A murmur rose from the gathering crowd, and with a final vicious thrust from Darius, the other man slid backwards out of his saddle and crashed to the ground. A collective moan filled the air from the surrounding soldiers, both in sympathy for the force of the landing but also in worry at the clear advantage Darius now held.

Rather than seize the perceived advantage, Darius heard murmurs of surprise as he dismounted. He shooed the horses away while the older officer collected himself and rose to his feet. For the first time, Darius noticed that the general carried a second sword slung across his back. However, as he rose, rather than draw the second weapon, he checked his shield. He seemed satisfied with its integrity and moved toward him. Darius, however, did draw his second blade and waited in a ready defense.

"So, you are *the apprentice?*" The general spoke for the first time and slowly circled, looking for an opening.

Darius was surprised and it took him a moment to respond. "I suppose you could call me that."

The general looked him up and down, inspecting his swords, stance, and attire. Then the officer sneered. "How appropriate that a gutter rat like Alamay would take another of his kind under his wing."

Finally, it struck Darius—the man's finery, his air of command, and the obvious contempt that he held for Arthengal. "You must be General Sharav."

"That's Commander General Sharav to you. It's time you were taught a lesson and put in your rightful place." Sharav attacked suddenly in the middle of his sentence.

Darius was prepared and defended with Lazy Viper. It was a tactic designed for use with a shield but worked just as well with two swords. The general attacked with the shield variation of Striking Adder. His form was efficient and concise. Darius began to worry that he may not have the advantage on the ground. After a couple of attacks, Darius switched to Willows in the Wind, using the two blades to alternatively block and attack. This turned out to be a mistake as Sharav charged forward and easily broke through his defense.

Darius was driven back a few steps and the crowd of imperial soldiers cheered.

He's good, Darius thought as sweat beaded on his forehead. He realized that his adapted single sword or sword and shield forms were not going to be adequate, so he switched to a dual-weapon stance.

Darius attacked first with The Hawk and The Dove. The general countered the high strikes easily with the shield but struggled to block the low blows and was forced to give up ground. Darius felt a surge of confidence at the success of the attack, but it was short-lived.

"Alamay has taught you well." Even the compliment felt condescending to Darius. "But it won't matter, you will die here today as will your little rebellion."

"We'll see." Darius changed tactics again and went on the offensive with the quickly alternating slashes and thrusts of Twin Dervishes. The general was placed on the defensive. Darius felt a momentary glimmer of hope but then realized from the expression on the officer's face that he was only using the opportunity to study Darius's movements and wear himself out. His heart sank as he realized the tactic was working. Darius could already feel his arms beginning to tire from the high-energy attack.

His elbow dropped slightly, and the opposing general struck. He stepped to the left, taking Darius's right blade on his shield and then thrust under Darius's guard. Darius managed to turn to the side at the last moment and the sharp blade only managed to score a long slash on his side rather than pierce his ribs. It was Darius's turn to disengage and circle defensively.

A cruel smile crossed General Sharav's lips. He attacked with a powerful overhand strike. Darius blocked the attack with crossed blades but then Sharav leaned into the attack adding the weight of his shield. Sharav bore down on him. Darius was surprised by the other man's strength. The initial blow almost forced Darius's knee to the ground. As the imperial pressed forward, Darius felt his feet slipping. He needed to act fast or he would be driven to the ground.

He relented slightly and then twisted to the left and let the momentum of the general's attack carry him past on his right. Darius switched to a combination of blows that targeted his opponent's sword and shield rather than trying to breach their defense. He followed with a sweeping attack that forced the general to block low and move slightly off balance. Before Sharav could recover his footing, Darius spun with a double-bladed strike that shattered the general's shield.

There were cheers from shadow soldiers and moans of despair from the imperials. However, Darius surprised the crowd again by stepping back and allowing his opponent to free himself from the broken shield and draw his second sword. It was not an unselfish move, even if the onlookers didn't realize it. Darius needed to catch his breath and flex his tired shoulders. He also took the chance for a quick glance at his side. The wound was bleeding but not as badly as he had feared. His breathing returned to normal, and his heart slowed slightly in the time it took the opposing general to reset his gear.

General Sharav held his two swords aloft. "Do you like my weapons? Do they seem at all *familiar?*"

At first, he hadn't noticed. The swords were well-constructed, utilitarian blades without much in the way of accoutrements. But now that the general mentioned it and held the swords out for inspection, Darius noticed the familiar cross guards, the worn comfortable hilt wrapping, and the slight nick near the point of the second blade that Darius had never quite been able to smooth out.

"Those are my swords," Darius said angrily.

General Sharav laughed. "A gift from Emperor Lao. They are good blades, and I appreciate the nostalgia of claiming something that had always been so highly valued by Alamay. But now, it seems, I have the opportunity to win the right to wield them as well by defeating their former owner."

Darius growled but refused to be goaded into an impetuous attack. He slipped into a defensive stance while he struggled to force his anger down. He used slighter movements, taking the chance to extend his rest and assess the other man's form. Darius quickly realized that the imperial general was not trained in dual weapons. Similar to what Darius had done when he was first learning, he merely adapted the single-weapon forms to his needs.

General Sharav was clearly a master and matched Darius stroke for stroke, but Darius began to see the gaps in defense that Lord Misrak had pointed out in Kasha Marka. After more than two years of practice with dual weapons, Darius saw that the small things he had always thought he was accommodating for were the glaring holes in form that they actually were.

Darius switched cautiously to the two-weapon offensive

forms. He attacked warily at first to see if his opponent was disguising his skill on purpose. He was not. Darius breached the defense of Lazy Viper and scored a strike at the elbow in the gap between the shoulder pad and the bracer.

This slowed the general's responses and Darius used the next opening to slash at the thigh just below the padded skirt. Darius dented the conical helmet and opened holes in the leather armor to expose the chain shirt underneath. Darius attacked again with The Hawk and The Dove, but his opponent anticipated the low slash this time and locked up Darius's left blade with both of his. The general twisted violently, applying opposing pressure with the two swords, and snapped Darius's sword in two, leaving him a much-shortened weapon.

General Sharav laughed again. "It seems we near the end."

Darius took a step back to readjust his posture. Thanks to Cheung Po's repetitive drilling, he was able to change his strategy to a sword and dagger defense. He saw the look of surprise on Sharav's face as he countered his next attack easily. Darius blocked and dodged, watching for another gap in the general's form.

Then, as the imperial attacked with a series of alternating thrusts and slashes, Darius recognized the form and anticipated the opening that he had been waiting for. The sweeping block of Sun and Moon lifted his opponent's left arm with his fractured blade just enough as he twisted in the form to expose the narrow gap above the chest armor in the armpit. Darius thrust the second blade with as much force as he could muster. The other man cried out as the sword struck the tender flesh, then Darius leaned into the blow. Sharav's eyes went wide as the steel of the weapon penetrated his heart.

There was a gasp from the crowd as the imperial general slumped to his knees. Both of his weapons clattered to the ground. There was a brief look of confusion on his face before his eyes glazed over and he fell to the ground dead.

Darius didn't notice what happened next because his eyes were focused on the two weapons that had fallen from the general's grasp. Shadow Crown archers formed up at the far end of the valley where they had emerged from the wooded hillside. Soldiers and horsemen aligned themselves to protect the archers and prepared to engage the imperial troops as Darius discarded his own weapons and enfolded his fingers around the leather-wrapped hilts.

Imperial soldiers began to fade into the trees first in ones and twos and then in larger groups. Even though they still outnumbered the shadow soldiers by two to one, the defeat of their general had broken their morale. Imperial officers tried to take charge and rally the troops as Darius felt the smooth texture that molded perfectly to his hands. A shudder ran through him as he felt the familiar grip and the perfectly distributed weight.

The efforts of the imperial officers were in vain as more soldiers fled, but Darius didn't notice as he reverently held aloft the blades that had shaped his hands and his form for half a decade. He glanced quickly at the general's attire, looking for the telltale scabbards with the web of silver and gold threads and the embossed head of a roaring bear, but they had been replaced by a more standard imperial issue.

Darius flexed his wrists, rotating the blades in opposing circles. Tears filled his eyes as he remembered years of training with Arthengal using these very weapons. Finally, he looked up. He noticed the half-cleared field. He saw the imperial officers trying to rally their troops. He caught the eye of one such officer, and his gaze caused the man to stop mid-sentence, frozen by the intensity of Darius's glare.

Darius took a step forward. The officer glanced briefly at his retreating army and then back at Darius before turning his horse to ride south, away from the field. Other officers followed suit now, and once the officers started to retreat, the rest of the imperial army fled in a full rout.

Shadow Crown soldiers cheered and began chanting Darius's name. "Dar-i-us, Dar-i-us, Dar-i-us."

The noise drifted over Darius, and he watched with satisfaction as the enemy troops fled. He sheathed Arthengal's blades, leaving the other two swords discarded on the bloodied grass. He felt warm breath and then a wet muzzle against his hand. He looked down and then smiled as he scratched Antu's broad head.

Chapter Forty-Four

Devastated

Lao Jun's hand trembled as he accepted the written report from General Kalin. He managed to maintain strength in his voice as he spoke. "Leave me to consider the impact of this news, General. Please send for Guo Wen on your way out."

Once the general had left, Jun collapsed in his chair. He read the news again, hardly believing it. Commander General Sharav was dead, killed during a conflict with the Hand of the Shadow. Slain by the enemy commander, who, by the description, could be none other than Darius Kabir.

Waves of grief passed over him as he struggled to maintain his composure. He was surprised by the intensity of the emotion. Sengiin Sharav had been a surrogate father to him after the fall of Emperor Chen's empire, but their relationship was always a complex one. He had disagreed with Sharav's stance on many political issues, but he was a strong commander and loyal to a fault. Jun had not missed Sharav's presence in Kasha Marka, but now that he was gone, he found, to his astonishment, that he missed him intensely.

There was a brief knock at the chamber door, and Guo Wen admitted himself.

"Sharav is dead," Jun said simply.

The surprise of the news took Guo Wen off guard, and he started coughing violently before he could respond. He raised a kerchief to his mouth, and Jun was sure he spotted red stains on the cloth before the older man stuffed it in a pocket.

"That is disturbing news," Guo Wen said once he had recovered. "Do we know how?"

"By all accounts, he was killed by Arthengal's apprentice," Jun explained.

"What was he doing leading forces that far from the capital city?" Guo Wen asked.

Emperor Lao shrugged and felt a pang of guilt as he spoke. "I guess he took my last admonishment personally and decided to take a direct hand in eliminating the threat of Shadow Crown."

"Do not blame yourself for Sharav's error in judgment," Guo Wen said, responding to the momentary look of pain on Jun's face.

"I don't." But even as he said the words, he could taste the lie in them. Then he felt a surge of anger at Sharav for being stupid enough to put himself at risk like that, and said more resolutely, "I don't."

"Did they at least kill the Kabir boy as a result?" Guo Wen asked.

"No," Jun said shortly. More anger welled inside. "The

commanders report that they 'withdrew from the field of battle to regroup and reorganize following the untimely death of the commander general.'"

"They ran," Guo Wen said, and then cut off any further reply as he started coughing again.

"Are you okay?" Jun asked with genuine concern in his voice.

Guo Wen held up a finger and nodded until he could speak again. "Yes, I'm fine. This troublesome cough just won't go away."

"It's been months, uncle. Have you seen the royal physician?" Jun asked.

"Yes, of course. They gave me a tincture of poppy and ginger to soothe the throat and a eucalyptus and horehound mixture to clear the lungs. It's just not working as quickly as I'd like. I'm not thirty anymore—it takes a bit longer at my age to recover."

Jun nodded uncertainly. "If you say so." Then he changed the subject. "What do you recommend we do in Shalanum?"

"Where are we at with the rest of the operations?"

"The Hand of the Shadow has been cleared out of most other areas. Only the group on the border to the north continues to cause trouble. And the pirates, of course, but they're another story."

"How so?" Guo Wen asked.

"They terrorize the Sea of Tears but don't seem to have a home base of operations that we can locate. They haven't ported at Lenwall Reach in months, and their ships are faster than ours. They have been making Admiral Kasumi look like a fool, and they continue to raid enough supplies from merchant ships to sustain themselves."

"Can General Nowak take command in Shalanum?" Guo Wen asked. "He is next in succession after Hamazi."

Jun shrugged, "He is old and complacent. There is a reason we put him in charge of Eridu and didn't bring him here. We could recall General Volkov to take over."

"Not advised, nephew," Guo Wen shook his head. "General Hamazi will need him in Orlyk. What about General Kalin?"

"Perhaps." Lao Jun hadn't considered that. He relied on Kalin to administer Magora in Hamazi's absence, but he would be easier to replace than Sharav.

Guo Wen started coughing again. Jun waited for it to pass but the hacking continued. Guo Wen put a hand on the table for support while he held his handkerchief to his mouth. Emperor Jun rose and crossed to his uncle. He placed a hand on his shoulder and searched the older man's eyes in concern.

Guo Wen caught his breath briefly and pulled the cloth away from his mouth. It was soaked with blood.

"Guards!" Emperor Lao shouted. The doors opened immediately, and soldiers appeared, ready to respond. "Fetch the physicians!"

He guided Guo Wen to a chair as spasms wracked his body again. He fetched some water from a nearby pitcher and held it out for his uncle. Guo Wen tried to drink, but the coughing fits wouldn't allow him time.

When the physician arrived, he knelt at Guo Wen's feet and examined his face. He pressed an ear to the old man's chest and listened, then examined the bloody cloth. "Majesty, we need to get him to his bed immediately."

Lao Jun nodded and waved a couple of guards over to help the doctor. They lifted the old man and carried him from the room.

Jun paced endlessly for the next several hours. The light from the windows faded from midday to late afternoon. Finally, there was a knock on the chamber door. He broke all decorum and rushed across the room to fling the doors open himself.

The physician was standing there with a grave look on his face. "I'm sorry, majesty. We did everything we could. Eucalyptus vapors, poppy tinctures, even leeching, but Minister Guo did not respond to our ministrations. I'm afraid he has passed."

The news hit Lao Jun like a charging bull. He struggled to catch his breath, and he found it impossible to focus on a single thought. The doctor's words became a buzzing in his ears. Lao Jun didn't feel his knees give way, but he did feel the impact of the floor. The doctor's shouts were a distant whisper compared to the pounding in his ears.

His mind was blank with shock. The impossibility of losing both Sharav and Guo Wen in a single day overwhelmed him. He felt his head shaking from side to side as if his body expressed the denial that he couldn't force his mouth to voice. Hands grabbed him under his arms and his feet dragged along the floor. The guards deposited him carefully in his chair and the doctor knelt to examine him, looking for injury. More shouting and waving from the doctor were lost on him. Lao Jun was lifted again and carried to the chamber beyond where he sometimes rested between meetings.

The guards arranged him comfortably on the narrow bed. He accepted the cup of tea that the doctor offered him and sipped it mindlessly. A warmth passed over him, and his eyelids grew heavy. He relaxed into the pillows of the bed and welcomed the warm comfort of slumber.

"Emperor?" The physician's assistant spoke again.

Micah looked at the emperor's sleeping body with concern. He stirred at the sound of the assistant's voice but didn't seem to break himself out of slumber. "What's wrong with him?" Micah asked.

"Nothing to be concerned about," the assistant answered. "Doctor Alvida has been putting a little laudanum in his ginger tea to help him sleep. The shock of his uncle's death was quite traumatic."

Emperor Lao's eyes fluttered open slowly. Micah saw a look of confusion on Lao Jun's face when his eyes settled on the assistant. Then, confusion shifted to relief as the emperor shifted his gaze to Micah. "You're back," he said weakly, and a small smile crept onto his lips.

"Emperor Lao, Captain Kabir is here and says he must speak with you," the attendant said.

Jun nodded and waved the attendant away. "Is she dead?" Emperor Lao croaked as soon as the assistant left the room.

"No, majesty," Captain Kabir said.

Lao Jun's brow furrowed. "Of course, she isn't. Why would she be? That would mean the gods had decided to show him favor for once in this dismal week." Lao Jun turned away from Micah and buried his face in his pillow.

Micah was worried by Emperor Lao's reaction. He heard the news that both General Sharav and Minister Guo had died almost immediately after his arrival. Micah expected the emperor to be angry or depressed, but this complete lack of emotion and apathetic response was unexpected.

He quietly exited the room so as not to disturb the emperor and approached the physician's assistant in the foyer. "I think the medicine is having an ill effect on the emperor. It's dulling his wits. We need to stop."

"He is still suffering from shock," the assistant said in a condescending tone. "Doctor Alvida is helping him deal with a great loss. You shouldn't concern yourself. Soon enough, Emperor Lao will be right as rain."

"You need to stop," Micah stated more fervently. "We need the emperor at full capacity now. There are many important matters that need his attention."

"General Kalin is handling matters of the state while the emperor rests, *Captain*," the doctor's assistant said. "If you have anything to discuss, you can discuss it with him. Leave the medical care of the emperor to those who know what they're doing."

Micah wanted to punch the pompous man in the nose, but he resisted. Instead, he sought out General Kalin.

He found the general's offices and was forced by the general's aide to sit on the benches outside with the other petitioners. Hours went by before he was finally admitted. General Kabir sat behind a desk littered with reports and maps. The general's eyes were rimmed red, and he looked like he hadn't slept in days.

General Kalin glanced up when Micah entered. "What is it, Captain?"

"Sir, I am concerned about the emperor," Micah said.

"We all are," Kalin said shortly.

"No, I mean, I think the doctors are giving him too much medicine, and it's dulling his mind. I have news from Kasha Esharra that demand his attention, but he needs to be sharp. There are—"

"You can deliver your report to me, Captain Kabir," Kalin cut him off. "I assure you it will receive its due attention."

Micah hesitated before deciding to proceed. "Empress Ullani has a proposal of sorts that she—"

"*Empress* Ullani?" Kalin stopped him short again. "The pretense of such a title is treasonous. Does the pretender wish to surrender?"

"No, but—"

"Then what could she possibly propose that would be of interest to *Emperor* Lao?" Kalin emphasized.

Micah did not know General Kalin well. He wasn't sure if the general's reactions came from a place of loyalty, hubris, or exhaustion. But it was clear General Kalin wasn't seeing the whole picture. "She proposes an alliance of sorts. It could end the war peacefully."

"Ridiculous!" General Kalin shouted. "We will end this war when the barons and your pretender bow at the feet of the one true emperor, and he takes his rightful place on the throne in Kasha Esharra."

"Things hang in the balance right now, General Kalin," Micah tried to explain. "Please, the barons have the Rusticari on the run in the east. Kasha Libbu has fallen, and Empress Ullani's forces are prepared to spread into Merkar, which may pose a danger to Magora. General Hamazi is facing an impossible task in Orlyk."

"You overstep, Captain Kabir, and speak of things above your authority," General Kalin said. "General Hamazi will soon be victorious at Kasha Ekur. He will mop up the remnants of the rebels in the east and then deal with the pretender. Your doubt is *concerning*."

Hubris, then, Micah thought. His mind raced, trying to think of something that would force the general to reconsider. He came up blank. Then a desperate thought entered his mind. "Of course, general." Micah bowed in deference. "I will leave you to your duties, then."

The general nodded dismissively, and Micah exited the room.

With long, quick strides Micah retraced his steps back to the emperor's quarters. He strode past the assistant still sitting outside the bedchamber.

"Where do you think you're going?" the idiot aide asked.

"Urgent news from General Kalin," Micah said shortly and then opened the door to enter.

"His Majesty needs to rest," the man protested.

Micah turned on the man with anger in his eyes. "Do you question the orders of General Kalin?"

"No, but—"

"Then mind your business and let matters of the state be dealt with by those who know what they're doing." Micah threw the man's words back in his face, hoping he would back down.

He did. The balding man grumbled and then returned to his seat.

Micah closed the door behind him and threw the bolt. Then, for good measure, he took a sturdy wooden chair and wedged it under the door's handle.

Emperor Lao looked up wearily, "What are you doing, Captain Kabir?"

"It's okay, Your Majesty. I'm here to help," Micah

responded.

The emperor gave an unconcerned sigh and then settled back into his blankets and closed his eyes.

Several hours later, there was a banging at the door. "Who locked this door?" a shout came from outside.

"Emperor Lao does not wish to be disturbed at this time," Micah shouted back.

"It is time for his elixirs. Open the door," the command came.

"Leave it outside. I'll retrieve it shortly. Emperor Lao is busy at the moment," Micah answered.

"Nonsense." The disbelief was clear in the voice. "Open this door at once."

"Do you question the orders of your emperor?" Micah shouted back. "Leave the medicine and return to your other duties, Doctor."

There was a brief pause, and Micah could hear a low conversation on the other side of the door. "Very well, but I will be back in an hour to check on him. See that he drinks his tonics."

The shouting had woken Emperor Lao, who now sat up in his bed. He looked confused and his eyes drooped with exhaustion. "What are you doing here, Captain Kabir?"

"It's all right, Your Majesty. Go back to sleep. I'll take care of you," Micah responded.

The emperor looked at him dully. Micah noticed a sheen of

perspiration had started to form on the emperor's brow. He looked

pale. Micah thought for a moment that Emperor Lao was going to

protest, but instead, he collapsed into his bed with an unintelligible

murmur.

Micah pressed his ear to the door. He didn't hear anything, so

he moved the chair, unbolted the door, and opened it quickly. A

bewildered assistant still sat in his chair. Micah stooped to pick up

the tray at the threshold and then closed and secured the door.

He placed the tray on a table at the far end of the room and

then moved a chair to sit by the emperor's bedside.

An hour later, the knocking came again, and the handle

rattled. "Your Majesty, it's Doctor Alvida."

Micah rushed to the door. He opened it a crack and put his

face in the opening. He scanned the hallway outside. The doctor and

the assistant were alone. "Shh," he hushed the doctor. "Emperor Lao

is resting and doesn't wish to be disturbed."

The doctor tried to push his way in, but Micah held a foot

firmly at the base of the door to prevent it from moving. "Let me in,

Captain. I must examine my patient."

"No," Micah said simply in a muted tone. "He took his

medicine as you suggested, and now he is resting. He said you could

come back in the morning."

"What? No," the doctor insisted. "I must—"

"Go away," Micah hissed. "Emperor Lao was very clear that

no one was to be admitted. I will perform my duty with the utmost efficiency, *Doctor.*"

Doctor Alvida's eyes widened at the clear threat. "We'll see what General Kalin has to say about this," he huffed and then spun on his heels to stomp away.

Shit, Micah silently swore. Then he bolted the door and secured the chair.

As it turned out, General Kalin had very little to say on the matter, at least not that night, for the doctor never returned. In all likelihood, he was still waiting outside the general's office for an audience. Micah watched the emperor diligently all night. Lao Jun tossed uncomfortably in his blankets and sweat soaked his pillows. His fever broke in the early morning just before dawn and he settled into a more comfortable rest.

The first rays of sun were peeking through the windows when the knocking came again at the door. "Your Majesty, it's Doctor Alvida. I must speak to you immediately."

Micah returned to the door and spoke through the closed oak panels. "Emperor Lao is resting again, Doctor. He was up earlier, and we discussed the situation," he lied, "But now he is resting again."

"Captain Kabir," the commanding tone of General Kalin penetrated the thick wood. "Open this door immediately."

"My apologies, General. The emperor's orders were not to admit anyone and not to disturb his rest," Micah answered.

"Fetch the guard." Micah heard General Kalin's command.

"Break it down."

Micah swore under his breath. He glanced around the room frantically, and his eyes fell on a heavy mahogany dresser. He pushed it toward the door. He was sure the men on the other side could hear the unpleasant screeching of the feet grinding along the floorboards. He moved the chair that was blocking the handle and pushed the dresser into place to block the door.

Moments later, there was a pounding at the door. "Open the door, Captain Kabir."

When Micah didn't respond, there was a loud crash on the other side. The crash came again, and Micah could see the frame begin to split. Micah rushed to the emperor's side and shook him gently. "Emperor Lao."

The crash came again, and the frame buckled. The door opened fractionally before it was blocked by the chest of drawers. "Your Majesty, wake up," Micah pleaded and shook him more vigorously.

Several men on the other side of the door pressed against it. The heavy furniture groaned as it slowly slid out of the way. "Emperor Lao!" Micah shouted desperately.

Soldiers poured through the opening and swarmed Micah. They quickly subdued him and pressed him to the floor. Micah felt the cold metal of shackles as his hands were roughly bound behind his back. "Your Majesty!" he shouted one more time as he was hauled to his feet.

They were dragging him toward the ruined door when a weak voice stopped them. "Wait."

All eyes turned to Emperor Lao as he pushed himself into a sitting position. He looked tired but his eyes were clearer than they had been the day before.

"Your Majesty, this traitor," General Kalin pointed to Micah, "has been holding you captive all night. We will deal with him. You need not worry."

Lao Jun Qiu settled his eyes on the general. When he spoke, he sounded exhausted, but the tone of command was unmistakable. "I said wait, General."

"Your Majesty," General Kalin protested.

"General, there are few that I would trust more with my life than Captain Kabir. He is loyal to a fault. He has been on special assignment in Kasha Esharra at my personal command, and I will hear what he has to say." Emperor Lao's voice became stronger as he spoke.

General Kalin looked dumbfounded. It was clear that he had not been informed about Micah's mission and was at a loss for words. "But, majesty," he pleaded.

"Unbind his shackles and leave us, General," Emperor Lao commanded.

"Your Majesty, this man has withheld your elixirs," Doctor Alvarez spoke. "It is important that your treatment continues. The shock from your loss—"

"I'm fine, Doctor," Emperor Lao spoke confidently. "I appreciate your ministrations, but it is time for me to set my grief aside and resume my duties to the empire. That will start with my hearing Captain Kabir's report on events in Chugoku."

The general and the doctor looked at each other, trying to find an argument, but Lao Jun didn't give them the chance. "Leave us!" His voice was strong, and the commanding tone was sure.

"Yes, Your Majesty," the two men said in unison.

General Kalin removed Micah's shackles and led the soldiers from the room, closing the door behind him as well as it would.

"Now, Captain." Emperor Lao turned his tired eyes to Micah. "Whatever you have to tell me must be important indeed to cause this sort of ruckus."

Chapter Forty-Five

Convocation

Emperor Lao leaned back against the pillows on his bed as Captain Kabir finished relaying the bulk of his discussions with the leader of the Cult of Kisha. He was feeling better. More than two weeks had passed since Captain Kabir's dramatic return, and Lao Jun found that his appetite had returned and his mind was not covered by a perpetual fog.

"Your assessment of the situation is impressive," Emperor Lao complimented the young captain after he finished his report. He tugged on the point of his mustache while he thought. "If we press our advance in Orlyk, General Hamazi may very well be tied up until spring with an extended siege. On the other hand, if we pull his forces back to Magora, it gives the barons room to unify their forces and advance once Rusticar falls completely."

"It is more Empress Ullani's assessment than mine," Micah admitted. "Her ability to see the whole picture is incredible."

"Don't sell yourself short, my boy," Emperor Lao said. "I see your hand in the tactical evaluation as well."

"Remember too that Ullani grew up in Magora and has ties to the palace. If we don't figure out a way to ally with her, then Bedria Kess may," Micah added. Emperor Lao saw the captain's cheeks color slightly at the compliment.

"I wish Ito would commit," Lao Jun said. "With his forces combined with Hurasham's navy, there would be no contest, and the Aengals and their allies would be forced to surrender. However, my cousin has been adamant in his refusal to take sides in this conflict. It is a matter of honor for him, and he holds loyalty to both sides."

"Likewise, a clash between Empress Ullani and the Merkari may not end in our favor. Most of her followers are from Merkar, and they may turn the country to her side," Micah said. "If Merkar, Ullani, and the barons united in the center of the country, they would be very difficult to overcome, especially with natural barriers to the north and west."

"Her proposal for an alliance is an interesting one. I'm just not sure it's worth the cost we would pay," Lao Jun said. He found himself missing the council of Guo Wen, whose insight had been invaluable in situations like this. Without thinking, he voiced the thought and noticed that Captain Kabir shifted uncomfortably in his chair. Lacking both Guo Wen and Sengiin Sharav's company, Emperor Lao found himself confiding in the young officer more than what was probably appropriate. He had no doubts about Captain Kabir's discretion, however, and found it helped him to be able to voice his feelings with someone he trusted.

"In what way, majesty?" Micah asked.

"Based on what you have described, she seems committed to maintaining some vestiges of power. And I agree that, without her leadership to guide them, the zealots that follow her would run amok and create havoc. Religious wars are messy and tend to do more damage to both sides than good. It's best that we try to prevent that from happening." Emperor Lao tugged on his mustache again.

"You have an idea?" Micah asked.

"You say she is opposed to uniting the empires through marriage?" Lao Jun asked.

Micah's face betrayed a certain discomfort while he considered his response. "She is afraid that it would diminish her power. She is reluctant to let go of the reforms that she has implemented amongst her people. I think she feels that a marriage where she is not the dominant member would work against her."

Emperor Lao nodded, accepting the answer. It was a logical concern. "If we were to unite our kingdoms without a binding union, then inevitably, there would be division. Our two sides would work against one another for dominance, and ultimately, the people would suffer for it." He shook his head. "It's no way to lead a country. We would need a balancing force of some kind."

"Like what?" Micah asked.

"An instrument of equal power that worked for the betterment of the empire as a whole. A champion for the people," Lao said.

Micah gave him a confused look.

"What do you know of the Shadow Crown?" Lao Jun asked.

Micah shrugged. "I've heard rumors of Darius becoming involved with them."

"I've heard the same. They rescued him when he was held in Eridu, and it seems they may have recruited him to their cause."

"And what is their cause?" Micah asked.

"I've often wondered the same. At first, I thought it was to create chaos and to work against our goals. However, I've found several texts in the libraries here in Kasha Marka that may tell a different story," Lao Jun explained.

Micah tilted his head, showing curiosity, but didn't interrupt.

"An ancestor of mine, in the third dynasty, saw the dangers of corruption at the highest levels. The texts are incomplete on the details, but from what I can gather, a faction in the house of Chung grew greedy for power. They overthrew the current emperor and seized power for themselves, forming the Shian Dynasty. For several generations, they ruled through torment and fear. They oppressed the people and made themselves and their allies wealthy beyond reason."

"What happened?" Micah asked.

"The Huangs finally raised an army against them, and with the support of the people, were able to cast them out. Those who weren't killed were banished to the sea never to return. The Huangs formed a new dynasty built on the needs of the people and designed to build an affluent kingdom through the prosperity of its people. It was a golden age that lasted more than a thousand years. Part of its success was due to the foundation of the Shadow Crown."

"I don't understand," Micah said.

"Emperor Huang Shizi Xin created a secret organization called the Shadow Crown. He put his most faithful allies in charge and gave them the mission of keeping the empire pure and just. They battled corruption from the shadows using economic power, intimidation, and even assassination, not to the detriment of the people but in support of it. If political officials became too corrupt, it was their job to manipulate the instruments of power against them, and if that didn't work, to kill them. Nobody knew who the members were and any efforts to unearth them usually ended badly. The Shadow Crown continued through the transition of the next ten dynasties, and they did their best to provide balance to the empire. I've come to believe that they were instrumental in the defeat of my uncle, Emperor Chen, although there is no mention of them in the official recounts."

"You said that it was one of your ancestors. I'm not sure I see the connection to the Huang Dynasty," Micah said.

"The last Huang emperor had only daughters. He married his eldest daughter to a member of house Lao, and upon the birth of their son, the Lao dynasty replaced the Huang. So, you see, I'm a direct descendant of Huang Shizi Xin," Emperor Lao explained.

"Interesting. So, how does that help us with our problem

today?" Micah asked.

"I think it's time to bring the Sillu Aga out of the shadows," Lao Jun explained. "We could create a triumvirate with myself, Empress Ullani, and the Sillu Aga sharing equal power, working together for the betterment of the empire as a whole."

"That's a pretty bold suggestion, if you don't mind me saying, majesty," Micah said. "Wouldn't that be akin to giving up and surrendering, in a sense, to the enemy?"

"Perhaps, some might see it that way. But in the end, I only want what is best for the people. We have been at war for three years, Captain. It is time that we look for solutions that will allow the country to heal. I would have never expressed such ideas to Guo Wen or General Sharav. I do miss their council, of course, but maybe it is time to be open to other ideas." Lao Jun sensed that Captain Kabir was getting uncomfortable again with the level of confidence he was sharing and decided to change the subject. "In either case, it wouldn't work without the agreement of the barons and Ito. If we are to end the war, there must be universal agreement on our path forward," Lao Jun said.

"How do we accomplish that?" Micah asked.

"I like the term Empress Ullani used—a *convention*. A convocation of all of the current heads of power to come to terms and end the conflict peacefully."

"And who would represent the Shadow Crown?" Micah asked.

"Why, your brother, of course," Emperor Lao said, surprised that Captain Kabir didn't make the obvious connection.

Chapter Forty-Six

Triumvirate

"It's got to be a trap, right?" Darius asked as they surveyed the small valley on the Dalaman Plains. There were several tents already assembled, including a large spectacle in the center with several flags flapping atop its many poles. He noticed the serpentine dragon that represented the imperial house among them but also the blue and white fish chasing each other on a field of black that represented Merkar—and also the white crane of Yapon. He noted that Shalanum's golden lion and Magora's yellow eagle were missing from the lot.

"Would you look at that?" Cheung Po gave a low whistle as he pointed at one of the flags flapping in the breeze. It was black—like the painted coins that they left as their mark, and included a golden crown on one side and a winged lion on the other.

When Darius had received the *invitation* for Sillu Aga to attend the peace talks, he immediately sent for Cheung Po. The old pirate had arrived a few days earlier, and they made for the meeting place. Darius was also accompanied by Rose and Jenna, along with a handful of armed guards. They had left Arnon and the rest of the council behind at Koza just in case this went badly so they could plan an appropriate response.

It had clearly stated that each delegation should bring no more than twenty men at arms. Still, if each flag represented a delegate, there would likely be close to two hundred soldiers in the vale once everyone arrived.

As they approached, Darius saw a crowd leaving a collection of elaborately decorated tents erected below the flag that depicted a serpent intertwined with a flowering vine. He didn't recognize the coat of arms, but he did see a familiar face at the center of the group. They were moving toward the central pavilion. He turned his horse and heeled her to a canter. "Ullani!" he shouted as he drew nearer and raised a hand in greeting.

She looked different. She wore elegant silk robes adorned with patterns of golden thread. Her hair was fixed in dozens of braids, each adorned with assorted glittering gems. As he called out, her entourage immediately closed ranks around her, and weapons were drawn.

He pulled his horse to a stop several paces short of the group. "Ullani?"

"That's Empress Ullani to you, peasant," a swarthy-looking man with a closely trimmed beard spoke.

"Empress? Really?" Darius asked.

"It's okay, Ahmed," Ullani spoke softly as their eyes met.

She smiled pleasantly and continued to stare at Darius while she spoke to her advisor. "Darius is a friend and one of the delegates."

"Me? No, I'm accompanying Cheung Po," Darius answered.

"Surely not," Ullani said. "Emperor Lao was clear in his message that you would be representing Sillu Aga at the negotiations."

Cheung Po chuckled at Darius's side. "You are the new face of the cause, General Kabir."

Darius gave Cheung Po an annoyed glance. He hated that title.

"Speaking of the emperor, is he here?" Darius looked around at the various tents in the valley but didn't see anything that he would recognize as representative of the empire.

Ullani shook her head. "He sent men ahead to erect the pavilion and to welcome the delegates, but he hasn't made an appearance himself yet."

"Who else has arrived?" Darius asked.

"Representatives from Merkar, Orlyk, and Chugoku." She indicated herself as she said the last.

Darius raised an eyebrow. "There must be a story there."

"A long one," Ullani agreed. "But not now. I'll be happy to give you the details later."

"Who else is coming?" Darius asked.

"We expect representatives from Ito, Hurasham, and Aengal, and of course, Emperor Lao. I'm not sure who else," Ullani answered.

"What about Baroness Kess?" Darius asked.

Ullani shrugged. "She may attend with one of the other parties, but Magora, Shalanum, and Rusticar are considered conquered provinces, and the emperor didn't invite them to participate."

"Rusticar? That seems odd. Weren't they close allies in the past?" Darius asked.

"For sure," Ullani agreed. "It wasn't the empire that conquered them but rather the Aengals."

Darius nodded. "You seem very well-informed."

"I have to be," Ullani said. "My life depends on it." It sounded like a flippant statement, but Darius could tell from the tension in her eyes that she was deadly serious.

"Have you heard any word about my mother or Anna?" Darius asked hopefully. The news that reached him in Shalanum never had such details, even when he asked their operatives to keep their eyes and ears open.

"No, sorry," Ullani answered with a sad smile. "I'm sure they are fine, though," she added reassuringly.

"Where are you headed now?" Darius asked.

"The representatives from Orlyk have just arrived and are in the main pavilion. I was just going to welcome them. Come with me, and I'll introduce you."

Darius shrugged. He dismounted his horse and handed the

reins to Cheung Po, then fell in line beside her. He could tell that her guards looked uncomfortable by how close he was to her, but Ullani didn't give any sign of distress, so they remained silent.

Darius was creating a teepee of firewood above a bundle of tinder and kindling at the center of the firepit when he heard someone call his name.

"Darius!" He heard it again and scanned the camp. His heart jumped when he saw the two women approaching his tent. The first was older with flaming red hair shot through with a few streaks of gray. She had a youthful face despite the crow's feet that were forming at the corners of her eyes. The second woman was younger with long dark hair and a mischievous smile that brought back a flood of memories of summers spent with Arthengal at the Cherian farm.

"Mother! Anna!" He dropped the sticks and raced to them, enveloping them both in a massive hug. Tears formed in his eyes as he pulled them close. He felt Anna's arms wrap around his waist and her head pressed to his chest just below his chin. Cordelia reached an arm over his shoulder and patted his back.

"Okay, okay," Cordelia laughed. "Too tight! Let us breathe."

Darius loosened his arms and took a step back from his mother to look at her. Anna refused to relinquish her grasp and pressed herself against him. He felt shudders from her body as she buried her face in his chest and sobbed quietly. He squeezed her in response and smiled at his mother, who was looking at the two of them fondly.

After a few moments, Anna stepped back, wiping her eyes. She looked up at him with a tearful smile. Then, without warning, she punched him in the arm. "We have been so worried about you." Then she hugged him closely again as if she was afraid he would disappear if she let him go.

"I've been fine," Darius assured them. "I've been worried about you too. I haven't heard any word since you all fled Basara. I wasn't even sure you made it out of the city until now."

Anna leaned back and punched him again. "Why didn't you come and try to find us then? Isn't that what you do?"

Darius felt a pang of guilt. "We have looked. Ever since Kasha Marka fell, I have spies watching and listening for any word of you, but none ever came."

"Oh, Anna, leave him alone," Cordelia said with a smile. "We were on the other side of the continent. There is no way he could have reached us even if he tried."

"Where were you?" Darius asked.

"First Ito and then the northern provinces with Baroness Kess," Cordelia answered. "We have heard a few rumors about you, though." She smiled. "Raiders in the company of a giant bear roaming the countryside of Shalanum."

Darius's lips crept into a devious smile. "We've been giving the empire a hard time where we can." Darius suddenly became aware of the group that had gathered around them. "Mother, Anna, this is Cheung Po, Rose Thatcher, and Jenna Allister. They are my…" Darius paused, looking for the right word.

"Lieutenants," Cheung Po filled in and then extended a leathered hand toward Cordelia. "It's a pleasure to meet you, ma'am."

Cordelia accepted the hand with both of hers. "Thank you for looking after my boy," she said.

Cheung Po laughed. "More often than not, it's the other way around."

"We were just about to cook supper," Rose said. "Would you care to join us?"

Anna gave Rose and Jenna a suspicious look and hugged Darius a little bit tighter.

"We'd love to," Cordelia answered. "And you can fill us in on events from back home. It sounds like you all have been busy."

"Would you mind if I joined as well?"

Darius turned to see Ullani and a small retinue of personal guards, all women, emerging from the shadows.

"Please," Darius said. "Your company would be welcome. And maybe you can shed some light on all of this."

"So, all of this is really your idea?" Darius asked. The sun had set long ago, and the small group of friends was huddled around the campfire. Most of Ullani's personal guard had been dismissed to their beds, but her guard, Captain Ava, remained close by. Anna leaned against Darius with her head on his shoulder and appeared to be dozing. Cheung Po, Arnon, Rose, Jenna, and his mother rounded out the rest of the group.

Ullani shrugged. "Mine and Micah's. The idea of adding the Shadow Crown as the third member of the triumvirate was Emperor Lao's idea."

Darius furrowed his brow at the mention of his brother's name. "How did Micah get involved?"

"Oh, he was sent by Emperor Lao to keep tabs on me," Ullani said casually. "Then circumstances brought us together and we discussed different options for a peaceful resolution to the current political strife."

"What sort of circumstances?" Darius narrowed his eyes.

"He ended up in one of my cells," Ullani said dismissively.

"What for?" Darius was sure his opinion about Micah was about to be justified yet again.

"That's not important," Ullani waved a hand at the question. "The important thing is that once I discovered who he was, I was able to use his knowledge and experience to help me."

Darius opened his mouth again to dig deeper, but he was interrupted by Cheung Po. "It's an intriguing idea. And would allow Sillu Aga to resume its mission as it was designed."

"With the exception of a visible representative of the organization," Ullani said. She pointed to Darius. "Having someone that the people can identify with and to whom the local governors can appeal to for aid would make the Shadow Crown a more tangible force."

"Wouldn't that put such a representative and his family at great risk?" Darius asked with a quick glance at Anna and Cordelia.

"I would think the opposite," Cheung Po said. "Knowing that you have the support of an amorphous and powerful organization behind you would make you less of a target. Your adversaries would not know who to trust and would be in constant fear of retribution."

"Plus, unlike the imperial succession, which would happen through birth, you would have the ability to appoint your successors from those most devoted to the cause," Ullani added.

"I guess," Darius said uncertainly. "I still don't fully trust Emperor Lao's motives, though. It still feels like a trap."

"Don't be so cynical, Darius," Ullani said. "Give the peace talks a chance. If we can't agree on a resolution, then nothing is lost by trying, and there is much to be gained."

Darius was about to speak again when cries erupted from the other side of the center pavilion. He heard the sound of weapons clashing and then a loud horn call broke the silence of the night.

Darius was on his feet at the first sound of violence, followed quickly by the others. Rose and Jenna were already moving to rouse their men and Ullani followed Ava in the direction of their tents.

"What's wrong?" Anna asked in a drowsy voice.

"I don't know," Darius answered. "Stay here. Stay safe and out of sight. We'll go and check it out."

Rose returned from behind leading horses for Cheung Po and Darius. She handed them the reins before hurrying back to rally her archers.

Chapter Forty-Seven

Rescue Mission

General Hamazi was standing near the front lines surveying the fortified walls of Kasha Ekur in the distance when the messenger arrived. The message he bore had Hamazi perplexed. He'd already read the message several times, trying to find a hidden meaning. He read the message again and then addressed the messenger. "You say this arrived this morning and that the emperor's seal was unbroken?"

"Yes, sir," the courier responded.

"Have you reviewed it for coded messages?" Hamazi asked.

"Yes, sir. We checked all of the ciphers and discovered nothing. The message seems to be legitimate."

"And it arrived via pigeon?"

"Yes, General."

"Could it have been intercepted and replaced?" Hamazi asked.

The courier shrugged. "There is no way to know, General, but it is doubtful unless the enemy has somehow managed to replicate the imperial seal."

General Hamazi scanned the message again: *Cease hostilities. Peace conference underway. Hold for further orders.* Simple and to the point.

"Something doesn't feel right." General Hamazi looked around at the rest of the generals on the council.

"Could things have changed so drastically with the death of Commander General Sharav?" General Volkov asked.

"No," General Hamazi answered. "Not when we have Kasha Ekur under siege and are so close to victory."

"What about in the east?" General Malik asked.

"Rusticar has lost its capital, but they are holding the passes. The Aengals will have a long hard fight to reach us here. No, either something else has transpired or this is a call for help, and His Majesty didn't feel like the ciphers were secure."

"Could Ito have joined the barons?" General Volkov asked. "A large force of reserves from Ito could turn the tide."

"We would have heard," Hamazi said. Then added uncertainly, "Wouldn't we?"

"What are your orders, General?" Malik asked.

"For now, we follow the order," Hamazi answered. "But I need to investigate. General Volkov, you will assume command here. Secure our defenses and prepare to resume the siege at a moment's notice."

"Yes, sir," Volkov responded.

"I will take a company of light cavalry west at speed and try to reach Kasha Marka to find out what is going on."

By the end of the second week, they had reached the midpoint between Atasu and the Pusteli River. Areas that took weeks to pass in the spring were covered in a matter of days now that the heat of late summer and early fall had dried up the landscape. They swapped horses at Atasu but, otherwise, maintained a grueling pace. General Hamazi slowed his horse as he saw smoke in the distance. There was a small hamlet up ahead where they had left a garrison of troops. It was the first sign of distress they had encountered, and his thoughts turned again to the possibility that something drastic had happened and Emperor Lao was in trouble.

As they approached, they saw men wearing tattered imperial uniforms walking down the road headed east. Hamazi called a halt as the lead man reached them. "What happened, Sergeant?" he addressed the soldier.

"They overran us in the night, sir," the man answered. "Must be close to a hundred of them. They came out of the hills north of town."

General Hamazi felt a momentary sensation of relief but then became agitated. *Orlyk partisans.* "I don't have time for this!" he swore. "Captain," he called to the lead cavalry officer. "Prepare the men for a charge."

As they approached the town, Hamazi saw a large group of

men and women celebrating outside the hamlet. They were not nearly a hundred, but it was more than enough to overrun the garrison if they were caught by surprise.

Celebration turned to fear as the revelers caught sight of the column of horses riding fast in their direction. They scrambled for their makeshift weapons. A few hurriedly shot arrows whizzed past. General Hamazi barely slowed his mount as he reached the quickly assembled line of defenders.

The battle, if it could be called that, was over before it really began. Hamazi commanded a dozen of his men to remain behind to assist the infantry sergeant to reestablish order before resuming his journey west. As it turned out, the brief conflict was the only trouble they ran into. Hamazi was starting to reconsider his concerns when they reached the city of Zymova and heard rumors of an assembly forming on the Dalaman Plains. It was said that representatives from all of the rebel factions were gathering.

Maybe this is what Emperor Lao was referring to, Hamazi thought. *Maybe there are peace talks amongst the rebels, and he wished me to investigate without signaling the call for aid to anyone who may have intercepted the message.*

"Captain," Hamazi addressed the officer. "Send a few scouts to investigate. We'll continue south at a slower pace, but we'll be ready to change direction if we receive word of anything untoward."

"Of course, General." The officer rode off to issue his orders.

It only took a couple of days for scouts to confirm the rumors that a large group of rebel factions was gathering in a wide valley several leagues away. General Hamazi immediately ordered the column to turn west.

General Hamazi watched the valley from a small stand of trees atop a hill to the north. The flags of Aengal, Magora, and Yapon flew above the column that was riding in from the southeast. There were several camps spaced out around the large central tent. Several dozen armed guards roamed the camps and escorted the diplomats but just as many looked like civilians. He was surprised by the number of women who were included in the camp, particularly under the waving flags of the winged lion and the twisted serpent and vine. Some of them even appeared to be carrying weapons, but he dismissed them as ceremonial.

Hamazi saw the imperial banner flying over the pavilion but didn't see any sign of Emperor Lao. *Is it possible he actually intends to engage this rabble in peace talks?* He dismissed the thought almost as soon as it entered his mind. However, just to be certain, he ordered scouts to survey the surrounding area to see if there were any signs of a delegation from Emperor Lao.

Maybe he lured them here to take them all out at once. A plan like that would be consistent with what Hamazi knew of Guo Wen's advice. Maybe the imperial advisor had spurred the emperor into action. General Hamazi amended his order to have scouts also look for expeditionary forces hidden in the surrounding hills.

If they didn't return with news by the evening, Hamazi was determined to attack once the sun went down. This was too perfect of an opportunity to pass up to deal a death blow to the resistance. Hamazi's forces were outnumbered by the armed men by a thin margin, but the element of surprise and the fact that they were mounted would add to their advantage. He had no doubt that he could end the battle, and ultimately the war, with one swift stroke.

The campfires below were dying down. Only a few still had anyone sitting around them. General Hamazi had heard from all but two of his scouts and none had reported any sign of imperial troops. It was odd but didn't mean this wasn't a deftly laid trap. Guo Wen was known to have a devious mind and was an expert at tactics. Hamazi was sure there would be some sort of attack in the upcoming days, but it would be his honor to beat them to it and deliver the emperor the heads of his enemies as a tribute to the eventual success of the empire.

He assembled his men at the edge of the trees. They had removed any loose metal or gear to allow the horses to move more quietly. They would approach from the northeast at a walk and would only raise the charge when they were close enough to prevent any significant response. The delegation from Orlyk had assembled their tents closest to Hamazi's hiding place so he would strike them first. Then he would attack Merkar and Aengal. Those three camps had the largest number of trained soldiers and would pose the greatest threat. There didn't appear to be any troops from Ito, and the ceremonial guard from Kasha Kyoshu was not known for their battle prowess, so he could deal with them last. The other two camps, assembled near the unfamiliar flags, seemed to be mostly comprised of desert nomads and a hodgepodge of ill-equipped commoners. He expected that most of them would flee into the hills at the first sign of danger, but he could round up whoever remained as prisoners once he had dealt with the legitimate military forces.

Hamazi guided his men through the darkness toward the camp. Torches resting in bracketed sconces mounted atop poles formed a perimeter and lit the spaces inside each camp. As they approached the edge of the light, Hamazi raised his arm in a silent signal. Then he dropped his arm and urged his horse into a charge. The thundering hooves of eighty war horses drew the immediate attention of the camp residents and a few scrambled to their feet and out of the tents.

The imperials tore through the Orlyk tents like rice paper. Cries of alarm and panic rang out through the night as they trampled or cut down the Orlyk soldiers and emissaries. It was too dark for flags to communicate, so General Hamazi signaled his drummer to sound the next order. As one, the column of riders turned and charged the Merkari tents. A few of the enemy soldiers had managed to arm themselves and put up a brief but spirited defense. General

Hamazi was getting ready to signal for the attack on the Aengal camp when a pair of arrows flew from the darkness and hit his signal officer in the side where his leather armor was weakest. The soldier's eyes glazed, and he slipped from his saddle with a low grunt. He was dead before he hit the ground.

General Hamazi searched the flickering torchlight and saw a handful of archers emerging from the camp of the winged lion. He was surprised to see that the group was led by an auburn-haired beauty in her twenties. The archers drew back again and delivered another attack with deadly accuracy. He made the split-second decision to abandon the attack on the Aengal camp for the moment to focus on the undefended archers.

"Attack the bowmen!" General Hamazi commanded. The order was passed quickly, and his men reassembled for a charge to the west.

As the cavalry bore down on them, the archers continued to fire. A dozen or so spearmen quickly assembled in a half-circle in front of the bowmen and drove the long shafts of their spears into the ground, holding them firmly with a foot. The first group of Hamazi's men crashed into the line of spears, and the wails of wounded horses filled the night air. He ordered his men to flank the small defensive line to get at the archers who continued to fire one deadly volley after another.

On the right flank, Hamazi's men were met by a group of women holding staffs and daggers. The charge had been broken, so the horses were moving at a slower pace as the women moved to engage. They worked in pairs. One would parry the strikes of the mounted warriors with her long staff, while the other darted in under the defenses to strike at the legs of the soldiers or the sides of their mounts. Several of the horses began to panic as they were wounded and the battle for the right flank descended into chaos.

Meanwhile, to the left, Hamazi's men encountered a smaller force of mounted soldiers wielding swords and javelins. They were surprisingly adept with their weapons for untrained fighters. General Hamazi heard a battle cry behind him and realized that the Aengal forces had assembled and were getting ready to charge from behind. He realized that he had underestimated his foes and had been outmaneuvered. He was about to call for the retreat when he saw a flash of brown and black fur out of the corner of his left eye. The force of the blow toppled his horse, and his right leg was pinned below the fallen animal. Hamazi heard and felt the cries from his warhorse as the monster of a bear ravaged it.

"Antu!" a shout came, and the bear retreated.

Hamazi stared up at the thickly muscled form of a blond horseman above him. The man dismounted and stood above Hamazi, pointing a sword at his head. "I knew you imperials couldn't be trusted. Emperor Lao will answer for this betrayal." The young man spoke with an unmistakable air of command. Serious doubt overcame General Hamazi for the first time. *Have I made a huge mistake?*

Chapter Forty-Eight

Armistice

Micah reached the pinnacle of the hill with the midafternoon sun at his back and was granted his first view of the camp. Rather than the well-assembled encampment that he had expected, the scene below was one of organized chaos. Nearly a third of the tents were in tatters. Bodies were being laid out at the northern end of the valley and funeral pyres were being constructed. Others tended to the wounded near the central pavilion.

As more horsemen rode up beside Micah, someone pointed up at them and shouted. The camp suddenly became a flurry of activity as warriors retrieved weapons and assembled at the edge of camp nearest to Micah and the imperial entourage.

Micah turned to one of the soldiers next to him. "Send word back to Emperor Lao. Have them hold where they are. Tell them not to approach the camp until I find out what's going on."

"Yes, Captain." The soldier saluted and then turned his horse to the southwest.

There were not many in the valley below, but they had

gathered into a solid defensive square with pikemen on the outside and archers in the center. A dozen or so riders garbed in a variety of armor and clothing formed up to the left prepared to meet a charge. Even at this distance, he recognized the tall man in front of the horsemen. *Darius*.

"The rest of you stay here," Micah commanded. "I'm going to ride down to find out why we are being greeted with such a hostile welcome."

Micah trotted his horse down the low hill and approached the mounted men and women. As he drew nearer, Darius seemed to recognize him. He spoke briefly to the other riders and then guided his horse out to meet Micah.

"Darius," Micah said in a friendly tone once his brother was close enough to hear. "It's good to see you."

"If you are coming to gloat, you needn't," Darius said in return. "We defeated your sneak attack last night, and we are prepared to defend ourselves if you try again."

"What are you talking about?" Micah said, genuinely confused.

"Don't pretend like you don't know," Darius accused. "Your *emperor* sent almost a hundred calvary last night in an attempt to wipe us out before the conference could even start. I knew this was most likely a trap, but I had hoped otherwise. Call me an idiot for being fooled by the prospect of peace. Don't worry though, it won't happen again."

"Darius," Micah complained, "I honestly don't know what you are talking about. Emperor Lao has been traveling with me for the past week. We haven't had any contact with any other imperial troops, and I promise you we didn't ambush you in the night. Not again."

Darius laughed. "Then you are the fool, Micah. We are holding General Hamazi prisoner. He all but admitted that he planned to destroy us 'for the good of the empire,' as he put it."

"That's impossible," Micah said. "General Hamazi is in Orlyk. Emperor Lao ordered him to stand down and await further orders. I penned the emperor's message personally and saw that it was sent."

"Well, apparently he didn't listen," Darius said angrily. "Because he attacked us last night, and a lot of good people died."

"No." Micah pinched the top of his nose between his thumb and forefinger and looked down at his saddle. "I promise you, Darius. Emperor Lao did not order the attack. He is willing to come to terms of peace. This was not a trap, Darius. We honestly think we have a solution that everyone can agree to."

Micah watched as Darius's accusing eyes studied him. His brother had changed. The open, curious boy that he had grown up with was gone, and in his place was a hard man, shaped by years of hardship and pain. Micah could see it now. The capture of their mother, the death of his mentor, his capture and imprisonment, and the past year or more fighting against the empire had shaped Darius and molded him into iron.

Micah was simultaneously proud and sad for his brother. He was proud that Darius had overcome the obstacles in his life and had grown into a man of strength and determination. But Micah also felt remorseful that Darius had lived such a hard life and that he hadn't been there to support and help Darius in his times of strife. "Please, Darius," Micah said softly. "Give this a chance."

Micah could see the inner conflict play out on Darius's face. Finally, Darius broke his gaze and shook his head with a sigh. "Everything in my being is screaming 'No!' Micah, but fine. We will hear what he has to say, but only because Ullani spoke so passionately about the prospects of peace before we were attacked last night. We'll give him one chance. But only you and he will be allowed into the camp. We will not put more lives at risk for betrayal."

"No, the emperor's safety cannot be trusted without protection," Micah complained.

"You have lost that trust, Micah. Don't you understand? If he is truly willing to negotiate for peace, then I will guarantee his safety. But if this is a trick, I promise you, the two of you will be the first to pay the price."

"Can you do that?" Micah asked curiously. "Guarantee his safety, I mean."

Darius nodded. "Yes. No one here will act against my orders. I promise you that."

He didn't know why or how, but Micah believed him. Darius, his little brother. The boy who once helped him gather eggs on the cliffs near Koza. The boy who he taught to shoot the bow could command the barons and even the Empress of Kisha and they would listen. They would respect his wishes and honor his code. Micah also knew that each and every one of them would follow Darius to destroy the empire if they felt they had been betrayed.

"Very well," Micah said. "I will relay your terms." With that, he turned his horse to return to his emperor.

Darius sat at the far end of the table, opposite Emperor Lao, who sat at the head. His arms were crossed over his chest, and he could tell by the sidelong glances he had received from Ullani and Bedria Kess that his face wore an expression of cynicism and impatience. *Good,* he thought, and he felt the furrow in his brow deepen. *Let them all know that I don't trust a damn thing about any of this.*

Emperor Lao cleared his throat and stood, pushing his chair back slightly. "Welcome, honored members. We have hope that, through our efforts here today, we can secure peace for our great nation and put her once again on a path to prosperity."

"Who is we?" a tall, well-muscled man with a thick red beard spoke with a tone of dissention in his voice.

At least I'm not the only one, Darius thought.

"Excellent question, Chief Dobhailein," Emperor Lao

answered. "Empress Ullani brought the idea to me, and I worked with my best advisors to shape the idea into one that I think will be appealing to all."

All eyes shifted briefly to Ullani, who, despite the sudden attention, seemed calm and assured.

"What is the overall premise of your proposal Emperor Lao?" A handsome man wearing the insignias of Ito and house Lao spoke.

Darius suppressed a laugh. *What should the antelope do? Says the jackal to the lion.*

"In its simplest terms, the idea would be to form a triumvirate," Emperor Lao explained. "Empress Ullani and the followers of Kisha would form one branch, and I would serve as her equal. Together, we would make the administrative decisions to govern Chungoku, and we would rely on regional governors to enforce the law and govern locally."

"And the third member of the triumvirate?" Bedria Kess asked.

"Long ago, in the third dynasty, an ancestor of mine saw fit to create an organization that would act in the best interest of the people." Emperor Lao said. "That organization, the Shadow Crown, operated in secret and independently from imperial oversight. We would propose that the Sillu Aga be brought into the light and speak for the will of the people as an equal but separate branch of the government."

"And who would lead this *shadow* organization?" Bedria Kess asked.

"Darius Kabir." It was Ullani who answered the question. All eyes were suddenly on him.

Darius shifted uncomfortably in his chair, sat up straighter, and uncrossed his arms in an attempt to reflect the same level of confidence that Ullani projected.

"And you support this idea?" Bedria directed the question at him.

"I have yet to be convinced," Darius answered simply, not wishing to remain the center of attention.

Emperor Lao smiled at him. "Then I shall endeavor to do so. Through a centralized government, we hope to promote the betterment of all who live in Chungoku. We wish to promote a society of opportunity and enlightenment."

"And equality," Ullani added.

Darius sat stiffly at first as Emperor Lao explained his ideas for trade schools, better roads to improve trade, and government-sponsored programs to care for the elderly and infirm who did not have familial support. He found himself relaxing and placed his elbows on the table when Ullani presented ideas of equal rights for women—an idea that did not sit well with the representatives of Hurasham and Merkar—an integrated defense force, and orphanages that would educate and promote the welfare of displaced youth. He was surprised to find himself leaning forward and actively listening with his chin supported on clasped hands when Emperor Lao talked about improving trade with other countries across the Great Sea and beyond.

"These ideas are all very grand," Bedria said once they were done. "But how do we ensure that the people have a voice in these decisions? One man, even one as impressive as Darius Kabir, cannot represent all of the many interests and cultural differences of the people of Chungoku."

"Sillu Aga will not be just one man," Emperor Lao corrected. "He would only be the face of a vast organization that could ensure that the voice of the people was heard."

"Setting policy has never been the intended objective, Sillu Aga," Cheung Po spoke now. "But rather ensuring that the policies that are set are enforced fairly and that corruption and greed doesn't endanger the people or the empire. It was never meant to be the voice of the people but rather their protector."

"Exactly," Bedria echoed.

"What is it that you propose, Baroness Kess?" Ullani asked.

"The baronies were established to recognize the cultural differences that must be allowed to thrive in a free society," Bedria explained. "Granted, some of my compatriots have demonstrated more success in that regard than others. However, if the will of the people is truly to be heard, then they must have direct representation in the decisions that will affect their lives."

"How would you accomplish that?" Ullani asked.

"A duly elected House of Lords," Bedria said. "Each region would appoint representatives who, together, would be empowered to influence imperial policy."

"An interesting suggestion," Emperor Lao responded. "I hadn't considered that."

The discussion continued well into the night before breaking to allow the members to rest. The following morning, the conference continued past noon until, at last, Ullani took advantage of a break in the conversation to address Darius directly. "Darius, what are your thoughts on all of this?"

He considered the question, studying the faces of everyone else at the table. The others seemed to show varying levels of acceptance or excitement at what was being proposed. Even Chief Dobhailein seemed to have come around based on some of the ideas he had presented. Finally, Darius shrugged, "If everyone else is in agreement then who am I to stand in the way of peace."

"So, we are agreed," Emperor Lao spoke. "The Empress of Kisha and the Emperor of Antu will rule side by side from equal but separate palaces in the city of Kasha Esharra. Each region of the empire shall appoint representatives to a House of Lords to petition for the interests of their people."

"And Sillu Aga will rule from the shadows," Empress Ullani added. "To ensure that corruption is punished and that the *good* of the empire shall never again be imperiled from within."

Those gathered around the table nodded in agreement. It had

also been agreed that neither the Empress of Kisha nor the Emperor of Antu would know the identity of any members of Sillu Aga. It was assumed among those assembled that Darius would lead the order, at least for now, but he would neither confirm nor deny that assumption.

The council continued as they ironed out the finer details of the treaty. Darius stood and moved toward the exit. He pushed the tent flaps aside and stepped outside. The minutia didn't concern him, and he was ready to be on the road. Antu rose from where he lay outside the pavilion and ambled to Darius's side.

Darius scratched the bear behind the ears. "So, did it all turn out how you and your sister wanted?"

Antu grunted, probably from the scratching, and moved off toward the other side of the encampment. Darius followed.

Jenna, Rose, Kal, and Anna stood as they approached and untethered the horses. Their gear was already packed, and it would be a long ride back home.

"Are they done?" Jenna asked.

"As done as I care about," Darius answered. "They'll be there for days still fine-tuning the treaty, but I'm ready to go. Cheung Po said he would stay until the end and will brief us back in Koza."

Ander and Cordelia joined them as Darius swung into his saddle.

"Hear, hear," Anna said with a smile. "I'm ready to finally

see this valley that you and Arthengal have raved about for my entire life. Of course, we'll need to stop at Eridu first. Mom, Dad, and Nasha should be getting back soon, and they'll need help setting the house right."

"Of course," Darius agreed. He pulled on the reins and turned the horse southwest.

"And Dad might need help if there is any fruit left on the trees," Anna continued.

"Yep," Darius nodded.

"And we'll have to talk to Mom about setting the wedding date. I'm thinking spring under the cherry blossoms," Anna said.

"I wouldn't have it any other way," he agreed with a smile, and then kicked his horse into a canter as the troop continued east.

Epilogue

Cordelia rocked in the chair on her front porch. She leaned her head back and closed her eyes, feeling the cool breeze coming off the cliffs and the warm sun of late summer on her face. She smelled the salt air and listened to the gulls calling from above as they circled, hoping for scraps from today's catch.

Her attention was drawn by the sound of a wagon wheel squeaking as it approached the house. She opened her eyes and turned to observe the man guiding the two mules at an even gait down the cobblestone road. The long locks of his youth had been cut short so that his hair fell just above the collar of his simple linen shirt. His calloused hands gripped the rope firmly as he turned the wagon past the gate. He was tall, and a steady diet of manual labor kept his well-muscled physique in shape. The scar that ran across his left eye was still visible but had faded with time.

"Darius!" Cordelia shouted.

"Hey, Mom." The man climbed down from the wagon and circled to the back.

"What brings you to Koza?" she asked.

"I needed to bring some more rope for the shop," Darius

answered. "And I thought I'd bring you a few supplies while I was at it."

"Thank you." She smiled. "How is the shop?"

"Good," Darius said. "Kal says business has picked up a lot since they extended the pier into deeper water and larger ships can make port. I see they're expanding the wall again."

"Yep, we keep growing every day. We'll never be the size of Eridu, but I can't believe this is the same little village where I was raised," Cordelia said. "How are Anna and the boys?"

"Good." Darius smiled. "Artie is taller than Anna now." He laughed.

"You'll have to bring them by soon," she said.

"We will, we will, but the hemp crop is coming in strong, and we'll need to harvest soon. I promise we'll make it over before winter sets in, though."

"Anything else new?" Cordelia asked.

"They just finished the final touches on the governor's residence and Governor Thatcher moves in next week," Darius said. "Oh, and they finished digging out the tunnel, so the road goes through again between the valley and Anbar Ur."

"That's good. Is it a nice house?"

Darius rolled his eyes. "Too much house for me, but Rose seems happy with it."

"It should be something fitting for the office," Cordelia said seriously.

"That's what I'm told," Darius said.

"How is Antu?"

Darius smiled. "As spry as ever. I left him hunting rabbits in the fields north of town."

Cordelia shook her head. Antu had to be more than twenty-five, which was ancient for a bear. She wondered, not for the first time, if Darius's theory about the beast was true. Another thought occurred to her, and she said in a conspiratorial tone, "I hear that Empress Ullani is going to marry Emperor Lao's captain of the guard."

"It's about time," Darius laughed. "Emperor Lao and Princess Nabila of Hurasham already have six children. Ullani needs to catch up."

"Darius!" Cordelia said in mock admonishment.

Darius shrugged. "What? I'm not wrong. She's nearly thirty-five. Time's a wasting to produce an heir."

Cordelia rolled her eyes. "You know having children has never been Ullani's primary ambition. And besides, under the new accords, she can appoint an heir." Cordelia paused to consider. "It would be nice to have another grandbaby though."

Darius laughed and then asked, "So, who told you about the impending nuptials?"

"Emperor Lao's captain of the guard, of course. You really should talk to your brother more."

He looked at his feet at the accusation and sighed. "I know."

"It's been fifteen years, Darius, and they have abided by every stipulation in the treaty. When are you going to finally forgive him?"

Darius looked up. "I forgave him a long time ago. It's just...hard to see him. Every time I do, it just brings back painful memories. It's just easier not to."

"Easier on you, but not on him. He misses you very much, you know."

"I know." Darius sighed. "I have to go to the capital next spring. I'll see him then."

"Well, now you'll have another reason to go besides Shadow Crown business. Ullani wants a spring wedding."

"Under the cherry blossoms, I suppose." Darius smiled.

"Well, of course. Who wouldn't want that?" Cordelia said as if it was the most obvious thing in the world.

They fell to silence while Darius worked. Cordelia watched as Darius unloaded the barrels and sacks from the wagon and stored them in her cellar.

"Will you stay for dinner?" she asked once he was done.

"Yeah, I'd like that," he smiled.

"Good. Lianna!" Cordelia turned her head to shout inside the house.

The young blond woman emerged onto the porch. "Yes, mistress?"

"Hello, Lianna," Darius said with a smile.

The woman smiled shyly and responded in a quiet voice. "Welcome, Master Darius."

"It's good to see you," Darius said. "You seem well."

"Thank you. You as well," Lianna answered.

"We'll be having guests for dinner," Cordelia waited for the pleasantries to end before continuing. "I think I'll invite Mayor Allister over as well, and the two of you can catch up, Darius," she added.

"I'd like that too. I'm going to go around back and wash up." Darius headed toward the side of the house.

"Lianna, will you be a dear and bring some of the salted pork in from the cold storage and get a fire going in the stove, then run over to Jenna's to invite her over?" Cordelia said.

"Yes, mistress," Lianna curtsied and hurried away to complete her tasks.

Darius returned and climbed the stairs to the porch. Cordelia rose so she could give him a hug. He squeezed her tightly and rested his cheek against the top of her head. "I've missed you, Mom."

Tears glistened in Cordelia's eyes. "Me too," she said and patted him on the shoulder. Then, before the tears could spill down her cheek, she placed her hands on his chest and pushed him away. "All right, all right—enough of that. Sit down and tell me more about what those grandchildren of mine have been up to."

"Yes, ma'am," Darius said with a smile and released his mother.